1

Sheldrake was a mage. His wife, Maud, was a shape-changer. They lived in a large, thatched cottage, grandly named Batian House, surrounded by an idyllic cottage garden, situated less idyllically, on the main road out of Highkington, the capital of Carrador. Behind the cottage lay stables and a working farmyard that opened onto paddocks stretching to distant bushland. All day long and most of the night, carts, carriages, horses and pedestrians passed within fifty yards of Sheldrake and Maud's front door. After a festival, the sounds of wheels, hooves and feet would be compounded by voices raised in song, chatter and argument.

For years, Sheldrake and Maud Batian had considered growing a hedge to deaden the noise, but firstly they were proud of their garden and liked to give passers-by the chance to admire it and secondly, they watched with interest the parade of life that passed along the road. They would often sit out in their front garden and wave to people they knew. Sometimes one or the other of them would lean on the front gate and exchange words with people, friends and strangers alike, as they passed, not letting on for a moment that their interest was as professional as it was friendly.

But not tonight.

On this cold, dark, rainy night, no one was travelling past their front gate and so did not hear the screams that issued from the idyllic cottage. Maud was giving birth.

Tall and spare, Sheldrake generally tried, often unsuccessfully, to appear phlegmatic. Right now, he paced the corridor outside, firmly banished from the bedchamber by his wife and their head groom, Beth, who was assisting with the delivery. Clive, their butler, trod heavily up the stairs, bearing a crystal decanter filled with a particularly fine whisky and one glass on a fine silver tray.

Sheldrake frowned in irritation at the tray. "Clive, you can't expect me to drink alone. I need moral support. Go back and get a glass for yourself."

Clive placed the tray on a small inlaid table, then grinned as he withdrew a second glass from his pocket, with a slight flourish. "One must be prepared for all eventualities, sir."

Sheldrake gave a snort of laughter. "Good man." He ran his hand over his immaculately neat black hair. "This is the most harrowing experience of my life. I had no idea Maud had such a loud voice...or would have to endure such pain."

Just as he was taking a filled glass from the tray, another scream rent the air, making his hand shake so much he nearly dropped it. Clive's big hand came down on his shoulder. "Easy does it, sir. She'll be all right. My Beth's in there looking after her and she's birthed hundreds."

"But Maud is not a horse."

"That's right, sir. Not at the moment," said Clive in a

calm, comfortable voice. He gave a reminiscent smile, "Eh, but she's a fine galloper when she is, though. Isn't she, sir?"

Sheldrake gave a reluctant smile. "Yes she is. But she is her true human form now, just as she must be, to give birth, and I don't know that Beth has as much experience with people."

"Don't you worry, sir. Animals are all much the same. It will be fine," Clive said, just as he would to any child, dog, or horse in distress.

On the other side of the door, Maud lay on a heavily carved four-poster double bed, her long, dark brown hair in a tangled halo across the pillows, her teeth clenched as another wave of pain began its crescendo. As the contraction reached its peak, Maud opened her mouth and howled.

"That's it, pet. One last push. The baby's coming." A thin, dried up woman in her fifties knelt on the floor at the foot of the bed, the head of the baby already in her hands. She wasn't a healer, at least not primarily, but she'd brought hundreds of foals, lambs and calves into the world and she had known for months that this baby would be a boy. "That's it," she said, as the baby gushed forth into the world. "You've done it. Good girl."

For long moments, tense silence filled the room before healthy little lungs bellowed in distress at the sudden change in circumstances. Both women smiled, tears of relief in their eyes. Beth tied and cut the umbilical cord, then gently wiped the child over with a soft damp cloth before wrapping him in a warm blanket and handing him to his waiting mother. Once Beth had tidied away the afterbirth and straightened the bed covers, she opened the door and beckoned Sheldrake to enter.

"Come and meet your new son, sir."

Sheldrake nearly catapulted into the room in his eagerness to see his wife and new child. Clive was close behind him, relieved despite his calming words. Sheldrake sat on the edge of the bed and together, he and Maud looked fondly down at the bright pink, scrunched up face of their first born, marvelling at the little nose and mouth and the perfect tiny fingers.

Then the child opened his eyes.

Sheldrake froze. Maud gasped in horror.

"What is it?" asked Clive urgently.

"His eyes," breathed Maud. "They're white."

Sheldrake frowned and leaned closer. After a close inspection, he shook his head. "No. They are not white. The pupils are black and the irises are a very pale lavender... hmm... but they look white."

"Can he see?" demanded Clive.

Beth intervened. "A new baby's vision is blurry anyway. He can't focus or track yet. So you probably won't be able to tell for a few weeks. He will be trying to focus on you, Maud, but if he turns his head to you, he could be just following your voice or the sound of your movement at the moment." She shrugged. "Most babies have bluey coloured eyes at birth and then often the colour changes. So maybe his will, too."

Even as they watched, the seemingly white eyes darkened to a faint lavender as the light reacted with the melanin in his irises, but they were still unnaturally pale.

Beth shrugged. "A small change often happens the first time the light hits their eyes, but you won't know his final eye colour for months yet."

Maud gave a strained smile. "Never mind. I will love him anyway. He is perfect in every other way."

But Sheldrake knew what she feared. "Don't worry, my love. The merit of a person is not determined by his eye colour. My grandmother's morals would have been just as bad, had she had blue or brown eyes."

"But the power, Sheldrake."

Sheldrake grimaced. "Yes, dear. Madison was powerful, but I do not know that any direct link was made between her eye colour and her particular powers. Besides, we too are powerful. So I think we can assume that our son will inherit at least some degree of magical ability, don't you? It would be stranger if he did not."

"But will he be able to manage it? Will he use it justly?"

"That will be up to us to determine, don't you think?" Sheldrake looked at Beth and Clive, before adding, "All of us."

2

During the following two years, Jayhan grew into an unremarkable toddler. Everything about him was normal, except for his eyes. He was a dear pudgy little boy, with a shock of blond hair that would darken to auburn by the time he was five.

Everyone, when they saw his eyes for the first time, drew back in consternation. Most adults tried to cover their reactions, partly out of kindness and partly out of courtesy. But many children, especially those in the village jealous of his privileged position, would stare unashamedly and whisper ostentatiously behind raised hands to their friends.

On the day after his eighth birthday, as Jayhan was trotting down the street holding his father's hand, a jeering voice called out "Spooky!"

Even before Sheldrake could turn around, the children had fled. The mage frowned ferociously around the empty streets but could see no one to berate.

Worse still, his reaction encouraged the jeerers. The voices continued their taunts from the cover of the side streets.

"Spooooky!"

"Ooh. Ghoul eyes!"

"Crow's eyes. Hey, your mother's a crow."

"He's a ghoul. He's a ghoul!"

"Back from the dead."

Jayhan didn't understand what they were saying but he knew why. When they arrived home, just as his father was thinking Jayhan hadn't noticed, the boy asked, "What's a ghoul? What is back from the dead? I thought when people died, they stayed lying down."

Sheldrake was discomforted by his questions and tried to fob him off. "They do, Jayhan, they do. Just ignore those stupid children. They don't know what they are talking about."

"They hate my eyes, don't they, Dad?"

Sheldrake huffed. "Nothing wrong with your eyes. You can see out of them, can't you? What more do you want?" After a moment, he said dismissively. "Ignorant people annoy me."

Jayhan glanced up at him but could tell he wouldn't get any more out of him. That didn't mean he would let the subject drop though, just that he would have to look for other avenues to find out.

Remembering the comment about crow's eyes, Jayhan took himself out into the garden and set himself up to play with a pair of wooden horses and a tiny carved carriage under a camellia tree where he was hidden behind a large lavender bush.

He watched a pair of blue wrens flit from branch to branch then onto the lawn for a while before flitting back into the bushes and disappearing. A black bird came and went, then two pairs of red-rumped parrots swooped in and pecked their way across the lawn before something startled them and they flew off in a flash of colour. For a while the lawn remained empty and Jayhan became so absorbed in his game that he nearly missed the crow when it landed in the middle of the lawn looking for bugs.

Jayhan studied its eyes. Their irises were bright white.

Jayhan sat back on his heels and thought about it. He had never particularly noticed the colour of crows' eyes before, but now that he had, he thought they were very interesting; different from other birds. Then he pondered the remark that his mother was a crow. He watched the glossy black, intelligent bird working its way across the lawn and decided that would be no bad thing. He knew his mother shape-shifted and could become a crow, if she wanted to, but that her true form was human. On the other hand, he doubted that the boys in the village knew that. More than that, he could tell they had been trying to upset him. He decided he would seek out Beth and talk to her.

He found her in the tack room in the stable, sitting on a stool next to a brazier, polishing a worn bridle that was nearing the end of its days. She looked up and smiled as he entered, no longer even noticing his pale lavender eyes.

"What have you been up to, young one? You have muddy knees again."

Jayhan grinned, knowing she didn't care. "Watching a crow. It has even paler eyes than mine. Bright white they are."

She looked at him a moment then said, "They must be beautiful then."

He put his head on one side and thought about it. "They look very bright because crows are so black. I like bright things." He scuffed the toe of his shoe in the dirt, "But Beth, the boys in the village called me Crow's Eyes and said my mum was a crow. I don't really mind either of those things but I think they were trying to be mean. And they called me spooky and ghoul and said I was back from the dead." He grimaced in memory. "What's a ghoul anyway? And I never died. So how can I be back? And anyway you can't come back from being dead... can you?"

"Jayhan, Jayhan, settle down. Too many questions." She put down the bridle with one hand while she held up the other to forestall his protest. "Give me time. No, you can't come back from the dead." She ticked her answers off on her finger as she talked. "A ghoul is make-believe evil spirit that digs up dead humans and eats them." Beth gave a brief laugh as Jayhan screwed up his face in distaste. "Yes, lucky they're make-believe, isn't it? And being spooky means..."

"I know what spooky is... and creepy," cut in the small boy. "I've often heard people say it when they thought I wasn't listening."

Beth looked stricken. "Oh Jayhan." She held her arms wide in invitation and Jayhan walked straight in and hopped up onto her knee. She hugged him to her and rocked him gently back and forth.

For a minute or two he let his head rest against her shoulder, mostly because Beth needed him to. Then he sat up abruptly and chortled. "I don't care if people get creeped out by my eyes. They're just being silly. Eyes can't hurt you no matter what colour they are." For a moment he looked uncertain. "Can they?"

Beth shook her head. "No young one, they can't." He felt her ribs tighten slightly as though she were about to say something more but she let her breath out and remained silent.

"But...?"

She gave a lop-sided smile. "You know me too well.

But... some eye colours are owned by particular people or types of people."

"Oh." He glanced up at her, then looked down. "So am I a particular type of person that gives people the creeps?"

Beth laughed. "No. You are a particular type of person who distracts me from my work." She lifted him off her knee. "Now off you go and entertain yourself for a while."

Jayhan obliged but he had heard a forced note in her laugh and knew that she had dodged talking to him about it. One more line of enquiry closed.

Jayhan gave up asking and no one noticed when he started to avoid looking at people or that his sunny smile had dimmed a little. And when his father invited him to accompany him to the village, Jayhan found excuses not to go.

After the fifth invitation was avoided, Sheldrake scowled at his son. "Your studies can wait. Don't you like to do things with me? Perhaps I should get someone else to tutor you in magic."

Jayhan's eyes widened in horror. "Oh no, dad. I love being with you. It's just...."

"It's just what?"

"I don't really like the village."

"The village has a lovely little shop with lovely little treats."

Jayhan produced a smile. "It has chocolate frogs, doesn't it?"

Sheldrake ruffled his hair. "Yes it does. So let's go."

As they walked through the village, Jayhan kept his eyes cast down until his father reproved him and told him to hold his head up. So when the village kids jeered at him he glared back defiantly, and the intense gaze of his pale eyes cowed them more than any rebuke his father could make.

3

During his lessons the next afternoon, as Jayhan dragged his way through a tedious page of arithmetic - his tutor was not a gifted educator - he thought about crows' eyes and the village children's taunts turning to fear. He pondered their reactions, surprised that just looking at them had turned the tables. He was just wondering whether they would have reacted in the same way if his father had not been there, when he was taken to task for having added every pair of numbers when he should have been subtracting.

He was brought abruptly back to the present by Eloquin demanding, "So, are you clear now on what you have to do?"

Guessing and hoping it was what she had said at start of the harangue, Jayhan nodded. "Yes Ma'am," and began the page of arithmetic all over again, this time subtracting. He was up to the fifth question when suddenly the image of a well-dressed middle aged woman swam into his mind; a woman with eyes like his. Where had that come from?

As he struggled his way down the column of subtraction

problems, the woman's face stayed in his mind. Perhaps he seen her portrait somewhere? Maybe. But where?

"Jayhan, if you want time to play before dinner, you must finish these questions and get every one of them correct." Eloquin was an attractive, dark-haired young woman who had been forced into the post of tutor as a consequence of her dissolute father gambling away the family fortune. She just wanted her young charge to complete his work in time for her to walk into the village to meet her sister, who was now working as a seamstress, and a rather interesting young man, who apparently worked somewhere in the city. She sighed in exasperation. "*Jayhan*, are you listening to me?"

The boy gave his head a little shake and let the image of the pale-eyed woman drift away as he applied himself to earning some play time.

He woke the next morning to the sound of honeyeaters squabbling in a bush outside his window. The sky was still grey, and colour had not yet crept across the lawn. Flowers and shrubs were shades of grey. Instead of bouncing out of bed in his usual fashion, Jayhan lay back and concentrated on remembering where he had seen that portrait. He let his mind wander the corridors of the house, around the entrance hall, into his parents' bedroom and, when none of these walls yielded the portrait, he changed tack and began to think of cupboards, spare rooms and the attic. He was just ruing his poor memory and from there, letting his thoughts drift to his difficulty in learning spells from his father when, with a jolt, he remembered where he had seen the portrait. It was in his father's workshop, the site of so many disastrous efforts by Jayhan to spellcast.

He had spent so many frustrating hours in Sheldrake's workshop, trying to master even the simplest of spells. Spellcasting did not come easily to Jayhan. He forgot the words or the gestures or some aspect of the spell that could cause problems. Just a week ago, he had levitated himself with a flourish, only to rise sharply upwards and hit his head on a beam. In the shock of the unexpected pain, he had lost control of the spell, sending him crashing to the floor. Sheldrake had not been pleased.

Jayhan waited until he had seen his father leave the house and walk through the front gate towards the village. Then he wandered casually across the back lawn, past the stables checking that Beth was not looking in his direction, and then along the paved path that led to his father's workshop. Even though the workshop contained many valuable artifacts, books and potentially dangerous chemicals, the door was not locked. A magical ward warned Sheldrake if family members, including Beth and Clive, entered his hallowed ground and immobilised non-family members before they could. Happily oblivious to this, Jayhan lifted the latch and pushed open the wooden door. Once inside, he meticulously closed the door behind him. Ignoring the temptations offered him by fascinating potions, vast arrays of tools and the marvellous scaled model of Carrador that dominated one side of the room, he walked to the back, right-hand corner.

There, partly concealed by a workbench, hung a large oil portrait, dulled by dust, cobwebs and neglect. Jayhan climbed up onto his father's stool and from there onto the work bench. Sweeping aside tools, nails, screws and bits of wood shavings, he knelt on the dirty wooden benchtop and studied the painting.

The woman in the portrait was standing in front of the side entrance to the stables Jayhan had so recently passed, holding the reins of a beautiful chestnut gelding. The cottage's front garden, in the full bloom of early summer, was visible in one half of the background. The woman wore a stiffly tailored green riding habit, her black hair swept up under a perky, impractical riding hat. Her straight black eyebrows gave her a stern expression that was lightened by a slight lift at the corner of her mouth. But it was her eyes that held Jayhan's attention. At first glance, they appeared to be stark white but when Jayhan leaned in closer and brushed a cobweb out of the way, he could see that they were actually, like his, a very pale lavender.

But who was she? Had she been teased by children in the village too? Maybe the lady in the portrait wasn't a real person, but a picture of one of these make-believe ghouls that ate dead people.

Na, he thought, *if someone was going to paint something scary like a ghoul, they wouldn't put pretty flowers in the background. Anyway, she doesn't look one bit scary.*

Actually, to other people, she did, but Jayhan had lived with his eye colour all his life and thought it looked perfectly normal.

A thought struck him and he peered down the small gap between the portrait and the workbench, trying to see whether there was a name plate at the bottom of the painting, as there were on the portraits that hung on walls in the house. He spotted a small golden rectangle, which he felt sure was the name tag he was looking for. He leant further down the crack trying to see. Suddenly his left hand slipped on something slimy that had been left on the bench and he plummeted head first into the gap. Then his trousers got caught on a nail sticking out of the benchtop and he was left dangling upside down, unhelpfully facing away from the painting.

It was at this unfortunate moment that the door was

flung open and Sheldrake stormed in. He had worked himself up into a lather of outrage, liberally laced with fear for his son's safety.

"What are you doing in my shed?" he roared, fully intending to give his errant son a reprimand he would never forget. Then he saw the legs sticking up from the back of his workbench and stopped short. "What on earth are you doing?"

Jayhan's heart lurched as he heard his father's roar, knowing full well he shouldn't be in the shed on his own. He knew his father could be stern but not deliberately unkind and as Jayhan was a plucky little lad, he said from his upside down position, "Hello Dad. Sorry Dad. I'm a bit stuck. Could you help me please?"

With amusement fast dissipating Sheldrake's anger, he managed to say sternly, "I should leave you hanging there as punishment for coming into my workshop when I have expressly forbidden you to enter on your own."

"Please don't, Dad. I'm starting to feel sick."

Sheldrake shook his head in fond exasperation. "You, young man, are a rapscallion of the first order." He leaned over the bench, grabbed two handfuls of Jayhan's trousers and pulled. This succeeded in detaching the trousers from the nail that had caught them but, from where he was standing, Sheldrake found it was impossible to lift Jayhan high enough to get him clear of the back of the workbench. "Right. I am going to have to lower you down, then you'll have to crawl out from there. Be careful of those boxes. Don't knock anything over on your way out."

Once this operation had been completed, Jayhan stood before his father and dusted himself off.

"And just what were you doing in my shed?"

"Nothing, Dad." When Sheldrake looked sceptical, he

shrugged. "I just came to look at that picture." Jayhan pointed. "See? She has eyes like mine... Do you think the village kids teased her too? Did they say she was a ghoul too? I don't reckon she was. She doesn't look like she eats dead people, do you think?"

"Who told you what a ghoul is?"

"I asked Beth."

"Hmph." Sheldrake looked into the cheerfully determined little face, as he realised that his son had sought his own answers when his father had dodged them. "You have an enquiring nature which is an asset in a mage... but no more sneaking into my shed. Understood?"

Jayhan beamed. "Yes sir."

Sheldrake turned to lean his elbows on his workbench to study the portrait and Jayhan copied him, although it meant his elbows were above shoulder height.

"That lady there is my grandmother, your great grandmother. Her name was Madison... and now you mention it, yes, I expect she was teased, though I must say I hadn't thought of that before... Perhaps that was one of the reasons she..." He looked sharply at Jayhan and stopped what he was saying. "Jayhan, we have all been teased by village children. They are envious of our lovely house, our well-cut clothes, our money and our status. Their parents are polite and respectful towards us as a general rule but the children, especially those who live on the streets beyond their parents' control, can be openly resentful and unkind."

"Really? You got teased too. What did they say?"

Sheldrake gave a short laugh. "I was a skinny little kid. They called me String, Slim, Stick, Scrawny, Pole... things like that. I disliked it intensely. I wanted to be big and strong and bulky." He looked down at himself. "But I never got any broader. I'm still as skinny as a rake." He gave a slow smile. "But I am strong now, though I mightn't look it."

Jayhan smiled at him. "Of course you're strong. You're my dad."

At that, Sheldrake actually put an arm around him and gave him a squeeze.

Jayhan thought about all the times people had recoiled from his eyes and knew the children's envy wasn't the only reason. "You know it's not just the kids in the village. Everyone hate my eyes, except maybe you and Beth and Clive. What's so spooky about them? Do dead people have white eyes? Is that what's wrong?"

"Your eyes are pale lavender, not that anyone notices. So were Madison's," replied Sheldrake. "And no, dead people's eyes stay the colour they were in life, Jayhan, just the cornea goes a bit cloudy after a couple of days."

"Hmph. Then why, Dad? I know you know."

Sheldrake heaved a sigh. "Ah Jayhan. Sometimes you are too inquisitive for your own good. I want you to be older before I tell you." Seeing Jayhan's face tighten, he held up a warning hand. "I will give you a compromise. I will tell you this much: People fear you because they feared your great grandmother."

"But that not fair. I'm not her," Jayhan protested hotly.

"Life is not fair, Jayhan."

"Humph." The boy looked down and scuffed his shoe back and forth along the ground, watching it drag a groove in the dirt floor. After a minute, he looked up and, rather to Sheldrake's surprise, smiled. "I guess that's true. It's not fair that we have a better house than the people in the village, is it?"

Having a sense of entitlement, Sheldrake was tempted

to take issue but decided not to. "That is what the villagers think and why they take delight in teasing us."

"So why was Great Grandma so scary?"

"I won't tell you that. Instead, I will give you several books which contain information about her. Only you may read them. Do not ask Beth or Clive or your mother to help you. Discuss their contents with me, as you need to."

"But Dad. I'm only just learning to read. I can't read big books."

Sheldrake gave a triumphant, mischievous smile. "Exactly. So now you have a reason to work hard at your reading."

4

The pile of books in the corner of Jayhan's room inspired him to study hard for a good fortnight. But at the end of that time, he opened one of the heavy leather bound tomes and found that he could read it no better than he had the day his father gave them to him. Disgruntled, he complained to his tutor, Eloquin, but she merely counselled him to have patience and study harder. Since he had given it his level best for the last fortnight, he knew he couldn't study harder. In fact, he was so peeved she hadn't appreciated his efforts that he decided it wasn't worth the bother. He dragged the pile of books into the back recess of his wardrobe, deciding to banish them from his mind and find other ways to learn about his great grandma.

After stowing the books, Jayhan stomped dispiritedly down the hallway and into the library where the ever-patient Eloquin was waiting to instil him the wonders of reading. With equal patience, he endured her uninspiring rendition of a dreary little story about a boy walking his dog. While Eloquin attempted to emulate a doggy bark, Jayhan heard the sounds of a large cart drawing up outside. Bryson, the carter, had arrived with their week's supplies of vegetables, meats, sacks of grain and kegs of ale.

Jayhan was manfully training his attention on the fascination of the dog wagging its tail, when a loud crash sent him running to the window to see what was happening.

Outside in the driveway, a horse was rearing between the shafts of a cart laden high. The horse's eyes rolled in fear as a large black cat stood stiff-legged in front of it, back arched and hissing her displeasure. The horse's owner was nowhere in sight, presumably inside the house with his first load for the kitchen.

Jayhan saw Beth arrive from the stables at a dead run, kicking her ferocious cat out of the way and lunging to grab hold of the horse's bridle. But the cat was not so easily dismissed. It spat and dug its claws into her boot as she kicked, unbalancing her.

Suddenly Beth was falling beneath slashing hooves. As Jayhan held his breath in horror, a small scrawny figure, dressed in tattered leggings and jerkin, catapulted himself at Beth, thrusting her out of the way just as the horse's hooves descended. The boy rolled lithely onto his feet, leapt up to catch hold of the reins and vaulted onto the back of the plunging horse. Grabbing the horse's mane with one hand, the boy leaned forward, crooning softly to the horse and stroking its neck in long, sure strokes. For a moment, the horse's ears flattened and its hindquarters bunched. Then, as the crooning voice penetrated its panic, the horse snorted, tossed its head, and came to a standstill, quivering with fright. As the firm stroking and gentle voice continued, the quivering gradually subsided.

Ignoring the protests of his tutor, Jayhan rushed out of the school room and down the stairs. He catapulted from the front door just in time to see the boy slide off the great horse's back and walk over to Beth, who was still sitting on the gravel. The boy held out a hand to help her up.

"Are you all right, ma'am?"

"I'm fine, thank you. I was just waiting for the horse to calm before making any movement in front of him. I'm quite capable of standing up in my own." Fright and irritation made Beth's voice harsher than she intended. She stood up and brushed gravel off her scraped hands.

The boy dropped his head. "Sorry, Ma'am. And sorry about Hoofer."

Suddenly, a great burly man pushed past Jayhan and strode over to the boy, grabbing him by the scruff of his shirt and dragging him away from Beth before bringing his other arm around in an arc, to hit him hard across the back of his head. The boy went sprawling.

"Sasha," he roared. "What do you think you're doing, talking to the patrons? You get back up on that cart and hand me down that sack of potatoes."

The boy pulled himself to his hand and knees, shaking his head in an effort to clear it. As he struggled to stand up, the big man strode towards him, hand raised, ready to hit him again.

"That's enough, Bryson," cracked a harsh voice.

The man stopped in his tracks and turned belligerently.

Dwarfed by him, Beth stood hands on hip, glaring up at him. "That child just saved my life. But even if he hadn't, you have no reason to use him so roughly."

Bryson towered over her, glaring but constrained by his need to sell his goods. "He's mine. I'll do what I like with him."

"If you keep hitting your son around the head like that, his wits will be addled before he is full grown."

The man spat to the side. "He's not my son. No whelp

of mine would be so small and scrawny by the age of eight. Sasha's a foundling, and I am looking after him out of the goodness of my heart."

"Cheap labour, more like."

Bryson shrugged. "The boy must earn his keep."

While they talked, Sasha had climbed nimbly up the wheel spokes, onto the top rim of the wheel and from there, onto the tray of the cart where he stood holding a corner of the sack of potatoes, waiting for his master to be ready to catch it. The side of his dark face was grazed from being hurled onto the gravel and a trickle of blood was drying, unheeded, on his cheek. He watched warily, knowing his master would be even angrier after Beth's intervention.

"Then he can earn it with me," said Beth firmly. "I need a new stable lad and this one has a way with horses I have rarely seen."

The burly man spluttered. "You can't just go taking my lad away from me. I've spent months training him up; teaching him how to drive the horse, how to pack up the merchandise and keep the cart in good order. There's a lot in it, you know. Not as easy as you might think, carting merchandise."

"How much?" asked Beth baldly.

Just as the carter opened his mouth to reply, Beth held up her hand. "Whatever you were going to say, halve it. It will save us both a lot of time."

The carter shook his head despondently. "You're a hard woman, Beth. But since my own lad's nearly ready to join me, I won't have to hire someone until I train up a new lad, so ten silver florins should cover it."

"Six," returned Beth promptly

"Nine."

"Seven and the deal is struck."

"Done," said Bryson, spitting on his hand and holding it out to Beth, who grasped it. "I'll be glad to see the last of him," he added spitefully.

A piping voice interrupted them from the top of the cart. "Now, hang on a minute. I'm no slave to be bartered around. I may be a foundling but I'm a free foundling. I've been working day and night for this bloke. Where's *my* money?"

"You don't get none, you halfwit reject," snarled Bryson.

"I'm not a halfwit and I'm not..." Sasha's voice died away.

"Huh. You see. You *are* a bloody reject. Just be glad you've had food and a place to sleep. Now finish unloading that cart."

Sasha, his face tight with resentment, directed his anger into the strength he needed to push the sack of potatoes off the cart into his master's waiting arms. Without another word, he waited sullenly for Bryson to deliver the potatoes inside then handed down each item as required. He avoided Bryson's gaze, and everyone else's. When the cart was empty, he pulled the ropes onto the cart and rolled them into neat coils at the front of the tray.

Jayhan watched the boy standing in front of the coils of rope, arms folded across his chest, a scowl on his face, and suddenly realised Sasha was frightened. No one had told him when he would come to work for Beth and if he went back with Bryson, he was facing another beating, Jayhan guessed. If Sasha stayed now, he was entering a new, uncertain world and although Beth had stood up for him, she had been tetchy to him and aggressive with Bryson and had not stayed to watch the end of the unpacking.

Jayhan walked quickly to the stables and called, "Beth. Bryson's leaving. Are you keeping the boy now?"

He found Beth with her head under her bed. "Tell them to wait. I will be out there in a minute."

Jayhan frowned and peered under the bed next to her. "What are you doing?"

"I need another shilling. It rolled under the bed here and I can't find it." She pushed him back. "Now go and tell Bryson to wait."

"I will." He hesitated. "Beth, I have two florins saved up. It's in my room upstairs. Do you want them? I don't want that boy to go home with Bryson. He's going to beat him again, isn't he?"

Beth pulled head out from under the bed. Cobwebs clung to the front of her hair and she used the back of her hand to wipe them away. "Oh Jayhan. You're a dear. Thanks. Just a loan, mind. I'll get it back to you. Now go and tell them to wait, then run inside and bring the money to me here. Got that?"

Jayhan nodded, pleased to have his offer accepted. He walked quickly to the front of the house and saw Bryson already sitting on the seat of his wagon, ready to leave. "Excuse me Bryson. Beth says, asks, could you wait a minute please. She will be out shortly."

"She'd better be quick. I've got to get back to the store house before dark," Bryson grumbled.

"She will be," said Jayhan as he shot into the house and up the stairs. He dodged past Eloquin and into his bedroom, pushing the door shut behind him with a little too much vigour. He opened the cupboard under his bedside table and took out a cloth drawstring bag full of colourful rocks that he had collected. At the bottom of the bag was another small cavity held shut by another drawstring.

Jayhan emptied the little rocks onto his bed then felt around for the small loop of the drawstring and from there, inserted a finger into the little hole that expanded to reveal the cavity beneath. His fingers closed around the silver florins.

With the florins clutched in one hand, Jayhan threw the door open, ducked past Eloquin who was just about to knock on his door. He muttered an apology over his shoulder as he sped off down the side stairs. He scooted through the kitchen, nearly scattering a bowl of shelled peas, and out through the side door across to the stables.

"Here," he said, panting, as he held his hand out to Beth.

As she took the florins, Beth smiled into his unnervingly pale eyes, noticing only his earnest, kind face. "Well done, young one. Now, off you go, back the way you came. Thank you."

As Jayhan emerged from the stairwell, he saw Eloquin down the other end of the corridor, gesticulating wildly as she told his mother of his behaviour. He slipped unnoticed into the schoolroom, crossing straight to the widow to peer down at the scene below.

Sasha had climbed down from the wagon and was now standing beside Beth as she farewelled Bryson. They watched as Bryson turned the cart and headed for the front gate without a backward glance. Then she placed an arm around the boy's shoulder to steer him towards the stable. Unexpectedly, Jayhan felt a stab of jealousy as he turned from the window and returned to his work table.

When his mother and Eloquin entered a few minutes later, he had already written a sentence about a boy walking his dog and was waiting for his next task.

He smiled cheerily. "Sorry Eloquin. It was important," he said, but refused to say what was important.

5

Sasha flinched as he felt Beth's hand come down on his shoulder. With an effort, he tried to relax his muscles under the pressure of her hand, but Beth could still feel the tension in them.

He was trying to appear nonchalant so he only glanced up quickly at the two storey cottage as they walked past. He didn't really see the beauty of the yellow climbing roses or the cosiness of the rooms that could be seen through the diamond panes of the leadlight windows. All he saw were tall whitewashed walls that lay between him and the family who lived there. Somewhere behind those walls were the people who could, if they chose to, make his life hell.

Then he risked a glance up at Beth and found her watching him. Fear knotted his stomach as he quickly dropped his gaze. He had often been belted for cheekiness and he didn't know what passed for cheekiness in his new world. His cheek still throbbed dully from his last beating.

"Come one, young one. I'm not going to eat you," said Beth bracingly. "Let's get that face of yours cleaned up and then we'll think about dinner. I bet you're hungry after all that unloading. That was heavy work for a small boy."

Sasha risked another glance up and saw that she was smiling at him. He nodded but said nothing.

He felt the change in texture under his bare feet as they crossed from gravel onto the brick path leading into the stable. He stared ahead at the well-kept wooden structure, smelling straw and dung and horses.

As they entered, Beth drew him into her office on the left side of the entrance. A wooden chair was pulled up to a large desk scattered with papers against the far wall, while along the right-hand wall was a long rough workbench, which Beth used for repairing and cleaning tack. The walls were hung with spare leather thonging, coils of rope, broken bridles and halters and, along the top of the wall, a row of rosettes and ribbons that nearly reached around three of the four walls. A fire burnt in a small hearth set into the outside wall and two chairs, one upright and the other a rocking chair strewn with knitted rugs, were set on either side of a small wooden table, on which a book and an empty cup of coffee had been left. A heavy black kettle hung over the fire, steam whisping up from its spout.

"Sit there," Beth said, indicating the upright chair nearest the door. She busied herself with pouring water from the kettle into two chipped cups and a bowl. She added coffee and milk to the water in the cups and ground willow bark to the bowl.

She found a clean rag and used it to gently cleanse his wounded cheek with the suspension of willow bark. Sasha held still, lips pressed together, expecting to endure pain. But Beth was gentle and as she pulled away, Sasha let out a soft breath of relief.

A knock on the outside door made Sasha jump but Beth

merely asked him to answer it. When he hesitantly opened the door, a young brown-haired blue-eyed maid from the kitchen handed him two steaming plates of what appeared to be beef stew.

"Here y'are, new boy. I'm Rosie, the parlour maid. Don't expect me to bring your food over every night. You can eat with the rest of us in the kitchen tomorrow."

Sasha nodded his head and mumbled his thanks.

When he re-entered the office, he handed a bowl to Beth and sat down, holding the other. He waited until she started eating. When he was sure that the bowl of stew he still held was for him, he picked up his spoon and began to eat. The stew's aroma almost made him giddy. Despite his hunger, he ate it slowly, wringing every last ounce of enjoyment out of its rich flavour. As he scooped the last spoonful slowly into his mouth, he gave a shudder of contentment. He looked up to find Beth's eyes on him, her bowl empty long ago.

He gave a little embarrassed grin. "Oops. But that was so... so amazing."

After a moment, Beth smiled. "Better than Bryson's fare, was it?"

"Oh yes, ma'am. I only ever had bread and cheese, sometimes an apple." He scowled. "Sometimes nothing at all, if he was too tired or drunk."

"Hmm. He didn't clothe you too well, either. We will have to find you some new trousers and a good warm shirt. You'll need boots too. Can't have bare feet round horses. I think young Master Jayhan may have some clothes he's grown out of that would fit you, until we can get you your own." She stood up. "But first, before you dirty new clothes or my stables, you will have a bath."

"*Now?* It's cold and dark and..."

"And you've never had one before, I'm guessing.

"I went swimming in summer, in the river," Sasha said defensively.

"Good for you. Now, there's a big metal horse trough outside. Throw out what's in it, get a bucket of water from the well and rinse it out. Then bring it in here. Once that's done, you can bring two more bucket loads of water from the well and put them in the trough. I will add the rest of the boiling water and by then we should have the makings of a bath."

Sasha stared at her for a few moments with his melting black eyes, then turned on his heel and followed her instructions to the letter.

As she added the hot water to make a shallow lukewarm bath, Beth nodded her approval. "Well done. You have a good memory." She handed him a piece of soap and a clean rag. "Now, undress and hop in."

Sasha baulked. "Not in front of you."

Beth frowned for a moment then shrugged. "Very well, I will give you twenty minutes. But when I come back, you had better have washed yourself thoroughly, including your hair. Otherwise, I'll be doing it for you."

6

At dinner that evening, the new stable boy was the main topic of conversation. Sheldrake, Maud, Eloquin and Jayhan were seated around a long mahogany table, being served with discreet efficiency by Clive.

Maud tore off a piece of bread and dunked it into her seafood chowder. "It was a little highhanded of Beth to employ someone without your approval, Sheldrake, don't you think?"

Sheldrake glanced at Clive, Beth's husband, whose face remained impassive, then back at his wife. "I believe the circumstance were unusual. The boy demonstrated quick reactions, intelligence and a remarkable affinity with horses. He acted without hesitation and with some courage to save Beth from that cart horse's hooves."

"And then his master beat him around the head so hard, he could hardly stand up again, just for talking to Beth," interrupted Jayhan hotly. "Of course Beth had to rescue him."

As Clive passed behind him, he felt the weight of something being slipped into his pocket. When he surreptitiously felt in his pocket, his fingers closed around two metal disks. His silver florins had been returned.

"No 'of course' about it. We cannot rescue every well-deserving battered child. We do not have the resources," responded his mother. She shrugged. "However, I understand Beth was prepared to pay for him with her own money."

"She was, although I have naturally reimbursed her, since he will be working for us," said Sheldrake.

"Why did she have to pay for him?" asked Jayhan. "Sasha said he wasn't a slave...but is he free to walk away from here?"

"Our society does not have slaves, Jayhan." Sheldrake's voice developed its didactic tone. "But we do have indentured apprentices, whose masters pay their parents for them in return for their labour. The apprentices can be given a small wage, especially towards the end of their training, but generally they work in exchange for training and board, so that they may eventually become tradesmen in their own right. Bryson would have paid the orphanage for this boy and raised the price because he had given the lad experience, even if carting is not an actual trade."

"But is he free to walk away?" he persisted.

Sheldrake gave a little cough. "Not exactly. His absconding would be broadcast and no one would take him in or give him work. An apprenticeship is a contract of trust, you see." Seeing Jayhan about to raise an objection, he added. "If the boy fled far away, he might be able to start again but he would have no money, no credentials and his chances of survival on the road alone would be vexed. A young lad is easy prey."

"Easy prey for what?"

Sheldrake glanced at him before taking a spoonful of

chowder to his mouth. He swallowed unhurriedly before replying, "Other societies trade in slaves. And a child on his own is not safe. There are those among us who would use and abuse a child with no connections."

"Hmph. Like that Bryson, you mean." Aware of his mother's eyes on him, Jayhan scooped a couple of spoonsful of soup into his mouth, careful not to spill it down his chin. When she looked satisfied and returned her attention to her own meal, he added, "Bryson didn't even pay him, you know, and the boy said he should have."

His mother asked for more wine and waited while Clive poured it before replying, "We will house him and feed him and Beth will teach him." As she saw a frown gathering on her son's face, she added hurriedly, "And I suppose we will give him a small wage. After all, a boy needs a bit of spending money, doesn't he, for his days off."

Jayhan let out a breath. "Of course he does."

Sheldrake smiled. "You seem to have taken this child's cause to heart."

"Dad, he saved Beth and I love Beth…and then that carter was so mean to him and…" his voice hitched… "I've never seen anyone be hurt like that before. It was so unfair." He suppressed a sob. "It was awful."

Sheldrake met Maud's eyes across the table as he put his arm around his son's shoulder. "The world is an unkind place for many people, Jayhan. We can't help everyone, but don't worry. We will look after your waif for you."

The boy leaned his head against his father's shoulder. "Thanks."

7

Next morning, well before dawn, Sasha sat up suddenly, starting in fright at an unexplained thump. After a moment, he remembered where he was, bedded down in a corner of the loft above the stables. He breathed a sigh of relief, as he realized that the noise would not preface Bryson's entry. He listened carefully, waiting to hear whether the thump would be repeated. After a minute, he heard the sound again and recognised it as a hoof being stamped on a bed of straw.

In an instant, he had thrown off his blankets and was climbing down the wooden ladder into the stables. He grabbed a pocketful of oats then crept quietly along the row of stalls, his bare feet hardly making a sound. He was sure the noise had come from further down. Sure enough, he heard the stamping of restless hooves three stalls from the end on the left hand side.

In the predawn monochrome, he could see a large draught horse filly, deep in her stall, tossing her head, ears back.

"It's all right," Sasha murmured, "What has spooked you, hey? No one else is upset."

Crooning softly, he walked forward and placed his hands on top of the half door of its stall.

"There now. Here I am. Nothing to be scared of." In actual fact, Sasha's heart was hammering in his chest, not because he was frightened by the great horse towering over him but because he didn't know what was spooking her. Was there actually some danger lurking that he couldn't see? Despite his efforts, the filly was still on edge. Sasha decided that something in her stall was upsetting her.

He took a long slow breath. Letting none of his own fear show in his voice or movements, he maintained a stream of soothing drivel as he felt his way to the bolt and carefully pulled it open, slithering in and re-bolting the half door behind himself.

The huge horse stamped her feathered foot and sashayed backwards from him until her rump hit the back of the stall. Sasha caught the flash of white in the semi-darkness as she rolled her eyes. The boy stood very still and waited for her to get used to him. After a few moments he started talking quietly to her again.

Her ears twitched forward at the sound of his voice but then she whickered and tossed her head. Suddenly Sasha realised that whatever was upsetting her was near the front of the stall. Talking all the while, he cast his eyes around, looking for the cause. His eyes lit upon the horse's feedbag which was hanging from a hook next to the door's hinges. He frowned. Was the feedbag moving, ever so slightly?

Heart in mouth, visions of snakes or sharp toothed rats in mind, he crept up to the feedbag and snatched away the top layer of hay. Two bright golden eyes looked up at him and blinked.

Sasha gave a low chuckle and patted a small ginger cat that lay curled up in the horse's feed bin. Under his hand, Sasha felt the vibration of a contented purr. After a minute, he left the cat and reached up slowly to stroke the filly's neck in long soothing movements. When she was calm, he placed the hand he had used to pat the cat under her nose, all the while stroking her with his other hand. The horse snuffed and snorted, perhaps at the cat smell or perhaps because Sasha's hand did not contain a treat.

Sasha produced the oats from his pocket and gave them to her before walking to the food bin to retrieve the little cat. With the cat curled in the crook of his arm, Sasha walked the few steps to the horse. He presented the cat slowly to the filly, who eyed it askance for a moment before bending her head to sniff it. The cat rubbed its ear against the horse's muzzle. Suddenly, like a flame flickering into life, a connection bloomed between the small cat and the huge horse. The filly snuffled gently and the cat batted the end of her nose. After a few minutes, Sasha sat the cat carefully on the floor in front of the horse and moved slowly backwards to sit himself in the corner of the stall to watch.

When Beth entered the stables an hour later, all but one of the horses popped their heads over the doors of their stalls to greet her. Immediately concerned, Beth crossed to the gap in their ranks and looked into the stall. Sasha was sitting cross-legged in the corner, sound asleep, with a small ginger cat curled up in his lap. Her fractious filly's head was lowered, watching them and from time to time, gently nosing the cat.

Beth was so bemused by the sight that, for a few minutes, she simply leaned on the door and gazed at them. But time was short and there was the day's work to be done, so eventually she cleared her throat and murmured, "Sasha," as quietly as she could.

The boy's eyes flew open as he jerked awake. The filly snorted and flung up her head but as Sasha, with a supreme effort, did not make any further move, the horse lowered her head again and nudged Sasha under the chin.

Sasha grinned and, disentangling one hand from the cat, pushed the horse's big velvety nose away. "Get away from me, you big brute." He placed the cat on the straw next to him and stood up. "There. You can have Apricot to play with. I have to go." He glanced apprehensively at Beth and pulled his forelock. "Sorry ma'am. I didn't mean to go to sleep." He ducked under the horse's head, drew the bolt and slipped out to join her. "I'm late, am I? What do you want me to do? I'll get right onto it. I'll skip lunch to make up the time. Sorry Ma'am." He took a quick breath. "Please don't send me back to old Bryson. I'll do better tomorrow."

"Stop!" Beth held up a hand which made Sasha flinch. She noted the movement but betrayed no response to it. "Stop, Sasha. I will not send you back to Bryson, whatever happens. At the very worst, if things don't work out here, I will find you a new position where I know you will be safe." She put her hand on his shoulder, again ignoring the flinch she felt beneath her fingers. "Now calm down and tell me how you come to sleeping in Flurry's stall?"

"Is that her name? It suits her." When he had given a brief explanation, she asked for more details. He finished by saying, "I supposed I should just have removed Apricot but, you know, Flurry has to start being brave about cats sometime. It's just a pest if she shies at a cat when you're driving her. It could even overturn whatever she's pulling or she could hurt someone. Look what happened with Hoofer."

Beth brow creased. "How old did you say you were?"

Sasha shrugged. "Bryson told you, ma'am."

"You don't talk like an eight-year-old."

Sasha scuffed his foot through wisps of straw that had drifted out into the walkway. "Sorry Ma'am. I didn't mean to be cheeky."

"It was not meant as censure. You seem wise beyond your years, that's all."

Sasha lifted his head and smiled, his face lighting up. "Thanks."

"I am not angry at you for sleeping in. You did well... Better than you know." She dug into her pocket and produced a small leather disk, stamped with a B. She handed it to him and gave his shoulder a final pat. "Now, off you go to the kitchen and give this to Hannah, the cook. Get some breakfast then come back to me for instructions."

"Yes Ma'am. Thank you Ma'am." Sasha couldn't believe his luck. He was still going to have breakfast. He ran as fast as his legs would carry him.

As he scooted into the kitchen, a large, comfortable, middled-aged woman turned from the stove and frowned at him. "No running in my kitchen, young fella."

"Yes Ma'am. Sorry Ma'am. Beth gave me this to give you and said I could have some breakfast." Seeing her frown deepen, he added hastily, "... if it's all right with you."

The cook took the leather disk and put it in her pocket without looking at it. "You're a bit late. The others have already eaten and are off about their jobs." Her face softened when she saw Sasha's face drop. "Jug of milk's still on the table. Get a glass and help yourself. Then sit yourself down and I'll rustle you up some hotcakes and honey. How does that sound?"

Sasha's breath came out in a rush. "Oh. That would be wonderful, Ma'am." Once he had poured himself a large glass of milk and slugged down half of it in one go, he asked, "Did you make the stew we had last night? It was marvellous, Ma'am."

The cook looked at him quizzically. "It wasn't stew, young fella. It was beef and red wine casserole, but I'm glad you liked it."

"My name's Sasha, Ma'am." He beamed at her. "I am going to be working with Beth in the stables, you know."

The cook smiled in amusement. "Yes, I did know. I hear you saved our Beth from the hooves of a plunging stallion yesterday."

Sasha shrugged and looked down, a little embarrassed. "Yes Ma'am. I suppose I did." He drank some more milk, which left him with a white moustache, "Mind you, it was our horse's fault in the first place. Hoover never could abide cats. I wanted to teach him to, but Bryson wouldn't let me near the horse once I'd taken off his harness and rubbed him down."

As he chatted, Sasha peered around the kitchen until his eyes fell on a basket in the corner containing a large tabby cat.

"Another cat!" he exclaimed. "Seems like this place is crawling with them." Immediately he hopped out of his chair and went to pat it. "Hello there. You're a handsome one, aren't you?" he said as he chucked it under the chin.

"Not crawling exactly, but we do have six of them. This one's the grand old man. His name's George. Now come back to the table. Your hotcakes are ready."

"Oops sorry, Ma'am."

"And stop calling me Ma'am. I'm not your mam. My name's Hannah."

A dull red darkened Sasha's cheeks. With none of his previous jauntiness, he came back to the table and sat down quietly. When the cook served him his hotcakes, he forced a smile and said, "Thank you Hannah."

Hannah could have kicked herself as she belatedly remembered where Sasha had come from. She put her arm around his little shoulders, stiff and resistant beneath her touch. "I'm sorry, lad. I didn't mean to be unkind. I know you were only saying Ma'am as a title of respect. I shouldn't have said what I did."

Sasha didn't know what to say, so he stayed silent. After a minute of munching, he said with a shade more warmth in his voice, "These hotcakes are very nice. I've never had them before."

"Good. Now wash up your plate and glass when you've finished. Then you'd best be on your way."

As he was about to open the door to leave, he was nearly bowled over by Rosie who shoved the door from the other side and swept into the kitchen. She took one look at Sasha, sniffed the air and scowled. "How come he gets a late breakfast?'

"Because I say so," stated Hannah baldly, crossing her arms and omitting to mention the leather disk. "My kitchen. I decide."

Rosie flounced. "Fine. But don't expect any favours from me," she said to him as she moved to the cupboard, reaching in to get out a tray.

Sasha looked startled. "No, Ma'am."

"I am not a Ma'am, I'm a Miss."

"Yes Miss."

"You're not Miss to Sasha," said Hannah, thumping her spoon against the edge of a giant pot she was stirring on the stove. "Don't you go getting airs above your station, young lady. If he calls me Hannah, he calls you Rosie and that's the end of it."

Rosie had placed the tray on the bench and was now filling it vehemently with a teapot and cups ready for morning tea.

"And," added Hannah forcefully, "if you break any of that crockery because you're cross, you'll pay for it out of your wages."

Rosie straightened, took a deep breath, not looking at neither of them and continued her work more carefully. Sasha saw her cheeks flame with chagrin and decided that he would be wise to avoid her until she had time to forget that cook had championed him against her. He suspected that might be a very long time.

8

It wasn't until late in the afternoon when Jayhan had finished his studies that he could get away to the stables. He was dying to meet the new stable boy and a small, unacknowledged part of him wanted to assert his prior claim to Beth.

With a flash of inspiration, he detoured to the kitchen and wheedled a small basket of rock cakes out of Hannah. He entered the stables, clutching his rock cakes and found Beth in her office, poring over accounts.

She looked up as he entered and smiled. "Hello, young man. I was wondering when you would get here."

He gave a little frown. "Were you?" He held out this arms. "Here. I brought you some afternoon tea."

Her smile broadened as she took the little basket from him and placed it on the bench. "Lovely. I'll put the kettle on."

Once they were settled with the tea and rock cakes, Jayhan finally asked, "So where's Sasha? I thought he would be here."

"He's out cleaning the dung out of the top paddock. He should be finished soon."

Just as Beth finished speaking, Jahan could hear the scrape of iron on paving as a shovel was leant up against the wall. Moments later, Sasha poked his head around the corner of the door jamb. His hair was hanging in untidy strands and his dark brown face glistened with sweat.

Sasha produced a small bunch of wildflowers from behind his back, a shy smile on his face and held them out to Beth. "These are for you. To say thanks for getting me away from Bryson."

"Thank you, Sasha." Beth gave him a warm smile as she took the flowers from him.

To cover his awkwardness, he ran the back of his hand across his forehead and said, "Phew. It's warm out there. What do you want me to do next?"

"That's enough for today." Beth indicated the other occupant of the room. "Come in and meet Jayhan."

Sasha's eyes widened and his dark face flushed with embarrassment as he realised his gesture to Beth had been observed. He straightened up resolutely as he turned to face the boy sitting on the other side of the office. Jayhan and he exchanged stares as they surveyed each other. With undisguised curiosity, Jayhan studied Sasha's dark brown skin and deep liquid brown eyes, noted that Sasha was wearing his own cast off clothes and that they were a bit big for him. At the same time, Sasha's gaze roved over Jayhan's auburn hair, lightly tanned skin before coming to rest, with no overt reaction, on his pale lavender eyes.

Once the inspections were over, Sasha gave a small formal bow and said, "Good afternoon, Master Jayhan. I apologize for interrupting. I didn't realise you were here."

Jayhan felt uncomfortable with the boy addressing him

as Master Jayhan but wasn't sure what he was allowed to do about it. He directed a small frown towards Beth, hoping she would understand what he was trying to convey. Beth, who was a bit of a genius with small boys as well as horses, gave a tiny nod and smile in return.

Jayhan relaxed. "Hello. Just call me Jayhan. You're Sasha, aren't you?" He gave a little grin. "Nice flowers. Wish I'd thought of that. I just brought rock cakes." He waved his arm around him. "So, what do you think? Do you think you'll like it here?"

"I do so far. The food's great."

Jayhan blinked. "Is it?" He grinned and proffered the little basket of rock cakes to Sasha. "Here. You'd better have one of these then. I brought them over for afternoon tea."

Just as Sasha reached out a hand, Beth said firmly, "Oh no you don't. Not until you've washed up. Off you go. There's a cake of soap next to the pump in the court yard. Come back when you're clean and then you can have one... and I'll have a cup of tea ready for you as well."

Sasha gave a comical grimace that made Jayhan laugh as he shot off to do Beth's bidding. When he returned, his black hair was slicked down and his hands and face were dripping. He stood in the doorway shaking the excess water off and grinning. "No towel."

Beth threw him a scrappy old towel. "Here, young one. Dry yourself off and sit down. Your tea's there. So's your rock cake."

`"Thanks." Once he had dried himself off, and taken his first sip of tea and first bite of rock cake, Sasha let out a long sigh of contentment. He saw Jayhan watching him and sat up straighter in his chair. "Sorry. I'm just a bit tired, that's all." Then he said inconsequentially, "You have very interesting eyes, you know. Just the opposite to mine. Yours are nearly white and mine are nearly black."

"They don't spook you?"

Sasha looked surprised. "Spook me? No. Why would they? I like them." He scrunched his face up as he thought. "I think they are very rare. I've never seen eyes like yours... but that makes them special, not spooky." Suddenly he jumped up and crossed to the chipped jar on Beth's desk that now held the little bouquet he had brought in. He plucked out a tiny pale orchid with a deeper lavender centre and presented it to Jayhan. "Look," he said grinning, "Just like your eyes."

Suddenly Jayhan's eyes filled with tears. "Thanks," he said thickly.

Sasha's face fell. "I didn't mean to upset you." He sent a worried glance at Beth but she just smiled.

"You didn't upset him. You accepted him."

The little boy looked a little confused by this. After a moment, he shrugged and grinned at Jayhan. "Deadly eyes. This orchid is called Pale Death." He chortled and said, "I don't think there is a dark brown orchid but there's a dark brown mushroom called Black Velvet and it is *fatal*.' He spread his arms wide. "So we both have deadly eyes."

For the first time in his life, Jayhan didn't feel a knot of tension as someone commented on his eyes. Sasha was sharing in the menace of his eye colour, even revelling in it. A tiny smile appeared on Jayhan's face. "What about Beth's eyes? They are deep blue."

"Oooh," exclaimed Sasha, "the deadliest of them all. Larkspur flowers are deep blue and *very* poisonous." He gave Beth a cheeky grin. "Much worse than Pale Death."

"You, young sir, are becoming far too comfortable far too fast." Her twinkling eyes belied the severity of her words. "You've only been here a day and you're teasing your boss. Now off you go, the two of you, and play outside. I need some peace and quiet to tackle these accounts."

And so began a friendship that would last their lifetimes. They wandered out past the stables then, by some unspoken mutual agreement, broke into a run.

"Race you," shouted Jayhan. "First to the fence on the other side of the paddock."

Jayhan, full of beans after a day behind his desk, won by a couple of yards. It occurred to neither of them that Sasha might be tired after hours of physical work.

"Cheat!" shouted Sasha joyfully. "You'd already started running when you said "Race you.""

"No, I didn't."

"Right then. Race you!" yelled Sasha, grabbing a definite head start. "To the tree line."

The tree line, which marked the edge of the forest, was a considerable distance and after a hard run race, both declared roundly that they had won. They caught each other's eyes and laughed before leaning over, gasping for breath. In no time at all they had recovered and Jayhan invited Sasha to come and see a wombat hole he had found.

As they drew near, Jayhan put his finger to his lips and whispered, "Shhh. It's nearly sunset. If we are very quiet, we might see it come out in a bit."

They hunkered down behind a bush about twenty yards from the hole and waited... and waited... and waited. After what seemed like an hour but was actually six minutes, Sasha began to reach his hand out slowly. Jayhan frowned and mimed, "Shh," to which Sasha mouthed back "I know, I know," and continued to move his hand. Jayhan gave an irritated shrug and turned his attention back to the wombat hole.

Minutes passed. Although he could still feel Sasha moving at his side, he had to grudgingly admit that the boy's movements were silent. Soon he felt a gentle dig in the ribs and turned to see Sasha gesturing that he should look at something on the ground while Sasha watched the wombat hole. Jayhan found two faces, made from rubbed lines in the dirt, twigs, leaves and pebbles, smiling up at him. No attempt had been made to define skin colour but one had white quartz eyes while the other's were obsidian. A decorative circle of twigs and leaves surrounded the two faces.

A broad smile split his face and his eyes teared up as the acceptance of this one child brought home to him how lonely he had been. Sasha glanced at him and his eyebrows twitched in concern when he saw the tears. Jayhan waved his hand in a gesture that meant not to worry and kept smiling. He raised his thumb to show he liked the pictures.

Suddenly the faint snapping of a leaf drew Sasha's attention to the hole on the other side of the bushes and he dug Jayhan excitedly, and less gently this time, in the ribs. As they watched, a broad hairy muzzle emerged from the hole and sniffed the air. Beside him, Jayhan saw Sasha stiffen in consternation then relax as he quickly licked a finger and raised it, feeling the breeze against the wombat side of his finger. They were downwind of it.

Sensing no danger, the rest of the wombat soon followed. For a minute or two, it gave a few desultory scratches in the leaf fall near its hole before trundling off, scratching from time to time with its powerful claws and rootling around with its nose among the detritus and roots, until it disappeared out of sight through the trees.

The boys heaved a sigh of satisfaction.

9

"White quartz is very powerful, you know," said Sasha a few days later as, once more, they wandered through the bushland on the other side of the paddocks. The weather was turning cold and they were both rugged up in warm coats and boots.

"So?" Light dawned. "Is that what you used to make my eyes on your drawing?"

Sasha nodded. "Yep. White quartz. Stores and channels energy. Even makes thoughts clearer, stronger somehow."

Jayhan frowned. "How do you know all this stuff?"

Sasha shrugged.

When it was clear that Sasha wasn't going to answer, he asked instead, "So what about the black stone you used for your eyes? Does it have any special powers?"

Sasha bent down and picked a small piece of it up from the ground and began to toss it in his fingers. "Yep. It protects you. Keeps you safe from mean people."

Jayhan eyed him for a moment before saying, "Didn't do much to protect you from that bastard, Bryson."

Sasha stopped tossing the stone and looked at him.

"You'd be surprised. My time with him wasn't good but it could have been a lot worse." He gave a little smile. "And look!" he said sweeping his arm around him. "I'm here now, aren't I? Not with him."

"Huh," snorted Jayhan. "That's because you were brave and you're good with horses, not because of some little black rock. Besides, you didn't have a little black rock then. You just had your dark eyes."

In answer, Sasha pulled a silver chain out from inside his shirt. Hanging from it was a polished black stone, held by a small ornate claw of silver. When Jayhan looked closer, he could see a series of lines cut into its surface; a triangle bisected by a long line that continued past its base. As he frowned, Sasha said proudly, "It is my family's symbol; a fire tree."

Jayhan looked puzzled for a moment before his brow cleared and he gave a short laugh. "You have a funny way of speaking sometimes. You mean a *fir* tree, don't you?" He nodded. "I can see now. It does looks like a fir tree."

Sasha huffed impatiently. "No. I don't mean a fir tree. I mean what I said... and my accent isn't funny... It's a *fire* tree. You know, like flames. In summer, it is covered in red and orange blossoms...looks like fire. Get it?"

"All right. Sorry, sorry. We don't have fire trees around here. At least I don't think we do." He thought for a minute. "So where are your family and you from? Somewhere they have fire trees, I'm guessing."

Sasha chortled. "Well done. Quick as a flash."

Jayhan grinned. "Thanks." After a moment, he prompted, "So go on. Where are you from?"

Sasha glanced at him then away. "From across the Najabi desert. From the Eastern Plains that run to the foothills of the Darkstone Mountains."

Jayhan's eyes grew round. "Wow! That is far, far away. How'd you end up here?"

"I don't know." Sasha gave an unhappy little grimace. "I was too young to remember… and no one can tell me."

"Did you ask them?"

"What do you think? Of course I asked them. I asked everyone at Stonehaven orphanage but all they knew was that I was left on the front steps sometime during the night. Old Tom told me that the delivery man found me the next morning lying wrapped in blankets in a very large basket made from woven grasses."

"So how do you know where you come from?"

Sasha looked at him a long moment, waiting to see whether he would figure out something so obvious. "My colouring and the basket," he said finally, "And my amulet."

Suddenly Jayhan stood up and started walking back towards the edge of the bushland. As Sasha caught up with him, Jayhan said, "So you've never seen those fire trees, have you? Someone just told you about them."

"So what?"

"And being dark coloured doesn't mean you have to have come from these Eastern Plains of yours. People with dark skin also come from the Western Islands, Kimora, Pangetti, Booralee. Just like paler skinned people like me come from here, Eskuzor, and Asthania."

"The Eastern Plains and the Darkstone Mountains are *in* Kimora, you idiot. Anyway, what about the basket?"

Jayhan stopped and put his hands on his hips. "What about the basket? Even if it comes from the Eastern Plains… personally I wouldn't have a clue where baskets come from…who's to say someone didn't buy it from the local market to put you in it. Goods travel between lands, you know. So do people for that matter. You could be from anywhere."

Sasha's face puckered as he stamped his foot and yelled, "I didn't know you could be so mean." Tears streamed down his cheeks. "I hate you."

Jayhan was struck dumb. Before he could recover, his little friend took off back the way they had come, dashing his way between sharp-leaved tea trees and clambering over a granite outcrop. Before Jayhan knew what was happening, Sasha was lost from view.

"Hey, Sasha," he yelled. "Come back." He set off in pursuit, muttering to himself, "What did I do? What on earth happened? What's got into him?"

By the time Jayhan reached the other side of the rocky outcrop, Sasha was nowhere in sight. He stopped and listened. A cold breeze crept down into his coat and made him shiver. After a few moments, he thought he heard leaves scrunching to his right. He turned and started in that direction but a wattle bird flew out from a bush almost under his feet and he realised that it was the bird and not Sasha that he had heard.

He grimaced in disappointment and stopped to listen again. The bushland around him seemed deathly quiet but slowly he tuned in to the drone of insects and, as he waited quietly, bird calls started up.

But no sound that he could interpret as being Sasha.

Suddenly he was startled by a pair of rainbow lorikeets, their orange, purple and green plumage flashing in the sunlight as they swept low over his head and disappeared at breakneck speed between the trees, shrieking as they flew.

Maybe Sasha disturbed them, thought Jayhan, heading further still to his right in the direction they had flown from. After a few minutes, he found himself at the edge of the bush but there was no sign of Sasha. He scanned the fields and ran his eyes along the tree line but nothing. Pushing down a confused sense of panic and frustration, Jayhan decided to head for home, hoping that Sasha had returned ahead of him, and if not, to get help looking for him.

By the time he reached Beth's door, it was full dark. He peered in the window and his heart sank as he saw no sign of Sasha. Still, perhaps he had gone inside the house for dinner already. Jayhan knocked and pushed the door open.

"I've lost Sasha," he said in a rush. "Has he come back here?"

Beth's eyes widened in alarm. "No. Not as far as I know. Why isn't he with you?"

Jayhan grimaced. "Tell you the truth, I don't know. He just got upset and ran off. I've been looking for him but I couldn't find him. If he hasn't come back here, I think he's still somewhere in the bush."

Beth grabbed her coat and strode out to join him in the darkness. The wind had picked up and snowflakes were swirling past them. She quickly checked the stables, calling Sasha's name as she ran.

"No. Not here. Where did you last see him?" When Jayhan described the location, she frowned. "The weather is closing in. The ground will freeze tonight. It will be a long, cold, lonely night for him if we don't find him." Seeing that Jayhan was already on the verge of panic, she didn't voice her fear that Sasha might not make it 'til morning. She took a deep breath as she collected her thoughts. "Right. We'll need a couple of horses saddled. You start on that while I round up some helpers. I'll let Maud know what is happening."

Twenty minutes later, two farmhands, Jake and Thompson, Leon the surly coachman and Beth were assembled outside the kitchen door, carrying lanterns. She handed Jayhan a meat pie. "Here. You and I will ride on ahead. Eat this on the way. I know you're probably tired but we need you to show us exactly where you were." She turned to a burly bearded man. "Jake, you two spread out and search the fields on your way to the trees. Jayhan and I will begin looking within the tree line but won't go out of sight until you join us."

Just as they had mounted up, Sheldrake stuck his head out the kitchen door. "Just a minute. Do you have any clothing of Sasha's? Something that carries his scent?"

"Up in the hay loft," replied Beth, nodding at Jayhan to fetch it.

As he returned with Sasha's spare shirt, a huge thickset bloodhound emerged from the kitchen and sniffed at it.

Beth gave a lop-sided grin. "Hello Maud. Good of you to join us. You can lope along next to Jayhan and me, if you like. The boys will meet us at the forest edge."

10

Sasha ran through the scrub, furious and distressed all at once. Underlying it all was a sense of panic. He had thought he knew at least something about who he was and where he was from, but Jayhan had taken it all away with a few thoughtless words. He had treated the meagre clues to Sasha's life as an interesting puzzle, casually challenging the scraps of knowledge that Sasha had woven together to create his past. For Jayhan a casual pastime; for Sasha, his whole identity.

As he rounded a corner, a stick rolled under his right foot. He fell heavily, his left leg folding under him. When he tried to rise, his left knee felt jarred but held him. He stood quietly for a moment, his forward impetus broken by his fall. He looked back the way he had come and realised he could no longer see the forest's edge.

Better go back before I get lost, he thought.

But as he moved his right leg forward, his jarred left knee buckled.

"Ow!" he yelped as he just managed to save himself

from falling. He stood with his weight distributed carefully between both feet, feeling unable to move.

"I need a stick," he said firmly. He hopped a few steps to a partly fallen dead tree and dragged a dry branch towards him. The bark held it to the tree by a determined thread. He pulled hard and as the bark gave way, he lost his balance and toppled backwards, banging his head on a raised patch of hard earth.

"OW! Again!" He sat up rubbing the back of his head, tears starting to his eyes. For a moment he felt woebegone, but with the determination bred from a hard life, he clamped down on his feelings, gave a defiant sniff and climbed gingerly to his feet.

He grasped the stick in his right hand to give him support as he put his weight on his left leg. After a few practice steps, he nodded his approval and set off back the way he had come. Long shadows striped the ground and he used them to keep his direction as constantly north-west as he could, given that he had to wind between trees, logs and the odd boulder. After twenty minutes, he could just see the last glimmer of evening shining through distant gaps in the trees, showing him the edge of the forest. But even as he watched, the light faded. With his eyes adjusted to the dark, he could still see, but he knew he didn't have long before it would be too dark to keep going.

Sasha tried to hurry but didn't want to risk falling again so his speed barely increased. Even so, he caught his right foot on a root that had grown under his path, making pain flare in his knee. From then on he stepped carefully, using his stick to feel out indistinct variations in the ground's surface. There were no longer any shadows to help him and this area of bush was dry, no moss on the south side of the trees to guide him.

In the distance he heard a dingo howl. He stopped to listen, guessing it was in the opposite direction from habitation. According to his own calculations that was almost right. A dark shape loomed and he realised it was a large boulder he has passed on his way in. Good. He was still heading towards home.

Home? Was it home? It was the closest he had to a home. Maybe after tonight, it wouldn't be any more. His stomach clenched. Oh no! What had he done? He had to get back and explain.

He stopped dead in his tracks. Explain what? That Jayhan had upset him? Would they even understand? And even if they did, would they then turn their anger on Jayhan? He didn't want that. And what would it do to their friendship if he got Jayhan into trouble? Jayhan may be an insensitive idiot, but Sasha still liked him... and he was the only friend Sasha had.

Suddenly a deep throaty howl sounded up ahead.

Sasha's face split with a grin. "Maud! Maud! I'm over here," he yelled. He started to hobble-run and promptly fell over a log and landed in a heap on the ground. "Oh, not again." He pulled a stick away that was jabbing into to his arm, raised himself on one elbow and yelled again. "Maud, over here."

Moments later, an enormous bloodhound bounded up and thumped him back to the ground with huge paws on his chest. Sasha beamed up at her and flung his hands around her neck. "Oh Maud, I'm so glad to see you. I was trying to get back as fast as I could, but my knee is sore and it's dark and..." He sniffed, then before he could stop himself, he was sobbing into the soft warm fur of her neck.

It was not long before Sasha heard voices and saw lights bobbing up and down as the rest of the search party approached. Maud gave a couple of ear-splitting howls, which guided the search party to them.

Sasha drew in a few shuddering breaths, trying to pull himself together before the others arrived, but the streaks from his tears shone on his cheeks in the lamp light. He looked up at them, his arms still round Maud's neck, his hands fondling her long ears.

"I'm sorry. I hurt my knee and couldn't get back fast. I tried. I really did." He sniffed and threatened to dissolve into tears again, scared of what would happen to him. He didn't seem to connect that he was drawing comfort from the mistress of the house while fearing the retribution of her staff.

They all stared at him, speechless.

Finally, Jayhan said, "You do realise that's my mother you're holding?"

Sasha gave a little smile and nodded. "Yes, I know. Maud found me."

Beth frowned. "How did you know it was Maud?"

Sasha looked puzzled. "What wouldn't I? Maud is Maud. You are you. It doesn't matter what shape you are. You're still the same person."

"Did you know Maud was a shapeshifter? I didn't tell you." Beth turned to Jayhan. "Did you?"

"No one told me," interrupted Sasha, before Jayhan could reply. "I didn't know until I heard Maud howling for me."

"Huh. Well, that's very odd. *We* only knew it was Maud because we don't have a bloodhound, so it had to be her." Beth gave herself a little mental shake and became businesslike, "Now that you've found him Maud, we can give you some privacy if you want to concentrate on changing back."

In answer, Maud shook her heavy head, flapping her long ears in Sasha' face before nuzzling him under the chin. Sasha chortled. "Stop it. You're tickling me."

Jayhan watched, feeling a twinge of jealousy. His mother had never been so warm with him.

Finally, Maud heaved herself off Sasha and rose to her feet. Leon, a hefty, broad-backed man, put his hands under Sasha's armpits and lifted him easily to his feet.

"There you are, young fella, me lad," said Leon gruffly. "Do you need a hand walking?"

Beth and Jayhan exchanged looks. Never had they heard Leon say more than a few grudging words.

"Thanks," said Sasha, as Leon handed him his stick. "I think I can manage." He set off, stick in one hand, his other arm draped across Maud's shoulders. Beth held the lantern to light their way. Sasha hobbled along as quickly as he could, not wanting to hold everyone up.

Jayhan came up beside him. "Don't feel you have to rush. It's not far to the horses. You can ride from the forest's edge," he said, eager to be helpful.

Sasha glanced at him, saw the worry in his face and let the residue of his anger melt away. *Just an idiot, not malicious,* he thought.

"Thanks," he said. "I'm glad you came."

Jayhan shrugged, a bit embarrassed, and said in a low voice, meant only for Sasha's ears. "I'm sorry I was unkind. I didn't realise..." He grimaced. "Beth explained to me what I did."

Sasha gave a little chuckle. "Burnt ears, huh?"

For a moment, Jayhan looked confused then realised what Sasha had meant and laughed. "Very burnt ears... most of the way from the house."

"Well, I'm glad you told her what happened. It saved me having to come up with a story to explain why I ran off."

Jayhan frowned across at the great bloodhound padding next to Sasha. "You realise my mother is listening to all of this?" he whispered.

Sasha grinned and patted Maud's back. "Doesn't matter. Whatever I did when I got back would be wrong. Either I would have to lie to cover up for you, or dob on you for being mean... even if you hadn't meant to be." He added hastily seeing Jayhan about to protest. "So, obviously, I would have had to lie."

Suddenly Maud gave a howl, making the boys jump. When they looked at her, they saw she was wagging her tail, although whether it was in appreciation of Sasha's frankness or his choice to shield her son was unclear.

11

The next morning Sasha was summoned to confront the family upstairs while they breakfasted. Beth had bound his knee so that he could walk without the aid of a stick, but he still favoured it. Heart hammering, he climbed the polished staircase. He had never been up to the first floor and he was overawed by the richness of the dark wood panelling and the portraits that seem to glower at him as he passed below them.

By the time he reached the top of the staircase, his knee was hurting and he was using the bannister to pull up as much of his weight as he could. He waited a few moments to compose himself before stepping forward to knock on the dining room door.

"Enter," came Sheldrake's voice.

Sasha tried to read what emotion tinged the single word but couldn't. It was neither angry nor welcoming.

Sasha opened the door and stepped in to stand at the foot of the table. The whole room seemed to glare as light from the window reflected off the blindingly white table cloth and bright, silver cutlery. Sheldrake, Maud and

Jayhan put down their knives and forks and turned to look at him. Unsure what to do, he bowed to them. He realised his legs were trembling as he put his hands behind his back and waited.

This is it then. They are going to send me on my way. I'm just a big pest. I put all those people out last night. Six people wasted their evening to look for me. Tears sprang to his eyes. *Oh what an idiot I am! Such a nice place; almost a home. And now I've ruined it. I'm not going to beg, though.* He took a deep breath and quelled his tears. *I will just thank them for all they've done for me and leave.*

"Good morning, Sasha," said Maud in a cool voice.

Sasha nodded his head in her direction. "Good morning, Madam." *Madam, not Ma'am,* he thought bitterly. *I learnt that mistake.*

"You are more respectful this morning, young man," she said, appraising him. "I thought you said a person was the same person, no matter what shape they took."

"Yes Madam. We are the same people as yesterday but in different roles today."

Maud gave her head a slight shake and murmured, "Such acumen in one so young," She looked across at Sheldrake. "I believe you have some questions?"

Sheldrake cleared his throat. "I understand, Sasha... that is, Jayhan has told me, I hope you don't mind, that you wear an amulet around your neck that you have had from birth and that gives you some protection. Is that correct?"

Instinctively Sasha's hand flew up to cover the place where the amulet lay against his thin chest. "Yes sir."

"Perhaps Jayhan has mentioned to you that I am an authority on such things and have many in my possession."

"Your pardon, but I do not wish to sell it, sir."

Sheldrake gave a slight smile. "That is well, because I do not wish to buy it."

Sasha looked panic-stricken but stayed silent. If Sheldrake decided to take it from him before turning him away there was nothing he could do about it.

Sheldrake frowned. "Do you think so poorly of me, lad? I would not force it from you. But I would feel honoured if you would trust me enough to show it to me. I might even be able to tell you more about it than you know yourself."

Sasha hesitated only for a moment before pulling the chain from around his neck and handing over the amulet. "I believe it is from the Eastern Plains near the Darkstone Mountains, sir, and bears my family's symbol of a fire tree..." He sent a baleful glare at Jayhan. "but I may be wrong."

Sheldrake glanced at Sasha then Jayhan but said nothing, dropping his eyes to the smooth, black amulet in his hand. "Hmm. Interesting... and beautiful. You are right. This is a symbol of power that is carved into it." He looked up and gave Sasha a surprisingly understanding smile. "I don't think it is a fire tree, however. I think the triangle represents birth, life and death but the line through the middle? I am not sure. I need to research it. Do you mind if I copy this symbol or perhaps keep your amulet for a few days?"

Sasha swallowed. "You may keep it for a short time, although it is my protection, but I must have it back before I go away... sir."

"What? You're leaving us?" demanded Sheldrake. "Jayhan wasn't that unkind to you, was he? I thought you two were friends again."

"No, he wasn't. Yes, we are. I mean..." Sasha's throat ached with unshed tears. *I won't let them see me cry. I won't.* "I thought you called me up here to send me away."

There! He had said it and blast it all! Now he *was* crying. "I'm sorry," he mumbled, sniffing furiously.

"Oh for goodness sake!" exclaimed Maud, getting up and coming around the table She put her arm around his shoulder and led him to the table. "Where's Rose? Get this boy a cup of tea. Sit down, Sasha. Here. Have a napkin. Of course we're not sending you away. Oh dear! We must have seemed like judge and jury to you, you poor boy."

Sasha nodded and hid his face in the napkin, unable to shut the floodgates that he had kept so firmly locked. Finally, the thought of how annoyed Rose would be at having to serve him a cup of tea tickled his sense of humour enough to dam the tide. To everyone's surprise, when he raised his head he was grinning. He gave a final sniff and put aside his damp serviette.

"So, was Rose cross?" he asked, as he sipped his tea.

Maud frowned in recollection. "Now that you mention it, she did seem to flounce out of the room."

Sasha gave a satisfied little chuckle and took another sip of his tea.

"So Sasha, do you feel up to continuing our conversation?" asked Sheldrake, helping himself to a now cold slice of toast. "Toast?" he offered as an afterthought.

"Yes please," Sasha took a slice from the toast holder and placed it on the plate near him. Sheldrake handed him the butter and jam as he finished with them. "And yes, especially if it's not about me leaving."

Sheldrake took a bite of jam-laden toast, then setting down the remainder, steepled his fingers. Once he had finished chewing, he asked, "So Sasha, how did you know that the bloodhound was Maud? Most, in fact *all*, of the people I know cannot see through a shape-shifting. Did you just deduce it must be her because we don't usually have a bloodhound and despite what you said, you really did know that Maud is a shape-shifter?"

Sasha's little body stiffened and his eyes glittered. "I am not a liar, sir."

"No need to get huffy. After all, you yourself admitted last night that you would lie to protect Jayhan."

He relaxed a little. "That's not the same at all, sir. I might lie to protect someone. I wouldn't lie to make myself seem cleverer than I am."

Sheldrake nodded slowly. "I see. A nice distinction. So the question still remains; how did you know the bloodhound was Maud?"

There was a lengthy pause as Sasha was munching a piece of toast. He swallowed as fast as he could, nearly choking himself. "Whoops! Sorry sir. I just knew it was Maud. To me, it's the same as seeing you in a different suit on a different day. You're still the same person underneath."

"But you acted differently with my wife?"

Sasha gave a little smile. "So did she. Now it's back to usual." He thought for a moment. "I guess it's like fancy dress. When you're in fancy dress, you act the part and people around you join in. Then tomorrow it's back to normal." Sasha cocked his head. "Does that help?"

"It makes it clear how it seems to you but not how you do it. But I suspect you don't know how," replied Sheldrake. "However, whether you understand it or not, the ability to see through shape-shifting and disguises would be very valuable to me."

"Now Sheldrake," remonstrated Maud, wagging a finger at him. "Don't you go involving this little one in your nefarious doings. He is too young and innocent."

Sheldrake appeared shocked. "Really Maud! I wouldn't put the child in danger. I would arrange things so that he could see the people in disguise without them seeing him. Regardless of whether I use him, I think we should do some training and experimenting in the meantime. If Sasha is agreeable, of course." He turned to the stable boy. "Would you like to join Jayhan in his magic studies, Sasha? While he studies with his tutor in the morning, you can fulfil your duties around the stables then meet us in the afternoon at my workshop. What do you think?"

Sasha looked from Sheldrake to Jayhan, who gave an excited nod. He turned back to Sheldrake, his dark eyes shining. "I would be honoured, sir.... I hope I'm worth your time. I will try my very best."

Sheldrake gave one of his rare smiles. "You are already worth the effort, whether you realise it or not."

PART II

12

BANG!
Jayhan went flying backwards and landed in an untidy heap on the ground. On the bench in Sheldrake's workshop, a beaker of murky grey fluid issued an innocent wisp of smoke but, above it, a thick grey haze wafted near the ceiling.

"Jayhan! What on earth do you think you're doing? You will get us all killed!" roared Sheldrake.

"Jayhan! Are you all right?" cried Sasha, as he ran to kneel beside him.

Jayhan turned a sooty face to Sasha and grinned. "Whoops!"

Sasha heaved a sigh, partly of relief and partly of exasperation. "You idiot! I told you to wait a minute to give it time to work, after you said the incantation. When you said it again, it doubled the force." Once Jayhan had sat up, Sasha helped him get to his feet. "All right?"

"Yes, just grazed my elbow, I think." Jayhan tried to manoeuvre his arm so that he could inspect the damage. He pulled at the tattered hole in the sleeve of his jacket, but frowned in frustration when he couldn't see his elbow. He dabbed at it with his fingers, which came away red and wet. "Yep," he said with some satisfaction. "It's bleeding."

Sheldrake glanced over from where he was concentrating on constructing a knife that could elongate to become a sword. "So, despite the excessive dramatics, did your potion work?"

Jayhan gave a little grimace. He would have liked some sympathy from his father but knew the best he could hope for was to avoid a lecture. *Soldier on until the job is done,* was his father's mantra. He reluctantly lowered his arm, giving his sleeve a shake to put it back in place and wiped his fingers on his trouser leg.

Shrugging off the whole incident, Jayhan turned his attention to the beaker and carefully decanted the grey liquid and a residue of crushed quartz into another beaker, leaving a small rounded oval object in the bottom. He placed a piece of white cloth on the bench then tipped the grey object onto it. Jayhan and Sasha peered closely at it.

"Hmm. Isn't it supposed to be white?" asked Jayhan dubiously.

Sasha used another cloth to wipe it, revealing white beneath the grey. He wet the cloth and tried harder. A stone of iridescent white, with sparkles of red, green and blue shone up at them. A jagged line of black, like a lightning strike, ran down the middle of it.

"Oh look!" breathed Sasha. "It worked. It's turned to opal. It's beautiful."

Jayhan grunted. "Huh. A beautiful marred opal. I wrecked it, didn't I?"

"Well, it's not pure, but I think the black streak looks great."

"Show me," said Sheldrake, not looking up. "Bring it over here."

Jayhan duly presented it on a piece of white cloth to his father and held his breath. Sheldrake finished inserting a tiny piece of metal into his construction and straightened, arching his back against stiffness. Only then did he look at the opal.

He picked it up and held it up to the light, angling it this way and that, so that the colours sparkled. He returned the stone to its place on the white cloth and smiled.

"Well done! Not perfect, but well done."

Jayhan let his breath out in a rush. "Thanks."

Sheldrake's smile broadened. "Son, you could kill yourself, holding your breath like that."

Jayhan grinned. "I didn't realise I was."

Sheldrake looked across at Sasha, who had remained standing at the bench. "Well done to both of you. You are right that the black streak is effective but I want you to be able to create one without. Then you can move onto creating a black opal." He patted Jayhan on the back. "That's enough for today. You can try again tomorrow. Besides, you need to get some antiseptic and a bandage onto that serious wound of yours. Tidy up, then go and see Beth." He gave his son's shoulders a squeeze before sending him off.

Jayhan and Sasha arrived at the stables just as Beth dismounted from a solid brown mare, whose flanks were dark with sweat. Sasha bounded up, took the reins from Beth and stroked the mare along her neck.

"Hello Maud. You look like you need a drink and good rub down." Sasha laughed as Maud tossed her head. "Go on. You know you'd love it. Let's start with a drink and see how you feel then."

Jayhan glanced at Sasha then raised a hand in greeting to the horse. "Hi Mum," he said awkwardly, far less at ease with his mother in other shapes than Sasha was.

As Sasha led Maud to the trough, Jayhan presented his elbow to Beth, who inspected it with due gravity. "I think that definitely needs a bandage. Let's go to my office."

Once he was settled on a chair, Beth dabbed his grazed elbow with a lotion infused with cinnamon bark and thyme.

"There," she said when she'd finished. "Now, you'll have to take your shirt off if you want a bandage."

"Do I need one?"

Beth considered. "Not if you wear that same shirt with the hole in the elbow for a day or two. But if you have to put on a new shirt, your graze may stick to it." She shrugged. "Up to you."

"Hmph. Up to Mum, you mean. If it were up to me, I'd just wear the same shirt."

Beth thought for a moment. "Yep. Better put a bandage on it. Off with your shirt. Anyway," she added, "this will stop it sticking to the table if you lean on it."

Jayhan, secretly delighted to warrant a bandage, took his shirt off with alacrity. While Beth was bandaging his arm, he let his eyes wander around the room, checking out the tack and rosettes, the cobwebs in the corner and the piles of paperwork. Noticing a small stack of books in the corner, he frowned. "Aren't they my old readers? What are they doing here?"

"I borrowed them from Eloquin," said Beth. "I hope you don't mind. I gathered you had finished with them."

"Oh, I don't mind. They're as dull as ditch. Can't think why you'd want to read them, that's all."

Beth finished tying his bandage and patted his arm.

"There you are. You'll have to keep your arm out of the bath or get a new bandage if you get it wet. Promise?"

Jayhan nodded abstractedly, still thinking about the books. Suddenly he asked, "Are you teaching Sasha to read?"

Beth grimaced. "Yes, in the evenings after dinner. It's supposed to be a secret."

"Why?"

"Well, partly because Sasha is embarrassed that he can't read."

Jayhan snorted. "I don't know why. I can't read very well myself, not hard books anyway. If he's already up to those books, he's not far behind me. He could do his lessons with me. I'll talk to Mum about it."

"No, Jayhan, don't. That is the other reason he has kept it secret. He is already sharing your tutoring time for magic. He doesn't want to seem as though he is angling to share your academic time as well. After all, he does have to pay his way. He is not, like you, the son of the house."

Jayhan looked troubled. "But that's not fair," he protested.

Beth smiled warmly at him. "No Jayhan, perhaps not. But life is not fair. Sasha would not feel good about having no time to pay his way. He already frets that he is not doing enough in the stables with the time he spends with you and Sheldrake in the afternoons."

"But Dad wants him to do that so he can help in the future. It is like he is a magic apprentice as well as a stable apprentice... and I hadn't thought about it before, but he'll need to be able to read when we start using spell books."

"He will be ready... in his own way and on his own time."

Jayhan brooded for a minute or two. "He works awfully hard, doesn't he? Can I help? What can I do to help?"

"You are a dear boy. You have already helped him by being his friend and accepting him. Don't worry. He is happier now than he ever has been."

Jayhan was not appeased. He would think about it.

13

Three weeks later, to the horror of both boys, Sheldrake entered the workshop carrying a small leather book, worn and dog-eared, and announced that it was time for them to start following their own formulae.

"This," he said, "was my first spellcaster's book. It is a primer, if you like." He handed it to Jayhan. "You will have to share, of course, since there is only one. Now today, begin with something simple and innocuous. I want you to make up an antiseptic lotion, probably similar to those Beth uses. Turn to page 4, the recipe is there. Most things you need will be in the labelled jars on the shelves but ask me if you need particular ingredients."

The boys took the book to their place on the bench.

"Well," said Jayhan, "Finding page 4 should be easy enough."

They opened the book and studied the ingredients on page 4. After a couple of minutes, by mutual agreement, they took the book to the shelves so they could match words to labels on jars. Two ingredients stumped them. They whispered together trying to find labels to match but eventually decided they need to ask. Then ensued a heated whispering match about who would ask, both valiantly insisting on taking the fall. Finally, Jayhan won by simply walking over to his father and saying, "We have everything but 'Hone-ee' and 'Thime.'"

Sheldrake looked at him for a long moment before saying mildly. "Well done on the other words. I think you will find honey and thyme in the kitchen. Ask Hannah."

As they walked to the kitchen, Jayhan said disparagingly, "How are we supposed to know that? Why don't they spell them as they say them? Stupid books."

Sasha gave a jaunty laugh. "Yeah, stupid books."

Jayhan glanced at him then threw his hands up. "Right. Confession time." He stopped and faced Sasha. "I saw my readers in Beth's office and she told me about you learning to read. She tried to avoid it but I figured it out myself from seeing the books there. So, if we have to read bloody recipes, it will be better if we both know where we stand. I am not a great reader. In fact, you seem to have nearly caught up to me already, which is just shocking as far as I'm concerned, but ask if you need help and I will try.... Might not succeed, but I will try."

Sasha let out a sigh of relief. "And you won't tell your Dad?"

"No. I've known for a couple of weeks and haven't told him. I completely understand why you wouldn't want to waste your mornings in the library with Eloquin and me. Much more fun mucking out the stables."

"Absolutely," said Sasha, with a relieved smile.

Over the coming months, both boys' reading improved as they used it practically. They realised that Sheldrake wasn't going to bite their heads off if they didn't know particular words and, in fact, would prefer them to check with him if they were uncertain, rather than wreck a potion. Unbeknownst to the boys, Sheldrake was leading them through their little book based on the reading level rather than on the relative difficulty of the potion-making.

"Jayhan, you're nearly ready to continue your research, I would think," said Sheldrake, one sunny afternoon as the boys proudly presented a concoction designed for reducing swelling.

"What research?" asked Sasha.

Jayhan looked puzzled for a moment before his brow cleared. "Oh. I'd almost forgotten about that. I put the books in the back of my wardrobe because they were too hard for me." He explained to Sasha about his search for information about his light-eyed grandmother. He shrugged and gave little self-deprecating smile. "I think the books are probably still too hard for us, but I suppose we could have a try. I'll bring them down tomorrow."

The next afternoon, Sasha walked into Sheldrake's workshop to find a daunting pile of books piled on top of their bench. He glanced at Jayhan who nodded permission. So he reached out, but instead of opening one and attempting to read it, he laid the books side by side along the bench. Then he stood back, surveying his handiwork.

"Hmm. They look pretty old." He looked at his friend and grimaced. "Thick, aren't they?"

"Yep. And full of hard words."

Sasha suppressed a sigh. "So what are we looking for? Stuff about your grandmother?"

"Yep."

"So what was her name? Madison?" Then with a surreptitious glance at Sheldrake, whispered, "How do you spell it? Write it down for me."

Jayhan found a piece of chalk and wrote the name carefully on the bench next to the end of the line of books.

Sasha peered at it then grinned triumphantly. "So all we have to do is start by looking for the name 'Madison' in the books and read in front and behind it."

"If we can read the stuff in front and behind," responded Jayhan gloomily.

Sasha gave him a reproving punch on the arm. "Don't be such a gloomy-guts! I come up with a great idea for cutting down on hundreds of pages of reading and all you can do is whinge."

Feeling Sheldrake's eyes on him, Jayhan forced a smile, worried that either his friend might get into trouble for hitting him or he might get into trouble for sulking, "All right. Good idea, I guess. A good start, anyway." He picked up the nearest book. "So we can take one book each, write down its title and then look through it for Madison's name. Then we just write down the page numbers where her name appears and come back to it when we've gone through all the books. What do you think?"

Sasha smiled. "Great idea." He leaned in and added, "And puts off the time when we have to be able to read them."

"Splendid!" Both boys started, finding Sheldrake suddenly standing right behind them. "Of course, you will do this investigating in your own time. We have more important things to do here." As the boys began to protest, Sheldrake raised his hand. "This is Jayhan's project, not mine. You will do it in your own time or not at all."

"Oh." The colour had risen in Jayhan's face, more from embarrassment than anger. Without a word, he packed up the books and put them in a pile near the door.

"Today," continued Sheldrake, "we will spend some

time on investigating Sasha's amulet. Would you mind showing us your amulet again please, Sasha?" When Sasha had pulled it out from beneath his shirt and placed it in Sheldrake's hand, he continued "I have made a copy and have been researching it but now, I want both of you to draw it as accurately as you can. Here, Sasha, have it back."

Sash breathed a sigh of relief as he regained possession of his beloved amulet. "Thank you, sir." He laid the amulet and its chain out, almost reverently, on the bench so that Jayhan and he could copy its markings onto pieces of paper. As soon as they had finished, he put it back on and let the amulet dangle within his shirt, once more out of sight.

Sheldrake walked over to inspect their work and nodded his approval, before handing Sasha an old leather-bound book entitled *Symbols and badges of guilds, sects and dynasties*. "Look through this and see whether you can work out the meaning of your amulet's symbol."

"Do you know, sir, what it means?" asked Sasha.

"Yes, I do now," said Sheldrake, looking over his spectacles at him, "but it has taken some considerable effort to find out. The book I have given you is the product of weeks of searching. I give it to you now so that you can enjoy, as I did, finding the last part of the puzzle. When you have discovered its meaning, we will talk further."

Sasha glanced at him uncertainly, perhaps sensing some undercurrent in his words, but the mage turned away and went back to his own work on the other side of the shed. When he turned his attention to Jayhan, he saw his friend's eyes alight with curiosity.

"Well, come on then," Jayhan said impatiently. "Share."

Sasha smiled at him and placed the book on the bench. "Well, come on then, yourself."

Together, they worked their way through the book, past

sections on heraldry, stonemason's marks, insignias, watermarks and even the seals made by signet rings belonging to the more prominent houses in Carrador.

"Look," said Jayhan suddenly. "That's my mum's mark. See? A centaur; half woman, half animal. That's because Mum shape-changes."

"Where's Sheldrake's seal?"

"I don't know. Wait. Yes, I do. Here it is."

Sasha peered down at an angular S within a diamond within a circle. "Hmm. I've seen that before. It's on some of Beth's paperwork." He smiled. "It suits him."

Jayhan tilted his head, thinking about it. "What? No nonsense? With sharp angles? But with an air about him?"

Sasha laughed. "Exactly."

"Come on you two. What are you up to?" came Sheldrake's voice from across the shed.

"Nothing." They chorused, then laughed. Smothering a fit of the giggles, they turned back to the book and flipped a few more pages.

Suddenly, there in front of them was the symbol from Sasha's amulet, although the vertical line only began half way down the triangle, whereas Sash's began at the top point. Beside it was a drawing of a small bush covered in red and yellow flowers.

"Huh! See?" exclaimed Sasha, "It does represent a flame tree."

"Read the small print," said Sheldrake dryly, from the other side of the shed. "One day, missing details might get you killed."

Two heads, one brown, one black, leant over the book, reading the small writing beneath the symbol.

"Oooh. That's tricky' isn't it? Most people wouldn't notice that extra bit of vertical line but it completely changes the meaning. It's like secret code. Amazing," said Jayhan grinning. He looked at Sasha speculatively. "So what does that mean about you, I wonder?"

Sasha shrugged, looking uncomfortable.

"It means," said Sheldrake, right behind them again, in that disconcerting way he had, "that our little friend here is a shaman, from a long line of shamans... and he is, as he told you, from the Eastern Plains, which is indeed from whence this symbol originates."

Jayhan almost winced when he asked the next question. "And how do you know that someone didn't just put the amulet round his neck?" He grimaced at Sasha. "Sorry. Just need to know. Then you can be sure."

Sasha just cocked his head at Sheldrake and waited. In answer, Sheldrake requested him to take off his amulet again. "Just a small demonstration. I won't keep it long this time." He handed it to Jayhan. "Put it on over your head, just as Sasha did."

Glancing at Sasha who gave a small nod of agreement, Jayhan lifted it. But as the silver chain passed above his head, his hands burned and his head felt as though someone were driving spikes into it. He yowled and dropped the amulet. Predicting the reaction, Sheldrake caught it well before it could fall to the floor.

Sasha's eyes grew round. He looked knowingly at Sheldrake. "Is that what happened when you tried to put it on?"

Sheldrake smiled. "Yes. Exactly the same. And I believe the same would happen to anyone other than you."

"Wow. That's wonderful, isn't it?" Sasha beamed. "Something that is really, truly my own and nobody else's."

Sheldrake and Jayhan, who both owned so much, exchanged a glance of shared sympathy for Sasha. The mage put his arm around the boy's shoulders and gave him a squeeze, "Yes. It is rather wonderful, isn't it?" After a pause, he added, "Your amulet has other properties too. Your mother or father, usually the mother, would have passed it on at the moment before her death to the heir of her bloodline... and with it, all the knowledge of generations of shamans."

"But it's supposed to protect you. That's what Old Tom said," protested Sasha. "How could my mother die if she was wearing it?"

"It didn't stop you from hurting your knee," Jayhan pointed out.

"No, but I didn't die and you found me."

Sheldrake was looking thoughtful. "You have raised an interesting point, Sasha. From what I've read, it does indeed protect you. But how much, I don't know. I will see what else I can find out."

"So is that why Sasha can tell it's my mum when she is in different shapes?" asked Jayhan. "Because he is a shaman?"

Sheldrake directed his response to Sasha rather than to his son. "You are not yet a shaman, just as Jayhan is not yet a mage. You both need guidance to develop your potential. However, in your case, Sasha, I believe your amulet is gradually imbuing you with knowledge as you mature. Hopefully, what you learn from me will enhance that." He gave a little smile. "I think those flashes of wisdom that you produce that seem far beyond your years, can be attributed to your connection with the wisdom of the shamans of your ancestry."

"Huh. Not as brilliant as you thought you were," chortled Jayhan.

"Huh yourself. It may the wisdom of my ancestors but it was me who drew on it." Sasha gave a little smile. "At least I have ancestors. That's a good start. Excuse me Sheldrake, sir, do you have any books about the people and shamans I come from? I don't know anything about my family and people, or shamans or anything."

"I do have some books, but more than that, I know of a woman, an ambassador for the Eastern Plains, who resides at the Kimoran Embassy in Highkington. I will see whether she might be willing to talk to you about your people."

"Wow! Really? That would be wonderful. Could Jayhan come too?"

Sheldrake smiled at his enthusiasm. "I'll see what I can do."

On their way out of the workshop, Sasha bent down to pick up one of Jayhan's books to work on, but Jayhan forestalled him.

"No, don't Sasha." Jayhan said awkwardly. "I thought we would be doing it in our magic lesson time. I don't want to you to spend your spare time on these stuffy old books. You have enough to do. It wouldn't be fair."

"But..."

"No. We'll leave it for now," said Jayhan firmly. He managed a smile. "Anyway, we'll be busy learning about shamans, won't we?"

Sasha glanced at him but, reading the determination on his face, subsided.

Later that evening after dinner, Sasha sat down with a jaunty little book, *The cat that lost its tail*, in his hand, ready to read it to Beth, who was sewing an insignia onto a saddle cloth. Instead of reading, he said, "If I could get hold of some of Jayhan's books, I could help him find out about his great grandmother. He's put them away again in his wardrobe, but it won't feel good if we're only looking at my history and not his. I would have said that to him, but he had that stubborn look on and I knew he wouldn't listen... We could make the books into my reading lessons," he suggested hopefully. He cocked his head. "What do you think?"

"I think you two are lucky to have each other as friends. So, just how were you thinking you might get any of these books *out* of Jayhan's wardrobe?"

Sasha gave a little smile. "Clive?"

Beth put down her sewing to look at him. "Now Sasha, Clive is a respectable, trustworthy member of the household..."

"Yes, but it wouldn't be stealing. It would be borrowing... and to be helpful. I'm sure Clive wouldn't mind."

"Clive wouldn't mind what?" asked a third, deeper voice.

Sasha turned melting, dark eyes on the new arrival and beamed. "Hello Clive."

Beth rolled her eyes and resigned herself to the inevitable.

14

For another fortnight, Sasha and Jayhan slogged their way through the potions primer that Sheldrake has given them, finally reaching some interesting formulae near the end of the book. They had discovered a potion that changed the pitch of a voice and had smuggled some out to use with great effect on George, the cat in the kitchen, who subsequently sounded more like a mouse for twenty-four hours. Amid gales of laughter, the poor cat had retired in high dudgeon to its bolthole under the house and refused to come out, even to be fed, until his voice had returned to normal.

The following afternoon, as they were about to enter the workshop, Sheldrake appeared in the doorway. "Good afternoon boys. We are having our lesson today out in the back paddock."

He led two intrigued boys past the back of the walled kitchen garden. As they passed the passionfruit vine that covered the red brick wall, Sasha pointed out a small nest.

"Look, Jayhan. A honeyeater's nest."

"How do you know?"

"I just know about birds' nests," said Sasha airily.

Jayhan's eyes widened. "Really?"

Sasha grinned. "What do you think? I saw the honeyeater there this morning."

"Oh." He gave a wry smile. "Fine. So, do you reckon there are eggs in it?"

Sheldrake turned around. "Now boys, you are not to touch that nest. We don't want to scare the parents off, now do we?" As the boys shook their heads, he continued, "Let us talk as we walk. Today I am going to teach you how to discover whether the person or animal you see before you is, in fact, that being's true shape. Am I right in assuming, Sasha, that you can tell what a being's original shape is? For instance, when you saw Maud as a bloodhound, did you know whether human or dog was her true shape... or did you simply know it was Maud? What if you had met her first as a bloodhound and only later as a person?"

Sasha thought about it. "I knew the essence of the bloodhound was Maud," he replied finally, "and I had an image of her human self somewhere inside the bloodhound. But when she is human, I don't see any essence of anything else."

"So you can tell that her original form is human?"

Sasha smiled. "I suppose I can. I hadn't thought about it before."

"So, given that you don't see any essence of anything else inside her, did you know Maud was a shapeshifter when you first met her?"

"No, sir... But I would now. I mean I would know another shapeshifter if I met one." He frowned slightly and glanced at Jayhan standing beside him.

Sheldrake drew his attention back, "And how would you know?"

"She's thicker," said Sasha, then blushed furiously. "Whoops. That didn't come out right. I didn't mean to say that Maud's fat. She's not at all overweight, at least not very, only a little bit tubby. What I mean is that she's..."

"Denser?" suggested Sheldrake, suppressing a smile.

Sasha breathed a sigh of relief. "Yes. Like thick cream instead of thin. Like there are a lot of layers underneath."

"Fascinating." Sheldrake stared at him, clearly entranced by this explanation. They had arrived at the top paddock and Sheldrake pulled himself together to unhitch the gate. Pushing it open, he gestured that they should go in. In front of them was a flock of sheep, idly grazing. A few of them eyed the intruders and moved further away, but most of the sheep ignored them.

"Now," said Sheldrake, "whatever you were going to say, Sasha, and I can guess what it is, keep it to yourself for the moment please."

"I wasn't going to say anything," Sasha protested. "If I gave away which one was Maud, Jayhan couldn't practise, could he?"

Sheldrake gave him a pat on the back. "My apologies for underestimating you." He turned to his son. "Now Jayhan, I want you to figure out which, if any, of these sheep is not in its true form. Here is how you do it." He held his fingers straight out but with the middle finger crooked between them, "This is called, rather melodramatically, the claw of truth. Now you place your fingers, held like this, somewhere on their skin or fleece. If their image is a glamour, you will feel a tingling sensation. Do you understand?"

When his son nodded, Sheldrake suggested that Jayhan try it on Sasha first. Sasha obligingly pushed up his sleeve so that Jayhan could lay his three fingers on his arm.

Jayhan shook his head. "No, nothing."

Sheldrake rubbed his hands together. "Good. So now we know our little friend here is not someone else in disguise."

Sasha frowned. "Of course I'm not," he said indignantly.

Sheldrake gave a slight smile that did not fully appease him. However, Sheldrake's mind was on other things. The mage muttered a few obscure words under his breath and waved his hand to encompass the grazing sheep. "Now Jayhan, I have just placed a gentle spell on the sheep so that they won't fear you, as long as you move slowly and are gentle. One of them, as you have gathered, is Maud. I want you to find out which one."

Jayhan worked his way diligently through eight sheep with no results, but happily, before Sasha could die of boredom, Maud made sure she was next in line. As soon as Jayhan touched her, he sprang back, his eyes widening in shock. "Yikes. That almost stung, it was such a strong tingle."

Maud tossed her head and Sheldrake said calmly, "Touch her again and see whether you can do it without betraying that you have noticed."

Jayhan steeled himself and placed his hand, with its longest finger crooked, gingerly on Maud's woolly shoulder. When he was ready for the sensation, he was quite able to withstand it and could remove his hand with more dignity and less haste.

"Hmm'" he said. "Well, that was interesting." He turned to Sasha. "Are you going to have a try, even if you know anyway?"

Sasha shrugged. "Might as well, I suppose." He placed his hand on Maud's shoulder but nothing happened. He looked disappointed. "Hmph. Doesn't work."

"Never mind. You don't need it anyway." Sheldrake smiled at him. "You're an interesting little character, aren't you? Magical, but in a different way from us. I must see what I can find in the library about shaman magic... and I think we might visit Old Tom and see what he knows."

15

Sheldrake and Maud departed for Highkington the next morning, leaving the boys in Beth and Clive's care. Each of them had business in town and the Spring Garden Party was coming up. They took the lumbering old carriage, which was roomy and comfortable, but not at all fashionable. Maud's sumptuous, deep green dress filled most of the interior so that Rose, whom she had brought as her maid, had to ride on top with Leon, the driver. Sheldrake sat across from her, dressed in his usual austere black, although the coat he wore today was exquisitely tailored as befitted a visit to court.

As they watched fields give way to cobbled streets and the stately stone homes of the northern sector, Maud leaned forward and tapped Sheldrake on the knee.

"Now my dear, I will ask Rose to glean what she can from the Kimoran Ambassador's staff. The woman has an excessive number of staff. All show. Quite pointless, in my opinion. However, I shall ensure that she receives an invitation to the King's garden party. Gavin won't mind. He's such a dear boy. So delightfully malleable."

"He's not, you know." Sheldrake smiled at her. "Only where you are concerned. While you get to know Lady Electra, I will look up my network's latest dispatches from Kimora. As I recall, things have been stable there since the current monarch ascended the throne." He frowned. "But I seem to remember some serious unrest preceded her reign. Anyway, I'll also see what anyone knows about shamans and their powers." He nodded at a sprawling mansion whose rooves and chimneys could be seen through the trees of its manicured grounds. "Look! The Academy of Mages. I haven't decided whether we should send Jayhan there or not."

"*You* haven't decided??"

Sheldrake actually winced. "Whoops! I beg your pardon, my dear. Of course we will decide together. I just meant that for my part, I have not yet reached a conclusion."

"Hmm. You only just slipped out of that one." Although Maud's eyes had narrowed, she flipped open a green brocade fan and began to fan herself to hide a smile. "I think his pale eyes will make him the butt of unwanted attention. I suspect that he may prefer to learn from home."

"Perhaps. But he will have to take his place in the world someday and learn to cope with people's reactions to his eyes." Sheldrake gave Maud a wry smile. "And one day, you too will have to come to terms with his eyes. He is a dear boy, if a little impetuous. I have seen him watching you with Sasha when you are in other guises... not with jealousy exactly, but wistfully."

Maud sniffed. "I do not dislike Jayhan, but I don't feel comfortable when those pale eyes turn my way." She threw up her hands. "I know. I'm his mother. I should love him without reservation but, well, I don't. I do love him, but not without reservation." She watched Sheldrake anxiously for his reaction.

The mage patted her knee. "I know, my dear. You are not a cruel woman. I know you do your best."

Outside, the rhythmic hoof beats changed to the sounds of stamping followed by silence.

"Ah," said Sheldrake. "We have arrived."

A footman opened the door and handed out Maud, Sheldrake descending behind her. Before them, the broad white marble steps of the palace rose to huge carved wooden doors set into walls of cream sandstone.

Despite the relative cosiness of their own small mansion, Sheldrake and Maud didn't even give the palace's grandeur a second look. They had two adjoining apartments within the palace; one in which they lived whenever they were in town and the other which housed Sheldrake's office and the deceptively small number of staff and records that he allowed the public to see. In reality, the King's Spiders, his network of informants, was spread far and wide, not only through the Kingdom of Carrador, but also through every surrounding country. Maud, to all intents and purposes, was a social butterfly, attending soirees, balls, garden parties and drinking tea or sharing wine with nearly everyone who came to court. Between her servants and herself, very little escaped her, especially since she could, unbeknownst to her acquaintances, change form when it suited her purposes. But while Sheldrake was the gatherer of information, she both gathered and used it. Sheldrake organised the Spiders but Maud decided what and how to tell the king.

For two days they innocuously caught up with business and friends. But on the evening of their third day in town, Sheldrake stood in his study wearing a very worn, grubby brown coat, a rumpled shirt and scuffed shoes below a saggy pair of leggings. A woollen cap hid his black neatly trimmed hair. Jayhan would have gasped in shock. Never had he seen his father look anything other than neat and trim. Beside Sheldrake stood a solid brindle dog of indeterminate parentage, her shoulder on a level with his thigh. Her tail waved gently back and forth as she waited.

Sheldrake pulled out the third book from the fourth shelf of his bookcase and pushed on a seemingly featureless part of the rear panel. After replacing the book, he depressed a rosette in the wooden carving running down the bookcase's left-hand side. With a click, the bookcase swung away from the wall, revealing a flight of stairs disappearing down into the darkness.

"Ready, Maisy?"

The dog wagged her tail and nudged her muzzle under his hand.

After a final glance around his study, he threw his tote bag over his shoulder and stepped onto the landing, Maisy right beside him. Once he had flicked his fingers to produce a floating orb of light, he pulled the bookcase towards him until it clicked back into place.

With the dog trailing behind him, Sheldrake descended the steps to a long passageway which ran under the rear of the palace and the street behind it. They climbed another set of stairs at the other end and minutes later, emerged from an inconspicuous door in a nearby alley. Maisy sniffed the air and the wall, then squatted for a pee while Sheldrake politely looked the other way. They spent the next ten minutes making sure that no one was following them before making their way to the Wayfarer's Inn.

The inn was a cheerful establishment mainly catering to lower-middle and working-class patrons. Merchants, tradesmen and travellers chatted and drank around dark wood tables, creating a genial hum of conversation that conveniently masked any individual discussions that might take place. Rory the barman, a small but very tough man, knew Sheldrake's real identity but always treated him as the down-at-heel travelling salesman he purported to be. He had no idea that Maisy was anything other than a dog but was happy to allow Sheldrake's dog into the bar, provided she behaved herself.

Sheldrake ordered a beer and wove his way through the crowd, slowly so that he could catch snippets of conversations as he passed. As he drew level with the third table, he laid his hand on Maisy's shoulder and moments later, she sat down to have a good scratch. Then she found a few well-trampled morsels, which led her under that particular table. Unnoticed by the patrons deep in conversation, she lay down under the table and put her head on her paws.

Sheldrake continued on his way until he reached a table just inside the far door. An old farmer was already seated there, nursing a pint.

"I heard you were looking for sacks to bag up your wheat," said Sheldrake.

"Only if they are good hessian and good value," came the reply.

Sheldrake's face relaxed into a smile as he sat down. "Good to see you, Kristoff." He leaned in closer. "Why the disguise? Have you struck trouble? Good wig, by the way."

Kristoff shrugged. "A bit. I visited The Hidden Lantern on the other side of town. You know it?"

"I know *of* it but have never been there. Some oddball magic makers group meets there occasionally, as I recall. Any shamans among them?"

For a moment Kristoff ignored the question. "They call themselves the Research Society. From what I saw, they are collectors of information about different types of magic use. A genuine group of enthusiasts, I think, with regular presentations by a variety of magic users from all over the world." He took a pull on his beer. "And yes, they have had shamans present to them in the past but..." Here he leaned in. "when I asked whether there was a shaman I could talk to, the atmosphere changed. They closed ranks, so to speak, and told me that no shamans had visited their Society or the Hidden Lantern for some time. I am certain they were lying."

"Interesting. Go on."

"And when I left, I was followed. I let her tail me until I could duck into a doorway in an alley and get a good look at her. She was a young woman, late twenties, I'd say. Fair hair, brown eyes. I recognised her from the Hidden Lantern. She had been drinking at the bar, near enough to listen, but not a Society member, as far as I could tell." He took a pull on his beer. "I thought of tackling her but that would have given away that I was skilled enough to rumble her and that I had more than a passing interest in shamans. So instead, I threw this dirty old smock over my clothes and donned the wig. Always carry a spare disguise in my tote bag."

Sheldrake gave a brief smile and touched his own tote bag, which lay at his feet beside him.

"Hmph. Of course you do. I suppose you take those things for granted; things I think are clever." Kristoff looked embarrassed.

"You're doing very well, Kristoff. Please, go on.

Kristoff gave a wry smile that acknowledged the praise for the sop it was. "When she gave up looking for me, I followed her. And, to cut a long story short, she ended up at the rear entrance to the Kimoran Embassy."

"Which she entered."

"Exactly." Kristoff pulled out a folded piece of paper. "I sketched her, in case you or one of your contacts knows her."

Sheldrake smiled. "You have done very well. I did not expect this little assignment to become so fraught. It seems we are not the only ones interested in shamans."

16

Sheldrake was just cutting the top of his boiled egg when Maud walked in, dressed in a deep red and blue tapestry gown, blue lace around the neckline and cuffs.

Sheldrake smiled. "Good morning, my dear. I do admire those colours on you. Lovely."

Maud smiled in return. "Why, thank you. A cup of tea please," she said to the maid as she sat down. "And perhaps an egg, bacon and a couple of sausages, I think."

"Now Maud," said Sheldrake, as soon as Rose left the room, "you don't need that much. It's the hungry dog aspect still influencing your thoughts."

Maud gave a little frown of annoyance, contemplating Sheldrake's egg as her thoughts moved inward. After a moment she sighed. "Blast you, you're right. Oh well, I shall save what I don't eat and feed it to the next stray dog I see." She gave a little grin. "Did Sasha really say I was tubby?'

"Oh no, my dear. Not completely tubby. Only a little bit tubby." He chortled and nearly spilt his tea. "But he really meant that you were dense." That did it. His tea spattered all down his pristine, white shirt as he succumbed to laughter. "You know," he clarified, "Thick."

Maud crossed her arms in mock admonition, but she couldn't stop a smile from playing around her lips. "Obviously, he means I have depths to me, unlike the shallow, uncomplicated mage sitting across from me."

"Cutting, Maud," said Sheldrake, smiling as he tried to wipe down his besmirched shirt. "Very cutting. Look at this! I'm going to have to change my shirt now."

Rose returned and laid Maud's breakfast out in front of her. Once she had left, Maud continued, "And you were also right about that table last night. I picked up some interesting scraps of information," she dimpled, "and some delicious scraps of beef pie." She laughed at Sheldrake's pained expression. "Ah my dear. You are so easy to tease. Anyway, as you must have gathered, they are merchants recently arrived from Kimora. They were complaining about the increasingly high bribes they now have to pay for their goods to enter the country. Every year it has been getting worse."

"Has it? That does not reflect a strong, ethical regime, does it?"

"No. Unless it is just an isolated pocket of corruption." She grimaced. "Unlikely, I think. Besides, the merchants were talking about unrest among the guilds; forced curfews, higher taxes, raids on guild meetings."

"Anything about shamans?"

Maud shook her head. "No. Perhaps you, or we, should visit Stonehaven Orphanage and talk to Old Tom."

"If you wouldn't mind, my dear, I think your talents might be more useful in becoming acquainted with the Kimoran Ambassador, what's her name?... Lady Electra?"

Maud gave a short laugh. "Sheldrake, there is no point in acting vague around me."

"And," continued Sheldrake repressively, "I wonder if you might infiltrate the Research Society when they next meet. The day after tomorrow, I understand. Kristoff was stonewalled when he asked about shamans and was followed when he left, by a fair-haired woman who returned to the Kimoran embassy."

Maud frowned. "We had better be careful. We don't want our little Sasha being discovered as a shaman until we know why the interest and why the protectiveness."

Sheldrake ate his final piece of toast and wiped his fingers. He glanced towards the door to check that it was closed and leant in a little closer. "And watch young Rose, if you are going to use her. She does not like our little shaman. I don't want her making mischief for him."

"Hmm, good point. Leave it to me. I'll sort it out." She bit a piece of sausage off the end of her fork with relish and waved the remainder in the air as she spoke. "I shall go to the Society as a cat. A mouse would be more subtle but I don't want to risk being eaten by a cat if the Hidden Lantern happens to have a mouser. Much better to fight on equal terms if they do."

"Maud, put the fork down," Sheldrake shook his head, "You do it every time you think about being an animal. Your manners evaporate."

Maud smiled sunnily and returned the fork to her plate. "Oops. The social veneer is thinner when I am not thinking as a human."

Sheldrake left soon afterwards to change his shirt, so Maud was left to eat her sausage as she liked. When Rose returned to clear the table, Maud asked her, "Have you had a chance to talk to any of Lady Electra's servants?"

"No, Ma'am. But my mother's second cousin, Petunia, is stepping out with a footman at the Embassy."

"Indeed? And does this help us?"

Rose finished stacking the breakfast dishes onto an ornately carved wooden tray. "I hope so, ma'am. I am having tea with Petunia this afternoon.... provided you don't need me, of course." She added quickly.

Maud smiled. "I need you to have tea with your mother's second cousin. Well done, Rose."

"Is there anything particular you wish me to ask, ma'am?"

"I don't want your Petunia realising our interest so don't ply her with questions until we are more sure of her discretion." Maud paused for a few moments. "Now Rose, one more thing before you go. I have noticed that you do not seem kindly disposed towards Sasha. Is there a reason for this?"

"No, ma'am," Rose said tartly. "I'm just making sure he knows his place in life."

"Which is?"

"He's a foundling, dependant on the charity of your house and an outdoors servant. He's on the bottom rung in the household and should remember it. That's all."

"Are you aware that he saved Beth's life?"

Rose shrugged. "That's the only reason he's with us at all, instead of where he belongs, with the likes of Bryson."

"I see. So you do not approve of our decision to employ him?"

"It weren't... I mean, wasn't your decision in the first place, ma'am. Beth just went ahead and did it, and you had to back her up."

With a flash of acumen, Maud asked, "And did you have someone else in mind for the stableboy's position?"

"Not my place to say, ma'am."

"Perhaps not, but I am asking you nevertheless."

Rose put down the tray she had been holding during this conversation and wiped her hands nervously on her apron as she gathered her resolve. Then she straightened and said defiantly, "That were... I mean was, my little brother's job, by rights. He was going to start as soon as he turned eight. Ma was depending on that extra money coming in, now that me da's dead."

"Rose," Maud's voice was gentle. "I didn't know your father had died. Why didn't you tell us?"

"Ain't none of your business, that's why. Our business is our own." Rose dropped a quick curtsy and modulated her voice. "Beg pardon, ma'am."

"Then you can hardly expect us to take it into account when we make staffing decisions, now can you?"

Rose dropped her eyes. "No ma'am. Just unlucky, that's all. I knew Beth was thinking about getting a new stable hand and I was going to bring Edgar into work, so Beth could meet him. Sasha got there first."

"Had you arranged this with Beth?"

"Not yet. Wasn't urgent, as far as I knew and Edgar don't... doesn't turn eight until next month." She looked up, her eyes moist with unshed tears, "Like I said, just bad luck. We'll get by. We always have."

Maud patted the chair next to her. "Come and sit down, my dear. The dishes can wait."

Rose wiped her hands again and sat down diffidently next to Maud, her hands clasped tightly in her lap.

"Would you like a cup of tea?' asked Maud, who thought tea was the solution to every emotional issue.

Rose managed a small smile. "No thanks, Ma'am. It'll be stewed by now."

"Oh. Well, never mind." She clasped Rose's stiff hands between her own. "So now that this situation has been brought to my attention - and I wish I had known sooner - I have two things I need to say to you. Firstly, you may tell your brother that he may start work with us the day after his eighth birthday.

Rose frowned fiercely. "We don't want no charity, ma'am."

"I'm sure you don't, my dear. However, Beth will need your Edgar soon because Sasha will be working more directly with Sheldrake as he gets older. Already Sasha is only working for Beth in the mornings. And Clive isn't getting any younger. He needs a young helper to run errands for him."

"Really? Are you sure?"

Maud snorted. "Of course I'm sure. Now secondly, before I let you loose with your mother's second cousin, I need to know that I can trust your complete discretion and your loyalty to our household."

"Of course you can, Ma'am. None of us servants ever gossip about you or your husband. It's part of our employment conditions, right from the start." She gave a little grin. "Not like other households, I can tell you. I expect to hear all sorts of things this afternoon."

"I am pleased to hear that, Rose, and I expected no less. But our household is not just comprised of Sheldrake and me."

"Oh yes, and Jayhan as well," said Rose quickly.

"And you, Rose, and Beth and Clive and all the staff. No one is to be talked about to Petunia."

Rose frowned. "Won't that seem a bit strange?"

Maud thought for a moment. "Yes, true. Well, talk about general things but if you mention any names, make sure what you say is unimportant. Think before you speak. Do you understand?"

Rose nodded slowly, obviously thinking it through.

"And, in particular, say nothing about Sasha."

Rose's eyes widened. "Why not?"

Maud looked at her for a few long seconds. "I am trusting you, Rose. Don't you let me down."

"No ma'am."

"Sheldrake has discovered that Sasha is a shaman; a type of magic-wielder found in other countries but not here. Our initial enquiries about shamans have been met with resistance and until we know why, we want no one to know about Sasha. So don't mention him at all; his age, his colour, how he joined us, nothing. Clear?"

"Yes ma'am."

Maud smiled. "Now, off you go. I look forward to hearing your report."

17

Sheldrake descended from his carriage and turned to look at the large, tired old grey building barricaded behind tall iron gates.

"Not very welcoming, is it?" he observed to Leon, who was holding the door for him.

"No sir, although the lawns and gardens seem well kept."

"Hmph. Well, ring that monstrous black bell. Let's see what sort of reception we get."

Leon did as ordered, and the harsh clang brought a small girl, dressed in a well-pressed smock, her fluffy light brown hair pulled into high pigtails, running down the driveway. She peered through the bars of the gate at them and smiled. "Hello." She paused then said, as though the words were unfamiliar, "May I help you?"

Sheldrake smiled and gave a little bow. "Hello young lady. My name is Sheldrake and I would like to speak with Tom, if he is available."

The girl nodded, "Do you mean Old Tom?"

"Yes. I think I do."

"Do you want to know my name?"

"Of course I do," he waved at his driver, "and this is Leon."

"My name is Joanne," she said and beamed.

"Well, Joanne, do you think you could get Tom for us?"

She nodded vigorously, said, "Yes," and shot off back up the driveway.

Sheldrake sent Leon a wry smile and rubbed his gloved hands together as he waited. "It's getting cold, Leon. Winter is closing in early this year."

"Aye sir, the horse dung was steaming this morning."

"Hmm. Perhaps too much information."

Leon snorted with laughter. "Such a delicate stomach you have, sir."

Sheldrake smiled vaguely and was about to make some reply when he spotted a great hulk of a man striding down the driveway. "Good heavens, Leon. Have we offended in some way? I fear we are about to be trounced. Be prepared to make a quick exit."

The huge man reached the gate and looked down at Sheldrake from at least a head taller. He was broad shouldered, deep chested and reached forward to open the gate with hands like hams. Then he smiled and it was as though the sun had come out.

"Good morning gentlemen. What can I do for you?"

Sheldrake let out a breath and dissipated a little spell he had been developing in case of trouble. "Good morning. My name is Sheldrake. I live out of town to the north and have recently employed one of your past children." On closer inspection, Sheldrake could see that the man's face was lined, partly from care but also from kindness and laughter, but not so much that one could think him old. "Would you be Tom?"

Tom's smile broadened. "Yes. Spit it out. Old Tom, they call me. I've been called Old Tom since I was fifteen years old. There used to be another lad here called Tom who was ten years younger than me. So I was Old Tom and he was Young Tom." The side of his mouth lifted in a grimace. "Sadly he died before he could be anything but young. Nice little kid." He pulled the gate wide. "Come on in. Leave the horses there. They'll be fine. No one much comes along this road."

Leon glanced at Sheldrake who gave the merest nod in return. So they both followed Old Tom up the driveway towards the front door.

Long before they reached it, Joanne came bounding up to them and tugged on Sheldrake's coat, "Do you want to see my picture I drew?" Anticipating his answer, she disappeared to return within moments with a scrawled series of lines on a piece of paper.

Sheldrake attempted to look impressed. "Oh well. That's very good, isn't it? Did it yourself, did you?"

Joanne nodded enthusiastically. "And you know what that is?" she asked, pointing at one particular squiggle.

"I would say," cut in Leon, rescuing Sheldrake in the nick of time, "that that is the lantern on the front of the carriage."

"Yes," replied Joanne as though it were the most obvious thing in the world. "I like lanterns a lot. I like carriages, but I *really* like lanterns."

"So I see," enthused Leon.

"Now, Joanne, let our guests be. See if you can organise cups of tea for us."

A few minutes later, they found themselves in a small reception room to the right of the entrance hall, Tom and Sheldrake seated around a polished mahogany table, Leon standing by the door. The chairs and table were of good quality, without being excessively valuable or ostentatious. Everything in the room was clean and well cared for. The walls were hung with portraits of children, exhibiting a wide range of skill in their execution.

Old Tom saw Sheldrake's gaze wandering and said, "Some of our past children have been very fine artists. All of these paintings were done by past residents."

Sheldrake nodded. "Impressive." He gave a little cough. "At least, some of them are impressive."

Old Tom laughed. "Yes. Not all, by any means, but at least they try."

"Is the rest of your establishment as well kept as this lovely room, or is this room kept particularly well to impress visitors?"

Old Tom gave a shout of laughter that made Leon jump. "You don't mince words, do you? What's on your mind? Do you think I'm running a slave labour camp out the back?" He waved his hand. "Help yourselves. You are welcome to tour the place, if you'd like to. In fact, the more people who see this place, the better chance I have of receiving donations to help the little ones."

"I beg your pardon," said Sheldrake stiffly. "I did not mean to offend. I am merely trying to gauge what sort of young life Sasha led. He is a talented young lad."

Old Tom stilled. It was only for a moment, but Sheldrake and Leon were both trained to notice the slightest nuance in people's reactions. "Ah, young Sasha. That is who you have working for you, is it? How did that come about?"

Sheldrake recounted the incident that had led to Sasha changing employers.

Old Tom grimaced. "I am sorry to hear that Bryson

treated Sasha so poorly. I had my doubts about Bryson, but he promised to look after Sasha until he could set him up somewhere. And at the time..." He shrugged. "Never mind. I won't place any other children with him."

"I'm pleased to hear it." Sheldrake accepted a cup of tea from Joanna which she had carefully transferred from a large tray held by a small boy.

"This is Mikey," she said, blithely interrupting the conversation. "He is my friend."

Sheldrake inclined his head and Leon murmured a greeting from the doorway. Joanna placed a plate of sultana scones on the table and delivered a cup of tea to Old Tom and one to Leon on the way out.

"Bye," she said cheerily, as she left.

Sheldrake took a sip of his tea before saying, "Sasha seems to have some particular talents, magical talents. And since I am a mage, I have begun to include him in my son's training. However, his type of magic is not familiar to me and I was hoping to find out more about his background, with a view to developing his potential."

"As to Sasha's origins," Old Tom shrugged. "the baby was found wrapped in a blanket inside a woven basket, which was found on the front steps here."

"On the front steps?" asked Sheldrake. "What about the gate, and don't you have a tall stone wall surrounding this building?"

"No. Only on the side facing the street. Behind us are fields of wheat and corn. We also grow our own vegetables. The fences around them are sturdy and high enough to keep the little ones in, but not high enough to keep out adults. We are not a jail. If the older children want to leave, they can choose to do so any time, although I try to make sure they have some future to go to. No wall is high enough to keep an unwilling child in and we have never had issues with marauders."

Sheldrake smiled. "The more I hear and see of this place, the more I like it." He sipped his tea then put it down so that he could pick up a warm scone. He took a bite and spent a moment savouring it. "Hmm. Very good. You must have an accomplished cook here."

"I do, and he teaches the children how to be kitchen hands and chefs. They need training to find work when they leave here."

"Most commendable. And do you keep in touch with the children once they have left?"

Old Tom nodded. "I do. At least I try to. Not all children want to remember where they have come from, but they are always welcome to visit. When we place children in employment, usually at ten years old, we like to visit them within six months to see how they are going."

"So Sasha left early, did he? He's still only eight. And you haven't followed up his progress, as you have others?"

Old Tom stirred his tea, round and round, taking his time. Finally, he raised his eyes and looked directly at Sheldrake. "No, but I would like to. Sasha was always special and always different. They all are, in their own ways, but Sasha more than most. I would love to see Sasha again. Perhaps you will allow me to visit you and we could talk more then."

Sheldrake watched him as he sipped his tea. "And do you know anything of shamans?"

"I have seen nothing of Sasha's magic, if that is what you are asking."

"Not exactly, but it will do." He took a final sip of tea and put down the cup as he rose. "I think we have taken enough of your time. Thank you for hospitality and your cooperation. I shall send you an invitation to call upon us so that you may assure yourself of Sasha's welfare."

Old Tom smiled and nodded at both of them. "It was a pleasure to meet you and to hear that Sasha is safe. I look forward to your invitation."

18

As the carriage rolled back towards the centre of Highkington, Sheldrake leant back against the cushioning and reflected on their encounter with Old Tom. The man had seemed friendly enough, but Sheldrake felt sure that he was not being completely honest, or at least not completely open, with him.

Sheldrake lurched suddenly as the carriage took an unexpected turn. As it took another, he heard Leon's boot thump down twice on the roof, a pause then two more thumps. They were being followed.

Sheldrake thumped three times on the roof with the end of his cane. A short time later, the carriage drew to a halt outside a bakery in Tanner's Field, a poorer quarter of town, once redolent with the smells of the tannery but less noisome now that the tannery had moved further out of town. Nevertheless, the narrow twisting street were littered with refuse and, in places used at outdoor urinals, producing their own rank odour.

Sheldrake drew in a breath before exiting the carriage. He descended the steps, ignoring Leon who was holding the door open for him, and made a show of inspecting the array of cakes and buns in the window before entering the bakery. Behind him, Leon went to the horses' heads and made a fuss of them stroking their noses and crooning at them, all the time watching the road behind them.

A solitary horseman trotted around the corner of the previous intersection. His surprise at seeing the coach pulled in to the side, showed in his mount tossing its head as he jabbed on the reins. Recovering himself, he didn't slow but passed the carriage at the same steady trot, touching his hat in greeting to Leon as he passed and turning down the next side laneway. Leon caught a view of a wiry, fair-haired young man, dressed in merchant's clothes that were well-kept but not expensive, in keeping with the quality of the horse.

As soon as the horseman was out of sight, Leon moved. He entered the doorway of a building to the right of the bakery, ran straight down the corridor between doors on either side and emerged into the back yard. He vaulted the back wall and landed in an alley that ran parallel to the main road. Keeping close to the wall, he slipped along the cobblestones until he reached the crowded laneway the horseman had entered. Leon peered cautiously around the right-hand corner and sure enough, there was the horseman, dismounted and appearing to make adjustments to his saddle girth while keeping watch on the road for the carriage to resume its journey. From where the horseman stood, Leon figured he could just see the horses, so would know if the carriage turned around or continued down the street. He wondered how long the horseman could maintain the pretence before shopkeepers or passersby would begin to notice how long he had been there for so little effect.

Leon threaded through the crowd, slid up behind him

and pressed a very sharp knife to the young man's ribs. Even though the lad was significantly taller than him, Leon knew a well-handled blade mattered more than size.

"Now," murmured Leon, "Let's assume I know what I'm doing and that if you move to attack, I will counter you, and at the very least, you will become the centre of attention. Now, ask yourself, is that what you want?" The young man stilled. Leon waited four heartbeats before continuing, "I want you to walk quietly with me across this lane, then down that alley over to our right. If you cooperate, I will not stab you." He glanced at the cloth merchant watching from the nearest window and nodded towards the horse. The merchant, held up her thumb in a gesture of understanding. "Your horse will be here when we return. Karin will mind it."

Leon tensed as he felt the young man take in a deep breath, but whatever he had been going to do, apparently he decided the better of it. Instead he simply nodded and turned to walk in the direction Leon had indicated. Once back in the side alley, Leon guided his charge past the wall he had scaled and ushered him though a gateway in the wall behind the bakery.

"Came like a lamb to slaughter, he did," murmured Leon to someone in the shadows.

A few minutes later, the young man found himself in a dingy room, seated at a table with two men facing him. Leaning his shoulder against the wall inside the door was the dagger-wielding coachman, while seated opposite him was the lean man he had seen entering the carriage. The fact that neither had bothered to disguise themselves worried the young man. Perhaps they weren't planning to let him live. He repressed a shudder and grasped his hands together tightly in his lap, keeping his eyes down.

As though reading his thoughts, the older man said, "There is no point in us disguising ourselves since you already know what we look like. You have, after all, been following us since you left Stonehaven. And whether you live or not will depend on whether we can come to some arrangement. Firstly, what is your name?"

The young man raised a frightened face to look at Sheldrake. "Jon, sir. Sir, I had no plans to harm you."

Sheldrake grunted. "Not directly perhaps. But your information about us may harm us. Had you thought of that?"

The young man half shook his head then dropped his eyes again. "No, not exactly. I'm just supposed to look out for unusual visitors to Stonehaven, find out who they are and report back."

"To whom?"

Jon shrugged. "Dunno." He looked up. "I really don't, sir. It's my brother's job, this. He took ill this morning and asked me to fill in for him. There's a few shillings in it, so I said I would. Didn't know I was risking a knife in my ribs. Seemed straight forward to me at the time."

Leon stood with folded arms against the wall. "That explains why you've been such a rank amateur at tailing us."

Jon shot him a resentful look but didn't say anything.

In the end they decided to let him go, after ringing a promise from him that he would not mention their presence. They plied him with a couple of dire threats and six florins to seal the bargain before Leon led him back to retrieve his horse. Young Jon looked dazed at his good luck at escaping, not only unscathed but richer.

When Leon returned to the room in the back of the bakery, he said, "I can see why you didn't ask him to find out who his brother is working for. He is too wet for words. Would have given the game away."

"Yes. Not cut out for subterfuge, our young Jon." Sheldrake stood up and lifted his long coat from the back of the chair. "But I think we need to know. Set someone to follow the person spying on Stonehaven and see what we can find out, preferably without them knowing that the watcher is being watched."

Just as they turned to leave, the cloth merchant burst into the room, wild-eyed and out of breath.

"He just vanished," she gasped.

"What! Who?" asked Leon, a horrible suspicion forming in his mind.

"The lad whose horse you asked me to keep an eye on. As soon as you walked away up the lane, he mounted his horse and then..." Karin snapped her fingers. "Gone! Right in front of my eyes."

"Gone? You're sure?" pressed Leon. "He didn't just gallop away quickly while you weren't watching."

The cloth merchant put her hands on her hips. "I think I would have heard that," she said caustically. "Anyway I happened to glance up at him just as he disappeared. No doubt, I'm afraid. He simply disappeared."

Leon's hand crashed down on the table, making the other two jump.

"Leon, please," remonstrated Sheldrake mildly.

"We have been taken for a right pair of chumps," fumed Leon. "Too wet? Not cut out for subterfuge? He's a bloody master. We couldn't have been more helpful. Blast! Blast! Blast!"

Karin's face split into a grin.

PART III

19

As Sheldrake and Maud departed for Highkington. Sasha had stood proudly at the horses' heads, waiting until Leon had climbed onto the driver's box, taken the reins and given him a nod. Leon had given him a tiny wave of appreciation that had left Sasha beaming from ear to ear, while Jayhan stood at the front door, waving as his parents left.

When they had disappeared from sight, Jayhan trudged inside to study while Sasha skipped across to Beth, still smiling, and cavorted around her as they headed towards the stables.

"Sasha, stop," said Beth, laughing. "You're like a big puppy. Run up to the top paddock and bring Flurry in for a brush down. That should burn some energy off you."

Completely unabashed, Sasha shot off to do her bidding.

After lunch, Jayhan was at last released and immediately raced to the stables to collect Sasha. Beth looked up as he bounded into her office.

"You don't have magic training, do you, while Sheldrake

is away? So Sasha can work in the stables in the afternoons."

Jayhan's face fell ludicrously but he rallied. "Then I will work in the stables too. What can I do?"

Beth thought for a minute. "Fair enough. If you share his work, then you can both finish early. Sasha has just taken Flurry back up to the paddock but when he returns, you can muck out all the stalls together. As soon as you have finished... and mind that you do a good job... you can go off and play."

"Yes!" Jayhan grinned. "Great. Thanks, Beth."

Beth laughed. "You're as bad as each other. Now, if your hands start to get sore using the shovel, put gloves on. You don't want to get blisters or it will hurt worse tomorrow."

Jayhan rushed off to meet Sasha as he walked down the gravelly track from the top paddock. He waved as he got nearer and yelled, "Hi. Beth says I can help you muck out the stables so we can play sooner."

To his surprise, Sasha frowned. "You can't do that. That's my job."

Jayhan hesitated only for a moment before saying, "Well, in exchange, you can help me look through those books about Madison. Deal?"

Sasha glanced sideways at him and smiled. "Already have."

Jayhan boggled. "What? How did you do that?" He waved his hand. "Never mind. Tell me later. So that means I definitely have to help you. So there! No more arguing."

By mid-afternoon, the stables were spotless and Jayhan was exhausted. He propped the shovel against the wall and leaned against the wall next to it. He eyed Sasha as he bounded up, still full of energy. "How do you do it? And you usually do it all on your own. This is only half."

"And I did stuff this morning. I cleaned all the dung out of the top paddock while Flurry was down here, filled the watering troughs, fed them all." Sasha grinned. "Don't worry. You'll get used to it... if you want to keep doing it, that is." He patted Jayhan on the shoulder. "Come on. Beth has some lemonade and scones waiting for us."

Jayhan heaved himself away from the wall. "Yeah, I'll keep doing it. Probably good for me, all this exercise."

"Probably is."

Once they had bolted down their scones and lemonade, Jayhan asked about the progress Sasha had made finding out about Madison.

"I've been through all the books and made a list of the pages where her name appears," Sasha replied, smiling proudly.

"Really? All of them? That's amazing. But how did you get hold of them? I left them in my wardrobe."

Sasha did a little cough. "Well, you have to promise not to tell if I tell you..."

"Of course."

"Clive snuck them out for me, a couple at a time. He put one lot back each time he got the next lot."

Completely unconcerned by Clive's questionable behaviour, Jayhan asked, "So where are the books now?"

"Oh. Back in your wardrobe. I finished going through them all and thought I'd give it a rest for a bit before reading and making notes. That's going to be the hard part."

"I'll say." Jayhan frowned as he thought. "We need to lay them all out again but we can't get into Dad's workshop while he's away and there's not enough room in Beth's office." He grimaced. "It'll have to be the library where I do my lessons, I'm afraid. Do you mind too much?"

"Mind? I'd love to look around your library. It's Eloquin

who might mind."

Jayhan blithely waved this objection aside. "Don't worry. She'll just be rapt that I'm spending extra time reading." He pulled a face. "She is so dull."

Firstly, they laid the books out in colour groupings, then from largest to smallest, then in alphabetical order and finally, in chronological order.

Sasha stood back and surveyed their work. "Yep. That makes more sense. So take a book each and compare notes when we've finished?"

"And if we don't understand a word, we write it down and look it up later. Agree?"

"Fine."

They slogged away at it until Jayhan was called for dinner.

Sasha gave him a quick smile. "Whoops. I'd better go too or I'll miss out. See you tomorrow."

They left out the contents of meetings and legal jargon because they had no idea what they meant, but after two days, they had pieced together the main features of Madison's story:

Madison was born in this cottage, just as Jayhan was. Her parents were well-to-do landowners but had their eye on the adjoining property. So, when she was old enough, they arranged a marriage for her with the neighbour's son, Brian, who was, unfortunately, a drunk and a gambler. When he got drunk, which was often, he would come home and beat Madison. One night, according to an eye-witness account by the maid, the husband had slammed Madison against the wall, and as she sank down in fear, he had stalked towards her, anger unabated, a poker in his raised hand. Suddenly, it was as though the extremity of her situation unleashed an inner strength. She raised her head and glared with those pale eyes of hers, straight at her husband. He fell back, clutching his throat and begging her to stop. She said nothing, just kept staring at him as he stumbled out of the room and down the stairs. She didn't kill him, but she hurt and terrified him somehow. From that day forward, her husband stopped drinking and never laid a hand on her again.

But Madison had been controlled and belittled, firstly by her parents and then by her husband. The only person who had loved her without wanting to use her was her nanny, Brenda, who had been dismissed as soon as Madison turned twelve. Now, for the first time in her life, Madison had power and there was no one who could pull on her heartstrings to rein her in. She used a mild form of her power on her servants, just to see what she could do. The eye-witness maid said that when her mistress turned her pale-eyed, power-imbued stare on her, Madison seemed to grow in stature and the need to please her was irresistible. Town officials and other people in the community reported that Madison could dominate a meeting and bend everyone to her point of view by staring them down. Suddenly other people would think their own views valueless in the light of hers. She did not instil fear in them as she had in her husband. Instead, she overwhelmed them.

When Sasha had read the scarps of writing and copied text that comprised this summary, he sat back, looking unconvinced, "She might just have been one of those strong people who can talk people around."

"Yeah, maybe, but what about her husband? She hurt him."

"That's only what the maid said. But maybe this Brian fellow was horrified at what he had been about to do."

"What? And choked on it?" Jayhan snorted. "You're too

nice. You always think the best of people."

"Huh. Didn't think much of Bryson."

Jayhan chuckled. "That's the best anyone could think of him."

Sasha scratched his head. "Well, I don't know. She doesn't sound as bad as you thought. Sounds more like someone who just got sick of being pushed around." He smiled at Jayhan. "And no one even mentions her eyes until that maid talked about them."

"True. But people mind about my eyes now. Grownups always pulled back when they see them and then pretend to smile at me. And the kids in the village used to tease me about them. Dad would get angry but they'd just run away laughing. Then one day, I stared back at them and they all looked scared and stopped." Suddenly sombre, Jayhan stood up and started to pack the books into a pile, not looking at Sasha.

Sasha grabbed his arm and pulled him around, staring straight into his pale eyes. "Well, here am I, looking straight into your eyes," he grinned suddenly, "and all I can think of is Pale Death." He laughed and ducked away. "And Black Velvet," he added hastily, chortling.

Jayhan laughed and threw a pencil at him. "You're an idiot. I'm trying to be serious."

"Far too serious." But despite his words, Sasha stopped laughing and said, "Look, if you're really worried about your eyes, why don't we experiment? Maybe you can actually do something with them. That would be exciting, wouldn't it?"

"Huh. I never thought of that." Jayhan placed the last book in the pile. "I'm sick of these old books anyway." He heard his name being called for dinner. His pale eyes were shining with excitement. "All right. Tomorrow. We'll go into the bush and try it out. See you."

20

Once they had finished their chores, Beth said they could take ponies to ride along the dirt track to the bushland, on the proviso they only walked and trotted them. "If you do well this time, I will let you canter for a short distance next time."

Jayhan saddled his own pony, Sasha keeping a weather eye on his progress. Once the ponies were saddled up, Sasha led them out into the yard, talking to them and patting their necks as he walked. Tosser, the pony Sasha would ride, was a brown and white mare who tended to toss her head and snap at any unwary person who strayed too close, while Jayhan's dark grey gelding, a gift for his seventh birthday, was quiet and if anything, a bit sluggish. Jayahn had enthusiastically named him Storm, but gradually Jayhan had come to refer to him as Slug. Sasha loved them both dearly. He dutifully helped Jayhan mount and gather his reins, before springing nimbly onto his own mount.

"Show off," said Jayhan with no heat at all.

Sasha just grinned.

They rode past the sheep paddock, the fields beginning

to turn gold under the slanting yellow rays of the late afternoon sun. Raucous cries made them look up to see two yellow-crested cockatoos cut and weave their way to land in the branches of a dead gumtree.

Sasha nudged Tosser with his heels and she increased her speed to trot. Jayhan did likewise and Slug grunted and kept walking. Jayhan increased the strength of his kicks but Slug just kept walking.

"Sasha, wait," called Jayhan to his fast disappearing friend.

Sasha pulled in and turned in the saddle, then brought his horse back to Jayhan's side. "Right," he said, "This naughty horse needs stronger persuasion."

He dismounted and, letting the reins drop to signal his horse to stand, rummaged around beside the road until he found a thin stick about the length of his small arm and trimmed the twigs from its sides. He approached Jayhan so that Slug couldn't see what he was doing and handed the stick up to Jayhan. "Here, a switch. Just tap with it. If you hit him too hard with it, he might take off."

Jayhan waited until Sasha had remounted. Once Slug was walking, he kicked and used the stick simultaneously. Slug reluctantly increased his gait to a trot... for forty yards. Then he slowed to a walk and huffed as though he had just galloped for miles.

"Blast him!" exclaimed Jayhan, fast losing patience. "Is he sick, do you think?"

Sasha shook his head. "I'll bet he'd trot if you turned his head towards home. Come on, let's swap for a bit."

Carefully avoiding Tosser's teeth, they swapped horses. Tosser immediately trotted at Jayhan's command, and to Jayhan's annoyance, Slug responded to a kick from Sasha, without even the need for the switch.

As they entered the bushland and shadows from overhanging branches dappled the path ahead of them, disguising possible potholes, they slowed their horses to a walk.

After a few minutes, Jayhan asked, "So what am I doing wrong? You can make Slug do anything you want."

Sasha smiled. "That's what I like about you. No, that's one of the things I like about you. You are happy to accept your... hmm... the things you can't do and want to get better at them. Lots of people would just blame the horse."

Jayhan grinned. "I do the blame the horse. He's a pain in the neck. But obviously that's only part of it. So how come he behaves better for you?"

"To start with, I spend more time with him because I live and mostly work in the stables. I give him treats and pat him and talk to him on the way past." Sasha shrugged. "But mostly, hmm... you have to know you're the one in charge, that your will is stronger." He pulled up at a low branch, lifting it to allow Jayhan to pass before lowering it behind his own head so that he too could pass. "You have to centre yourself and know who you are. Then your horse will feel safe, knowing you're in charge and that you know what you're doing. All the switches in the world won't work as well as believing in yourself."

Jayhan eyed him, "That sounds awfully grown up. Is that Shaman stuff?"

"I dunno. Maybe. Don't care really. It's what I think, wherever it comes from."

They rode in silence for a few minutes until Jayhan asked, "So how do you centre yourself?"

Sasha leant over and patted Jayhan's stomach, just below the ribs. "Here's your centre. Just focus on it. All your power comes from there. If you need to, you can feel power radiating out from there to heal parts of yourself."

"Hmph. You didn't miraculously heal your jarred knee."

"No. It's not that miraculous. Just a bit. If you focus when you're hurt, I think it speeds healing." He gave a shy little smile. "And if you're getting sick, you can focus really hard and usually, but not always, you can send strength to yourself and stop yourself from getting sick."

Jayhan leant forward and patted Tosser's neck as he thought about it. "What if you're already sick?"

"It works to make you better quicker but problem is, you have to be well enough to get the energy up to centre yourself."

Just then, a kookaburra landed in the next tree along, threw its head back and sent forth its laughing call. Tosser shied violently, tossing his head and pulling hard on the reins, striving to break away.

"Centre!" Sasha's voice was low-pitched but loud, cutting through Jayhan's shock.

Jayhan focused on his centre, the world taking a step back. He realised he was keeping a firm, but not panicked, grip on the reins and was talking to Tosser, soothing him with his voice. He felt grounded, his legs melded to the horse's flanks.

Tosser stopped trying to pull away and after giving a few snorts of displeasure, pranced past the tree containing the kookaburra and settled to a calm walk again.

Sasha brought the unruffled Slug up beside him, grinning from ear to ear. "Well done! You handled that amazingly. I was already rehearsing in my mind how I was going to explain to Beth that I had let you ride Tosser who had then bolted with you on board."

Jayhan laughed and patted Tosser on the neck again, far more confident and relaxed. "I get it. I really do. Probably would have taken me ages if I hadn't suddenly had to master it. I didn't have time to think. I just did."

Behind them, the kookaburra's voice rose in laughter echoed by its mate somewhere further to their right, deeper in the bush. Tosser flicked his ear but otherwise didn't react.

"Stop soon?" suggested Sasha.

"All right. What about at the creek? It's not much further."

Another half mile brought them to a small creek, choked with rushes and lined with old river red gums whose limbs twisted and curved and whose hollows provided homes for scores of birds and possums. Even though the nights were cold, today the sun shone warmly and a dragonfly zig-zagged past as they dismounted and untied the food packs that Hannah had provided. They each found a comfortable fork in a tree to sit in while they ate their sandwiches.

"So, how are we going to test your eyes?" asked Sasha.

"Well, I reckon centring would be a good start..." When Sasha nodded his agreement, Jayhan shrugged. "Other than that, I guess I just look at something and ... what?"

"Hmm. I guess you have to decide first what you want to do with it." Sasha took another bite of ham sandwich, chewing for a while before saying, "That Madison great grandmother of yours. She could maybe choke people and scare them." He looked around. "No people out here except me and you're not trying it on me. Don't even think about it. So what can we use?"

"Not horses. A bird?"

Sasha grimaced. "I suppose, if one comes close enough. But you don't want to kill it, do you?"

"Course not. Maybe just try scaring it?"

"Yeah. Good idea. Start with that."

They sat quietly and soon noticed a dozen rainbow lorikeets riffling among the leaves high in the gum tree above them. Three wrens, one of them a brilliant blue, hopped and flew in and around a nearby bush, while a magpie standing in the next tree along, cocked its head to get a better view of them. On the other side of the creek, a white-faced, grey heron picked its way upstream.

"Hardest part will be getting the bird to look at you. Best bet is that magpie. Try it."

Jayhan carefully centred himself, then stared at the magpie. Before he could think of anything scary, let alone think anything at it, the magpie opened its beak and let forth its beautiful warbling song.

Jayhan rolled his eyes. "I don't want to scare it. Listen to it. Nuh. This is hopeless."

Sasha chuckled. "One thing's for sure. You're no evil genius." He swung down from the tree fork and dusted his hands. "Maybe try breaking a rock or a stick with your eyes?"

"What? The rock's going to know I'm looking at it, is it?"

"No. But who's to say what the power is? It might be a physical force of some kind. Maybe Madison's husband choked from a physical pressure on his throat and maybe those people changed their minds because they were scared of what she might do, or because she put some sort of physical pressure that made them feel scared?"

Jayhan jumped down from his perch in the tree and grabbed a stick. "Right. You hold this and I'll try."

"No," said Sasha firmly as he bent down and started to pick up small rocks. "Let's set up the stick between two piles of rocks. Then you can try when I am well away from it."

"Oh. Sorry. Good idea."

They tried everything they could think of for the next hour but nothing interesting happened. Finally, Jayhan gave up.

"Well, that was a bit of a fizzer." He sighed despondently. "I'm hopeless at spellcasting too, you know." He headed towards the horses, leaving Sash to pack up the remains of their lunches to stow them behind their saddles. As an afterthought, he turned back and asked, "Do you want a hand?"

"Not your job," said Sasha shortly. He finished strapping on the little leather luggage rolls, before looking up to meet Jayhan's eyes. "You're not too bad at spellcasting. Just a bit gung-ho sometimes." He gave a little smile. "But you do have a special talent that no one, including you, knows about."

Jayhan's eyes grew round. "Really? What?"

Sasha grinned. "You're a shapeshifter. I realised it when I told Sheldrake how I knew Maud was. You're thicker than other people, sort of layered. Not as much as Maud, but I don't know if that's age or power."

"Oh fantastic! How exciting! Maybe I could become a bird and fly... or a horse and gallop really fast... or a lion stalking across the plains..." Jayhan jumped up and down mimicking the movements of each animal as he thought of them.

Sasha laughed at his antics until he had calmed down enough to listen. "Come on Zoo Man. It's going to be dark soon. Let's head back. You can try out your shape-shifting tomorrow."

As they rode back through the gathering shadows, birdsong quietened as the birds settled for the night. But near the tree line, Sasha pulled his horse up and sat still listening. Jayhan, watching him, did likewise. Sasha gave him a brief smile but continued to listen.

After a couple of minutes, Jayhan asked quietly, "What's up?"

"Not sure. Just seems too quiet, even for this time of day." Sasha shook his head. "Don't know. Just a feeling. Something's not quite right."

Jayhan leaned closer. "Well, if something's not right, shouldn't we get home as fast as we can?"

"Suppose so. Doesn't feel threatening exactly, just... It's like someone is watching us."

Jayhan gave Slug a good kick that urged him into a trot. "Now you're giving me the creeps. Let's go."

21

"But Maud, how did he just disappear?" Sheldrake shook his head. "I can't do that. Can you?"

Maud savoured a mouthful of pheasant and leek pie before putting down her knife and fork. When she was quite ready, she replied, "No dear, unless I turned quickly into a small animal like a mouse, but I couldn't make the horse seem to disappear as well."

"Hmm. So no." Sheldrake took a sip of red wine and sighed. "I believe a select number of sorcerers in Eskuzor can translocate, but even they would struggle with the horse, I would think. Still, an outside possibility."

"Perhaps," said Maud slowly, "a shaman can do it. Did he look Kimoran?"

"Not everyone form Kimora is dark, you know, so I don't know whether he looked Kimoran" said Sheldrake irritably. "But who's to say what he can do? Perhaps he can disguise his colouring? After all, if Sasha can see through disguises perhaps he can also disguise himself... but just hasn't tried yet." He cut into his pie with unaccustomed savagery. "Blast it?! He was such a nice, unassuming young man."

Maud smiled sympathetically. "Rather like Sasha then?"

An arrested look came into Sheldrake's eyes. "Very much like Sasha, now that you mention it."

"Now don't go overthinking yourself. Just finish your pie while I tell you what Rose discovered." Once he had nodded, she continued, "Her mother's second cousin is stepping out with a lovely young man, apparently, called Jon."

"JON?" Sheldrake choked on his mouthful.

Maud smiled broadly as she delivered several belts on his back to help him recover. When she was sure he would live, she said, "Yes, Jon. By all accounts, he is tall, fair and handsome, but that may just be a besotted girl's view of him."

"So our tail was also employed by the Kimoran Embassy. Just as Kristoff's was, the other night. Interesting."

Maud gave a little cough, "Not necessarily, my dear, at least not in his capacity as your tail. He did say, if you remember, that he was filling in for his brother."

Sheldrake rolled his eyes. "Which may or may not be true. We are getting nowhere fast."

"I haven't finished." She waited while he let out an exasperated breath and refocused himself. "Rose asked about shamans, hopefully in a way that did not arouse suspicion. The Queen of Kimora is a shaman, apparently, a very powerful one. Many members of her family were also shamans but they seem to have been largely eliminated when she rose to power."

"But presumable there are other shamans outside her family?"

"Yes. But they are strictly monitored. All shamans must be registered by the crown. Unregistered shamans are hunted down, and either imprisoned or killed, depending on the circumstances. They are considered a threat to the crown if they are rogue," Maud gave a little cough, "that is, unregistered."

Sheldrake frowned. "Her jurisdiction does not cover Carrador. Are we to assume the Kimoran government is hunting down shamans within Carrador? Surely the King would not sanction this?"

Maud shrugged. "It would depend on the rationale presented by the Kimoran ambassador. If shamans are indeed dangerous, I can imagine Gavin might be happy to be rid of them."

"This is most disturbing, Maud." Shaking his head, Sheldrake pushed his plate away, suddenly not hungry. "I have become fond of our little Sasha. I don't want anyone hunting him down, but equally I don't want our family endangered by harbouring someone who could grow to be a threat."

"Like Jayhan, you mean?"

"No," snapped Sheldrake. "Just because my pale-eyed grandmother was an evil old woman does not mean Jayhan will be. Powerful perhaps. We shall see. But inherently evil, no." He let out a breath and slowly smiled. "Cunning, Maud. You must like Sasha too, if you're standing up for him. So provided we keep him away from any adverse cultural influences of fellow shamans, there is no reason that Sasha should become dangerous as he grows into his powers."

"Except for mistakes, of course." Maud tilted her head to the side as she thought about it from every angle. "I think that is right. Do you?"

Sheldrake leant forward and took a slow pull on his wine before setting the glass down. "I would like to think so, but in truth, I don't know. Can people be born evil? Or do they perhaps have a tendency towards evil that circumstances nurture?"

"Evil is such a strong word, my dear. And so all encompassing. People are not usually evil, so much as power-hungry, or selfish, or uncaring, vengeful, jealous…"

"Some are just plain sadistic. They enjoy seeing people suffer."

"Yes, that is quite bad, I agree. But other qualities can be equally as destructive."

Sheldrake sighed. "So where does all this leave us? Is Sasha a threat or not? Perhaps shaman magic makes the wielder become obsessed in some way…"

"Before you get carried away, do more research. I am sure there must be books in the great library on shamanism. I thought shamans were supposed to be healers or witch doctors, something along those lines, not malevolent forces. And I think you should gather more information about Kimoran politics."

"All of this, without letting anyone know our interest in shamans."

"Now I must prepare for the King's garden party." Maud rose from the table and added with smirk, "I believe the Kimoran ambassador will be there."

"Well done, my dear. And I have recalled one of my senior agents from Kimora but he will not arrive for several days. Meanwhile, I will visit the library." He put down his napkin and stood up. "Good luck this afternoon and even more so this evening." He grinned. "Try not to get into any cat fights."

22

The garden party was held in the rear garden of the palace. Velvety green lawns dotted with majestic river red gums swept down to a small lake. Although most guests tended to stand chatting as they circulated, a few small chairs and tables were provided for those who could not stand for too long. Liveried servants threaded through the throngs bearing trays of drinks and savouries.

Maud drifted artfully through the nobles and distinguished people who had been graced with an invitation, listening briefly to conversations as she passed. She spent a few minutes as part of the group around the King, observing who was intent on speaking to him and why. King Gavin was a slight man in his mid-twenties, his wavy, auburn hair not quite reaching his shoulders. His blue eyes twinkled benignly at those gathered around him. His father had died two years before from pneumonia, contracted after being caught in a torrential thunderstorm during a day of hunting. So Gavin had ascended the throne unexpectedly, and before he felt ready. But as Sheldrake had said, Gavin was no pushover. He listened to people but formed his own opinions and made his own decisions. However, Maud had been his father's advisor and Gavin was wise enough to retain her counsel. He trusted her above anyone to steer him into his new role, knowing she had a perspective that he still lacked. Not wishing to appear dependent, he did not have her always at his side, but he did consult with her from time to time and usually accepted, or at least considered, her advice.

Maud exchanged smiles with him and commented on the success of the party before excusing herself to intercept Lady Electra soon after she had arrived and had been introduced to the mingling crowd.

The Kimoran ambassador wore an exquisitely cut gown with a modest, bowed neckline and billowing skirts in soft shades of orange and yellow, which contrasted beautifully with her rich brown skin. Maud eyed it enviously, thinking that, had she worn it, she would have looked either jaundiced or insipid, or both.

"Lady Electra, how lovely to see you. I wish I could wear those colours. They look stunning on you."

The ambassador raised an eyebrow. "Thank you, but I think the green you are wearing becomes you most admirably. You are Lady Maud, I believe." She accepted a glass of pale green sparkling wine from a passing waiter. Maud nodded but just as she was about to speak, Lady Electra looked her up and down and frowned. "And unless I am much mistaken, you are a shapeshifter."

Maud caught her breath and glanced around quickly to see who was within earshot. Fortunately, the hubbub had covered Electra's pronouncement.

Seeing Maud's reaction, Electra smiled disarmingly. "I beg your pardon. I can see from your reaction that this is not common knowledge. I must assume that the magic wielders in Carrador cannot discern your gift, as I can."

Maud deftly replaced her empty glass with a full one as another waiter passed within reach. By the time she had taken a sip, she had herself well enough in hand to smile in return. "No, it is not generally known. Are you a particular type of magic wielder that you can see it?"

"Of course. I am a shaman, as are many of my countrymen and women. Shamans have an affinity for animals and the more adept shaman are sensitive to their...hmm... I suppose you would call it, essence. Your essence is complex, almost layered." She seemed impressed. "You have the potential to be many things, I would think. Very unusual and very powerful." She leant in closer. "Do not worry, my dear. I will keep your secret. I can imagine it is very useful for one so close to the King."

To her annoyance, Maud felt herself blushing. "You seem to know a lot about me and yet, I barely know you."

Lady Electra laughed. "My dear, you underestimate yourself. You are known far and wide as the power... no, not quite that... as the mind behind the King."

"I do not control the King," said Maud stiffly. "And Gavin has his own mind, thank you very much."

"Of course he does," said the ambassador placatingly. "But you do, I think, exert some significant influence."

Maud glanced around again before saying, "I like to think he heeds my advice from time to time." She took refuge in a sip of wine. This woman was unexpectedly difficult.

Lady Electra raised her eyebrow again, an intimidating gesture. "So why did you wish to meet me?"

Maud choked. In the time it took her to stop coughing, she had come up with a response. "We value the trade that occurs between our two nations. So Sheldrake was concerned to receive reports from some merchants saying that tariffs have risen for goods going into Kimora. Actually, since we are being so devastatingly frank, I will say that I mean bribes, not tariffs. It seems there are some issues with governance and we would like to clarify what this may mean for our trading arrangements with your country. You also have some problems with the guilds, I believe."

"I see. If your husband could supply me with the particular entry port where these bribes were demanded, I can arrange to have the matter investigated." Maud noted with no surprise at all that Lady Electra knew who Sheldrake was. "The unrest among the guilds is more difficult. The Queen has had to enforce strict measures because of ongoing discontent. We believe that someone is behind it, trying to incite the guilds into civil disobedience."

"Really? Any idea who?"

The ambassador shook her head. "No. Not at this stage."

Maud was not sure she believed this but she also knew that she couldn't press. They were discussing internal Kimoran politics, after all. She changed the subject. "And I believe, unlike Carrador, you have a registration process for your magic users. Is the King aware that you are tracking down unregistered shamans within the boundaries of his realm?"

Lady Electra raised those finely arched eyebrows of hers. "Who told you that?"

Maud smiled vaguely. "We, like you, have our sources."

Instead of stalling for time by taking a sip of her drink, Electra simply held up a finger and said calmly, "Just a moment. Let me think."

Impressed, Maud waited.

"Our queen is, not unreasonably, wary of magic users. She came to power by right of her own shamanic magic and although she has now ruled for over ten years, still fears that other shamans may be plotting to overthrow her." Electra gave a gentle shrug. "Hence our interest in unregistered shamans."

"But, is she not the daughter of your previous queen? Wasn't her claim legitimate?"

"Yes, Toriana became the heir after her older sister, the Princess Corinna, and her family were killed by bandits, only weeks before their mother, Queen Suriana, died. It was a very hard time." Electra looked away. When she turned her head back, Maud could see that her eyes were shiny with unshed tears. "I'm sorry. Corinna and I were dear friends. I still mourn her."

"I beg your pardon for upsetting you." When Electra waved this away, Maud continued, "However, we are far from Kimora's seat of power here. Surely it should be safe for anyone at odds with your queen to be in exile here, both from your perspective and theirs?"

The ambassador studied Maud for a long moment. "When a shaman is registered, they are bound to the Queen's service both by oath and by power. This limits what they are able to say or do."

Maud frowned. "Are you saying that a shaman's power needs to be controlled to be safe?"

Electra looked startled. "No. Not at all. A shaman's powers need to be controlled for the Queen to feel safe." She took a little breath. "You missed my point. Perhaps if I remind you that I, too, am a shaman."

"Oh." Maud's brow cleared. "Oh, how dim of me. Can you answer me this, then? Does the King know you are hunting shamans in his realm? Because I give you fair warning, he will soon, for Sheldrake or I intend to inform him."

"I cannot stop you and in fact, do not wi..." Electra gagged suddenly. She swallowed and produced a wan smile. "Ahem, perhaps some bubbles went down the wrong way." Since she had not touched her sparkling wine for several minutes, this was unlikely. "I will prepare our apologies. It was a pleasure meeting you." She gave a formal nod of her head and moved away, leaving Maud gazing thoughtfully after her.

23

In strict accordance with the invitations, the garden party ended at four o'clock and carriages bore the invitees away. By a quarter past the hour, the garden was nearly empty. Maud spoke briefly to the King before she left, making a time to see him on the morrow to bring him up to date and to confer with him on any pressing issues.

She returned to her room and rested for a couple of hours before ordering an early dinner. Sheldrake had not yet returned from the library, but she wanted time to check out the area around the Hidden Lantern before entering it later in the evening.

Once darkness had fallen, she retired to her room and produced the image of a cat in her mind: its shape, its movements, its habits, attitudes and tastes. Slowly Maud shimmered into particles and almost disappeared, before coalescing into a rather solid grey cat, sporting white paws and a natty white patch on her chest. She strutted up and down in front of her mirror, conceding that Sasha might be right about her being a little tubby. Nevertheless, she thought herself rather dapper and rubbed appreciatively against the mirror before jumping lightly onto the windowsill, then out into the night.

Maud scampered across roof tops, heading east towards the docks and the Bohemian quarter. As she passed, she peered through windows to see families at dinner, servants preparing trays for their employers, a young man ardently declaring his love for a modest serving girl who looked uncomfortable and... Maud stopped and watched while the girl's protests became more strident and the young man's approach more determined.

Maud spotted a balcony above her, bunched her muscles and leapt. She climbed nimbly up a drainpipe and over the railing. The balcony door was closed but not locked. She leapt up and grasped the handle, pulling it down with her weight and holding on as the door swung open. Maud let herself drop before dashing in and down the stairs. The door to the room was closed and this door had a knob that was not so easy for a cat to open. Inside, she could hear the girl protesting and a thump as something was knocked over.

Maud sat on her haunches and yowled at the top of her voice. In moments, a voice from upstairs demanded to know what was going on. The door to the room was flung open and the young man strode out, glaring for the source of the noise. Maud slipped between his legs and entered the room, while he yelled up the stairs that nothing was wrong, that it was just a tomcat in the alley.

Maud ran straight for the girl who was cowering in the corner beside the fireplace, white with fright, holding up the torn bodice of her dress. Maud clawed her way up the girl's skirts and onto the mantelpiece. When the young man re-entered the room, he was confronted with a grey ball of fury, claws slashing whenever he tried to approach the girl.

Gaining courage from having an ally, the girl grasped the nearby poker. "Keep away, sir." He swayed a little closer, so she raised the poker. "Away, sir. I work here for honest money. I can't afford to lose my job but I will leave, if staying means being your plaything."

Suddenly the fight went out of the young man. He backed into a chair and put his face in his hands. "Oh, no. What am I doing? What was I thinking?" He raised his head and looked at her "And where did that come from?" he asked, pointing at the grey cat that stood on the mantelpiece with back arched. He shook his head. "It doesn't matter. I'm sorry, Larissa. I should never have done that. If you wish to leave the household, I will give you a good reference and will pay to get you settled somewhere else."

Larissa lowered the poker. "I prefer to stay, as long as this doesn't happen again."

The young man shook his head. "It won't. You have my word of honour."

"If you leave the room now, we will say nothing of this."

He stood. "Just a minute. Stay there."

He left and returned a few minutes later with another dress. The cat was still on the mantelpiece but sitting with her tail curled around herself. He held the dress out to Larissa, keeping as far away as he could. "Here. I beg your pardon. I had to enter your room, but you need a change of clothes. I am more sorry than I can say. I do love you, I think." He held his hand up. "but, I know. You don't need to tell me. I have a poor way of showing it." He gave a wistful smile. "Thank you for your forbearance."

With that, he left the room. Maud waited while the girl stroked her and made a fuss of her. When she had had enough, she jumped down and crossed to the window, scratching at the glass.

"Oh. You want to get out, do you?"

Quick as a flash, thought Maud.

Larissa opened the window and Maud slipped into the night.

Ten minutes later, she was slinking along shadows on the opposite side of the road from the Hidden Lantern. Chunky, a fearsome tomcat, so called because he had lost chunks of hair during his long, vicious history of fighting, was the local dominant male but he would only challenge other males, so was no threat to her. Female cats were a different matter, but she had made it clear to those who had met her that she was only in the area for a short time and a specific purpose.

As she rounded the corner, she noted a small low door in the wall of the Hidden Lantern, which presumably led to the cellars for delivery of ales, and a drainpipe leading down from the roof near the corner, past an upper storey window. She jumped the fence into the rear yard and found herself facing a closed back door and an open, street level window. Empty barrels were stacked along the wall of the inn.

She crossed to the wall and leapt lightly up onto a barrel and sat down, her tail curled around her feet listening to the sounds of the night, her ears flicking back and forth. After a few minutes, she took a deep breath, gathered herself and sprang up to the windowsill. She stood balanced on the narrow sill as she listened and looked for people, other cats or, horror of horrors, a dog. The coast seemed clear. A scullery and an open trapdoor with a ladder leading down into the cellars was to her right while straight ahead, she could see a crack of light shining under the door at the end of a dark passageway. After a moment's thought, she jumped down and slunk towards the light. As she neared, she could hear voices but the heavy wood of the door precluded her from hearing what was being said. Her tail twitched in irritation.

Suddenly heavy footsteps approached from the other side. Maud whipped to the hinge side of the door and pressed herself against the wall. The door opened and the inn keeper walked through carrying empty jugs. Maud slid behind him and through the doorway before the heavy door swung shut in his wake.

She found herself in a private parlour, hung with ancient tapestries depicting scenes of war and witchcraft, interspersed with ornate mirrors. Eight men and four women, each wearing a different style of dress, were seated on carved wooden chairs around a large round table. One of the women was dark like Sasha and Maud wondered if she was a shaman. To Maud's immediate left was a heavy sideboard on raised legs. She slunk beneath it and hunkered down to listen.

For a while they discussed mundane things such as the treasurer's report and cost of the venue, which apparently was subject to increase from time to time. Then each magic-user reported on new developments in their field. Maud found it interesting but dry. She would rather see and use magic than hear about it. Finally, a round-faced man in a crimson, embroidered robe said, "Now that we have heard all the reports, I think the next matter on our agenda is two-fold; someone has been watching our proceedings from the bar and another person is asking about shamans."

"And Teleman told me," chimed in the dark woman, nodding at a thin man wearing a ragged, brown linen coat, his beard and moustache long and wispy, "that the person asking about shamans was followed by the watcher from the bar." She huffed, "So now it looks like we have two separate parties interested in shamans."

"Don't worry Yarrow," said the round-faced man, "you know we will not betray your presence nor that of any other shaman who visits us. This society stands for the freedom to develop magical potential. We learn by working together."

Yarrow waved a ring-laden hand. "Thank you for your reassurance Donian, but it is not the Society members I am worried about. I am worried about the watcher from the bar, since we know she is from the Embassy. But even more so, the stranger who enquired concerns me. Where is he from? Clearly not from the Embassy, if she followed him. So who does he represent and what are their intentions?"

"Perhaps he is an ally or simply a researcher of shamans?" suggested Donian. "Perhaps we should have spoken to him."

Certainly would have helped us if you had, thought Maud.

Suddenly a scratching sound attracted her attention and before her eyes, a little mouse scurried out of a hole in the wainscot beside her. It did a doubletake when it saw her, its eyes widening in horror. Without the interception of thought, Maud pounced. The mouse, whose life was on the line, was quicker and scrambled back into the hole. But not fast enough. Maud's claws slammed down, catching the end of its tail. Maud was so intent on keeping her tenuous grip on the tiny bit of tail as she tried to stretch her other paw into the hole that she froze with shock when a hand grabbed her from behind and hauled her out from under the dresser by the scruff of her neck.

Oops.

As she hung in mid-air, staring into the indigo eyes of a finely built man wearing a coat not unlike Sheldrake's, Yarrow exclaimed, "Marvis, be gentle. That cat is a human shapeshifter," she walked around to look into Maud's eyes. "... who has a bit of explaining to do."

The last thing Maud wanted was to shape-change back into human form in front of a roomful of strangers. She focused frantically on the shape and size of a flea. Six legs was a challenge. So too was the size; so small. She felt as though she were changing into a dress six sizes too small for her.

Suddenly, the man's hand closed over thin air.

For an instant, Maud gripped his thumb with her tiny toes then used her multi-jointed legs to push off in a jump that landed her on the shaman's skirts. The next jump took her to the floor and the next, deep under the dresser. She waited for a few moments to draw breath and accustom herself to her new shape, listening to the exclamations and shouts issuing from the magic makers. A huge hand swept in under the dresser, but before anyone could invoke any sort of spell, she was out and under the door in two quick leaps.

She was nearly trampled on by the innkeeper who arrived at the door with filled jugs of ale, just as she emerged. A dollop of foam dropped on her as he paused to open the door and she found herself deep within wet clouds of froth that slowly popped and fizzed around her to become an amber puddle. Before it had time to submerge her, she pushed off from the floor and sprang further down the corridor.

For a while, she just stood there on her chitinous legs, dripping with sticky beer, tired from the unexpected style of exercise and shocked by the nearness of her escape. When her heart stopped hammering and her breathing had slowed, she began to think through her options. Before anything, she needed to get dry.

She jumped her way down the corridor and around the corner until she found an old rag lying discarded against the wall of the scullery. She burrowed into its folds, ruing the pungent smell of hops, until she had wiped off most of the beer. She listened for sounds of the inn keeper returning but from the noise issuing from the room, he was probably being berated for his lack of security.

She drew a couple of centring breaths then imagined her true self in her favourite green gown that she had worn as she shape-changed into the cat form. As she coalesced into her human shape, she swayed and had to prop herself against the wall. She hadn't noticed before how high a human's centre of gravity was. Not a good sign, feeling disoriented in her own body. She usually only shape-changed once a week or less, not three times in a few hours, and not in a tearing hurry.

She steadied herself, shaking her arms to become used to their length and moving her her weight back and forth from one foot to the other until she felt more secure in her body.

Just then, she heard the door open and the inn keeper's footsteps coming down the corridor towards her. Checking her hair briefly in her reflection in the window, she tucked in a few stray wisps, took a deep breath and surged around the corner.

She swept past the inn keeper, saying in her most assured manner, "Bring another glass, would you, when you return with more ale? Thank you so much."

The inn keeper, his hands full of empty jugs, goggled at her as she passed but made no move to stop her.

Maud knocked peremptorily on the door and entered without waiting for a response.

"Good evening," she said, smiling her most brilliant,

social smile. "You may remember, we met briefly a few minutes ago." She held up her hand to quell the voices that had begun to speak. "Having listened to the contents of your meeting, I believe an open exchange between you and me is justified. With any luck, I can answer your questions, while you can answer some of mine." She turned her smile on the shaman. "How do you do, Yarrow. My name is Lady Maud Batian and as you can tell, I am a shape-shifter."

They all started talking at once while Maud stood before them, the picture of calm, friendly assurance, saying nothing and simply waiting for them to sort themselves out. Eventually, the man called Donian, who seemed to be their chairman, called them to order. Once they were silent, he turned to Maud and said formally, "Lady Maud, it is an honour to have you here although the manner of your arrival, was," he coughed, a little nervous but determined to do his duty, "somewhat reprehensible."

Maud smiled with unabated cordiality. "It was, wasn't it? However, I did not have to return to face you all and in fact would not have done so, had I decided you to be untrustworthy. I have, you understand, the care of others to consider."

"Indeed, ma'am. Could you be more explicit?"

"Certainly, but firstly may I join you at your table? Do you think another chair could be procured?"

Just then, the rear door opened to reveal the innkeeper lugging a chair in one hand and an extra glass in the other. Maud beamed at him "Oh well done, sir. You have anticipated my need. Thank you very much."

"I will be back shortly with more ale," he said to no one in particular and left.

"Now," said Maud, clasping her hands before her on the table. "Perhaps you would like to hear why I am here."

"I'm sure we would," replied Yarrow dryly.

"It is nothing nefarious, I assure you, and neither was my associate's enquiry about shamans the other day. Sheldrake and I simply want to learn about the powers of shamans."

"Sheldrake?" exclaimed the man with the indigo eyes, whose clothing resembled Sheldrake's. "*The* Sheldrake?"

Maud raised her eyebrows delicately. "Is there another, Marvis? Sheldrake is my husband, as I assumed you would know."

Clearly from the murmurs around the table, not everyone did know.

Yarrow frowned fiercely. "Isn't he, and aren't you, involved in the King's Sp... information service."

"Not I, only Sheldrake. But the King did not commission any investigation into shamans, if that is your fear. And since you people were unresponsive to a straightforward enquiry, I have had to ask elsewhere for the information I am seeking. So today, I had a talk with Lady Electra, the Kimoran ambassador. As you probably know, she is a registered shaman." Maud paused for a moment, her eyes sweeping around the circle of shocked faces. "Hmm. Before I go any further," she turned again to Yarrow, "are you registered or unregistered? Don't worry. Anything you say to me will remain with me, unless I have your agreement otherwise."

Yarrow drew a deep breath then tilted her chin up in an unconscious defiance. "I am an unregistered, free shaman, ma'am."

"Oh good. That's a relief." Maud smiled around the group, who had all relaxed at her words. "Which is why you need protection. Correct?"

Teleman leant forward and replied tersely. "And not

only Yarrow. Any unregistered shaman has our support and protection. If you are harbouring, as I suspect you are, an unregistered shaman, I hope, I sincerely hope, you did not give Lady Electra an inkling of it."

"So too do I," replied Maud. "After our associate was stonewalled by you and followed by the Embassy's agent, I made every effort to disguise the true nature of my enquiry. In fact, I made it clear to her that the King would not look kindly on Kimora chasing unregistered shamans within Carrador's boundaries." She gave a cheeky grin. "And I can assure you I wasn't followed here."

This turned the discussion to her shapeshifting skills which were of great interest to the Society, since they were so rare, particularly to the extent that she commanded them.

Eventually, Yarrow broke across the conversation, asking, "Lady Maud, will you tell us who you are protecting?"

Maud fidgeted with her cuffs then put her hands below table level to hide her tension. "Before we began to make enquiries, we did not realise that he needed protection. Knowing what we do now, I am loath to tell you, but in fairness, I think I must. We recently employed a young lad, who apparently arrived as a baby on the doorstep of Stonehaven Orphanage some eight years ago. He wears an amulet that denotes his origins as a shaman from Kimora." She smiled. "We first became curious about his magic when he saw straight through my shapeshifting," she looked at Yarrow, "as can you."

"Eight years ago? You are sure?" asked Yarrow, suddenly intent.

"Yes, as far as I am aware. Sheldrake visited the orphanage yesterday to check the story and it was just as Sasha had said."

Yarrow leaned back, the tension draining from her. "Oh. No, the timing is wrong. Don't worry. Just someone I'm looking for."

Maud smiled sympathetically. "I gather things have been hard on shamans under this Queen's rule. Is there, as Electra suggests, someone behind the guilds' unrest in Kimora?"

"Many someones, My Lady. Many people, not just shamans, are unhappy with the current monarchy."

"Yarrow, I would not want to put you at risk but if there is any chance that you could find time to teach Sasha a little of his heritage, we would be grateful. We had intended to ask the Kimoran ambassador but..." Yarrow's eyes widened in alarm, but Maud waved a reassuring hand. "But clearly, if we want Sasha to maintain his independence, that is not an option."

"No, it is not," said Yarrow vehemently. "I would be pleased to teach a fellow countryman and shaman. We," she waved her hand to encompass the assembled company, "will find a safe way to communicate with you. Be careful that you are not followed home. Remember that most shamans can see through shapeshifting."

"Hmm. Good point. Is that girl in the bar a shaman, do you think?"

"No. I would know if she were. It is a particular skill I have."

Maud stood up with decision. "To be safe, I will return the way I came." She let her gaze travel around the group. "Have you ever seen a shapeshifter change?"

Amid headshakes and mumbled 'no's, Donian gave a slight laugh, "Except from cat to flea, ma'am. None of our members has that skill."

"I have been impressed by your Society and believe you

nurture the development and diversity of magic. So, if you like, for the sake of erudition, I will show you. In return, please tell no one of my particular talent."

Donian stood and gave a small bow. "We would be most honoured, Lady Maud."

"Goodbye then. Please make sure I can get out the back window." With that, she focused her whole being on her grey and white feline counterpart, shimmered and merged into her new shape. She gave a proud "Proww," and rubbed her side against Yarrow who opened the door for her. Without a backward glance, mostly because she was embarrassed, she scampered down the corridor, leapt onto the windowsill and out into the night.

It was nearly midnight when she reached their apartment at the palace. She leapt lightly in the window and slunk quietly across the carpeted lounge room to her bedroom, in an effort not to disturb Sheldrake. She need not have bothered though, because he was seated in an armchair in her room, reading a book. Despite her care, his head rose from the pages as soon as she entered, and his face lit with a relieved smile.

"Ah my dear. You are safely back. I am so glad. I'll get us both a nightcap, shall I?" Not expecting an answer, he rose from his chair and headed for the door, tactfully leaving her to shape-change in private.

When he returned bearing two crystal glasses containing hefty serves of brandy, Maud was sitting up in bed wearing a gold and green silk night gown, with a cream woollen wrap thrown round her shoulders.

"Thank you, Sheldrake. I hope I didn't worry you too much. I have had a very adventurous night." She gave him an entertaining version of events before saying, "I am concerned about our little stable boy's safety. I think we should consider curtailing our visit and return home tomorrow after I have spoken with Gavin. What do you think?"

Sheldrake sipped his brandy, aware that her mind was already made up but happily finding himself in agreement. "I was watched in the library this afternoon; not because it was me but because someone was watching for interest in the section on shamanism. I hope I spotted the woman before she spotted me, but I am not sure. Once I knew she was there, I tried to look as though I was browsing all kinds of magic, shamanism least of all. But I don't know how convincing I was. I agree with you. We must return home and review our security arrangements."

24

The next day, happily unaware of any impending danger from the Highkington, Sasha and Jayhan saddled up the ponies as soon as their chores were done and headed off to the bush. This time, Jayhan carefully centred himself and found that he could raise a trot in Slug even heading away from home without the use of a switch; not an enthusiastic trot admittedly, but a trot nonetheless. Slug even managed a short canter but Jayhan had to work hard for every moment of it.

By tacit agreement, they did not speak of magic until they had made their way to the same spot beside the creek that they had stopped at the day before. Dismounting, they climbed into the lower branches of a twisty red gum to eat their sandwiches. Sasha had a whole day of physical labour behind him and was content to eat slowly and relax for a little while, but Jayhan was could hardly contain himself.

As soon as he had swallowed his last bite, Jayhan jumped down and began to pace back and forth below Sasha.

"So, what do you reckon? How do I do this?"

Sasha finished his last bite then leaned back along the branch he was seated on and put his hands behind his head. "No idea."

"Aw, come on. You must have some idea."

"Why? You've had years more magical training then me."

"Yeah but," Jayhan frowned up at him, "But you know about shapeshifters. From being a shaman. Maybe you can concentrate on your amulet and ideas might come about how to shape-change."

Sasha sat up straighter on his branch, held out his amulet on its chain around his neck and peered down at it. "I've never thought of taking in the knowledge from the amulet on purpose. I just let it happen or not. It's worth a try. In fact, maybe I should be trying to draw knowledge from it."

Jayhan, with rare patience, sat down on a nearby log and waited while Sasha concentrated on his amulet.

Firstly, Sasha centred himself. When he felt ready, he studied the bisected triangle symbol on his amulet, running his eyes around the three points which, according to Sheldrake, represented birth, life and death. As he ran his eye down the central stroke, he began to think about Maud and the layers he saw behind her human form. He thought about how she had appeared to him in the shapes of bloodhound, horse and sheep that he had seen her in, her true form clear to him within her outside appearance. Then he thought about her again in her human form and compared it to what he saw in Jayhan.

Something was different. In Maud, Sasha saw a depth and complexity of the other shapes that was lacking in Jayhan. He visualised Maud and Jayhan side by side then he realised the difference. Maud's layers contained a myriad of shapes and colours but Jayhan's contained a wide variety of colours but only slight variations in shape.

With a sinking heart, Sasha looked up at his friend who was waiting so patiently, eager to try out different animal shapes.

"Well?" prompted Jayhan. "How do I do it?"

Sasha shook his head, realising he hadn't even focused on that aspect. "Just a minute. I need a bit longer."

Jayhan huffed but said nothing.

Sasha had never seen Maud shape-change. So he just imagined her as her real self then as the blood hound, cutting back and forth between the two images. Suddenly, from deep within him, the knowledge of how to change welled up. He raised his head, dropped the amulet back onto his chest and leapt down from the tree, to land in front of Jayhan.

Jayhan, who had been amusing himself by watching a large ant struggle to carry away a crumb of bread twice its size, looked up startled.

"I've got it! I know how you change!" Sasha yelled triumphantly. Before Jayhan could replay, Sasha held up his hand. "But..."

"But what?"

"But it's not all good." He winced as he anticipated Jayhan's disappointment. "I don't think you can shapeshift into other animal forms. I think you can only shapeshift into other human forms."

Jayhan's face fell. "Oh." He stood up and scuffed his toe along the ground. "So no flying, or galloping across the plains, after all."

"No, I don't think so. I might be wrong. After all, I'm new to all of this but...no. I'm pretty sure, no."

Jayhan put his hands in his pockets and walked around

the edge of the clearing, scuffing his feet through the grasses and leaves, his head bowed. After a while, he sat on a log and said glumly, "Wouldn't you know I'd come up second best?"

"No, I wouldn't know, as it happens. I think you're great." Sasha came to stand in front of him with his arms folded across his chest. "Except that you whinge about yourself too much. Anyway, you still have a special talent most mages lack, even your father. Don't you want to try it out? It could be fun... in a different way." Sasha grinned. "You could pretend to be me and trick Beth."

At that, Jayhan raised his head and looked at Sasha, his eyes narrowing as he thought about it. He gave a lop-sided smile. "Hmph. Not quite as good as flying but hmm, could be fun." Suddenly he smiled, his sunny nature reasserting itself. "And I could become Hannah and pinch whatever I like from the kitchen when she's not there and become Eloquin and tell Mum that I, as in I Jayhan, had done great work and deserve a holiday." He chortled. "So come on then. Tell me how to do it."

Sasha explained how to centre himself then to focus hard on the person he wanted to become, imagining every aspect of their appearance and behaviour, until his real self faded and the image took over.

Jayhan took a deep breath. "All right. I'll try it." He waved his hand. "Go over there somewhere so I don't have you watching me. And look somewhere else. I'll come and show you when I've done it... or at least when I think I've done it."

Ten minutes later, Jayhan blew out a long breath and looked himself up and down before walking over to tap Sasha on the shoulder.

"What do you think?" he asked, torn between embarrassment and amusement.

Sasha turned and found himself staring at himself; dark skin, soft dark brown eyes and curly black hair. After a moment, he cocked his head as he studied particular aspects.

"Well?" pressed Jayhan.

Sasha grinned. "Pretty good. Really good if someone wasn't expecting it."

Jayhan frowned. "What's wrong with it?"

"Well, the face is a bit lopsided. That little mole I have on my cheek is on the wrong side."

Jayhan frowned even harder, then laughed. "No, it's not. You always see yourself in the mirror. And I bet it's not lopsided. It's just the other way around."

"And is my nose really that snubby?"

"It's not snubby. It just turns up a bit at the end."

"Hmph. All right. Come over to the creek and we'll look at our reflections side by side in the water."

Two little Sashas parted the bull rushes and knelt on the muddy bank, staring down into the water, comparing the two reflections. Suddenly the real Sasha grinned and slapped Jayhan on the back. "Well done. That's fantastic, especially for a first time. Let's go home and trick Beth."

They pulled their hoods up as they neared the house and waited until they saw Beth come out of the side door of the stable and walk towards the front garden. As soon as she disappeared around the corner of the building, they trotted their ponies the last hundred yards, flung themselves off and hitched them to the post beside the water trough.

"Quickly," hissed Jayhan. "I can hear her coming back."

They ran quickly down the aisle between the stalls and snuck into her office. Sasha hid behind her comfortable armchair while Jayhan stood near the table ready to look as though he were collecting a curry comb. As she entered, his stomach lurched at his audacity.

"Hello," he said cheerily. "We just got back. I'll just brush down the horses before I put them away."

Beth frowned at him. "Will you now? And where is Jayhan? He is supposed to be learning to look after his own horse."

Whoops. Jayhan waved his hand airily, in what he suddenly realised was one of his own gestures. He hoped Beth wouldn't notice. "I know, but Eloquin called him. Don't know why. He'll probably be back to help me soon."

Beth relaxed a little and asked, "So, did you two enjoy yourselves? Did that lazy horse manage a canter?"

Jayahn grinned. "Yes, for a bit. Jayhan's getting better at managing him, but he's hard work, even for me."

A suppressed snort of laughter issued from behind Beth's chair. Beth whirled around and strode over. "What's going on? Who's here?"

Sasha stood up slowly, grinning his head off. "Hello Beth. Pretty good, hey? Can you tell us apart?"

She thought for a disappointingly short moment before saying, "Well, I would say I have been talking to the false Sasha who was trying to see whether he could trick me. So that means that you're the real Sasha, who is becoming very cheeky for an apprentice, and that naughty ratbag with the curry comb in his hand is Jayhan."

Sasha's smile faltered. "Sorry Beth. I didn't mean to be cheeky."

Beth ruffled his hair. "Don't be silly, Sasha, I'm only joking. You are very clever to have worked out how to do this, all on your own. Your father will be very impressed, Jayhan."

"And with Sasha," said Jayhan, quick to stand up for his friend. "He taught me how to do it."

"When I said you, I meant both of you." Beth put her hands on Sasha's shoulders and looked into his eyes. "Well done, Sasha. You are generous with your growing knowledge."

Sasha smiled up at her, knowing she was trying her best to make up for his lack of parents. "Thanks. You are both really kind to me. Everyone is, except maybe Rose. I trust you a lot." He swallowed. "So, there is something I have to, want to tell you."

And into the fraught silence that followed this pronouncement, walked Sheldrake and Maud.

PART IV

25

At first, Sheldrake and Maud only saw Sasha looking earnestly up into Beth's eyes. Feeling the tension, Sheldrake asked, "What's going on?"

"Hello," said Jayhan from the other side of the room, having completely forgotten that he was currently looking like a second Sasha. As soon as he said it, he remembered, blushing and grinning with pride at his accomplishment.

Sheldrake raised his eyebrows so far that they threatened to climb into his hairline. He and Maud looked back and forth between the two Sashas several times, studying them so hard that Jayhan's grin faded and both boys began to feel awkward. Beth let her hands drop from Sasha's shoulders and he walked over to stand, hands behind his back, beside Jayhan. They glanced at each other and a small smile passed between them.

"So is this what you were about to tell Beth? That you have a twin brother? When did he turn up? Does *he* need a job too? What with you, Rose's brother, and now your twin brother, we are going to have a lot of new staff," said Maud, sounding none too pleased.

"No, ma'am," said Jayhan stiffly, miffed on Sasha's behalf. Without conscious effort, he assumed the role of Sasha's fictitious twin brother. "I do not need a job with you. Our family would not wish to cause you any further imposition. I'm sure neither of us would wish to stay where we were unwelcome."

Sasha goggled at him. He dug Jayhan in the ribs, as surreptitiously as he could, hissing, "Shut *up!*"

Jayhan looked at him. "What? She's being mean. I'm just standing up for you."

Sasha rolled his eyes and whispered, a hint of desperation in his voice. "Stop it. *Please.* I can't afford to upset people. I need my job."

Jayhan looked at his mother then at Sasha then back to his mother. "It is easy to be unkind, isn't it, when a person can't answer back."

Maud was turning a dark shade of red.

"That is enough, young man," barked Sheldrake. "You are clearly not cut out for our household. Sasha, however, may remain if he chooses. In fact, I hope he does. We have come to value his work, his knowledge and his good cheer."

Jayhan stared at his father, then remembered who he was and what they were really doing. Slowly he began to laugh. "Whoops! Sorry Dad. Sorry Mum. I just got carried away. I've never been spoken to like that before and I..." he shrugged. "I just didn't like it. That's all."

Sheldrake and Maud goggled.

"Jayhan???" they said in unison.

Jayhan grinned and nodded his head. "Yep. I can shapeshift. But not animals though."

Suddenly Maud clapped her hands, making them both jump. "Well done, Jayhan. Magnificent. Even if you were insolent to your mother."

"And Sasha, we have you to thank for teaching him, I take it?" asked Sheldrake.

Sasha nodded, looking down and scuffing his foot.

"I thought we might. You're a clever little fellow and so is Jayhan. I am most impressed." He rubbed his hands together. "So, before you change back, Jayhan, do you mind if we try a couple of things?"

Maud rolled her eyes. "Sheldrake, we have only just walked in the door. Can't it wait?"

"It could my dear, but it won't take long ... and it is so interesting. Don't you think?"

Maud gave a reluctant smile. "Yes, I suppose it is."

"Now," instructed Sheldrake. "Could you both walk outside, muss your hair about, dirty your clothes a bit or something, so we don't know which of you is which. Then come back in and we will try to work out who is who."

"You had better take your pendant off, Sasha, or it will give the game away. Here," said Beth, stretching out her hand. "I will hold it for you."

"And I will turn into a bloodhound. I suspect I will be able to smell the difference," said Maud. "Just a minute."

With that, she retired to a horse's stall to change shape in private while the boys scuttled outside and swapped tops but not pants and mussed their hair.

Once they had reconvened, Sheldrake and Beth went first, debating which was which. In the end, they picked out Sasha because he was still feeling unsure after Jayhan's little sortie and his diffidence reflected in his demeanour. Maud padded in once they had made their choice and after sniffing both, went straight to Sasha. Sasha gave her an uncertain smile and had to have her nose pushed under his hand before he would pat her as he usually did.

Maud retired to resume her true form. When she

returned, she came to stand beside Sheldrake, her arms folded. She looked grim. "Sasha, as we entered, you were about to say something of significance to Beth. It was not, as we first thought, that you have a twin. So, what was it?"

Sasha went stock still. He glanced at Beth, standing beside him, and his eyes went to his amulet. Without a word, she proffered it and he placed it around his neck.

"One way the amulet protects me is by hiding who I am," he said. "But I wasn't wearing it when Maud, in her bloodhound form, smelled me and I think she now knows what I am."

"You're a shaman, correct?" asked Sheldrake, frowning.

"Yes, from what you've told me. But I am also... It's hard to explain, but ever since I was a baby, I've had to hide who I am. Old Tom said people were after me and I had to stay hidden. I don't know why."

"Maybe because you are a shaman," suggested Sheldrake. "I gather the Queen of Karoka is hunting down shamans. She either kills them or binds them to her will somehow. Nasty business. I just hope our questions have not alerted anyone to your presence here. In fact, that's why we have returned earlier than we planned. To make sure you are safe."

"It isn't just that, Sheldrake," said Maud quietly. "Is it, Sasha?"

Sasha looked steadfastly at the floor. "No, ma'am, I mean, madam. I was going to tell you. I just had to be sure I could trust you all. Old Tom said so. I never trusted Bryson and the amulet kept me safe, at least mostly." He took a deep breath and raised his head. "I am a girl, not a boy."

Jayhan swivelled so fast to look at Sasha that he nearly

fell over. "You're WHAT?" He gaped. "You're a girl? No. Can't be. Really?"

Sasha put her hands on her hips. "And what is wrong with that exactly?"

"Did I say anything was wrong with it? *No.*" Jayhan heaved a breath as his bewilderment threatened to overcome him. "I'm just boggled..." he shook his head from side to side. "and confused... and trying to think about what we've done together ...and all that time you didn't trust me..."

Then as his understanding of who Sasha was faltered, so did his shape-shifting. His features blurred and for a moment both Jayhan and Sasha's features intermingled on his face. Then Sasha's features were gone and it was just Jayhan standing there, looking lost and a bit forlorn.

Impulsively, Sasha stepped forward and wrapped her arms around him. "I'm sorry. I truly am. I didn't mean to hurt you. I've been your friend ever since I met you and I still am, I hope."

Jayhan endured the hug for a minute then pushed her away. "We've never been huggy. Why start now?"

Sasha smiled at him. "Because you looked sad, that's all... and I caused it."

"I'm too young to have a girlfriend, you know. I'm only eight."

Sasha rolled her eyes. "Oh for goodness sakes, you idiot. I'm not your girlfriend. I'm your friend who's a girl. Completely different."

"Oh."

"Hmm. And would I be right in guessing that you are also older than we were led to believe?" asked Beth dryly.

Jayhan and Sasha had been so intent on each other's reactions that they had forgotten they were ringed by adults.

Sasha's head whipped around to find three sets of adult eyes regarding her. Her cheeks reddened. "I beg your pardon. I forgot you were...that is, Jayhan needed, um..." She stuttered to a stop and frowned. "Er, what did you ask me?"

"How old are you?" asked Maud baldly.

"I am ten years old."

"You're what?" demanded Jayhan. "No wonder you can ride better than me and learn to read better than me and... well, everything better than me."

"Jayhan," interrupted Sheldrake in a tone of mild reproof, "This is not all about you. Please let others have a chance to speak to Sasha."

Jayhan mumbled an apology, then whispered "Cheat!" over his shoulder as he walked to stand, with his arms folded, by the wall and distance himself from the conversation.

Sasha was left standing on her own, facing three very serious adults.

The silence stretched out as Maud, Sheldrake and Beth tried to get their heads around their stable boy being a stable girl.

Eventually Sasha spoke, "Does it matter? I'm sorry I deceived you. I never lied about it because I didn't need to. Do you want me to leave?"

"No," said Sheldrake sharply. "We would not send you out into possible danger when you have... honoured us with your trust," he gave a rueful smile. "even if it has taken you so many months to do so."

Sasha took in a deep breath that hitched on a sob. "Oh good. Because I have nowhere to go, you see. And no one to go to, because Old Tom said it would be too dangerous for me to go back there, to Stonehaven, even though I loved it there." She wrapped her arms around herself. "I had to leave when I was nine. Everyone else could stay until they were at least ten, but not me. I had to leave when I was nine. Someone came and talked to Tom and the next morning, they hid me under the sacking on Bryson's cart and sent me away to live with him. I didn't even get to say goodbye, except to Old Tom."

She looked around in surprise when she felt an arm across her shoulders and found Jayhan standing next to her. He smiled at her, took a breath as though to say something, but then just smiled more warmly. She smiled back, even as tears filled her eyes and coursed down her cheeks. Suddenly Maud and Beth had both encircled her in their arms and Sheldrake even went so far as to pat her on the head and say, "There, there."

After a while she took a deep shuddering breath. "It is such a relief to tell you. It felt so lonely being the only one who knew."

Maud gave her a final squeeze. "We must still keep your gender and age a secret until we know what we are dealing with. I see no need to tell Hannah or Rose. Sheldrake, you may need to tell Leon as he is privy to your investigations and of course, you must tell Clive, Beth. But no one else. For the time being, we will carry on as before. Agreed?"

This last was addressed mainly to Sheldrake, who replied, "Indeed. And we will not broadcast, any more than we have, the fact that you are a shaman, Sasha."

26

"I must talk to Leon about security today," said Sheldrake to Maud the next morning, as he rose from the breakfast table, placing his napkin neatly on his side plate. "I have a magical ward around my workshop but perhaps we need one around the whole perimeter. Anyone could walk in off the street."

As if to demonstrate his point, the front doorbell rang. A few minutes later, Clive appeared. "A gentleman has asked to see you. I have put him in the front parlour, while I ascertain your availability. He would not give his name, which I found distinctly odd, but he said you would know him when you saw him." Clive paused. "Do you, in fact, *wish* to see him?"

Sheldrake frowned. "Extremely odd... but intriguing. Yes, I will see him, but I had better take precautions. Ask Leon to join us, would you?"

Clive gave a slight bow, his formality a sure sign that he did not approve of such goings on.

Sheldrake trotted down the stairs and into the parlour, not waiting for Leon before entering. A tall, willowy, young man, dressed very correctly in morning attire, his blond hair neatly pulled back at the nape of his neck, turned at the sound of the door opening. A whimsical smile lit his face.

Sheldrake, who prided himself on being able to maintain a neutral visage, was saved the embarrassment of gaping in astonishment by the young man, who stepped forward and bowed, giving him time to recover.

"Jon, I believe," Sheldrake managed, congratulating himself on the steadiness of his voice.

The young man straightened, his blue eyes shining with laughter. "Indeed, sir. I see you remember me."

"And to what do I owe the pleasure of your company?" asked Sheldrake dryly, waving Jon to a chair.

Suddenly the laughter was gone from the young man's eyes. "You have in your charge, in your employment, a very special person."

Sheldrake saw no point in prevaricating. "Sasha?"

"Indeed. And your enquiries have incited the interest of the Kimoran Embassy."

"Where you, yourself, are employed. Are you here on its behalf?"

Jon inclined his head in acknowledgement of Sheldrake's knowledge. "I am a plainsman from Kimoran and am loyal to the welfare of Kimora but I do not hold with... hmm, how can I put it?... *leashing* shamans."

"I see." Sheldrake heard Leon slip into the room and turned to him. "Were you in time to hear that?"

Leon, his mouth tight with suspicion, nodded shortly and took up residence against the wall.

Sheldrake returned his attention to Jon. "My question remains unanswered. Are you here on behalf of the Embassy?"

Jon stood up abruptly, making Leon straighten, and

began to pace. "No, I am not and just be glad I'm not, for Sasha's sake."

"Why were you watching Stonehaven?"

Jon stopped in the window embrasure and studied Sheldrake. "Suffice it to say, that when someone enquired about shamans at the Hidden Lantern, word was carried to the Embassy." His mouth quirked. "Being a footman has its advantages. Generally, I am ignored unless they require me to run an errand. When I heard Marsha's report to Lady Electra, I determined to watch Stonehaven to check whether the enquiry was linked to Sasha. If Old Tom indicated it was, I could then follow you."

"I see. And why follow us?"

"Two reasons. To verify that you were who you said you were to Old Tom. Secondly, to gauge your quality."

Sheldrake raised his eyebrows. "And how did you verify who I am from our encounter?"

Jon gave a sunny smile. "Oh, I continued to follow you after you let me go, watched you return to the palace and asked the guard who you were. Then I rode on out here. I was just approaching the house from the bushland at the back when I saw Sasha and a boy - maybe your son? - riding back to the house. As soon as I had seen that Sasha was all right, I left. I decided it would be better mannered to visit openly through the front door."

Sheldrake exchanged glances with Leon, who looked as though he were restraining himself from throttling the young man. Sheldrake returned his attention to Jon. "And what did you think of my quality?" he asked dryly.

Jon sat down again removing his height advantage, deliberately, Sheldrake suspected. He leaned forward, looking earnestly into the mage's eyes. "I have not yet decided. You are clearly wealthy and can afford an impressive cottage, which is bigger than it looks from the road... I was impressed with your clemency when we last met... Your network and tactics are admirable..."

"Oh very," interrupted Sheldrake, with awful sarcasm. "We were totally bamboozled by you, weren't we? Hardly admirable."

A snort of agreement issued from his coachman.

Jon leant back and grinned. "I shouldn't have let you see me disappear, should I? But I have a playful streak that I just don't seem able to repress. I would have loved to see your faces when Karin reported back to you."

Sheldrake and Leon found themselves at a complete loss. The young man had made complete fools of them, supposedly masters of subterfuge, but was now inviting them to share in his mirth. Finally, Sheldrake demanded, "Do you know what I do?"

"Do you mean as a mage or as the head of the King's Spiders?" asked Jon.

Sheldrake spluttered. "No one knows I am head of the King's Spiders except the King and Maud and a very few trusted agents."

"Lady Electra does, and therefore, so do I." Jon was not smiling now. "Kimora's intelligence service, like any country's, has a vested interest in finding out information such as this."

Sheldrake gave a wry smile. "I suppose they do. After all, I know the identity of the heads of all of their intelligence services." He turned to Leon. "Could you send for tea please?" He turned back to the young man. "So, am I right in inferring that you are particularly concerned for Sasha's welfare, over and above your care for all shamans?"

"Oh yes. I brought Sasha out of the chaos that preceded

the current queen's reign and hid h... the baby at Stonehaven."

Sheldrake frowned at Jon's hesitation and wondered how he could broach the question of Sasha's gender without betraying her trust. After a distinct pause, he asked, "Does Sasha know you?"

Jon nodded. "Mostly I have kept away from Stonehaven, but from time to time, I have slipped in to spend a few hours with the child. It was dangerous. The Kimoran Embassy must never know where... Sasha is."

Sheldrake noted that Jon carefully avoided using any pronouns that would give away Sasha's gender. He was becoming increasingly convinced that Jon knew she was a girl.

Clive entered with a silver tray bearing a novelty teapot that was a facsimile of their cottage, a milk jug that resembled Sheldrake's shed, and two quite mundane white cups.

As Clive set down the tray, Sheldrake murmured, "Thank you. An unusual choice of crockery for a new guest??"

"I understand he is playful, sir," replied Clive, completely deadpan.

Sheldrake gave an embarrassed cough and glanced at Jon, whose face, he was relieved to see, was lit with laughter. He returned his attention to his butler. "Hmm. Could you ask Sasha to join us please?"

"Certainly, sir." Clive bowed and retreated with withering dignity.

Jon gave a short laugh. "I see I do not meet with your butler's approval."

"Apparently not. My staff are unnervingly willing to express their views... and I'm afraid I am not the master to quash them." He leant forward and poured a cup of tea for

Jon, "I hope you don't take sugar. There seems to be a lack of it on the tray."

"He probably does not deem me worthy of such a luxury."

Sheldrake frowned. "Hmm. But I do. So if you would like some sugar, I will procure it."

"Thank you, but no." Jon accepted the cup with a nod of thanks.

For a few minutes they sat in silence, sipping their tea until a knock sounded on the door. At the sound, Jon put down his teacup and stood up, tense with anticipation.

As the door opened to reveal Beth and Sasha, Sheldrake raised his eyebrows. "Good morning, Beth. Are you being protective or is Sasha feeling unsure?"

Even before Beth could answer, Sasha let out a whoop of joy, ran across the room and catapulted herself into Jon's arms. Jon threw his arms around her, grinning and hugging her tightly.

"Hello, young Sasha." he said, as he held her. "I am glad to see you too. Very glad." He whispered something in her ear, to which she nodded in reply. "Good." He whispered something else and again she nodded. "Oh good. Even better. Old Tom was worried, you know, after Sheldrake visited. He referred to you as a boy, you see."

Sasha pulled out of his embrace enough to smile at the other three. "I only just told them. I haven't been here all that long." She scowled. "And I never told Bryson. He wasn't very nice."

Jon gave Sasha a final hug and let her slide down to stand beside him. "Bryson was rough. Too rough, I gather. I'm sorry, Sasha, that you had to endure him." He looked at Sheldrake. "I heard that Kimoran intelligence was closing in on the orphanages in their search for Sa...for shamans. We had to get her out of there quickly. For all his faults, Bryson is willing to help Kimoran shamans. His wife is from Kimora and her sister is a shaman who refuses to submit to the Queen's will."

"So, did Bryson contrive the accident with Hoofer?" asked Beth.

Jon shook his head. "I doubt it. Bryson hasn't an ounce of magic in him. He would just have seized the opportunity to move Sasha on to a new placement, one with no connection to Stonehaven."

Sasha pouted. "And why didn't you visit me sooner? I haven't seen you for ages." Suddenly her indignation faltered. "I thought you might have forgotten me."

Jon folded his long frame into a crouch so that his blue eyes gazed earnestly into her dark ones.

"No, Sasha," he said quietly. "I would never forget you. You are too important to me... and to Kimora." He took a breath. "Bryson vanished, leaving no word of your whereabouts. I don't know what has happened to him or his family, and until this week, I didn't know what had happened to you either. I have been beside myself with worry." He stroked her hair, ending with his hand under her chin. "Old Tom and I have been trying to track you down but we had to be subtle about it. Other people are seeking you too." After a moment, when he was sure Sasha was no longer upset with him, he looked at Sheldrake and gave a rueful smile. "You have no idea, sir, how welcome your visit to Stonehaven was.

27

Upstairs in the library, Jayhan was keeping himself from becoming completely comatose by having one eye on his books and the other watching events in the yard below. As his eyes travelled over the stables, he thought about Sasha and the amazing fact that she was a girl. He looked at Eloquin and tried to imagine Sasha wearing a long flowing dress with her hair long enough to be tied back with a bow. Now he thought about it, Beth didn't wear flowing dresses either. He had seen her in dresses occasionally, but they were unadorned riding habits. Mostly, she wore trousers. Hmm. Now he thought about it, Beth was unusual in that way. Hannah the cook, Rose the maid and Maud all wore skirts or gowns. He wondered how Sasha would go climbing trees in a dress. She might get her skirts snagged and end up hanging upside down. Jayhan gave a little chuckle, which earned him a frown from Eloquin. *Oops. Better look like I'm reading*, he thought.

As he struggled through a tedious book about a family picnic, he saw the tall stranger arrive. The book family was just packing up their picnic and heading home, when he spotted Beth accompanying Sasha across the yard towards the house. Now what was happening? Why was she taking Sasha in to see the stranger? Jumping to the wrong conclusion, Jayhan made a quick apology to Eloquin as he dodged around her, scooted down the stairs and burst into the front parlour.

"You can't take Sasha away. Sh... Sasha's my friend."

Five people turned to stare at him and Jon straightened slowly from where he crouched beside Sasha.

"Shut the door, Jayhan." Sheldrake's voice was like verbal concrete, cold and hard. "Let me introduce you to Jon, to whom you may address your apology."

Watching this interchange, Jon decided that it was Sheldrake's inclination, not his inability to quell, that allowed his staff such leeway.

Jayhan, flushed both from embarrassment and concern for his friend, bowed stiffly. "I beg your pardon, sir, for intruding." Order obeyed, he brought his pale gaze to bear on Jon and continued in a rush, "But please don't take Sasha away. He is happy here and we are happy with him here....and he is my friend."

Jon stared in return but not with the discomfort that usually characterised an adult on their first view of Jayhan's eyes. If anything, he seemed a little stunned. However, he recovered quickly, so quickly that Jayhan wondered whether he had imagined it, and glanced briefly at Sheldrake, Leon and Beth, before returning his gaze to Jayhan. "And you are a good loyal friend who is keeping her secret, but as it was I who suggested that she should masquerade as a boy to keep her safe, her secret is safe with me... and with all of you, I think."

"Yes, it is," replied Sheldrake gravely.

"And does anyone else know of it?" asked Jon.

"My wife, Maud, and Beth's husband, Clive, my butler."

Jon nodded. He looked down at Sasha and placed his fingers under the amulet hanging around her neck, lifting it slightly. For a moment, his hand closed around it before he let it drop back into place. "You have taken this off, haven't you? At least twice." When Sasha nodded, he said, "No one but you can take it off, just as no one but you can wear it. Don't ever take it off again. You and the amulet are the past and future of Kimora, but each without the other is meaningless."

"Well, that's not very nice," protested Jayhan. "Sasha means a lot to us whether she is wearing her amulet or not."

Jon gave a rueful smile. "I beg your pardon. I meant meaningless to Kimora's future. She means a great deal to me also."

"Huh. Should have looked after her better then."

"Jayhan, that is quite enough," interposed Sheldrake sharply. "You are being rude to someone you have just met without knowing anything of the circumstances."

"But..."

Sheldrake's glare would have melted metal. Jayhan subsided into a huff as his father turned to Jon. "I apologize for my son's behaviour." Jayhan found this even more humiliating than having to apologize himself. "However, he is concerned, as are we all, about your intentions regarding Sasha."

Jon looked down at Sasha who was watching his every move. He stroked her hair and smiled at her before replying. "Sasha's welfare matters to me above all else, but I cannot care for her in my current position as footman in the Kimoran Embassy and my... hmm... other activities would also place her at risk. If you are happy to continue having her here, I also would be content."

"So we have passed muster, have we?" asked Sheldrake dryly.

Jon grinned, regaining some of his previous light-heartedness. "Yes. Besides, how could I drag her away from her gallant defender?"

Jayhan reddened and sent a little smile and a shrug to Sasha, who laughed in return.

Sheldrake watched this interchange, feeling a little manoeuvred by Jon's comment. After a moment he sent Jayhan and Sasha out to play, with the promise that Sasha could see Jon again before he left. "In fact, Jon, the decision is not yours alone to make. I think Maud and I need to speak to you in private. Beth, could you send Maud to join us please?" Seeing Leon scowl, clearly reluctant to leave, he added, "Until we have the boundary ward set up, Leon, I would appreciate it if you could keep a close but distant eye on Sasha, if you know what I mean."

Leon's eyes narrowed as he considered whether Sheldrake was fobbing him off. He must have decided there was at least some merit in the request, because after an uncomfortably long pause, he nodded curtly and left in Beth's wake.

It was not long before Maud surged into the room, her green skirts billowing around her. "Ah, here is the young man in question. Jon, I believe."

When Jon nodded, she presented her hand for him to kiss, which he did with a little more flourish than necessary. When he straightened, he smiled at her, "Pleased to make your acquaintance, ma'am."

Maud did not return his smile. She was all business. "Now, you may assume that I know all that has been said, since I was briefed by Beth before entering. So shall we continue as though I had been here all along?" She sank into an armchair, indicating that Jon should also be seated. "I have a question I wish to ask you. When I visited the Research Society, I met a shaman named Yarrow, who seemed excessively interested in the timing of Sasha's arrival at the Orphanage. I assured her that Sasha did indeed arrive there eight years ago, since your friend Old Tom had verified Sasha's story. However, since then, Sasha has changed her story and appears to have arrived at Stonehaven nearly ten years ago." Maud raised her eyebrows. "I presume that Old Tom backed Sasha's original story because Sheldrake had referred to her as a boy." She paused. "Correct?"

Jon, rightly assuming that this was not yet the question she wished to ask, merely nodded and did not attempt to interrupt her flow.

"So, my question is this: Why does it matter that she arrived ten years ago? In fact, what matters so much that you hid her gender and age to cover it up?" Before he could answer, she added firmly, "And you might like to be more explicit about the nature of Sasha's importance to Kimora."

Jon, reeling beneath this barrage, glanced at Sheldrake to find him stifling a smile. Seeing no help from that quarter, the young man hitched a breath and returned his attention to Maud. He stared at her for a moment as he made his decision. "Lady Maud, Sasha is the only surviving daughter of the Queen's elder sister. By rights, Sasha should be on the throne, not Queen Toriana."

Had he been expecting Maud to gasp in amazement, he would have been sorely disappointed. Maud merely nodded. "I thought it must be something like that. It does not seem to me, young man, that you have done a very good job of looking after your liege. Bryson's behaviour towards Sasha was appalling. And then you lost track of her completely. Most unimpressive."

Jon grimaced. "I agree with you, ma'am. I began well, but in the last couple of years, the search for Sasha has intensified and it was a close call when we smuggled her out of Stonehaven. I thought she would be safe at Stonehaven and indeed she was for eight, nearly nine years. But two years ago, the Queen employed a clever, powerful shaman hunter who thought of scouring the orphanages of Carrador and other nearby countries to find her."

"To find Sasha or just any shaman?" asked Sheldrake.

"It is not common knowledge that Sasha survived, but the fact that the amulet has not surfaced suggests that a true descendant of the High Shamanic line still exists. So the Queen's public position is that she is searching for rogue shamans but in actual fact, this shaman hunter has been employed to find Sasha specifically and, even more so, her amulet. Without that amulet, Queen Toriana's right to rule will always be in question. The amulet has been worn by the reigning monarch since time immemorial... and only the rightful Queen can wear it."

Sheldrake and Maud glanced at each.

After a significant pause, Maud said quietly, "You have thrust, or are trying to thrust, a huge responsibility onto us, aren't you, young man?"

"And has it occurred to you," asked Sheldrake, "that we work for the Kingdom of Carrador? How much will it compromise our loyalty to our king to be harbouring a pretender to the Kimoran throne, however legitimate?"

Jon looked from one to the other, visibly shaken. He stood up and moved to the window, looking out over the garden with his back to them. Maud and Sheldrake waited patiently until Jon heaved a breath and turned back to face them. To their shock, they realised his eyes were bright with tears. "If you will not keep her, I don't know what to do." He sniffed and groped in his pocket for a handkerchief. "Sorry about this," he said as he wiped his cheeks. He attempted a wan smile. "You are absolutely right. She is a huge responsibility. I love her dearly but she is a huge responsibility... and as you so clearly pointed out, one I have failed." His tears threatened to overwhelm him again, but he sniffed them away. "But you are also right that she is not *your* responsibility." He took a deep breath and squared his shoulders as he began to think through options. "I could take her to the resistance group. They live in the forests just within the Carradorian border but they are ill-disciplined, bitter and poorly resourced at the moment. I really wanted to protect her from that until she is older and they are better organised." He shrugged. "I suppose I could take to the roads with her. I was only twelve, you know, when I brought her out of Kimora as a baby. That was very hard, but it should be easier to look after both of us now that we are both older." He nodded firmly as this idea took roots. "Yes. That is what I must do. I will leave my post at the Embassy. In time, we will find someone else to infiltrate it." He shrugged again and gave a wan smile. "Besides, Sasha is far more important. Without her, there is no point in gathering information anyway."

"Now, just a minute, young man," interrupted Maud. In her usual response to tears, she had risen and moved to the door to call for more tea. When she turned back, she said, "We didn't say we wouldn't keep her. We are just pointing out the difficulties."

"Oh, but I thought..." Jon frowned at Sheldrake. "Didn't you say it's a conflict of interests?"

Sheldrake waved his hand in irritation. "Yes, I did and it is, or at least it may be. Just let me think it through." He stood up and began to pace back and forth in front of Jon as he thought, waving his forefinger in the air to underline each point. "It would not be politic for King Gavin to be seen as complicit in undermining the reigning monarch of a neighbouring country. The same, of course, applies to us... This only becomes a problem if it becomes apparent that we *know* we are harbouring the pretender to Kimora's throne. So while Sasha's true identity remains hidden, there is no issue. In terms of our personal loyalty to Carrador, I can't see that having Sasha on the throne of Kimora would be counter-productive to Carrador. In fact, the emerging conflict within Kimora is beginning to affect our trading relations with her. So, in the end it may benefit Carrador to have a more stable monarchy in Kimora."

"And Jon, unlike you, we are used to huge responsibilities and have the resources to manage them," added Maud. She glanced again at Sheldrake, who gave a minute nod. "So even though our apprentice turns out to be more of a liability than we expected, we will keep Sasha and do our utmost to protect her."

Jon breathed a huge sigh of relief. "Oh, thank you." Tears sprang to his eyes again.

Maud frowned. "You're not related to Sasha, are you? Your colouring is completely different but you have the same buoyant but fragile air about you."

Jon gave the ghost of a laugh. "Yes. I am her older brother."

28

Outside, oblivious to the momentous disclosures taking place in the parlour, Jayhan and Sasha were busy around the back of the stables building a cubby house in a large spotted gum tree on the edge of the front garden. They had gathered planks, old bits of tin and bricks from around the yard and were hauling them up onto a large platform that had been secured with Clive's help in a high fork of the tree.

Sasha caught Jayhan eyeing her thoughtfully as she dragged a large piece of rusty tin from the scrap heap in the middle of the platform to lean it, rather precariously, against the trunk of the tree. She brushed her hands off, ignoring his look, and said, "Quickly. Get some bricks to put against the bottom of it so that it can't slide out."

"Maybe a long solid piece of wood might be better..."

Sasha shrugged and nodded. "And we'll need some long planks to lean against the trunk inside the tin. Otherwise it's going to sag."

"Some long sticks might do."

"No. They'll roll. Planks'd be better, I think."

Their final construction had sticks holding down the tin on the outside and planks holding it up on the inside. They stood back and surveyed their creation.

Jayhan grimaced. "It's not very high, is it? Not high enough to stand up in, I don't think."

Sasha frowned. "No." After a minute of thought, she suggested, "Maybe we should turn the tin around so its long side is going up instead of along, and get another piece to go next to it. What do you reckon?"

"Yeah. Good idea. Maybe two more bits. Except the trunk won't be wide enough to lean all of them against it" Jayhan screwed up his face while he thought. "Hmm. Maybe we can nail a cross beam to the trunk for them to lean on."

Once this suggestion had been implemented, they had created a lean-to that stood about five and a half feet high nearly five feet wide, taking up half of the platform. They ducked inside and looked around.

"Hmm, pretty good," said Sasha. She peered down over the side of the platform. "Maybe we need a back wall... so we don't fall off."

"Yeah. At least a few planks so we can lean against them and maybe hang some cloth from them."

"And one side as well. The other side is where we'll come in and out."

This idea turned out to be fraught with difficulties, since the wood had to be nailed from a position off the platform. Eventually, they spotted Leon lurking near the stables, chopping wood for the lounge room fire, and recruited him to find a ladder and then to help them with building the back and side walls.

His reluctance made Leon surly at first but once he saw what they were doing, he realised his role as Sasha's protector required him to be involved to make sure the structure was strong enough. He decided that Jayhan and Sasha's treehouse building was as much a threat to Sasha's safety as any outside danger could be. However, the two children thought they were doing an excellent job which, in many ways they were, and offered him friendly, helpful suggestions at every opportunity. Leon found this so irritating that eventually he snapped at Jayhan's latest suggestion. "If you know so much, you do it."

Jayhan's face fell as he replied earnestly. "We *are* doing it." He waved his arm to encompass the three of them. "We're all doing it together. If there's anything else you want Sasha or me to do, just tell us. We're busting to help. It was our project in the first place, after all. And then Clive joined in and now you have."

Sasha nodded. "And don't forget, Jayhan and I are experts on cubbies. We make them all the time." She looked up at the treehouse, squinting her eyes against the sun. "This will be the biggest and the best, but it's a bit tricky."

"Well, not the biggest. Remember the one that we built amongst the blackberry bushes down near the creak. The tunnels in it went for miles," objected Jayhan, blithely exaggerating.

"True but this one is definitely the hardest."

"Oh, definitely."

"What's the best cubby you ever made, Leon? Before this one, I mean," asked Sasha.

Despite himself, Leon couldn't resist being dragged into the conversation. Grunts and short answers were met with genuinely interested questions and before he knew it, Leon was waxing lyrical about a particularly grand cubby he had constructed from crates and planks, and had decorated with old pieces of rags. His mother had even given him a cast-off curtain for decoration and let him take his dinner in there for a whole week, by which time he was bored with having no one to talk to at meal time. His story was met with round eyes and an enthusiasm that he had rarely experienced as a child, since his siblings had been much older than him and treated his creations with disdain.

It was almost with regret that he banged the last nail into place and stood back to inspect the new slatted walls. "There," he said gruffly, "That should keep you safe and you can use some old blankets draped over it to keep the wind out when it's cold."

Sasha stood beside him, also surveying the results. "Great job, Leon. That's just what we need." She turned to Jayhan. "What do you think?"

"Yep. Really good."

Then Sasha leaned in and whispered in Jayhan's ear. His face scrunched into a frown and he whispered something back. After an intense minute of whispered discussions, he nodded enthusiastically and looked at Leon, smiling.

Leon scowled, unsure whether they were making fun of him or making up another hare-brained scheme. "What are you two up to?"

Sasha beamed. "We are going to call our treehouse the Joosoo Club. See? It has Jayhan's and my initials in Joosoo, and yours and Clive's in Club. Pretty good, hey?"

A slow smile lit Lean's face. He nodded. "I like it. So will Clive."

Sasha and Jayhan swung themselves up through the boughs of the tree, then onto the platform. They walked along the edge of the platform to the open end of their lean-to, then ducked inside.

Sasha nodded and looked around for a few moments before poking her head out and shouting down at their minder. "It's great Leon. You'd really like it up here." Then she put her head on one side and asked Jayhan diffidently. "Do you think we could ask Jon in here for morning tea before he goes?"

Jayhan considered the height of their roof and grimaced, "Well, we could, but he'd have to duck. Maybe if he came straight in and sat down…" He shrugged. "Anyway, he mightn't want to. I wasn't very kind to him before."

"He'll want to," she said firmly. She caught Jayhan glancing speculatively at her again and this time didn't let it pass. "What? What are you looking at?"

"Um, nothing. Um, just wondering what it's like to be a girl?"

Sasha folded her arms. "Don't know what it's like to be a boy so I don't know how it's different. I'm just the same as yesterday before you knew, if you're wondering."

Jayhan reddened. "Sorry. I'm not meaning to be rude. I just want everything to stay the same. You're my best…my *only* friend… Are you going to start wearing dresses?"

Sasha looked horrified. "Of course not. Besides, I'm still supposed to be a boy to everyone outside your family. Remember?" When Jayhan nodded unhappily, she added, "You are my bestest friend too. Even if things change, we will always be friends. Deal?"

She put out her hand and Jayhan grasped it. "Deal!" His face lit in a relieved smile.

"Come on," she said, "Let's go and see whether we can ask Jon to tea."

"Wait a sec." Jayhan swung down through the branches

and a few minutes later, returned to the bottom of the tree with four metal buckets. "Chairs!" he pronounced triumphantly, as he proceeded to throw them up to her. "And," he added, as he threw up the fourth one, "A table!"

29

Seeing Maud and Sheldrake's incredulous stares, Jon hastened to explain, "In our bloodlines, siblings can have different hair, eye and skin colour from each other. Males tend to be fairer, women darker but not always. Sasha and I are full brother and sister. I may be older but the right to rule passes through the female line. I am not a contender for the throne, no matter what. Sasha is the rightful ruler of Kimora and I will give my last ounce of blood to see that she is."

"Tell us what happened," asked Sheldrake quietly, "how you came to be in Carrador... unless it is too painful for you to recount."

Jon drew a breath. "It is painful but less so, as the years pass. I will tell you."

The tea arrived in the best silver teapot carried by Clive, who bent a reserved but accepting smile upon the young man.

Sheldrake raised his eyebrows at the teapot. "Hmm. You seem to have gone up in the world," he said, as soon as the door closed behind Clive. Once the tea had been poured, Jon and Sheldrake seated themselves once more and Sheldrake nodded for Jon to continue as soon as Clive had left the room.

"Our family was travelling from our estates in Burndale to the capital to celebrate the year's turning. We had camped for the night, and my father and older brother were standing around the campfire talking with the guards when arrows streaked out of the trees. One minute they were standing. The next, they had slumped to the ground. Just like that. I was in the tent with my mother, my little sister, Marina, and the baby, Sasha. My mother had asked for my help to feed and settle Sasha before bed. Sasha was in a travelling cot, a woven basket, against the back wall of the tent and I was beside her in the shadows, rocking the basket to send her to sleep. Through the tent door, we saw the men outside slump to the ground but only my mother knew what it meant.

"'Stay back,' she whispered urgently to me. A heartbeat later, two huge men... or so they seemed to me... swarmed into the tent. They wore no insignia but my mother knew them. They grabbed Marina by the hair and before anyone could move, they sliced her throat." Jon swallowed before continuing. "One of them growled, 'Now hand over the amulet or your baby dies too.'

"Our mother swept her arm before her in a wide arc, sending her attackers flying in a spray of sparks. But she knew it was only a short reprieve. There were too many of them. She dragged the amulet over her head and threw it to me. 'Protect her with your life, Jon.'

"I caught the amulet and held it over Sasha's head as my mother shouted the words of transfer, 'From Corinna to Sasharia! Karesh!' She flung out her hand, and blue light blazed, turning the amulet red hot in my hand. With a yelp,

I dropped it around the baby's neck. 'Now Go, Jon! Go! Don't look back."

"My heart hammered in my chest, so hard I thought I might be sick. I drew my dagger and sliced the tent wall. I was so scared, my fingers felt like sausages. Hugging Sasha in the basket to my chest, I threw myself through the gap onto the cold leafy ground outside." Jon gave a lop-sided smile. "For some reason, I have always remembered the leaves. It was autumn and even in the dim light from the lanterns and firelight, I could see they were yellows and red." He gave himself a shake. "Anyway, I shimmered to hide us from view and crept into the woods beyond the firelight. To my horror, I realised I was only a dozen yards away from one of the archers who had killed my father and the guards. So I had to hunker down for ages before the hunters dispersed. I nearly smothered Sasha keeping her quiet."

"What do you mean, you shimmered?" interrupted Sheldrake.

"Oh." Jon grinned and the air around him began to shimmer as it does in the desert on a hot day when travellers see oases that are not truly there. The shimmering increased until suddenly, Jon was gone. "It is my Plainsman heritage," said Jon's voice from the empty chair near the window.

"Can Sasha do that?" demanded Sheldrake.

Jon drifted back into view, shrugging. "I don't know. Shimmering is very rare. Usually it's paired with blonde hair, for some obscure reason. But you never know…"

"Well! What do you know?" exclaimed Sheldrake. "That is truly marvellous! And you can include objects or people or animals with you as well, can you?"

As Jon nodded, Maud cut in, "Sheldrake. Have a little sensitivity. Jon is in the middle of a very distressing story. Discuss his magic at another time, if you don't mind."

Sheldrake grimaced, but his eyes twinkled. "Sorry dear. Your pardon, Jon. Carry on with your tale."

Jon shrugged. "There is not much more to tell. I heard my mother cry out from the tent, then silence. Any servants in the open were cut down and every last one of their tents was fired. They all died, either from fire, sword or arrows." Jon shook his head, his eyes glistening at the memory. "It was terrible, truly terrible."

"And you were only twelve, you say?" asked Maud gently.

Jon nodded. "My mother died alone, facing those men to save Sasha and the amulet and me." A shudder passed the full length of Jon's body. "And there was nothing I could do to save her."

"But you did save Sasha."

"Yes. Only just. By luck, I found where they had picketed their horses. All eyes, even the guards', were on our campsite in the clearing trying to spot Sasha and me, so I was able to sneak behind them and lead a horse away. All I could do was ride hard and hope to find someone to help us. Sasha was starting to whimper with hunger. Eventually, I found a farmhouse in the middle of nowhere and the farmer's wife gave Sasha her pet goat to suckle on. Pretty weird actually, but it worked. She stopped wailing for the first time since we left the carnage. But then the farmer started asking awkward questions and we had to take to the road again. A few times, I found a sheep or goat to suckle her but I had to catch them first. Not easy. By the time we reached Carrador, Sasha hadn't eaten for two days."

"And how did you find Stonehaven?"

Jon shrugged. "Stonehaven is close to the border. I just kept asking people for directions to an orphanage because I knew I couldn't look after Sasha on my own. It was the first one I found."

Maud frowned. "And did you really just leave her on the doorstep? The future Queen of Kimora?"

Jon waved his hand dismissively. "No. Of course I didn't. I took her inside, met Old Tom, had a look-around and then left her in his care. He knew what to do. He'd had babies left there before. He gave me a meal and let me stay for a few days. I couldn't stay for long because I was too old, but he let me visit. Over time, I told him the whole story but we agreed not to tell Sasha who I was or where she was from, until she was old enough to keep secrets." He took a deep breath. "So that's it really." As though expecting their censure, he avoided meeting their eyes, by letting his eyes drop to his teacup as he took a slow sip of his now tepid tea.

"You are an impressive young man," said Sheldrake. "You have dealt with more in your short life than many would in a lifetime."

Jon raised his eyes and lifted one side of his mouth self-deprecatingly. "Not really. You just do what you have to, when you find yourself in a situation."

Sheldrake gave a snort of laughter. "Well, I wish some of my agents could do half as well as you."

"One question, Jon," asked Maud quietly. "Why was your mother wearing the amulet when she was not yet on the throne?"

"My grandmother was very old and knew she only had weeks to live - It's one of the less desirable shaman skills, foreseeing one's own death - and it is customary to pass on the amulet to their successor one moon's travel before their death. So my mother had been given the amulet but did not yet have the protection of the full Royal Guard. If my mother had held onto the amulet, it is unlikely that the warriors could have killed her, but she could not have borne seeing the rest of her children killed and so would have relinquished it. So her last act was a desperate gambit to save Sasha and the amulet from the hands of the usurpers."

"And thanks to you, it worked," said Sheldrake.

Jon laughed. "Thanks to me and the amulet. Never forget the amulet."

A knock sounded on the door and Sheldrake frowned in irritation. "I thought I gave instructions not to be disturbed."

Despite his words, the door opened slowly to reveal Jayhan, Sasha behind his right shoulder, peering in hopefully. "Hello Dad. We were just wondering whether Jon would like to have morning tea with us in our new cubby we just built. Sort of as a sorry present," he added with a flash of inspiration.

Sheldrake glanced at Jon and saw that his face was a picture of indecision, caught between the wish to go with them and the fear that he would offend his hosts.

"And Hannah has made us up a tray with a teapot and cups and milk and fruit scones," piped up Sasha.

Sheldrake smiled. "Well in that case, we can't disappoint Hannah. Jon, I'm afraid you will have to imbibe yet more tea. Perhaps Jayhan can show you the water closet on the way out..."

PART V

30

A week later, Rose sat at the kitchen table shelling peas, her mind on what clothes her brother would need for starting work with Clive. After years of practice, shelling peas was so automatic that she could let her mind wander unfettered as she worked. But suddenly she was called back to the present by the unusual feel of a pea pod in her fingers. She looked down and found the pod she had been about to open was a darker green, less rounded and felt like worn leather rather than the soft flesh of a pea pod. She peered more closely and discerned small letters, MAUD, stamped into it.

"Excuse me, Hannah, I think I have a message for the mistress," said Rose as she stood, ready to deliver the pseudo pea pod.

Hannah looked up from where she was rolling out the pastry for the evening's pie and, spotting the object in Rose's hand, nodded her permission. "Off you go then."

After years in Maud and Sheldrake's service, little oddities were commonplace for both of them.

Rose delivered the pea pod and waited while Maud

carefully sliced it open and unfurled the little message contained inside. When she had read it, she looked up at Rose and smiled. "Send Leon to me please. Prepare for an extra person at dinner and make the blue room ready for our guest, should she wish to stay."

"Yes Ma'am." Rose curtsied and headed off to find Leon.

It was a good twenty minutes before Leon presented himself. He entered, wiping his hands on the back of his trousers. "Beg pardon, ma'am. I was down behind the stables, chopping wood and keeping an eye on the little ones."

Maud raised an eyebrow. "I thought we had a magical ward in place right across the front of the property boundary now."

Leon grunted. "We do, but that doesn't stop Sasha and Jayhan from damaging themselves. Yesterday, I hauled them down off the roof where they were about to play hide and seek among the chimney stacks."

"Oh, I see. Well done then." Maud waved the little scroll at Leon. "I have received a communication from Yarrow. She will be waiting in the bar of the Blue Boar at sunset. Since she is a target for shaman hunters, would you go into the village and bring her back here as quickly as possible please? The sun is setting, even as we speak." As Leon was about to leave, she asked, "We have someone checking our front entrance for watchers, don't we? Are we under surveillance? Because if we are, you will not be able to bring her in through the front gates."

"Yes we do, Ma'am. And no, we are not. All agents are required to inform us as soon as any watchers are sighted."

Maud breathed a sigh of relief. "So far, so good then. It

is a little harrowing, having young Sasha with us, much as I am fond of her."

Leon gave her a thin-lipped smile of assurance. "Don't worry ma'am. Between the Spiders and our magical ward, she is safe from outsiders."

Before she could say anything further, Leon left.

An hour later, Maud peered out the window and saw Leon returning with Yarrow, who was wrapped in a nondescript black, woollen cloak covering a drab brown dress.

Maud swept down the stairs and opened the front door to greet her without Clive's interception. "Yarrow! I am so pleased you have come. Leon, take her cloak please. Could you also ask Clive to prepare refreshments and take them to the parlour? We will return shortly. Oh, and let Sheldrake know. I know he is keen to meet Yarrow. Come, my dear. I am sure you are dying to meet Sasha."

Looking a little bewildered, Yarrow was hustled by her hostess to the stables.

Just as they reached the stables, the door burst open and Jayhan rushed out shrieking, "Mum, Mum. Sasha's going to get me." Before anyone could react, a torrent of water sailed out behind him drenching him and splashing the other two. Jayhan pulled up short. "Oops." He grinned as, dripping wet, he performed a neat little bow. "How do you do? I am Jayhan." He looked behind him. "Watch out, Sasha. You're in trouble now. You just wet Mum and a visitor."

"Oh no," whispered Sasha hollowly. In an act of pure courage, she didn't run away but crept forward to face the music. She peered around the side of Jayhan before emerging. She straightened up and squared her shoulders. "I am truly very sorry. I didn't mean to wet you... Would you like a towel?" Without waiting for a response, she disappeared inside and returned with a grubby towel covered in horsehair.

Yarrow held up her hand. "Uh no. We will dry off quickly anyway. It was only a small splash."

Sasha looked anxiously at Maud. "Sorry Madam."

Maud smiled reassuringly. "No harm done. Look Sasha, I have brought someone to meet you. Yarrow is a shaman from Kimora. I told her," said Maud meaningfully, "that I have stable*boy* from Kimora working for me and she offered to tell you about your homeland."

"Wow!" breathed Jayhan. "So do you wear one of those amulets too? With the triangle with the line through it?"

Yarrow frowned. "Yes. How do you know of this?"

"My dad investigated the symbol on Sasha's amulet."

"Jayhan," interposed Maud, "go inside and change. You are dripping wet. When you are presentable, you may join us in the parlour."

Jayhan grimaced. "Yes Mum."

By the time he had achieved world's fastest change of clothes, Sheldrake, Maud and Yarrow were seated comfortably in the parlour. A side table carried an array of cups and the best teapot, waiting for tea to be served. Sasha sat nervously on the edge of a large lounge chair. Without a second thought, Jayhan crossed the room and squeezed in next to her. "Hello," he murmured, "Did I miss anything?"

Sasha frowned and surreptitiously shook her head. "No. Now shush," she whispered.

"I understand," Yarrow was saying to Sheldrake, "that you discovered the meaning of the symbol on Sasha's amulet. Is that how you became aware that he was a shaman?"

"It is. We became interested in his abilities when he was able to see through Maud's shape-changing."

Yarrow nodded. "That is indeed a shaman ability." Her voice held a note of reserve.

"So may we see your amulet?" asked Jayhan eagerly. "Do you wear it always, like Sasha does?"

"Jayhan," admonished Sheldrake. "Yarrow may not wish to show us her amulet. I am beginning to gather that it is a privilege to possess one and that I erred rather grievously in asking to borrow Sasha's."

Yarrow raised her eyebrows. "You *borrowed* it? Took it from him?"

Sheldrake looked a little flustered. "I asked him but, of course, I suppose he felt obliged to say yes, now I think about it." Seeing the severe expression on the shaman's face, he added in a rush. "I was just trying to find out about his origins and his powers... and he wanted to know too. I only kept it for a few days."

"What's done is done," intervened Maud firmly. "And if Sheldrake hadn't worked out that Sasha was a shaman, we wouldn't have known to ask you here to help him."

Yarrow took a breath and with a noticeable effort, relaxed. "True." As a peace offering, she turned to Jayhan. "Let me show my amulet." A chain hung around her neck but its end was deep within her bodice. She pulled it up until a milky grey amulet appeared in her hand. It carried the same symbol as Sasha's.

"Oh, that's pretty. They come in different colours, do they?" asked Jayhan.

Yarrow's brows snapped together. "No. All shaman amulets are crafted from moonstone. All but one."

"Oh," continued Jayhan, oblivious to the frantic efforts of his parents to silence him. "Sasha must have that one, then."

A resounding silence filled the room.

"What?" Jayhan glanced at Sasha beside him. "What? What did I do?"

Sasha shrugged. "I don't know," she murmured. She looked at the severe faces surrounding them and grimaced. "But whatever it is, it's not good."

Yarrow's eyes were wide with shock. She turned to Maud. "Did you lie to me? If you did, I can understand why. But did you?"

"Not exactly," replied Maud. "At the time, I thought I was telling you the truth. I only found out later, you see... last week, in fact."

Yarrow stood up and walked across to Sasha. "You're not a boy, are you?"

Sasha glanced at Maud, who gave a grimace of consent. She returned her gaze to Yarrow. "No madam, I'm not."

"And how old are you?"

Again she glanced at Maud who nodded. "I am ten years old, Madam." She noticed that the shaman was beginning to tremble. "Are you all right?" she asked in concern. "Can I get you some water?"

Yarrow waved away the request. Instead she said quietly. "And may I see your amulet?"

Sasha sent Jayhan a puzzled look before reaching down and withdrawing her amulet from within her jerkin. In her hand, the obsidian amulet pulsed with a dark light. As though in response, Yarrow's amulet shone with clear pale brilliance. At the sight of it, Yarrow sank to one knee.

"Quick Jayhan. Help me hold her up. She's fainting," said Sasha in a panic.

With a child holding each of her arms, Yarrow just knelt there, shaking her head from side to side. In a daze, she said, "No your Highness, I am not fainting. I am kneeling before my rightful Queen."

Sheldrake and Maud rolled their eyes heavenward, as they realized things had gone sadly awry.

Intent on keeping Yarrow upright, Sasha hadn't even register what she had said. Her face screwed up with the effort, she gasped, "Sir, madam, can you help please? She's too heavy for us."

Jayhan, however, had listened to the shaman's pronouncement. He tapped Sasha on the shoulder. "You can let go now. I don't think she's going to fall over. You have a different problem." He leaned closer to Sasha and chortled quietly behind his hand. "Either she's nutty or you're someone you didn't know you were."

"I'm afraid," said Sheldrake, "that your second surmise is right, Jayhan. As you say, Sasha is not aware of who she really is. But Yarrow does know... and so do we."

Jayhan's first reaction was outrage. "You *knew* and didn't tell Sasha?" Then he frowned as he remembered what Yarrow had said. "And Yarrow knows? Are you sure? Because she said..." Jayhan dug Sasha in the ribs. "Were you listening?" When Sasha shook her head, Jayhan said. "Well I think you'd better." He turned to Yarrow. "Could you say that again please?"

Yarrow grasped one of Sasha's hands in her own. "Your Highness, I said that I was kneeling to my rightful Queen."

Sasha just stared at Yarrow, dumbstruck. After a minute, a little frown appeared and she transferred her gaze first to Sheldrake and then Maud. Then she glanced sideways at Jayhan and her little grimace told him that she didn't know what to do.

"Excuse me, Yarrow," said Jayhan. "But it must be getting uncomfortable down there. I think Sasha's had a bit of a shock. She didn't know, you see. She probably needs a cup of tea... or some lemonade, maybe a cake," he added hopefully. "If you could just give her hand back and maybe sit down again..."

Yarrow seemed to come out of a trance. She gave an embarrassed laugh, stood up and moved away to reseat herself in the armchair across the room. She passed her hand across her eyes. "Sorry. Of course. I should have thought. I didn't realize..."

"Well," said Maud, rising to the occasion. "I think discovering your true identity calls for a celebration, don't you, Sasha?" She rose and put her head around the corner of the door. "Clive? Lemonade and cakes, if you please? And perhaps a bottle of champagne."

"So, who is she exactly?" asked Jayhan. "I don't quite get it."

Sheldrake addressed himself to his stable hand. "Sasha, you are the oldest living daughter of Princess Corinna who was heir to the throne of Kimora. As I understand it, Corinna's younger sister, your aunt, tried to kill your whole family but your brother escaped with you to Carrador. Since you were just a baby at the time and could not come forward to challenge her, she seized power on the death of your grandmother. You, however, are the rightful monarch, not she."

"Oh." This was far too much for Sasha to take in. Her head whirled with questions. After a long pause, she said slowly. "So that's why I had to, still have to, hide who I am."

Sheldrake merely nodded, purposely giving her time to think.

After another long pause, she asked, "And is my brother who rescued me still alive?"

"That lovely young man, Jon, is your brother," said Maud.

Sasha's face split into a smile. "Jon's my brother? Oh, I

wish I'd known. I wouldn't have felt so all alone... even if he couldn't be with me all the time."

A discreet tap on the door preceded the entrance of Clive, who replaced the unused tea tray with the makings of a celebration.

When everyone's glasses were charged, Sheldrake raised his glass high and proposed a toast. "To Sasha's illustrious identity. The road ahead will not be easy, no matter which course you take, but we will all support you as best we can."

Sasha, her eyes bright with tears, raised her glass and was about to take a sip when Jayhan nudged her, grinning. "You can't toast yourself. Wait a minute, then drink as much as you like."

"Get lost," she said and took a long draft of lemonade.

31

Once their tiny celebration was over, Sasha was sent away to have her meal with the servants as usual. Jayhan gave her a little wave as she left and turned to see Yarrow fairly quivering with indignation.

"Come now, Yarrow," said Maud bracingly. "You can either give her consequence or give her safety but not both at the moment. Sasha's future depends on maintaining her disguise as our stableboy. Once you have had an opportunity to change, you shall dine with us this evening and exchange knowledge with Sheldrake. Tomorrow, after Sasha has worked in the stables for the morning, you may share your shaman knowledge with Sasha... and with Jayhan and Sheldrake, during their afternoon magic lessons. The more we know of her powers, the more we can all protect her."

Tight-lipped with displeasure, Yarrow retired to dress for dinner.

When she reappeared, Yarrow was dressed as she had been at the Research Society, resplendent in a loosely fitting black dress, studded with bright stones of many colours and embroidered in swirling patterns around the wrists, neckline and hem. Her black hair, piled on top of her head and held in place by a scarlet scarf, was threaded through with beads. Everything about her shrieked mysticism and magic. Maud admired the woman's flair and was pleased that Yarrow felt at ease enough to display her true colours.

Still unthawed, Yarrow accompanied her hostess up the stairs to the dining room. As she sat down at the white-clothed dining table beside Maud, Yarrow prised her lips apart enough to say, "Shamanism should be women's lore, according to Kimoran custom, which is why I suspected Sasha wasn't a boy. I will not speak of women's business in front of a man and a boy."

Maud smiled charmingly, as though she had just been paid a compliment. "That is entirely up to you, my dear. I think perhaps you should consider however, before you become too huffy, that we have no reason to trust you. We only have your word for it that you are an unregistered shaman. Until we know you better, Sasha will be protected in your company. I'm sure you will concede the need for such precautions."

For a few comical moments, Yarrow simply gobbled. Then she drew a deep breath and let it out slowly. "Forgive me. You are right, of course." Clive serving the soup gave her time to think. Once he had finished and left the room, she said, "Hmm. I can prove that I am not registered. I can speak disparagingly of Queen Torriana and a registered shaman cannot."

Sheldrake sipped his soup. "Ah, pea and ham. One of my favourites." He dabbed his mouth with his serviette before saying mildly, "Although, as a registered shaman, perhaps you might still be able to disparage the Queen, if it were in service of her plans? What do you think?"

Yarrow spluttered and choked on her soup. After a bout of coughing and a drink of water, she sipped her soup in silence for a while. Sheldrake met Maud's eyes across the table and gave a slight smile, content to wait for Yarrow's next gambit. When it came, he was surprised.

"Well," said Yarrow finally. "I have thought hard and cannot think of a way to convince you. The Research Society has accepted me as an unregistered shaman but, as you say, I could be prevaricating as part of service to the Queen. I know how Sasha's obsidian amulet would react to a free and a fettered amulet, which it did. But if *you* don't know, then that will not convince you. Shaman lore is mostly unwritten and passed down by word of mouth. So you will not be able to scour your Carradorian libraries to find it."

"Then Sasha has missed much by losing her mother," murmured Maud.

Encouraged, Yarrow nodded. "Especially *that* mother. Princess Corrina would have known of powers privy only to the direct line of succession. Even Queen Toriana will not know of them."

"And nor will you," finished Sheldrake.

Yarrow shook her head. "No." She took a breath to add something but then thought better of it.

"But, you were going to say, she may learn purely through contact with her amulet," said Sheldrake. He smiled at her obvious surprise. "I learn by observation too, not just through books in Carradorian libraries. Sasha is wise beyond her years and her powers are gradually developing. I may be a mere male, but I have been helping her to tune in to her amulet and to teach her my magical knowledge. She is an adept student, more so than Jayhan, I fear."

"I beg your pardon." Yarrow smiled warmly, as she put

down her spoon and leaned back, nodding her thanks as Clive removed her bowl. "I can see that you've been generous with your knowledge while I was planning to be secretive with mine. I do not look down on men. We just have different roles, that's all. But I do thank you for taking Sasha under your wing and nurturing her talent."

He gave an embarrassed glance at Maud before confessing, "I was hoping to use her talents in the Spiders. Not yet, of course. When she was older. Her talent for seeing through shapeshifting and disguises could be most useful." He harrumphed. "Hmm. I may have to rethink that. But," he added hurriedly. "I will continue to teacher her nonetheless."

"In that case, I think it is only fair that I share some of my knowledge with you and your son, and of course you Maud, if you are interested." Yarrow gave a lop-sided smile. "Besides, you will have to guard Sasha against me for the time being." She shrugged. "I suppose I'm grateful that you protect her so well."

Jayhan watched this interchange silently from his place beside his father. He knew enough about kings and queens to know that Sasha wasn't being treated in the right way for someone who should be queen. He understood the need for secrecy, but still thought his parents were being unfair. Although he found Yarrow a little odd, he sympathized with her outrage and was sure she could be trusted. But how to convince his parents? He thought about what she had said about Sasha and her amulet reacting differently to fettered and free shamans and remembered how Sasha had worked out how he could change shapes just by focusing on her amulet. He needed to talk to Sasha.

He shovelled down his dinner and then unusually for him, declined desert and asked to be excused. He thought he had been quite tricky but four pairs of adult eyes, including Clive's, watched him leave the room.

"Hmm, off to see Sasha before bedtime, I'm guessing," said Sheldrake. "Perhaps you could saunter over to see your wife as soon as you have served desert, Clive?"

"Indeed, sir."

To Jayhan's frustration, Sasha had not yet returned from the kitchen when he reached the stables. Beth returned first and Jayhan rushed to hide in one of the stalls, worried that he would be sent off to bed if she spotted him. As she walked down the row of stalls, Beth noted a few shuffles and foot stomps in the straw and with little difficulty traced the cause to a pair of booted feet in the second last stall, easily visible if one bent a little as one walked by. She merely grinned and kept walking.

A few minutes later, Jayhan heard Sasha's light steps and, carefully pulling the bolt so as not to make noise, crept out to meet her. He put his finger to his lips and pointed with his other hand in the direction that Beth had gone. Sasha smiled and nodded, and by unspoken agreement, walked back out the way she had come and headed towards the paddocks. As soon as she was beyond the lights of the house, she turned. Jayhan was at her elbow.

He grinned at her. "Come on. Let's go to our cubby."

They skirted around the back of the stables and using the light of an almost full moon, hoisted themselves up through the branches of the oak to the tree house platform. Jayhan fumbled in the dark looking for the candle and flint they had secreted next to the doorway of the corner of their cubby. Once the candle was alight and carefully placed on their table bucket, they settled themselves on their metal bucket seats.

"So what's up?" asked Sasha.

"What's up?" repeated Jayhan, surprised. "You're what's up. You've had such a bundle of surprises today and then you couldn't even talk to anyone about it." He grinned. "And I knew you'd want to. Aren't you excited?"

Sasha chuckled. "Sort of. I'm very excited about having a brother, especially since it's Jon."

"Yeah, he's pretty good, isn't he?"

Hearing a note of reserve in his voice, Sasha punched him on the shoulder. "Don't worry. I have always loved him, even when I didn't know he was my brother... and Old Tom. But I love you too and I can't play with them as I play with you. Besides," she added grinning, "they all have boring eyes, compared to you."

Jayhan grinned. "That's true, of course." He found a stick and dipped it into the molten wax of the candle then held it into the flame to let the wax drip down again.

"Watch out," said Sasha, as the flame spluttered. "You'll put it out if you're not careful."

"No, I won't," he said, just before everything went dark. "Whoops!"

"Idiot!"

After a bit of scrabbling about in the dark, the flame was re-ignited.

"There. All better again" said Jayhan with an unrepentant smile, picking up a stick to fiddle once more with the candle. As he saw Sasha about to remonstrate with him, he pointed to the flint. "This time I know exactly where the flint is."

Sasha sighed, knowing defeat when she saw it. "Fair enough."

"So what about the queen thing?" asked Jayhan, his eyes intent on the stick and the candle.

"Hmph. Bit odd really, isn't it? I don't feel like a queen.

Queens always look so confident and grand and powerful. I don't feel any of those things."

"Well, you're not a queen until you're crowned, I don't think."

"You know what I mean."

"Yes, but at the very least, you're a princess." Jayhan grinned at her. The stick, unsupervised, promptly caught alight. He blew it out and dropped it without a thought for the dry wooden platform underfoot. "Amazing, hey?"

Sasha pouted. "I don't feel like one of them either."

Jayhan looked her up and down, quite unselfconsciously. "No. You don't look like one. Probably the clothes."

"And the boots and no servants, and no palace and…"

Jayhan waved his hand to stop her. "Yes, but I thought a queen or princess would look different from other people up close."

"How exactly? Hidden horns? A royal aura that glows in the dark?"

Jayhan looked pained for a moment before breaking into a grin. "Yeah. Or perfectly neat hair no matter what happens and clothes that stay miraculously clean." Another idea occurred to him. "And hands and face that never need washing and…"

Sasha punched him in the shoulder again. "You're an idiot."

They sat in companionable silence for a while until Sasha broke it by asking, "But you know a king, don't you? Haven't you met King Gavin? What he's like up close?"

Jayhan shrugged. "Oh, but he's just Gavin. He just treats me like everyone else does. Nervous of my eyes and trying to pretend he hasn't noticed them. Mind you, he stopped coming here after he became king. He still sees mum in town but he's busy all the time now."

Sasha scrunched up her nose. "That doesn't sound like much fun... being so busy you can't visit your friends anymore."

"No..." Jayhan trailed off into a thoughtful silence. After a while he glanced at her but didn't say anything.

Sasha rolled her eyes. "Not again, Jayhan! Stop worrying. I already said we will always be friends, no matter what. If it ever turns out that I'm a busy queen then you'll just have to be busy with me, won't you?"

"Yep. Suppose I will." Jayhan leant down and picked up his burnt stick and a couple of leaves he had spotted and threw them out into the darkness. "Tidying up," he said with a little smile.

"Hmm. I wonder if there's a bit of old carpet we could have for our floor?"

"Good idea. We'll ask around tomorrow."

"If we have time. We have that Yarrow lady coming to talk to us in the afternoon." Sasha leaned in close and said quietly, "She's a bit creepy, isn't she?"

"Yes, definitely odd... and," Jayhan added in a conspiratorial whisper "I think she likes you..."

"Stop it, you horrible boy," said Sasha, giving him another thump on the shoulder.

"Ow. That's the third time you've hit me in the same place."

"Serves you right, trying to spook me."

"Mum and dad don't trust her, you know. They think she might be a registered shaman pretending not to be. Yarrow says her amulet shone when it saw your amulet because it is a free amulet, but only she knows if that's true." Jayhan shrugged. "Anyway, *I* reckon, if you concentrated on your amulet, you would know if she were a truly free shaman. What do you think?"

"Hmm. Maybe." Sasha looked unsure. "I'll think about it...but what if I get it wrong?"

"Don't worry, no one's going to leave you alone with her. Dad and I will be with you, even though Yarrow wanted it be just you two." Jayhan chuckled. "Mum made Yarrow very cross about that, but she got over it." He scuffed the toe of his shoe through the dirt on the floor before asking diffidently, "So aren't you angry about having to stay being a stableboy when you're really not?"

"Oh, but I really *am* a stableboy, Jayhan... well, a stable girl. That's my job and my life. All this other stuff is other people's business. I don't know anything about Kimora or this dreadful Aunty-Queen I apparently have, who wants to kill me." Sasha gave an involuntary shudder. "And it doesn't sound to me like I can just wander in and start being a queen. I'm safe and happy here."

Jayhan eyed her, wondering whether she just hadn't had enough time to think it through, but on balance, he decided to let the topic drop.

32

The next afternoon found the four of them in Sheldrake's beloved shed. Yarrow was prowling along the benches, scowling at various half-made concoctions, peering at bottles of completed mixtures and running her hands over a scattering of herbs that Sheldrake had left lying about. She strolled over to one of his bookshelves and ran one long red nail along the spines of worn, dusty, little leather books, then flicked her fingernail clean with her thumb. Completely aware of their scrutiny, she finally swirled and looked at them.

"So, Sheldrake," she said condescendingly, "You do indeed have some knowledge of tinctures and remedies. Are you able to heal using only your hands?"

Jayhan could see that it was taking Sheldrake some effort to keep his temper. "No. I wish I could. Tinctures and bandages can only go so far."

"How very true." Yarrow smiled at Sasha. "Now you and I, Your Highness, can heal without the need for these..." she waved her hand around her at the Sheldrake's potions, "...material aids."

Sasha's eyes narrowed. In a hard little voice, she replied, "If, as you say, you value my life, do not call me that. And if you want my friendship, please respect my friends and their skills."

A shocked silence filled the workshop.

Suddenly the wind left Sasha's sails and she looked at Sheldrake in trepidation. "I'm sorry, sir. I should not have presumed to call you my friend."

Sheldrake smiled. "Oh, I think you have just earnt the right."

Yarrow sniffed, put her nose in the air and walked to the other end of the workshop.

Sasha glanced at Jayhan, who was still looking stunned by her outburst, and grimaced. After a minute, she followed Yarrow and tapped her on the arm. "Excuse me, Yarrow. I'm sorry if I upset you." She waited a few seconds but when there was no response, continued, "Could you please show me, us, how you do your healing? My amulet helps me to heal faster, I think, but I don't know how to heal myself straight away or how to heal anyone else. I would really like you to show me, if you would."

Yarrow's stiff shoulders sagged and she turned to face them. Jayhan was shocked to see that her eyes were red-rimmed. She sniffed and wiped her red-nailed fingers under one eye. "It would be my pleasure... Sasha."

Sasha beamed at her. "Oh thank you." She put her hand in Yarrow's as the woman walked back to the waiting man and boy. "Would you like me to hit Jayhan so you have something to heal?" she asked, with a grin in his direction.

Yarrow raised her eyebrows. "Certainly not. Oh. You were joking."

"She's only half joking," muttered Jayhan. "She hits me all the time."

"Only in a friendly way," Sasha assured Yarrow. "So, what else can we heal then?"

"I think we need to work through some basics first. I will explain it to all of you, but I think only Sasha will be able to do it."

Sheldrake smiled. "That's fine. Only Maud can shapeshift and only I can create magical wards. We don't mind knowing of skills that we ourselves do not and cannot possess. It helps us to understand one another."

Yarrow gave a perfunctory smile then looked at Jayhan. "And you can shapeshift into human guises, can't you?" As Jayhan nodded with a shy smile, she added, "And of course you have those marvellous eyes."

"I do?" Jayhan looked like a puppy being offered a bone. "I mean, I know they're unusual, but most people hate them."

"Not me though," piped up Sasha. "I've always liked them."

"And I," murmured Sheldrake in the background.

Yarrow gave a genuine smile. "You see? The people who know you, like them."

"My mum doesn't."

"Oh. Perhaps she fears their power."

"She does," said Sheldrake shortly. "A past relative used their power poorly."

"Ah, but I think those powers are in good hands with this young man, don't you?" Suddenly Yarrow squatted down in front of Jayhan so that her eyes were slightly lower than his. "Poor Jayhan. Here we are talking about your eyes in front of you and not including you. Something that has happened to you all your life, I expect."

Jayhan simply nodded.

"Well you, young man, are very special. Your eyes help

you see better in the dark. Have you noticed that?" When Jayhan just shrugged, she smiled. "You would assume everyone else saw things the way you do, wouldn't you?"

He shrugged again and after a moment's thought, nodded. "Sasha and I tried to get my eyes to push things away because we read that Madison flung her husband across the room only by looking at him. But nothing happened."

"You can't just summon the power. It is simply part of you. And if I tell you too much about it, you will become self-conscious and by trying too hard, block it."

Jayhan frowned. "Well, that's annoying."

Yarrow gave a friendly laugh, all attempts at airs and graces forgotten. "Yes, isn't it? Just have faith in yourself and who you are. And most importantly, learn to meet people eye-to-eye, and cope with their reaction. It is they, not you, who have the problem."

Yarrow patted his shoulder then stood up, her dress tinkling as little gems clashed against each other. "And now for you, young lady." She glanced around the windows of the shed and asked Sheldrake, "I know these windows are tarnished but they are still transparent. Is there anyone who might peer in while we work? Are your staff completely trustworthy? I am sorry to seem so untrusting, but I have been in hiding for years."

Sheldrake smiled reassuringly. "My staff are completely trustworthy, but I can place a shield around the shed that stops people from seeing in while you work." He waved his hand, muttering a few words under his breath and surprisingly, the world outside seemed to brighten, rather than fade away. At Yarrow's puzzled expression, he explained. "We can see out better but for them, it is like being in a well-lit room trying to see into the darkness."

"But you can't possibly have lit up all the surroundings..."

Sheldrake laughed. "No indeed. It is just an illusion, but it works for your purposes."

"Thank you, I'm impressed." Yarrow hesitated. "And I'm sorry... for before. I was just trying to align myself with the... with Sasha, and instead I alienated myself. Silly of me, really." She wrung her hands. "It's just, she matters so much to me and I have been looking for her for so long."

The strength of her emotion left everyone feeling a little uncomfortable. Into the silence that followed, she pulled on the cord around her neck and lifted her amulet from within the bodice of her dress. She said nothing but simply held it in the palm of her hand so they could all see it, then focused on Sasha.

After a minute, Jayhan said, "It seems to be giving off light but not a steady light."

"It is pulsing," observed Sheldrake. "It is subtle, but it is there."

"Yes," said Yarrow. "Sheldrake, hold your fingers over the vein in Sasha's wrist... if she doesn't mind."

Sasha obligingly held out her arm and Sheldrake grasped her wrist. He concentrated for a full minute then raised his eyes to Yarrow's. "Your amulet beats in time with Sasha's heart."

Yarrow nodded, tears welling in her eyes. *Oh no,* thought Jayhan *she's going to cry again,* but to his relief, she held herself together. "All amulets are linked to the High Shaman and her amulet. They beat in time to the one true ruler's heart. Now do you see how much Sasharia means to me?"

"And why Toriana can never be accepted as the rightful monarch," finished Sheldrake for her.

Sasha listened but made no comment. Instead, she slowly pulled out her amulet and asked, "Do you mind if I try something?"

"Of course not," said Yarrow.

Sheldrake nodded, "Go ahead."

Sasha grasped her black amulet in front of her. As soon as it appeared, the obsidian began to glow, eliciting a clear, answering light from Yarrow's.

Ignoring the light, Sasha gazed into Yarrow's eyes, focusing on the depths of the shaman as she had focused on Jayhan, when she'd realised he was a shapeshifter. At first, she could not see beyond the surface, so her impressions of Yarrow's character and talents were foggy and unclear. As she tried to penetrate deeper, she found her mind wandering off on tangents or swirling in circular thoughts. Suddenly she realised that Yarrow had made herself inviolate by wrapping herself in cloudy confusion.

Sasha mentally pulled back and gave Yarrow a little smile. "Please?"

At once, the fog cleared and Sasha was swept into the passion and knowledge and skills that lay beneath Yarrow's surface. It was far more complex and diverse than either Jayhan's or Maud's. Sasha allowed herself to whirl among images of ceremonies, herbs, invocations, spells, memories of performing rites, healing, teaching, comforting. She felt the mist within Yarrow trying to reform and push her away but it was too late. Sasha's mind spun more and more wildly as the kaleidoscope of images pressed in on her from all sides. She was drawn into visions of wild chases through the forest, the sound of distant hounds sending terror though her, images of fighting, burning villages, bloodshed and a body swinging under a tree, a noose around its neck.

In her hand, the black amulet roared to life, throwing a

pulse of power at Yarrow that sent her flying across the shed to hit her head with a resounding whack against the far bench.

At the same time, a flat oval of unreflective blackness suddenly appeared where Sasha had been standing. They couldn't see her, but Sheldrake and Jayhan both heard her crumple to the floor. They rushed towards her but could not reach her. The area around her felt soft but was impenetrable. When they pushed insistently, their hands began to tingle then burn.

They backed off, hands stinging but undamaged. When they tried to dodge around the patch of blackness, it appeared oval-shaped and apparently two-dimensional from every direction.

"Blast it! We can't get to her," said Sheldrake, shaking his head. "I've never seen anything like this before. It must be a shield of some sort." He turned as he heard a groan. "Yarrow! What did you do to her?" he asked harshly.

Yarrow sat up groggily and put her hand to her head. She brought her hand around to inspect it, but there was no blood on it. She shook her head and winced. "Ow. That hurt." She brought her gaze to bear on the blank oval of blackness, then looked at Sheldrake. "What you are seeing is Sasha's extreme protection. Most of the time, the amulet protects her in subtle ways such as helping her to make everyone believe that she is boy, healing her more quickly when she has been hurt. It can't deflect an unexpected physical attack but the wearer can consciously direct its power in her defence. But this," She nodded at the black patch, then winced again, "this is a full-blown healing shield. It is both protective and healing. It will keep everyone away from her until she is fully recovered."

"But what did you do to her?" demanded Jayhan, still

watching the black place where Sasha lay, hidden from view. "You hurt her, didn't you?"

"NO. Well yes, but not intentionally. She learnt too much too fast. The will of her amulet overpowered my defences." She sat on the floor, with her arms wrapped around her knees, making no attempt to get up. "At first I let her into my mind at her request, happy to show her some of my knowledge and skills. By the time I'd decided she had seen enough, the strength of her amulet, or her will, had gained such momentum that I couldn't reinstate my defences. My knowledge and memories streamed into her; the visions, sounds and feelings." Yarrow grimaced. "And some of my memories are filled with fear and horror."

"Oh dear. I see." Sheldrake's face was drawn tight with concern. He pondered for a moment then asked, "Will she recover?"

Yarrow hugged herself closer, tears springing to her eyes. "I hope so. It was so much information for a young girl to take in, especially all at once."

Sheldrake stepped away from the black oval and grasped Jayhan's arm to pull him back too. "And we can do nothing? Just wait?"

"I'm afraid so."

The wait was long.

For two hours, Sasha remained hidden by the strange black oval. Sheldrake sent a reluctant Jayhan, worried he would miss her awakening, off for supplies. Maud and Beth returned in his wake, helping him to bring in trays of tea, lemonade and rock cakes. Then the five of them waited, sustaining themselves with afternoon tea, but not leaving.

Slanting rays of late afternoon sunlight were streaming through the window when, without warning, the oval shrank rapidly and winked out, revealing Sasha lying curled up on her side, apparently asleep. It happened so suddenly that at first, no one moved.

Then Jayhan rushed over to her and knelt down beside her.

"Sasha, Sasha, are you all right?" he murmured. He reached out tentatively and patted her arm. "Sasha?"

Sasha's eyes fluttered then opened. For a moment, her eyes were as black as a fathomless pit, but even as Jayhan drew back in shock, they reverted to their normal dark, liquid brown.

"Phew!" he breathed. "Hello. Are you all right?"

The tapping of nails on the stone floor of the shed made Jayhan look over his shoulder to find himself looking up into the droopy, furry face of his mother. She nudged him aside with her nose and flopped down beside Sasha, putting her heavy bloodhound head and one paw on the girl's chest.

"Oof!" Sasha giggled. "Do you know how heavy you are?" She rolled partly onto her back so that she could use both hands to stroke Maud's long soft ears, then looked at Jayhan. "Hello to you too. Well, your plan worked." The folds around Maud's eyes moved as she looked at her son, still kneeling next to her. A deep growl vibrated in her chest. Sasha giggled again. "That tickles." She stroked Maud's ears soothingly. "Don't get mad at Jayhan. It was his idea for me to look into Yarrow so I could check on her loyalty. It was a good idea and I agreed to it."

"Check on her loyalty, hey?" murmured Sheldrake. "That is an odd way of phrasing it. I presume you mean honesty?"

Sasha's eyes met Yarrow's across the room. "Perhaps. But more than that, I found loyalty." She heaved a deep sigh and glanced out the window. "Is it really that light? I thought more time would have passed." Her gaze took in the presence of Beth and the tea tray. "How long have you been waiting for me?"

"*Ages.*" "Two hours," said Jayhan and Sheldrake simultaneously.

"Oh dear," Sasha gave an impish grin. "I am a troublesome stable boy-girl, aren't I, keeping you all tied up here for the afternoon." She did not, however, sound fearful of being dismissed as she would have previously. In fact, she sounded disconcertingly self-assured.

Her eyes travelled to the tray of cake and lemonade but her self-assurance didn't stretch to asking for some. The look of longing in her eyes was eloquent enough, however, and Beth brought her over a slice of cake and a glass of lemonade.

Sasha smiled. "Thanks. I'm starving. Just keep it away from greedy guts here," she added, gesturing at the huge hound sprawled over her chest. Maud raised her head a little, managed to look even more hangdog than usual and gave a little whine, but Sasha said firmly. "No. I bet you had heaps while you were waiting."

Maud dropped her head even more heavily onto Sasha's chest and heaved a sigh. Sasha laughed. Beth put the plate on the floor next to her hand, out of Maud's reach, and Sasha attempted to eat cake lying down with her head to one side away from Maud. After one awkward bite on which she almost choked, Sasha pleaded, "Come on Maud. Let me up. It's too hard."

After a final heave with her paw that nearly knocked the wind out of Sasha, Maud sat up, towering over the prone girl.

"Thanks Maud," said Sasha, as she sat up, then gasped in shock as Maud reached past her and with one lick of her enormous tongue, polished off the rest of the slice of cake. "MAUD!"

Maud wagged her tail and licked her chops, before wandering away off behind one of the work benches to change. It did not escape Sheldrake's notice, however, that Maud had provided comfort and distraction to Sasha after her ordeal. He mentally saluted her.

33

Although Sasha had seen many of Yarrow's memories, the amulet had intervened before she saw everything and she had not had time to fully comprehend the memories she had seen or their implications. So her knowledge was incomplete.

After considerable discussions, it was decided that Yarrow should continue to teach Sasha her heritage and shamanic powers. Sheldrake and Jayhan joined Sasha in these lessons most of the time, although Jayhan's attention tended to flag when the topics under discussion were the history or politics of Kimora.

At the end of the second week, a letter arrived from Jon, asking whether it was safe for him to visit. Sheldrake checked with Leon that their gates were still not under surveillance before sending a reply, inviting him for lunch two days later.

Sasha kept an eye out for him, driving Beth crazy by nipping out between cleaning each stall to check the gate. When he finally arrived, she was caught unawares, hard at work in the third last stall, Flurry's. Sasha had the great draught horse tied on a lead rope to an iron ring in the corridor while her stall was being cleaned and was concentrating on shovelling dirty straw into a big wooden barrow. Suddenly Flurry and the other horses up and down the stalls became restless, tossing their heads or stamping the feet.

"Hello, little sister."

Sasha spun around so fast that her shovelful of straw sprayed around the wall of the stall. She ran out of the stall and flung her arms around him, engulfing him in the smell of horses, straw and dung. "Jon, Jon. You're here, you're here. I've been waiting for you all morning."

"Looks like it," said Jon dryly, hugging her tightly in return even though he knew his clothes would be the worse for it. "Specially dressed for the occasion."

She hugged him even tighter and asked in voice muffled by his jacket, "Why didn't you tell me? I thought I was alone all this time."

Jon stroked the top of her head. "To keep you safe, little one. We have had to be so careful. We still have to be so careful. But now, at least, you're old enough to keep secrets."

"I always was."

A sob issued from the area of his chest and Jon realised Sasha was crying. He kept stroking her hair and hugging her. "I'm sorry, little one. Maybe I should have trusted you more... Maybe I should have done a lot of things differently. But people from Kimora were looking for a brother and sister who had escaped. I had to remove all trace of us. And Sasha," He gave her an extra squeeze which bent her ribs, "I couldn't bear to lose you. You are all I have."

She lifted her tear-stained face at that. "Don't you have a girlfriend, Rose's mother's second cousin?"

For a moment Jon looked taken aback. Then he shook his head. "No. We split up."

"Why?"

"Because I discovered she had been talking about me."

"Oh. That was Maud's fault. She sent Rose off on a fact-finding mission before she approached the embassy about me."

"Just as well she did. I wouldn't have wanted Lady Maud to breeze in and tell Lady Electra about you." He grunted as a big velvety nose nudged him in the back of the head. "Hoy you," he said to Flurry, who was peering at him enquiringly. He disentangled himself from Sasha and turned to stroke the great filly's neck. "She's a beauty, isn't she?'

Sasha beamed with pride. "She's a bit skittish sometimes, but she's better now that she's friends with Apricot."

"Who's Apricot?"

"The little cat who insists on sleeping in Flurry's feedbag.

Jon stroked continued to stroke Fluffy. "You have a little cat friend, do you? You're a funny one then." He looked over Sasha's shoulder at the mess of the third last stall behind her. "So what are we going to do about that?"

Sasha surveyed the stall and grimaced. "I'd better get to and finish it, I suppose. Maybe I'll see you after lunch."

"Hmph. I think I'll give you a hand." So saying, he took off his smudged, pale yellow coat and hung it on the iron ring Flurry was hitched to. "Come on. Let's go."

Just as they finished cleaning out the final stall, Beth came out of her office and walked towards them. There was no coincidence in this at all, as Beth had been keeping a discreet eye on their progress.

"Good morning, Jon. Thanks for your help." She smiled. "You are looking a little less dapper than when you arrived. Would you like to come into my office and sponge down your coat," she inspected him, "... and your shirt before going to lunch? Sasha can bring in a bucket of water."

Jon nodded and thanked her, following her back between the rows of stalls. Every horse watched him, whickering or tossing its head as he passed. Long before he reached Beth's office, he raised his hands in resignation, stopped and went back to the start of the row. He then retraced his steps, this time giving each horse a scratch on the forehead or stroking its neck as he passed.

When Beth turned around to watch, he shrugged and smiled ruefully. "I don't know what it is. Horses are always like this with me. Maybe it's the plainsman heritage."

Once he had greeted every horse, they settled down and were content merely to watch him until he was out of sight in the office.

"Sasha also has a way with horses," said Beth, as she handed him a clean rag, "not perhaps as extreme as yours, but certainly better than most. She wandered into Flurry's stall when she was being skittish, calmed her down and introduced her to little Apricot, the cat. No mean feat... And of course, you know she saved my life by pushing me out of the way of a rearing stallion then hopping onto its back to settle it."

"Did she?" Jon was still smiling, his blue eyes shining with pride, when Sasha entered the office lugging a heavy bucket of water.

Sasha set down the bucket and frowned, "What?"

"I have just been hearing about your heroics."

Sasha's cheeks reddened and she dropped her gaze. "Oh."

"And you, young lady, are going to have a wash and put on your best clothes. You are going up to lunch with Maud and Sheldrake today."

"Oh," said Sasha again, sounding more worried than pleased. She looked up at Beth. "Really? They're all going to be watching how I act."

"Don't worry so much," said Beth bracingly. "Yarrow has been teaching you, hasn't she? And no one is going to be critical."

Jon accepted a sponge and began to wipe the grime off his coat. After a few hard scrubs, he paused and said with a smile, "Just copy me."

Sasha scowled. "I just want to be a stableboy."

"I hear you're very good with horses." Jon turned his coat and studied it critically. "Can you see any more spots I need to clean?"

"No," snapped Sasha with barely a glance at his coat. "I like being a stableboy. In fact, I love it."

"I am pleased to hear it, since it will hopefully to be your lot in life for many years to come." Jon rubbed at another patch of ground-in horse dung then held his coat up for another inspection. "And one day you may rise to become assistant head groom."

"And what would be so bad about that?"

Jon finally raised his eyes from his coat and looked at his little sister. "It would be an honour to rise so high under Beth. I can tell she is a true professional."

"Hmph."

Jon laughed. "You can be a stable boy with good table manners, you know. The two are not mutually exclusive." When she didn't respond, the laughter died on his face. "I was looking forward to your company, but if you do not wish to come to lunch, I will give your apologies. I can drop back over here to see you before I go." He shrugged himself into his jacket and smoothed down the lapels.

Sasha's face reddened. "No. It would be bad manners for me to refuse an invitation when they have done so much for me. I will come. Just wait while I wash and change so we can go over together."

"As you wish," replied Jon, but his voice was cool.

Sasha's eyes swivelled from Jon to Beth and back again, her face taut with worry. "Sorry," she said uncertainly. "I didn't mean to hurt your feelings. Of course I want to have lunch with you. It's not you," she said in a rush. "It's the queen thing. It's pretty weird, you know, suddenly finding out I'm so important to all these people I don't even know." She grimaced. "And it's embarrassing, having everyone watching me practise how to behave as a noblewoman."

"Oh, Sasharia..." Jon took a deep breath then let it out in a long sigh. "I left Kimora when I was twelve. So I remember her, and I care for her and her people. You do not. Second-hand memories from Yarrow are not at all the same. I know that so far you have allowed Yarrow to teach you about Kimora, but if you want no further involvement with your heritage, then that is your choice. I have not, and will not, force you."

"Oh." After a moment, Sasha picked up a flannel, dipped it in the bucket and started to wipe down her arms with it.

"Out you go, Jon," said Beth briskly. "Wait for her at the

side door. Sasha needs a better wash than that if she is to be presentable for lunch."

When Sasha re-joined him, she was clean and garbed in fresh leggings and a soft cream shirt covered by a new brushed suede jerkin. "But," she said, as though their conversation hadn't been interrupted, "If I stopped having lessons about Kimora... and stuff, would you still visit me?"

Jon raised his eyebrows at her. "Of course I would. What do you think I am?"

"Sorry. Again. I just thought you cared a lot about this queen thing and saving shamans and maybe only wanted to see me because of your plans to save Kimora. And also that you'd be mad at me," she finished in a little rush.

"Angry? No. Disappointed? Yes. But I would never walk away from you. You are my sister and my..." He shook his head. "Never mind... And yes, my plans are important to me. I have a duty to Kimora that I will not relinquish. But I will simply have to find another way." After a moment, he produced an almost cheery smile and proffered his arm. "Shall we go in to lunch?"

Sash shook her head. "Not yet." She tucked her hand into his arm and asked, "Can we just walk to the paddock and back? It will only take five minutes."

Without a word, Jon turned his footsteps and looked down enquiringly at her as they walked.

"When I was at Stonehaven, I always did my chores as well as I could, to please Old Tom. Even with Bryson, I did my best," She gave a little snort of derision, "although that was partly to avoid being hit and even then, it often didn't work." She threw a resentful glance up at her brother.

"Sorry," he said quietly and squeezed her arm closer to him.

"Hmph. Anyway, then I came here and I tried my

hardest from the second I walked in the door. I was desperate not to be sent back to Bryson or to be turned out into the world with no job and nowhere to go." She kicked a little pebble then drew a breath. "Now I just do my best because they are kind to me and have helped me and because," she shrugged, "I guess I expect it of myself."

She stopped walking and withdrew her hand so that she could face him. "So I will do my best for you too, and for all those people."

Jon gave her a little bow of acknowledgement that made her giggle.

"Stop it! I was being serious."

Jon smiled. "So was I."

"Oh..." She shook her head. "And if I do become this queen person, how will I be supposed to act around Beth and Jayhan and Maud and Sheldrake, and how will they act around me and when will it change?"

Jon put his arm around her shoulders and hugged her to his side, chuckling. "You already are this queen person, as you call it. It's a bit overwhelming, is it? With people you know well, it need only change in formal situations. And just remember this. You will always be you, no matter how you act or how those around you act. You will always be you."

"Hmph." She thought for a moment, then tilted her head and smiled up at him. "I suppose that's all right. Tricky, but all right."

He grinned. "Of course, who you are is the rightful Queen of Kimora." She frowned and punched him in the ribs. "Oof!" he gasped playfully, his grin broadening. "But you always were and always will be, whether you knew it or not. Only difference is now you know."

Sasha took a deep breath and prepared herself for the

coming ordeal. Well, not quite an ordeal, she corrected herself, a challenge.

As they headed inside, Jon bent down and whispered, "By the way, I have a little surprise in store for you." She glanced at him, but he just gave a secretive little grin and kept walking.

34

When they entered the dining room, Jayhan gave her a smile, not of reassurance but of pure, excited welcome. It clearly did not occur to him that she might have reason to be worried. Although this probably sprang as much from his lack of understanding as from his confidence in her, his smile still calmed her.

She smiled back as she followed Clive's gesture to a place halfway down the table between Jayhan and Jon. Eloquin and Yarrow stood behind their chairs opposite her, ready to be seated, while Maud and Sheldrake were standing at either end.

"Good afternoon, Jon and Sasha, and welcome." Maud turned to Eloquin and Yarrow. "Jon knew Sasha at the orphanage, and now works at the Kimoran Embassy."

Yarrow's face tightened. She nodded curtly. "How do you do?"

"It's all right, Maud," said Jon, with a slight smile. "I know of Yarrow's allegiances and her work to help unregistered shamans though my own network. If we can trust her with knowledge of Sasharia, we can trust her with me too."

Maud breathed a sigh of relief and smiled. "Lovely. That will make lunch so much easier. Yarrow, Jon is Sasha's older brother, who brought her out of Kimora after..." She shook her head. "Never mind."

Yarrow gaped in shocked delight. "Oh, Your Highness. Oh, I'm so pleased you're all right. No one knew where you were." She sank into a deep curtsey.

Eloquin, standing beside her, looked a bit panicked as she wondered whether she too should curtsey. She sent a little frown at Maud who gave a slight shake of her head.

Clive discreetly trod to the door and closed it, making sure no other staff could enter until Yarrow had recovered herself.

Jon gave her a warm smile. "I am pleased that you too, as an unregistered shaman, are safe. I have heard of your work. Please rise. You endanger both of us with such gestures." His easy response, in such contrast to Sasha's panic a few weeks before, highlighted the fact that Jon had actually been raised, at least until he was twelve, as a prince while Sasha had no memory of a royal life.

Yarrow scrambled to her feet. "Oh. I'm so sorry. Of course. I should have realised. It's just..." Tears sprang to her eyes, making Jayhan look down firmly so that he didn't roll his eyes.

"Shall we sit down?' invited Jon.

Clive left his self-appointed post by the door and assisted Sasha and Jon to seat themselves, spreading their napkins on their knees, before moving to do the same for Yarrow and Eloquin, while Maud, Sheldrake and Jayhan seated themselves. Sasha, fresh from lessons with Yarrow, suddenly realised that Clive was meticulously giving precedence according to the rank of non-family members, now that it was acknowledged. She felt embarrassed and struggled to meet Eloquin's eyes.

Noticing this, Eloquin leant forward and said quietly, "Sasha, I do like your new jerkin. It looks very soft."

Sasha was forced to look at her and found her smiling warmly at her. "Thanks," she mumbled. Then she stroked the front of her jerkin and grinned in return. "It is soft. I love it. These are the best clothes I have ever owned."

A moment of awkward, sympathetic silence was broken by Jayhan who said blithely, "I bet they are. And if your jerkin's like mine, it has inside pockets. Have a look."

Sasha undid the top three buttons and peered inside. She looked up grinning, "It does too. I hadn't even noticed. That's handy, isn't it?"

The adults around the table collectively relaxed.

It was about then that Sasha noticed another place had been set between Yarrow and Sheldrake. As she pondered this, Clive re-entered the room and announced in a tone dripping with disapproval, "Old Tom, sir."

The huge man followed Clive sheepishly into the room, "I am awfully sorry I'm late... And I seem to have upset your butler. Not quite sure how."

"Old Tom," shouted Sasha and bounced out of her seat and around the table before anyone could object. She threw herself at him and wrapped her arms around his legs, which nearly sent him flying.

Staggering, Old Tom peeled her arms off his legs, grabbed her under her arms and swung her high in the air. "My little Sashakins! I'm so glad to see you. I thought we'd lost you and when I heard bloody Bryson had been mistreating you, well! It's lucky for him he disappeared. That's all I can say." He swung her back down so that she landed neatly on her feet, then looked around the table. "I beg your pardon. How do you all do?" He raised his eyebrows hopefully and Sheldrake rose to the occasion by introducing everyone.

"Lovely to meet you all," said Old Tom as he sat down. "You're looking very dapper, young Jon."

Sasha beamed. "Huh. You should have seen his shirt before Beth sponged it down. He helped me muck out the stalls, you know. And you should have seen the horses! So excited to see him and all demanding to meet him."

"Good gracious," exclaimed Maud. "How inconvenient for you."

Jon laughed. "Yes, it can be."

The first course of potato and leek soup was served by Clive, assisted by Rose, whose nose, Sasha was sure, was more in the air than usual. She did not once meet Sasha's eye.

Jayhan spooned a few mouthfuls without spilling a drop then sighed. "I wish I had such a way with horses. They just put up with me."

"You're getting better," said Sasha. "and let's face it. Slug is well named. Even I have to make an effort to get him going."

Sheldrake's head reared up from his soup. "Slug? I thought you named him Storm."

Jayhan met Sasha's eyes as he gave a little smile, "That was before I got to know him."

"Oh. I see."

The boy grimaced. "Sorry Dad. I know you bought him 'specially for me and I do like him. It's just he's..." Jayhan shrugged, "a slug."

Old Tom smiled at Jayhan with fellow feeling at this remark, showing no reaction to the boy's pale eyes.

Maud frowned. "Sounds like a lazy little pony. I might have a word with him next time I'm a horse."

Jayhan brightened. "Thanks Mum. You never know, that might help." He looked at Sasha who was carefully spooning her soup. He nodded at her. "You're doing well. Soup is the absolute hardest."

Sasha rolled her eyes and promptly clinked her spoon against the edge of her bowl, luckily not spilling any. "You're not supposed to comment, you idiot," she hissed.

"Language, please," said Yarrow.

Sasha's eyes narrowed but she said nothing.

"Of course Sasha is doing well," interposed Old Tom. "We are not savages at Stonehaven. All the children are expected to have impeccable table manners and to be able to hold their own in any company, high or low. I think you will find that Sasha adjusts her behaviour to suit those around her." He gave a slight smile and re-addressed himself to his own soup.

A stunned silence followed, in which everyone but Jon and Old Tom readjusted their view of Sasha.

"Besides, Sasha must be allowed to enjoy our company and the luncheon without the constant scrutiny, both positive and negative, that she is being placed under," said Maud gently but firmly. "We are here to enjoy a meal with Old Tom, Jon and his sister. That is all." She smiled at Jon. "And how are things at the Embassy? I do like your yellow jacket, by the way. Very smart."

"Thank you. Things are much the same. Lady Electra was pleased to be invited to another of the King's garden parties and is becoming better known at court. However, her mother is ailing, and she is becoming a little homesick even though reports of unrest in Kimora are becoming more frequent and more serious." Jon glanced at his sister.

"Although she doesn't or can't say it, I think the indiscriminate, vicious reprisals by Queen Toriana have shocked her."

"Can you be more explicit?" asked Sheldrake.

Just as Maud was about to protest, Jon replied for her. "No. Not in front of the little ones. Jayhan is only eight, as I understand it, and Sasha is only a little older. She will have to deal with unpleasantness while she is still young, but now is too soon. If I can protect her for a while longer, I will."

"Of course." Sheldrake motioned for the soup to be cleared away. "Thoughtless of me. Perhaps later."

"Certainly."

Sasha watched and listened but said nothing, giving Clive a quick smile as he removed her bowl. As he turned away with her bowl, he placed his other hand briefly on her back, a gesture which made her glow inside. Seeing it, Old Tom gave her a warm smile.

The next course turned out to be spatchcock. Each plate bore a whole small spatchcock glazed with a spiced apricot sauce and served with long beans, peas and small new potatoes. Sasha repressed a grimace as she contemplated the challenge of dismembering a bony fowl purely with her knife and fork, and spearing peas onto her fork without using her knife or overturned fork to scoop them up and without sending them careening across the table. She looked up to see Rose placing a similar plate in front of Eloquin on the opposite side of the table. As she straightened, Rose looked at her and a fleeting smirk of anticipation crossed her face. Sasha's spirit rose to the challenge. So Rose thought she would make a fool of herself, did she? Not a chance. She could do this. It would be difficult, but she could do it.

Sasha gave a grunt of amusement at herself. The triviality of it struck her. This parade of manners was nothing compared to the trials being endured by shamans in her country of birth. Barely worth the trouble of attempting it... and yet she knew that one day it might matter.

The volume of conversation dimmed as the diners concentrated on dismembering their fowls. Suddenly, a loud clatter next to her preceded a cascade of peas across the table from Jayhan's plate. Maud and Sheldrake frowned while Jayhan grinned sheepishly.

"Whoops. Sorry," he said as he reached out to scoop the peas back onto his plate.

Maud put up her hand. "No. Leave them where they are. Do not compound one error by another. Rose will clean them up before the next course." She studied his innocent little face before calling Rose over. "And Rose, could you procure a few more peas for Master Jayhan please? We wouldn't want him to miss out." She chuckled as he rolled his eyes. "No young man. You will not have your carelessness rewarded by avoiding green vegetables."

Jayhan gave a little huff and returned his attention to his dinner. After a minute or two, when the searchlight of his mother's eyes had moved on, he gave Sasha a little dig in the ribs and when he had her attention, raised his eyebrows in the direction of her meal. In response, she shrugged and gave a little smile. He spotted Eloquin watching her and gave her a guilty grin. To his surprise, she gave a slight smile and spoke to Yarrow, neatly diverting attention away from the two children.

"Do you have any relatives or friends who are still in danger in Kimora?" she asked.

Yarrow finished her mouthful, then picked up her knife and fork, ready to prepare her next mouthful as she answered. "Yes. A whole colony of shamans is living deep within the jungles. I know many of them personally. They are good honest people who use their powers to heal and help. Many of their family members have been hunted down for information. Those family members who are released, are watched and...," she glanced at the children, "harassed, often to the point where they feel forced to leave."

Sensing that Sasha had gone very quiet beside him, Jayhan glanced at her to see a tear trickling down her cheek. He put his hand under the table and squeezed her leg. She gave him a tremulous smile and a sniff, "Yarrow's best friend, Tara, lost her baby," she said sadly, "because they had to travel so hard and fast to escape the Queen's guards. The baby was only a few days old. And a soldier swung at Simeon's dad, but the sword missed his dad and sliced straight through the little boy's leg instead. And now he only has one leg...." She sniffed again, struggling to rein in tears. "Sorry," she added to no one in particular.

Yarrow grimaced. "Don't be sorry. It's I who should be, for allowing you to see my memories. I should have foreseen the danger." She gave a wan smile. "Yes, although she reached the safety of the hidden colony, Tara still grieves for her lost child. And little Simeon... " She shrugged. "He is learning to walk with a peg leg." In an effort to cheer Sasha up, she added, "But when they find out that you are still alive and in possession of the amulet, it will give them hope."

A look of panic crossed Sasha's face. "But I don't know what I'm supposed to do or how to help these people," she exclaimed. "I don't even know them or where they are." She heaved a deep shuddering breath to prevent herself from dissolving into tears and applied herself to the remains of her spitchcock, thus missing the minatory stare Maud sent to Yarrow.

An uncomfortable silence engulfed the table until Jayhan said cheerily, "Well, I know it's a bit tricky, but it's pretty good mattering so much to all these people. I mean, when you were with Bryson, you didn't matter to anybody; at least you didn't think you did. It's got to be better than that."

With her eyes still on her plate, Sasha actually giggled. "Yes it is, isn't it?" She grinned and looked up. "You're right. I've gone from having no one to having heaps of people I belong to. I should stop whingeing, shouldn't I, and just work out what to do."

Jayhan nodded and grinned back at her.

Jon and Yarrow caught each other's eye and a silent message passed between them. This was duly noted by Sheldrake and Maud, who were not so unsubtle as to glance at each other, as each knew the other would have noticed and they could discuss it later.

35

Old Tom left shortly after lunch but Jon was able to stay for the afternoon. He was absurdly pleased to be invited to their magic tutorial.

"Jon and I shall go ahead, I think," said Sheldrake, "You three may join us in an hour's time."

They briefly touched on the deteriorating conditions in Kimora as they walked down the path to the shed, but Jon lost the thread of the conversation as he entered Sheldrake's hallowed workshop in the mage's wake. He ran his gaze in awe along the shelves filled with jars of herbs, spices, and strange, unidentifiable substances, but he was particularly taken with the scaled model of Carrador. He studied it for several minutes, asking Sheldrake questions about its accuracy and how the information had been gathered for its construction. He leaned in closer, studying the positioning of minute figures on the model.

Jon looked over his shoulder and asked, "Do these figures represent your agents or areas of concern?" Seeing Sheldrake's face tighten, he gave an apologetic smile. "I beg your pardon. I shouldn't abuse your hospitality by prying, but it is such a wonderful device. It gives you so much better information about the terrain than a flat map does, even a topographical map. It is one thing to see from above that a mountain range is steep or gentle and quite another to be able to see it from every angle. Most impressive."

Despite himself, Sheldrake unbent under the warmth of Jon's enthusiasm. "The miniature figures can represent a variety of things. They can be, as you suggested, hotspots of trouble or my agents. But if, for example, we were considering a particular problem such as improving the transport system, they can represent poor roads that need attention or the way-houses and taverns available for travellers." He gave a little cough. "I had an idea you would be taken with my three-dimensional map. Could I just mention that I don't feel comfortable discussing my work with just anyone... Yarrow, for instance?

Jon nodded casually. "I wouldn't have mentioned any of this if she were here... or the children. And I thank you for taking me into your confidence by talking to me about this."

Sheldrake's eyes narrowed. "I keep forgetting what an astute young man you are. You have such a disarming manner."

The colour on Jon's cheeks heightened and he shot Sheldrake a sideways glance. Suddenly Sheldrake remembered that this apparently confident young man had had to bring himself up since the age of twelve with no family and no support, except for occasional visits to see Old Tom. On impulse, he put his arm across Jon's shoulders and said warmly, "You are almost as impressive as this map!"

Jon grinned, but his eyes glistened.

"And," continued Sheldrake, on a roll that he worried he might regret later, "you can count on Maud and me to look after you, should you ever need it; not politically, you understand, but personally. Sasha is almost one of the family and so too are you."

All expression fled from Jon's face. He closed his eyes and stood rigid within the circle of Sheldrake's arm. Feeling the tension, Sheldrake gave him an awkward couple of pats on the back and dropped his arm. Finally, Jon mastered himself enough to look at Sheldrake. "I wish someone had said that to me a long, long time ago." He drew a deep, shuddering breath. "But now I have to stay strong, for Sasha, for Kimora."

"You are strong, Jon. Maybe stronger than anyone I have ever met."

"I can't afford to fall apart," said Jon tightly.

Sheldrake shook his head. "Ah Jon, you won't stay fallen apart."

"But the others will be here any minute..." said Jon, trying a last-ditch stand.

"No, they won't. We have plenty of time but just to make sure..." Sheldrake waved his arm and muttered something that Jon didn't hear. Suddenly, a dull click sounded on the other side of the door. "There! My 'Keep out until further notice sign' is now on the door. They will go away when they see it." He patted Jon on the back. "You are safe."

As though a dam had broken, Jon spat out, "I am never safe. I have never been safe since my family died around me. If I remember when I was last safe, it is to remember the family I have lost and to know that safety was an illusion." To Sheldrake's shock, it wasn't sadness that poured out him. It was rage. "That woman destroyed my life, Sasha's life, the lives of countless others. For what? To sit on a big chair and dictate to destroy more lives." He shook his head. "I can't allow her to do that. Not for my own sake or for Sasha's, not even for the true line, but for the sake of the people." He straightened and glared at Sheldrake. "Oh, believe me, I have been sad. I have cried myself to sleep in alleyways, my stomach hurting from hunger. I have sobbed at the loss of my mother, my sister, my father and brother until I retched. I will always carry that grief." He drew a deep breath. "But it is the rage I must control. It is a poison that could leach into my friendships, my judgement and my actions. And I have a duty to my people that I must not jeopardize by marring it with anger."

Sheldrake looked into the intense passion that seemed to contract, even as he watched it, in Jon's blue eyes and saw him, for the first time, as the prince he was born to be. Sheldrake restrained himself from producing a bow of acknowledgement and instead, let out a long breath. "I admire your control. If you ever need someone to discuss your plans with, to make sure they are not too rash, vindictive or vengeful, I am at your disposal."

Jon scrutinized him for a moment, then he too let out a long breath and grinned. "I will take you at face value on that. I know your loyalties lie with Carrador but I have no intentions that threaten her so I can't see that you are being devious in your offer. Thank you."

"If I have any misgivings for Carrador, I undertake to tell you." Sheldrake smiled. "Besides, that is likely to be the quickest way to circumvent any potential issues anyway." He paused and added, "My other offer still stands too. We are here if you need us. I can't do anything about the lonely years behind you but I... and Maud, and Sasha, and Jayhan, and even Beth, Clive and Leon can be here for you now." He turned and began to fiddle with his map, moving a few pieces around, carefully not looking at Jon. "Then maybe your ruined lives can begin to heal. They will never be the same, even if Sasha regains the throne. And revenge will not repair the damage. But maybe our friendship can help to make them... better."

He heard a sniff and looked up to see Jon standing in the middle of the room with tears trickling down his cheeks. When he met Sheldrake's eyes, he used the palms of his hands to wipe the tears. "Aaah. Now look at me. More than anything, kindness undoes me." He tried to smile, but the tears kept coming. "Blast!" He put his hand over his face and his shoulders shook.

After a brief hesitation, the mage crossed to him and enveloped him in a bear hug. "Sorry about this," said Sheldrake gruffly, "But here is some more kindness. I think Maud would be ordering tea about now." He was rewarded with a watery chuckle amongst the sobs but didn't say anything more for quite some time.

As soon as he felt able to let go of Jon, Sheldrake clicked his fingers, a little flicker of magic that brought Rose knocking on the shed door. With a mischievous glance at Jon, he crossed to the door, opened it just enough to talk to Rose and order tea. When he returned, he was grinning hugely.

Jon chuckled between sniffs. "You two are incorrigible. I may end up drowning in tea!"

"That can only mean you will visit us often. Excellent." The tea arrived and after Sheldrake had poured it and they had spent some time sipping, he asked, "How are you feeling? Ready to face the little ones? And Yarrow?"

When Jon nodded, he removed the sign from his shed door with a wave of his hand. "They should be here in about five minutes, I estimate."

Sure enough, a few minutes later, the door burst open and Jayhan and Sasha tumbled in, eager for Jon to show them his shimmering they had heard about. Yarrow followed them more sedately.

Jon glanced at Sheldrake and Yarrow. "Do you mind if I do it, or will it distract you too much from your study?"

"All magic is our study," replied Sheldrake. "Go ahead."

When Yarrow also nodded her agreement, Jon's form began to waver, the waves in his appearance becoming faster and thinner until, in moments, he disappeared.

"Wow," breathed Jayhan, wide-eyed. "How do you do that?"

A chuckle sounded from where Jon had been standing. "I just think about the light bending past me instead of touching me. I did it slowly so you could watch it happen. It's an inherited ability, I'm told, just as your shape-shifting is."

Sasha stood with her arms crossed, frowning with concentration. "And like being a shaman."

"That's right," agreed Yarrow. "Of course, it is only women who are shamans, whose amulets are passed from mother to daughter down the generations, while it is only men from the royal line who shimmer."

"Why only men?" asked Sasha. "I share the same heritage as Jon."

"Just the way it is," said Yarrow, shrugging.

"Hmph," Sasha did not sound pleased. She walked a few steps and prodded at the last point she had seen him, her hand meeting resistance. "Jon?"

Her brother abruptly reappeared, laughing. "You're tickling me."

She beamed at him, her brown eyes shining. "Could you do that again, holding my hand please?"

"Of course. I can make anything I'm touching disappear

too." He offered his hand for her to grasp and the air began to waver around him.

"Me too?" pleaded Jayhan.

Jon grinned and as he took Jayhan's hand, he and the two children instantly shimmered out of sight.

"Wow!" exclaimed Jayhan from out of nowhere. "It's like standing behind a waterfall. Dad, you should have a go."

"I would like to, of course," Sheldrake sounded embarrassed. "But I wouldn't dream of imposing on Jon like that. He is not a funfair ride."

Abruptly the three reappeared. Jon was grinning hugely. "And would you like to try it too, Yarrow?" He didn't wait for her reply, simply letting of the children and grabbing Sheldrake and Yarrow by their arms. The light wavered around them for a few seconds, then they too gradually shimmered out of sight, a little more slowly than the time before. "I told you I like having fun," said Jon.

"Thank you," came Sheldrake's voice gruffly. "This is most interesting."

For a minute there was a silence then a faint sound of shuffling. Suddenly the three adults appeared behind the children and Jon tapped them on their shoulders, making them jump and squawk with surprise.

After a moment, Sheldrake frowned at Jon, whose face had paled. "Have you overdone it, young man?"

"Maybe." He gave Sheldrake a small private smile. "I was a bit wrung out when I started, you know." He shrugged. "But it was worth it. Each shimmering takes effort but staying shimmered does not, at least not to the same extent. Seems that three in a row was a bit much."

"Well, thank you," said Sheldrake warmly. "I really appreciate it. It is such a rare opportunity."

Jon gave a slight bow. "My pleasure."

Sasha snuck her hand into his and smiled up at him. Then she turned to Yarrow and Sheldrake. "So what will we show Jon?"

"Well Jon," asked Sheldrake, "what would be most useful for you to know about?"

The young man thought for a minute before saying quietly, "How to make something that will deaden the pain of wounds and stop them from festering."

The mood of levity that had accompanied the shimmering evaporated.

"A good choice, one which I think all four of us could provide you with. Yarrow, which formula would be easy yet effective, do you think?"

"Basil stops wounds from festering," Jayhan jumped in, eager to help Jon.

Sasha nodded. "And arnica and willow deaden pain."

"So does basil," added Sheldrake. "And it helps reduce swelling. Yarrow?"

"All good suggestions, to which I would add marjoram. Marjoram, like basil, reduces swelling but also speeds healing. In addition to pain relief, arnica reduces swelling and can stave off tiredness."

Jon was looking a little dazed as this barrage of suggestions hit him. "So...?"

Sheldrake smiled. "Definitely basil. And marjoram. Only problem with arnica is that it might keep someone awake when they might do better to sleep."

Yarrow shook her head. "No. It's the arnica leaves that give energy, the roots and flowers that reduce inflammation. So we just don't use the leaves."

"Good point. You can use comfrey on its own for broken bones but it doesn't need to be in the poultice we will give you for general wound treatment." Sheldrake moved to the shelves where he stored his dried herbs. "We have the ingredients here. We'll show you how to make up a poultice of basil, arnica and marjoram, for a start, and give you a jar of it to take away."

"Thanks." Jon smiled. "That will be great and I don't need to be a shaman to use it."

"No, you don't," agreed Yarrow. "A shaman could infuse the wound with healing power above and beyond the scope of this poultice, but this poultice will work quite well on its own."

They spent the next hour deciding on how much of each to include then using the mortar and pestle to crush the herbs into a fine powder. Next, Sasha poured this powder into a jar, leaving a small amount behind.

Indicating the remnants, Yarrow explained, "To treat a wound, you place the crushed herbs in a bowl and add a little water... Thank you Jayhan," she said, as the boy arrived with a small jug of water, "just enough to make it into a paste. Sasha, would you like to show Jon?"

Sasha poured the small quantity of crushed herbs into a bowl and added just a few drops of water. After a bit of stirring, she gingerly added a few more drops of water until a ball of green paste lay in the bottom of the bowl. She looked up at Jon and smiled.

"Your turn, Jayhan," said Yarrow.

Jayhan beamed at Jon before spreading a thin piece of cheesecloth on the bench next to the bowl. Then he tipped the paste onto on half and spread it out until it was about as thick as his little finger. He folded the cheesecloth over and held it up. "Look! This is what you put on the wound. Easy hey?"

Jon nodded. "Once you know how. Well done, you two."

"We'll give you a jar of the crushed dried herbs," said Sheldrake, "and you can add the water to make a poultice when you need it."

A thought occurred to Sasha. "Yarrow, can you infuse these herbs with shaman power to make them work better?"

"Yes, we can. It won't work as well as one of us working directly with the injured person, but it will make a difference." She drew out her amulet.

Jon raised his eyebrows. "That's moonstone, not obsidian like Sasha's."

"And look, Jon," said Sasha, holding out her wrist. "It beats in time with my heart. Amazing, isn't it?"

Jon took her wrist and after a minute, nodded. "Yes. That is amazing." While Yarrow drew her amulet across the mouth of the jar of herbs and muttered a few indistinct phrases, he continued to hold Sasha's wrist, feeling her heart beating in time with the pulsing light from Yarrow's amulet. When Yarrow had finished, he said thoughtfully, "I wonder whether Lady Electra's amulet beats to the rhythm of Sasha's heart, now that her power has been... harnessed?"

Yarrow's eyes narrowed. "Interesting question. I don't know the answer to that, since registered and free shaman naturally don't mix. After all, the registered ones would be bound to report the free ones, wouldn't they?"

"And what would happen," Jon mused, "if a registered shaman came within... I don't know... ten, twenty, one hundred yards of the true monarch's black amulet? Would she sense Sasha's presence?"

Yarrow thought back. "No, I don't think so. I can sense when someone is a shaman but it is a very rare gift. And even I could not tell that the black amulet was in the room until I was shown it. And I was quite close to Sasha by then, only a few feet away."

"And how close were you when your amulet began to pulse like that?"

Yarrow eyes shone with an almost religious fervour. "It always pulses, no matter where I am." She smiled at Sasha in a way that made her squirm inside, although she tried hard to hide it. "That is how I knew, all these years, that our true queen was still alive."

"I see." Jon frowned. "I didn't realise that. Hmm." He fell silent for several minutes, thinking hard.

Jayhan, growing bored, wandered off in search of a ball he had lost last time he had been in there. He spotted amongst it some cobwebs deep under the bench that held the model of Carrador. But as he ducked under the edge of the bench, he knocked a hanging bunch of herbs off its hook and in his momentary fright, reared up, banging his head on the bench. Almost in the same movement, as he turned his head to retreat, he ripped his forehead open on the head of a large nail that had been driven into the underside of the bench.

Jayhan yowled with pain and collapsed onto the floor crying and clutching his forehead. As Sheldrake and Sasha rushed to him, they were alarmed to see blood welling between his fingers.

"Oh Jayhan, what have you done to yourself?" exclaimed Sheldrake, as he sat on the ground, oblivious to the dust, and scooped his son into his arms.

Sasha paled and turned to Yarrow in a panic. "What do we do?"

"We staunch the bleeding, see if it needs stitches and worry about a poultice later." Yarrow grabbed a clean piece of cheese cloth, folded it quickly into a wad and handed it to Sasha. "Here. Hold this firmly on his wound."

For a moment, Sasha looked horrified.

"Do you want me to do it?" asked Yarrow, not unkindly but firmly, more concerned with a quick response than pandering to Sasha's uncertainty.

The girl took a quick breath and shook her head. "No. I'll do it," she said resolutely. Sasha squatted in front of Jayhan. "It's all right Jayhan. Move your hand away and I'll put this on it instead. Okay?"

Jayhan gave a little nod, even though he was still crying, and did as she asked. His whole forehead on one side was a bloody mess. Sasha stifled a dismayed gasp and pressed the wad of cheesecloth onto the area with the most blood. Her stomach felt queasy and she hoped desperately that she wouldn't make matters worse by vomiting.

She felt a hand squeeze her shoulder and looked up to see Jon. Then he leaned past her to wrap a towel around Jayhan's bloodied hand.

"So the blood doesn't go everywhere," he explained briefly, before retreating to the other side of the room.

As Sasha watched, blood seeped into the cloth she was holding, gradually dying it red. Just as she turned in panic, opening her mouth to speak, Yarrow was there, holding out another wad. "Here. Just keep holding it there until the bleeding slows. It will soon, I promise you."

"You see, Jayhan," crooned Sheldrake. "It will be all better soon."

"But it hurts," said Jayhan fractiously, wriggling to sit up straighter.

"Stay still. Of course it does, but it will be better soon." His father moved to ease the weight on his arm. "But you know, I think it may even need a bandage."

"Oh." Jayhan sank back and said, his defences down from the pain, "That's good."

Sheldrake met Sasha's eyes, and despite the gravity of the situation, smiled.

True to Yarrow's prediction, the bleeding did slow and the next wad of cloth did not turn red. Yarrow brought over a basin of warm water and bathed Jayhan's forehead with a clean flannel, revealing a two-inch jagged gash.

Sasha looked on in amazement. "That doesn't look too bad. I thought..." She shook her head, realizing she didn't want Jayhan to know that she'd been scared he might die.

Yarrow smile sympathetically. "That's head wounds for you. They bleed like stink, whether they're severe or superficial." She dabbed Jayhan's forehead. "Doesn't even need stitches." Seeing Jayhan frown, she added hastily, "But it will need a poultice and a bandage, wouldn't you say, Sasha?"

Jayhan, who had his eyes closed, missed the little smile that passed between them.

"Well," said Jon, advancing with the poultice in his hand, "I happen to have something we prepared earlier..."

"Lovely." Yarrow took it from him and placed it over the wound. "Now, Sasha, hold that in place and imagine drawing power from your amulet up your arm, through your hand into the poultice and from there into Jayhan's forehead."

Sasha nodded and concentrated. After a minute Jayhan reported, "It's gone all tingly."

Yarrow nodded her approval. "Good."

He disengaged his hand from the towel Jon had wrapped it in and raised it to place it over Sasha's. "Youch! The tingling just got much worse."

"Perhaps you're pressing too hard," suggested Yarrow.

Jayhan eased the weight off his hand but didn't take it away. After a moment, he shook his head. "Still the same. A bit too tingly."

"Take your hand away completely, Jayhan," ordered Yarrow.

As soon as he removed his hand, the tingling eased. "Huh." After a moment, he replaced his hand on Sasha's. "Yow. Too tingly again."

Sasha was too busy concentrating to think about what was happening, but Sheldrake and Yarrow looked at each other, frowning.

"I think that may be enough, Sasha," said Yarrow. "Remove the poultice, if you please, and we'll have a look."

When Jayhan's forehead was revealed, all that remained of his wound was a neat pink scar.

Sheldrake raised his eyebrows. "Oh dear, Jayhan. I don't think you'll be needing that bandage." He turned to Yarrow. "So what just happened here? Are Sasha's healing powers so powerful? It seemed to me that Jayhan himself played some part in this."

"I agree." Yarrow turned to Jon. "What do you think?"

Jon was about to shrug, when he thought back to his shimmering. Instead he frowned. "Jayhan, do you feel up to trying a bit more shimmering?"

Jayhan felt his forehead, running his fingers over the scar. Reluctantly, he nodded. "I seem to be all better," he said morosely.

Sasha laughed. "That's good, you idiot. If you needed a bandage, you might have had to stay inside until your head healed."

The little boy brightened. "True." He stood up and looked at Jon. "So, what do you want me to do?"

"I'm going to try a little experiment. Sheldrake, can you time this?"

Without a word, Sheldrake drew out his pocket watch.

"First, Sasha." Jon took Sasha's hand. "Ready Sheldrake? Now!" For a few seconds, Jon and Sasha appeared to waver before shimmering out of sight. A minute later, they reappeared. "Okay. Now Jayhan." Sasha stepped back and Jayhan took her place. "Ready Sheldrake? Now!"

Instantly they were gone.

"There we are!" came Jon's voice triumphantly. "Jayhan amplifies other people's magic."

"I didn't even have time to press the knob on my watch the second time," confirmed Sheldrake. "Huh. That is an impressive attribute, Jayhan." The two reappeared, Jayhan pink with pleasure at his father's words. "Hmm. You will have to learn how to control it, though. Some magic would be dangerous if it were magnified. Hmm, yes, very dangerous."

"And who knows what would happen with Mum," said Jayhan cheerily. "She might turn into a wolf instead of a bloodhound."

"Exactly," replied Sheldrake repressively.

They discussed the wonders and possible drawbacks of Jayhan's gift for some time.

Jon had gradually withdrawn from the discussion, lost in his own thoughts. Suddenly he interrupted them by asking Yarrow, "Excuse me. So, you said all the unfettered shamans' amulets beat in time to Sasha's heart, didn't you? Then they must all know the true queen is still alive. Right?" When Yarrow nodded, he continued, "No wonder the resistance is so determined. The shamans *know* Queen Toriana is holding the throne illegally and they will have told their companions."

"Yes, but they didn't know at the start," Yarrow clarified. "When she ascended the throne, Toriana sent out a proclamation saying that she had recovered the amulet. According to her proclamation, a special ceremony had enabled her to wear it, even though her predecessor had not been able to pass it onto her." The shaman unconsciously looked at Sasha as she continued, "But the heart rate generated by the true amulet was high, over one hundred and twenty beats per minute, even when she was sleeping. At first, people thought Toriana's heart rate must be raised by the distress of losing her sister and family. She made good use of that time and swore many shamans to her, using an oath laced with power. But weeks went by and the pulse rate coming from the true amulet remained too high for an adult, sometimes as high as one hundred and sixty beats per minute for extended periods of time." Yarrow drew her gaze from Sasha and began to tidy up, starting by wiping out the mortar. "People began to talk. They watched Toriana. It soon became clear that her moods, exercise and sleeping were not in tune with the heartbeat changes in unsworn shamans' amulets."

Sasha recorked the jars of herbs and placed them back on the shelves. "So," she concluded for Yarrow, "they could tell she wasn't wearing my amulet."

"Aha," said Jon, waggling his forefinger as he put the pieces together. "So that's when the unrest started! Shamans began to refuse to swear allegiance to her and those who had, found they were restricted by her power in what they could say or do."

"And then the shaman hunts began," finished Yarrow sombrely.

Sheldrake glanced at Sasha. "No wonder the Queen,

ahem, I mean Toriana, is so determined to find the true amulet and remove her opposition."

Jayhan disentangled himself from his father's arm and wandered over to Sasha. He put a friendly arm across her shoulders. "Don't worry, Sasha. We'll look after you."

"Huh!" she said, a surprised smile on her face. "You're getting quite huggy yourself."

He shrugged sheepishly. "I just figured I'd had a hug when I was upset and you're probably a bit worried and could do with one too." He smiled cheerily at her. "Anyway, I've just had this really good idea."

Sahsa immediately looked worried. "Uh oh."

"No really. It's a great idea, actually."

"Go on," Sasha said, her tone anything but encouraging.

"We should invite Lady Electra out here!" he declared with an air of triumph.

Four voices shouted, "What?" in unison.

Jayhan cringed but when nothing else happened, he gradually straightened and explained. "Well, you see, Yarrow said she couldn't detect Sasha's amulet. Right? So neither will Lady Electra. And if you want to know how Lady Electra's amulet acts, you ask to see it and then you can see whether it's beating in time with Sasha's heart. She doesn't have to see Sasha at all for us to test it out. We can be with Sasha watching through a window." He grinned at their stunned faces. "Mum can ask her out for afternoon tea or something."

Sheldrake was the first to recover. "Very ingenious, son. But do we really need to find out this information?"

Seeing Jayhan's face starting to fall, Jon intervened hastily. "I think so. If we are to have any hope of opposing Toriana, we need to find out how her power binds the registered shamans; whether it only affects the women themselves or their amulets, or both."

"Hmm," muttered Sheldrake, standing up and preparing to leave the shed, "Interesting. Let me think about it. We don't want to rush into anything that may endanger Sasha, now do we?" He patted her on the head as he passed. "I think we have done enough for today. Afternoon teatime," he said firmly.

PART VI

36

Jayhan was beside himself with pride and excitement as he waited next to Leon for the first of the carriages to arrive. Jayhan, Leon and Sasha had spent all afternoon setting up lamps in sconces mounted on the gates, house walls and on poles that had been placed at regular intervals along the driveway. He was dressed in a smart frock coat and long pants, his hair brushed and not a speck of dirt on him. His strange pale eyes shone in the glow of the lamplights. Looking down at him, Leon couldn't help smiling, even though he was on edge himself, keeping his eye out for any sign of trouble.

Maud had baulked at simply inviting Lady Electra to dinner or afternoon tea, saying that it would seem too strange on so short an acquaintance to invite her home. Instead, she and Sheldrake had hit upon the notion of Sheldrake's fortieth birthday being the perfect excuse to invite a wide range of dignitaries and friends to a party. Left to his own devices, Sheldrake would not have chosen to celebrate his birthday so publicly, but he was happy to sacrifice his preference to provide a pretext for Lady Electra's visit.

As the coaches rolled in, they disgorged their patrons at the front steps before Leon, with Jayhan standing beside him, directed them to continue on past the house to where Jake and Thompson, the two farmhands, were waiting to show them where to park in the paddock behind the kitchen garden.

Under strict instructions from Beth, Sheldrake, Yarrow, Maud, Leon, Jon and even Jayhan, Sasha was relegated to the loft above the stables while people arrived. She was disconsolate at first, until she discovered a crack in the woodwork that allowed her to peer through to watch the parade of carriages as they passed the stables to the back paddock. Once they passed, she could catch a glimpse of the guests just before they entered the front door.

The days were drawing in and the evening was frosty. Both men and women wore cloaks against the cold. The men's cloaks were mainly black or brown, but the women's cloaks were chosen to set off the colour of the gowns they wore underneath, which in turn were chosen to set off their hair colour and complexion. Sasha had never seen such richly coloured, sumptuous materials. She was dazzled by the clothes, the hairstyles and the jewellery and wished fervently that she could be closer to see them better. She grimaced as she imagined Rose telling her smugly tomorrow what she had missed.

At last, Sasha spotted Jon, resplendent in the deep blue and pale orange of the Kakorian colours, standing at the back of a carriage as it pulled up in front of the house. Even before the carriage had halted, Jon had sprung down, ready to open the carriage door and assist Lady Electra to alight. Unexpectedly, Sasha felt a surge of resentment that he should have to wait on someone, who, by rights, should be serving him.

Electra did not appear to even notice Jon - she certainly did not acknowledge him - but took a moment to glance around her surroundings, a slight frown on her face. As her eyes swept past Sasha's hiding place, Sasha felt a jolt and her amulet warmed against the chest. Sasha saw Electra's frown deepen as she looked away. The ambassador gave her head a little shake and trod the path to the front door while Jon was left to close the carriage door and remove himself to the kitchen where food would be provided for the waiting servants. Not once did he look up towards Sasha or betray in any way that he knew the layout of Sheldrake and Maud's property.

Once inside, Electra took a moment to adjust to the glare of a shining dome that hung from the ceiling in the hallway. As she squinted against the light, Clive took her cloak from around her shoulders and directed her to Maud and Sheldrake who were waiting to receive her at the foot of the stairs.

She arrived in time to hear Maud saying. "Oh dear, Sheldrake. I told you that your light orb would be too bright. Look! Poor Electra is nearly blinded by it."

Electra, whose eyes were quickly adjusting, waved her hand. "Not at all. It is merely the contrast with outside." She blinked a couple of times, trying to shake off a slight headache, and looked up at the sphere of pure light that Sheldrake had created for the evening. "It is rather wonderful, really. Do you have one in every room?"

Sheldrake gave a little bow. "Thank you. I am pleased with it. But no, it is something in the way of an experiment, so other rooms are lit with candles or lanterns, some of which can be redeployed here if my orb fails." He took her gloved hand and kissed it. "I am pleased that you could join us for the celebrations."

"As too am I," added Maud. "I had wondered whether anyone would bother to come all this way north from Highkington."

Electra raised her eyebrows, but her brown eyes twinkled. "Really, Lady Maud? But surely you are aware that an invitation to your country retreat is the height of social achievement?"

Sheldrake gave a crack of laughter. "Touché, my dear," he said to Maud. "You really say the most absurd things sometimes." He turned back to the ambassador, smiling. "Lady Electra, you're absolutely right. So, congratulations on reaching such dizzying heights."

Electra grinned and dropped a small ironic curtsy. "Thank you."

As she resumed her full height, a small frown line appeared between her eyes which vanished when she saw a short, thick-set, middle-aged gentleman walking with military stiffness from the front door to join them.

"Ah. Colonel... I mean Lord Argyve, how lovely to see you," gushed Maud. "You retired from the military some time ago, didn't you? Are you acquainted with Lady Electra, ambassador for Kimora?" She turned to Electra. "This is Lord Argyve, the Esukorian ambassador."

Electra curtseyed again as Argyve performed a neat bow and smiled at her, before turning to Maud, "Actually, Lady Maud, Electra and I have met on several formal occasions in the capital. Always a pleasure."

"Just Sheldrake and Maud will do here." Maud quirked an eyebrow at Electra. "Well, perhaps you can have a more relaxed chat at our little gathering this evening." She was amused to see Electra frown repressively at her while the colour in her cheeks heightened. Maud smiled mischievously and added, "Argyve, would you mind accompanying Electra through to the ballroom for refreshments? We will join you shortly, once all the guests have arrived."

"Of course. I would be delighted." Argyve proffered his arm, which Electra accepted with a tight smile. As they walked off towards the rear of the house, Maud heard him ask, "Are you all right, my dear?"

Just before they moved out of earshot, she heard Electra reply, "I think so. I just feel a little strange, head-achy. Nothing to worry about. I'm sure it will pass when I've had something to drink."

Maud gave Sheldrake a significant look. "Interesting, don't you think?"

"What? That he called her 'my dear' or that she has a headache?"

"Both." Maud leaned in towards Sheldrake so that they couldn't be overheard. "What do you think of her?"

"She is charming and intelligent. I like her. I hope she doesn't make things too difficult for us if she becomes aware of Sasha's presence, or reacts badly to her amulet."

Maud's face scrunched up with concern. "Oh dear. I hope so too. This is all very fraught, isn't it?"

Sheldrake's face softened. "A little, but we will do our best to bring them all through unscathed."

They had no time to say more as the arrival of new guests kept them busy for the next half hour, meeting and greeting. Once everyone had arrived, Maud and Sheldrake joined them in the ballroom at the rear of the house. A string quartet was playing in the corner, but it was no part of Sheldrake's plan for people to dance. It was a party, not a ball.

Large glass double doors led out onto a terrace at the rear of the house, where braziers had been set up to ward off the cold. Steps led down to a lawn that wandered up to a wire fence. Through it, sheep and couple of horses could be vaguely seen through the gloom, grazing in the home paddock. Already, many people had taken food and drinks outside to sit at the tables near the braziers. Sheldrake and Maud separated and chatted their way from group to group until the clock chimed nine o'clock. Then, with masterful choreography, they casually converged on Electra, who was still, they were pleased to note, in the vicinity of Lord Argyve.

"Hello you two," said Maud cheerily. "And hello Sheldrake. I haven't spoken to any of you all evening. Finally, I have managed to make it round to talk to you. I see you two have been catching up. Lovely."

Argyve frowned and gave a nervous cough. "Ahem. Just so. Electra and I have had trade agreements to discuss."

"Of course you have," said Maud spuriously.

"I hear, Argyve," said Sheldrake, cutting across his wife's teasing. "that you have acquired a high-stepping pair of bays. Did you bring them tonight?"

The ex-colonel gave a wry smile. "No. To be honest, they are a bit showy for a long journey. They impress around town, but they are so busy stepping high they don't seem to step along enough to have stamina over longer distances. I don't think I will keep them."

"Is that right? What a shame." Anyone who knew Sheldrake well would know this was not news to him. "So, are you looking for replacements?"

"Possibly. I am in no hurry, but if a good pair came up," Argyve shrugged, "I might be interested."

"Do they have to be bays or would chestnuts do?" asked Sheldrake. "I have a fine pair of chestnut geldings that I am planning to part with. We bred and trained them ourselves." He smiled. "When I say we, I mean our head groom, Beth. She is an outstanding trainer."

"I would certainly like to see them," responded Argyve. "At your convenience, of course."

Sheldrake glanced around to check that everyone seemed happily engaged in conversation and well attended. "Perhaps we could take a quick stroll to the stables now?"

He looked enquiringly at Maud who said, "We can have a nice cosy chat while the men are gone." Suddenly she frowned and murmuring an apology, raced across the room to where the servants were preparing drinks to hand around.

"Ahem, perhaps not this evening, after all, Agyve" said Sheldrake ruefully. "It would be churlish of us to abandon Electra... as my wife has just done."

Electra smiled cheerily. "Don't worry. I am not offended. I am surprised you have lasted this far into the evening without any hiccoughs. If I may, I would be delighted to accompany you both to the stables. I would love to see your horses. I have a horse stud back home in Kimora, you know."

"Do you indeed? Now why didn't I know that? I must be slipping."

"And," continued Electra, "would you mind if I sent for my footman to meet us there? He has an affinity with horses I have rarely seen."

"Why is he not your head groom then?" asked Argyve.

Electra shook her head regretfully. "I could not replace old Morgan, who has been my family's head groom and coachman since I was a small child. Besides, Jon is tall, athletic and good-looking which, as you must know, are very desirable qualities for a footman who is to be seen up behind one on one's carriage or serving in the dining room and salon. Jon helps with the horses when he has time between his other duties."

"Ah yes, I recall him now," said Argyve, "He is indeed a credit to your turnout. He must be a busy lad then." His mouth turned down, but his eyes twinkled as he said mournfully, "Alas, my Frederick is not even six feet and he's getting a little dumpy. Still, like servant, like master. I am no longshanks myself."

Sheldrake and Electra laughed.

"You are absurd, sir," said Electra. "Shall we stop this nonsense and go for a quick look at your horses?"

"Certainly. I'll send for your footman as we pass the passage to the kitchen." Sheldrake gestured to his right. "Let us go past the stairs and out the front door. The stables are just across the yard from there. Since everyone else is at the back of the house, we won't be commented upon or waylaid."

As they approached the front of the house, Argyve noticed a small furrow reappear in Electra's brow. He didn't comment but gave her arm a slight squeeze.

37

It had been a long evening for Sasha, stuck up in the loft. Once everyone had arrived, Jayhan had joined her while Leon had remained downstairs to keep watch. They talked excitedly about the dresses, horses and carriages they had seen.

"Did you see Jon?" Jayhan's pale eyes almost glowed in the gloom. The only light came through the crack in the wood. "He gets to stand up while they're going along. How much fun would that be?" His face fell. "Dad would never let me do that."

"I bet it's cold." When Jayhan shrugged, she added, "And what if it's raining or snowing or really windy? That wouldn't be much fun."

Jayhan glanced at her and conceded defeat. "No, I suppose not. And it'll be freezing by the time they leave tonight." He brightened. "Still it would be great on a sunny day."

A while later, Leon called up, "Jayhan, come down. Hannah has sent you over some party food."

With a quiet whoop. Jayhan almost threw himself down

the ladder and landed in front of Leon before he could draw another breath. Leon shook his head, smiling as he handed Jayhan a bulging cloth bag.

"Thanks." The boy's eyes strayed to another cloth bag sitting on the floor beside the door. "What about that one? What's in that?"

"Get away with you," growled Leon with mock ferocity, turning Jayhan by the shoulder and giving him a light tap on the bum to send him back up the ladder. "That's my little bundle of treats."

Jayhan grinned and scuttled back up with his booty.

They ate their way through salmon patties, tiny meatballs, little fruit tarts and an assortment of beautifully decorated tiny cakes, holding each item up to the sliver of light to work out what it was and admire it before eating it.

After their feast, time dragged. They played a few word games, but they couldn't see well enough to play board games or read. Despite entreaties, Leon refused to let them take a light up into the loft in case it attracted attention.

Finally, they heard Leon call softly, "They're on their way."

They peered through the crack to see Sheldrake accompanying a lady in a deep apricot gown, a warm but ornate cloak of velvet green thrown over the top.

"Wow!" whispered Sasha. "She's beautiful. What wonderful colours she's wearing."

"Same colour as you, under all that," observed Jayhan prosaically.

"Well, I think *she's* beautiful too, not just her clothing."

"Yeah. Of course. So are you."

Sasha blinked and looked at him. He just gave a little smile and shrugged.

"Who's that bloke with her?" he asked, completely unfazed by the compliment he had just given her.

"I don't know. Quick. Ask Leon before they get here."

Jayhan shuffled through the straw to the top of the ladder and called down sotto voce, "Leon. Who's that? How does he fit in?"

Leon turned an agitated face upwards and waved frantically with his hand. "Get out of sight."

Jayhan grinned. "I will. I promise. Who is it?"

"I don't know. Well I do. It's some bloke called Argyve who's a friend of Lady Electra. But I have no idea why you father decided to include him except as a pretext for getting the lady over here. He just got it into his head that we needed him." He glanced towards the doorway. "Now shush. Go away."

By the time they were halfway across from the house, Electra was leaning more heavily on Argyve's arm. Jon joined them from the direction of the kitchen and his appearance forestalled Argyve's query of concern. Jon simply nodded at Argyve and fell in behind them without a word, his tall willowy physique contrasting noticeably with Argyve's shorter muscular frame.

As they stepped into the lantern-lit stables, the horses moved restlessly in their stalls as they became aware of Jon amongst them. But he had no attention to spare for them as Electra clasped her hand to her chest, feeling for her amulet. Her breathing was becoming constricted and her movements stiff and uncoordinated. A patina of sweat had broken out on her forehead.

As she passed directly beneath Sasha, a pale blue light pulsed once from beneath Electra's fingers. She saw Argyve step back in surprise.

"What on earth is that?" he demanded. "Are you all

right?"

Electra pressed her hand more tightly to her chest. "It is my amulet. I'm not sure what it is doing. Perhaps that is why I'm feeling so..." She glanced down, as the light from her amulet began to pulse erratically, shining right through the bodice of her dress and through her hand. "Oh, look at it! What's happening to me? To it? It should be pulsing in time with the Queen's heart. Maybe she's sick."

She leant heavily against Argyve who held her up as her knees threatened to give way.

"Don't worry, my dear. I have you," he said bracingly. "Perhaps you should give me that amulet until it settles down."

"No," chorused Electra and Jon.

Argyve threw a repressive frown at Jon but addressed himself to his host. "What do you think, Sheldrake? You know about these things. Is it dangerous?"

Before he could answer, a strong firm rhythm began to super-impose itself over the amulet's erratic pulsing.

Electra looked around wildly. "Someone is taking over its rhythm." She stared in horror. "No. It can't be. They all died... My oath..."

Up in the loft, Jayhan whispered fiercely, "That's it. Focus...hard. Breath slow. Think about your heartbeat."

Sasha grasped her amulet in her hand and sent her heartbeat through her obsidian amulet down towards Electra. Suddenly, a vast stream of power sheared through the wooden floor of the loft, leaving a cut a foot long, before spearing down towards Electra. As the black stream coursed into her, Electra's whole body began to glow within a dark transparent cloud. Argyve was clearly unnerved but held onto her stoically. The glow built until, with a low whoomph, it detonated. A blinding flash of light completely obscured Electra. When the light subsided, her limp body was being held up only by Argyve's arms, the amulet's light beating with a strong steady rhythm that could be seen through the material of her gown.

"What on earth is going on?" demanded Argyve, as he laid her on the ground. "Get me something for a pillow," he ordered, his military background re-asserting itself in a crisis. "Find a healer."

Jon rushed into the office and returned with a cushion from Beth's chair, which he placed under her head.

Argyve frowned furiously as his eyes swept around Sheldrake, Jon, Leon and Beth, who had followed Jon out of her office. "What is happening here?" he demanded. "What have you done to her?"

Beth came over to kneel beside him and took Electra's limp wrist in her hand. "I am a healer of sorts although more used to horses than people." She gave Argyve a calming smile. "Her pulse is steady and strong. Jon, dampen a towel and bring it here."

Sheldrake squatted down in front of Argyve, so they were face to face. "I think we owe you an explanation."

Argyve glared at him. "If you have hurt her, an ambassador of Kimora, you will have not only Kimora, but also Eskuzor, to answer to."

"I hope she is not hurt. I think, in actual fact, her mind may be clearer than before. I can't be sure until she wakens, but I believe the magical constraints placed on her by her Queen have been broken."

As Argyve continued to glower at him, Sheldrake went on to explain Queen Toriana's deception of her people. While he was talking, Jon arrived with a damp towel which he placed on Electra's forehead. As yet, she was showing no sign of rousing.

"Hmph," Argyve grumbled. "These bloody royals. For every good one, there's a bad one. At least in Eskuzor, we now have a stable, moral monarchy, but the previous one was a nightmare. Your King Gavin seems pretty good too," he added hastily, suddenly remembering he was an ambassador to their court.

Sheldrake grinned. "Yes, we are fortunate in our monarchies, your country and mine. But Kimora is not."

Electra murmured something but by the time they had focused on her she was quiet again.

"Did you hear what she said?" asked Argyve.

Sheldrake shook his head.

Argyve heaved a sigh of frustration before asking, "So why are you involving yourself in another country's affairs... so blatantly, I mean? And why involve me?"

Instead of answering, Sheldrake stood and walked to the bottom of the ladder. "Come down, you two." He glanced at Argyve with a slight smile before adding, "I have a very kind, wise man I would like you to meet."

In moments the two children had scampered down the ladder and stood neatly at the bottom, hands behind their backs. Covering his surprise at their unusually exemplary behaviour, Sheldrake introduced them, "Children, this is Lord Argyve, previously a colonel in the Eskuzorian army and now their ambassador. This is my son, Jayhan, and this," he concluded with a flourish, "is my stable boy, Sasha, who turned out to be a stable girl, who then turned out to be the rightful Queen of Kimora."

"Good heavens!" Argyve looked thunderstruck but took only a moment to adjust. He rose to his feet and performed a neat bow. "How do you do, ma'am? And young sir." If he had any reaction to Jayhan's eyes, he did not betray it.

Sasha glanced uncertainly at Jayhan before bowing in return. "Pleased to meet you, sir."

Jayhan also bowed. "How do you do?" More used to civil greetings, he promptly looked past Argyve at Electra, lying on the floor, his brow crinkled anxiously. "Is she all right, Beth? She's not going to arrest Sasha, is she?"

Beth shook her head. "I can't answer either of the questions for certain."

"She has no jurisdiction to arrest Sasha within Carrador," said Sheldrake firmly, "and we will continue to keep Sasha safe from their agents who are seeking unregistered shamans."

As he spoke, Sasha slipped past Argyve and knelt beside Electra. She gently drew out Electra's pale amulet and held it in the palm of her hand.

"Birth. Life. Death... Always," she murmured slowly, then placed the amulet back on Electra's chest. Jayhan wondered whether she had learnt those words from Yarrow or just absorbed what to do from the amulet.

Electra's eyelids fluttered. Then she heaved a deep breath and opened her eyes. As she saw Sasha leaning over her, her eyes widened further. "You... You're... Who are you?" She closed her eyes again as confusion overwhelmed her.

Sasha gently stroked her hair. "I am Sasharia."

Electra's eyes shot open again.

"And," Sasha took a little breath for courage, "your liege."

Electra sat up so quickly she nearly head-butted Sasha, who pulled out of the way just in time but remained kneeling beside her. Electra grabbed for her own amulet and held it, feeling its pulsing.

"Give me your wrist," she demanded of Sasha, "And show me your amulet."

Sasha frowned, then looked at Sheldrake for guidance.

"Not the way to speak to your liege, I wouldn't think," murmured Sheldrake quietly.

"Please," snapped Electra.

Sheldrake nodded, so Sasha held out her wrist.

Electra felt Sasha's heartbeat as she watched her own amulet beat time with it. After a minute she shook her head and gazed up at Sasha, before saying more gently, "And your amulet? Please, may I see it?"

Slowly, Sasha withdrew her amulet. Electra's eyes widened at the sight of the obsidian, so different from her own moonstone. As she watched it, the black amulet sent forth a pulse of dark light. Just as Yarrow's had, Electra's amulet shone in response with clear pale brilliance.

Tears spring to her eyes. "And am I right in saying that no one else can wear this?"

Sasha nodded.

"I tried," said Jayhan from the sidelines. "It hurt and wouldn't go over my head."

Electra waved a hand. "So how...?"

"Would you like a chair, ma'am?" asked Leon urbanely, placing one from Beth's office beside her.

"Thank you. I would."

Argyve was instantly at her side, assisting her to rise and deposit herself on the chair.

She smiled at him warmly and thanked him before returning her attention to Sasha, simply waiting expectantly for an answer to her half-asked question.

Sasha stood before her, wringing her hands, not at all sure how to proceed. "Before I tell you, or others do, could I ask what you intend to do about...?" she waved her hand to encompass herself and the others then shrugged, "Well actually, mostly about me, because I understand you are hunting unregistered shamans, and I, of course, am one. In fact," she added with a little grimace, "I think I may be the person the Queen is really looking for ... and my amulet, of course."

A look of consternation passed over Electra's face. "Oh my stars! I didn't realize." Straightforward as ever, she said simply, "Give me a moment." She put her hands over her face for what seemed a long time to her onlookers but was probably only two or three minutes. When she emerged, she looked calm, clear and decisive. She looked around at them all, taking her time to assess them; Sasha, Sheldrake, Jayhan, Leon, Beth, Jon and Argyve. Finally, she asked, "And is my life forfeit if I give the wrong answer?"

"Certainly not," said Argyve. "They would have to get through me first."

"No," said Sheldrake calmly. "In fact, I included Argyve in the hope that he would give you independent support. We didn't know how your amulets would react, but we suspected it might be difficult for you... or Sasha." He shrugged, "If you remain determined to hunt down unregistered shamans, we will hide Sasha and inform our king of your renewed intentions. That is all."

"Hmm." Electra turned to Jon. "And are you part of this or an incidental bystander?"

Jon gave a little bow. "I work for the welfare of Kimora, as I always have."

"And that," said Electra tartly, "is no answer at all. But based on its ambiguity, I will assume you are part of this conspiracy."

Jon glanced at Sasha, who said, "You might as well tell her. She won't trust you any more after this anyway."

Electra raised her eyebrows haughtily at Jon. "Well?"

Jon grinned. "I am Sasharia's older brother."

Electra looked for one to the other and back again. "Oh my word!" she said, "I am sitting in the presence of two members of the royal family while they stand." Before anyone could react, she rose to her feet, Argyve's hands supporting her arms from behind. Once standing, she sank into a low curtsey. "Your pardon, Highnesses."

Jon laughed. "You've been doing it to me for years."

Electra rose, her face flushed partly with chagrin and partly with anger. "That is unfair. How could I have known?"

"That was not an admonishment. I merely find it funny. It is I who have chosen to endure it, not you."

"And are any other members of your family still alive?"

The laughter died in Jon's eyes. "No. All were killed. As the killers closed on my mother, she threw the amulet over Sasha's head, invoked the words of transfer and bade me escape with her to safety," he took a deep breath, "which I did."

Electra looked at him. "That breath speaks of months and years of lonely hardship. I am glad you survived it, Your Highness, and saved your sister. And I applaud your courage and ingenuity. How old were you?"

"Twelve."

Electra nodded. "It is no small thing for one so young to achieve such feats and to grow into manhood, alone and unacknowledged. I loved your mother. You have my sincerest thanks and admiration."

Jon's eyes shone with unshed tears which he tried to cover by bowing his appreciation. Sasha stepped over to him and put her arm across his bent shoulders before he straightened. He scooped her up and swung her into the air before settling her in his arms. She beamed up at him and he smiled back. "Hello, little one."

"Hello yourself, big brother. You have to tell me that story sometime, you know... when I'm older," she said in chorus with him saying, "When you're older."

They both laughed. Suddenly they realised everyone was waiting for them and Jon swung Sasha back down to land on her feet.

As though there had been no interruption, Electra said calmly, "I am now free of Toriana's compulsion and I consider myself free of my oath, since it was given under false pretences," said Electra. She went down on one knee. "So I hereby pledge my loyalty to you, Sasharia, and your brother, Jondarian."

Sasha smiled and drew her up. "Thank you. Thank you so much."

Electra smiled in return. "An unexpected pleasure, I assure you." She looked around the group. "So, where to from here?"

"I think," said Sheldrake, "that we have tarried here long enough. We are in the middle of a party after all, of which I am the host. Argyve, could you have a quick look at my chestnuts so that you can at least field any queries and then we had better return. Perhaps you would honour us with a visit in a week or so, Electra? Bring that rascally footman of yours, and perhaps you too would like to join us, Lord Argyle? Let Maud know convenient dates and she will arrange it." He smiled disarmingly. "Then we can give you a more complete story and work out our next steps."

"An excellent plan." Electra smiled and, in an effort to lighten the mood, added, "And just think. I will reach even more dizzying heights of social achievement with a private invitation."

38

At the end of the evening, when her coach rolled up to the front door of Sheldrake's house, Jon jumped down as usual to open the door for her. She frowned at him but he merely bowed and handed her in.

"We will discuss this later," she said, obviously uncomfortable.

When they reached her house, he was there to open the door and hand her down.

"Thank you," she said, unlike when she had arrived at Sheldrake's party. "I would like to see you in my study as soon as the horses are settled."

"Certainly ma'am." He bowed, but she thought she caught a twinkle in his eyes.

Half an hour later, he presented himself at the study and knocked discreetly on the door.

"Enter."

He did so, closed the door behind him and stood waiting, hands behind his back, as Electra rose from behind her enormous mahogany desk and walked round to stand in front of him.

Electra glanced around the room. "Is this room safe?"

"Nowhere has ever been safe, but with you on my side, this room is now safe."

"Oh Jon! I hope I have not treated you too badly. Please sit down," she said, indicating a straight-backed but padded chair.

Jon glanced at the door before crossing and turning the key quietly in the lock. He gave a lopsided smile as he sat down. "I can't afford to relax, if someone might walk in."

"True. Thoughtless of me. I am not very good at subterfuge. You will have to instruct me." She retreated to her chair behind her desk. She picked up a paperweight and fiddled pointlessly with it before raising her eyes to meet Jon's gaze. "Your Highness, I am most truly sorry if I have ever treated you unkindly. This is making me rethink how I treat all my staff."

Jon grinned. "That is no bad thing. I don't think you have ever been deliberately unkind, but you often take us for granted and at times do not consider our welfare. I remember I developed bronchitis two years ago, after standing behind your carriage on a long drive through a snowy evening. I doubt that you even noticed, except for the inconvenience of finding a replacement until I recovered."

Her face tightened as she remembered how annoyed she had been. She took a breath to apologize but he held up a hand to forestall her. "By the way, please do not use my title, even alone. If you start thinking of me like that, it will slip out at the wrong time. Call me Jon, as you always have." Realizing that Electra was looking stricken, he softened his tone and added, "Besides, you were my mother's friend and would have called me Jon in private anyway, had things not gone awry."

She nodded miserably and heaved in a breath. "Sorry,"

she whispered, and Jon realised she was trying to hold in tears.

In a moment, he was out of his chair and around the desk, holding her against him with his arm around her shoulders. "Ah, that was too harsh. I too am sorry. You were only fulfilling the role of a grande dame. I knew what I was letting myself in for." He stroked her shoulder, looking down at her. "You've had a hard day, haven't you? Your whole world has turned upside down. The last time that happened to me I lost my whole family except for my baby sister."

Something in her body's reaction alerted him. He squatted down next to her. "Is your family safe?"

Electra drew a shuddering breath. "Only as long as the Queen thinks I am true to her. She keeps shamans' families close."

"Hmm. How does your pledge of loyalty to my sister and me hold up against the safety of your family?"

She pulled away so she could look him in the face. "I knew that risk when I made my pledge."

"I see. Then I am even more honoured by your loyalty than I was before." He smiled at her. "We will not knowingly jeopardize your family. I have no immediate plans to change my current role. Sasha is too young still and we are not ready. And you will no doubt continue as Ambassador. I have watched you, as you know, and I think you are doing an excellent job."

Electra gave a watery smile. "Thank you."

Giving her a final pat on the shoulder, Jon stood up and walked back to his seat. "As long as the Queen remains unaware that your amulet is beating in time with Sasha's heart and not her own, you and your family should be safe. Is there any way she could tell?"

"I don't think so... as long as I follow her orders and don't deride her in front of people who report back to her." A look of distress crossed her face. "Oh dear! What about the hunters of unregistered shaman? I never liked that practice, but I like it even less now I know its real reason. I am supposed to facilitate their operations."

"You don't have to do this alone." Jon chuckled as he waved a hand. "I have been undermining their work for years. Now you will also have Sheldrake's services to misdirect them back into Kimora or elsewhere, plus King Gavin's intended ban, so the hunters will become the hunted."

Electra considered him for a moment. "I never knew you at all, did I? And what are we going to do about *us*?"

"What do you mean?"

"Well, how can I continue to treat you as a servant now that I know who you are?"

"Because by doing so, you will be serving Sasha and me and supporting the cause we all share. And if you don't, and the wrong people find out who I am, my life will be forfeit." Jon leaned forward, all humour gone. "Make no mistake. It may feel like play-acting, but it is incredibly serious. My life depends on it."

Electra was shaken by the intensity in his blue eyes. Suddenly she could see the determination that had brought him through ten lonely, dangerous years of exile. She took a deep breath and said, "You honour me with such trust. I will do everything in my power to justify it. And I will keep your warning in mind to wipe out any self-conscious smile that might threaten to emerge."

Then as quickly as it had come, his intensity lifted, and he smiled. "I must go. Already I will have to field questions about what you wanted with me. Perhaps we could say you wanted my opinion on the chestnuts we saw, in case Argyve does not choose to take them? They are excellent, by the way. I have seen them exercising and working with a light carriage."

"Their looks were certainly impressive." She rose from her seat and gave a nod of respect. "Goodnight Jon. My life, which was never dull, will now be even less so. I look forward to working with you."

"Goodnight, my lady." He gave a small bow, unlocked the door quietly and departed, leaving a very thoughtful ambassador staring at the last place she had seen him.

39

All night long, Electra tossed and turned. Her mind, for so long fettered by the Queen's amulet and oath, now felt clear and free to roam. She looked back over past events, reviewing them in light of her knowledge of the Queen's duplicity and again in light of Jon's true identity. She wondered how many agents Jon and the Queen each had working within the embassy, at odds with each other. Did Jon know all of them on both sides? She hoped so.

She felt at sea. So much of what she thought she had known turned out to be false. She considered each of her staff in turn, wondering whose side they were on. Ostensibly they all supported the Queen without question, apparently unaware that Sasha and Jon lived. But she knew unrest was growing in Kimora, presumably fuelled by Jon or his network. Was Jon in charge of that network? How many people knew his true identity?

So many questions. So few answers.

She looked back over the events of the evening and felt embarrassed by the number of times she had shown weakness, shock or tears. She prided herself on her self-control and her ability to remain phlegmatic whatever the situation. This evening, that had all fallen apart. She wondered what Argyve must think of her. She couldn't help liking him. He was a few years older than she, not at all flamboyant as she was, not tall, not slim although muscular, almost stocky. But he was warm despite his military bearing, he was wise, down-to-earth, and completely unflappable in a crisis. And apparently, he had maintained his hold on her while all the world exploded into light.

She realized that Sheldrake had shown rare sense in including Argyve while they turned her view of Kimora upside down. Argyve was uninvolved with both Carrador's and Kimora's politics, independent of both Sasha and Sheldrake. Without him as a solid rock to cling to, she would have felt beset on all sides. But with his strength beside her, she had been able to gather her shattered view of the world into some semblance of order and decide where her loyalty lay without feeling coerced. She wondered whether he was quite so unbiased about Kimora's politics after hearing tonight of the Queen's perfidy. She would like him as an ally, she decided... After a moment, she added, at the very least.

The next morning, she arose full of decision. She needed a way to be able to talk to Jon regularly without arousing the suspicion of the other staff. During the night, the answer had come to her.

Her morning was full of appointments so her plan would have to wait.

All the time that her maid, Jensen, assisted her with choosing her gown and dressing her, Electra wondered whether she was a spy for the Queen or part of Jon's conspiracy or neither. All she could do was to try to act as she had always done.

"Are you well, my lady? You seem very quiet this morning."

Oh dear thought Electra. *This isn't going well already.* She managed a smile. "Quite well, thank you. Just tired after Lord Sheldrake's party last night." *And now I've just said thank you. Would I usually do that? I can't remember.*

Once she had dressed, she took a deep breath before emerging from her bedroom into the likelihood of encountering Jon. Sure enough, there he was, standing outside the dining room, dressed in the embassy's deep blue livery with its pale orange piping, looking straight ahead. Steeling herself, she walked past him without even glancing at him.

Once she was seated at the table, he appeared at her elbow with a fresh pot of tea. He filled her cup, placed the teapot on the table and stepped back. Taking another breath, she resisted the urge to thank him. "I will have the eggs, bacon and tomatoes this morning, I think."

More and more it was being driven home to her, how little she acknowledged or thanked her servants. She found it excruciating having to continue as she had, now that she had become aware of it. She cringed inwardly as she remembered Argyve saying how busy Jon must be, working with the horses on top of his other duties.

When he had placed her breakfast before her, she said, "Let Morgan know that I will want the carriage after lunch. I will require you to accompany me."

"Yes, my lady." Jon gave a slight bow and retreated to stand by the door until required further.

Electra ate her breakfast with no pleasure at all, knowing her prince was standing behind her. Each mouthful was an effort. Several times she came close to throwing down her napkin and sweeping out of the room, but she persevered. When she had finally finished, she chanced a quick glance at Jon on her way out of the dining room, but he looked rigidly straight ahead. She couldn't help feeling chastened but reminded herself it was all an act.

Finally, with her appointments and another excruciating meal under Jon's eyes out of the way, Electra made her way down the front steps of the embassy to where Jon was holding the door of her coach open for her. She gave directions to Morgan the coachman, then nodded at Jon as he handed her in and, giving her no response, took his place at the rear of the carriage.

Forty minutes later, they pulled up outside a large workshop with a swinging sign over the doorway proclaiming it as Conway and Sons, Coachbuilders. As Jon helped her to alight, she said with a mischievous smile, "Jon, I would like you and Morgan to assist me in buying a phaeton."

Jon raised his eyebrows, but merely bowed before walking to the coachman's seat to relay her request.

Morgan scowled as he tied the reins and climbed stiffly down. "I hope she don't think she'll be driving it on her own."

"Why? Not good enough? Surely you trained her to drive horses when she was younger."

"It's just not proper, a young lady gallivanting around on her own."

Jon laughed. "Not so young and probably not planning to gallivant."

Morgan sniffed. "Well, all I can say is, you'd better make sure she takes you with her. Some ladies drive phaetons completely unaccompanied, but I won't hold with that and so I will tell her."

"Morgan, she is more likely to listen to you. You have the advantage of long acquaintance."

This sop to his vanity mollified the old coachman and he entered the coachbuilder's premises with a more open mind.

Lady Electra was already strolling along a line of twelve carriages of various designs by the time that Morgan caught up with her, slightly out of breath. The first four were coaches, designed to be driven by a coachman with the patron seated inside. The fifth was a very perky high-perch phaeton with yellow wheels and only one seat. Electra stopped to look at it, astonished by the small size of its body compared with the size of its enormous wheels.

"My lady, I think something with a double seat and a footman's seat behind might be more suitable," Morgan said repressively. "Then you could take a companion if you chose to or perhaps put a parcel in it if you need to."

Electra looked at him, her eyes dancing, "Do you not approve of this one?" she asked. When Morgan frowned, she smiled and relented. "I think it ridiculous, myself. But I'm sure some young lady will think she is cutting a dash in it. Let us move on." Jon, she noticed, stood back, waiting to be consulted but not offering an opinion.

The seventh vehicle was a red-enamelled phaeton, with a double seat for the driver and passenger, a small seat behind for a groom or footman and a roof that could be folded back. In the style of phaetons, the wheels were large but not ridiculously so. Electra walked around it, admiring the woodwork and the colour of the enamelling.

She turned to Morgan and Jon, "I like it. What do you think?"

Morgan's shoulder relaxed noticeably. "Very good, ma'am."

Jon inspected the groom's seat and grinned at Electra.

"Enough room behind the front seat for my long legs," earning himself a frown of disapproval from the old man.

"How many horses will I need, Morgan? These shafts seem designed for one and I would rather have two horse drawing it. What do you think?"

Morgan studied the ends of the shafts. "These are bolted to the body. I think the coachbuilder could easily change the front assembly to cater for two horses."

"Two horses would look smarter, Ma'am," said Jon, "They would last longer and draw your phaeton more quickly. More expensive, of course."

"True, but I might able to procure a matching pair such as those Sheldrake showed me last night."

Jon gave a slight smile. "Let us hope then, that Lord Argyve decides against them."

They were interrupted by the coachbuilder, who had dragged himself away from a work bench at the rear where he had been shaving a long piece of wood. He rubbed the sawdust off his hands on his big leather apron as he approached. "Good morning. I am Conway the Elder. Can I help you or would you like more time to look?"

Morgan explained Electra's wishes and began forceful negotiations with Conway, while Electra retired towards the front of the premises, with Jon trailing behind her.

"Does Morgan know about you?" asked Electra, once they were safely out of earshot.

"No. It would have created a conflict of interest for him. He is fiercely loyal to you but I suspect he would also be loyal to the true line which, while you were restricted by your link with the Queen, would have been in opposition to you."

Electra smiled. "I am glad you did not put him in that position, for his sake as well as yours."

A few minutes later, they saw Conway the Elder return to his work bench while Morgan stomped his way towards them.

"Can we tell him now?" asked Electra. "We can browse between these coaches."

Jon nodded. "From what I know of him, he deserves your trust... and mine. Just a minute, I will skirt behind the coaches just to check no one is working on them. Then I'll position myself where I can see the door, in case someone else arrives or Conway wanders up this way."

Morgan reached Electra, just as Jon disappeared behind the row of carriages. "All done, my lady. Fair price. Should be ready to pick up in two days' time." He frowned. "Where has that flibbertigibbet gone? He shouldn't be wandering off on his own. He's supposed to be attending you."

"Thank you, Morgan. Now come down this row," said Electra, ignoring his little diatribe. "I have something I want to show you." She led him a short way down the aisle between the second and third carriages before turning to him. "Actually, it is something I want to tell you. Just a minute." She put up her hand. "I'm waiting for Jon."

A soon as Jon appeared and took up his position at the front of the row, Electra began, "Morgan, you have always been faithful to me, my family and my wishes."

Suddenly Morgan seemed to deflate. "Ma'am. I know Jon's a natural with horses, but I have much more experience than him. I may be a bit stiff but I'm not too old to do my duties."

Electra looked shocked. Impulsively, she reached out and grasped Morgan's gnarled hands in hers. "No Morgan. I am not planning to dismiss you. Quite the contrary. I am planning to take you into my confidence."

Unconsciously, Morgan straightened. "I see," he said

gruffly, sending a less than friendly glare at Jon, who had witnessed his moment of weakness.

"As I was saying, you have always been loyal to me so I think it only fair to inform you of my own change of loyalty so, hopefully, you can continue to support me." Letting go of his hands before it became awkward, Electra hesitated, working out how to broach the subject. "Morgan, I recently, yesterday actually, discovered that two members of the true royal line survived the attack on Princess Corinna's party."

Morgan eyebrows shot together. "But it was announced at the time that they all died. That's what gave Toriana the right to be Queen."

"Exactly, Morgan. As you can understand, this information has far-reaching implications."

"Indeed ma'am. But how do you know it's true? Could be rabble-rousers stirring up trouble."

"Because, Morgan, my amulet's link to the Queen, which has fettered my thoughts and actions for years, was broken yesterday evening by a ten-year-old girl wearing the one true amulet."

For a moment Morgan was thunderstruck. Then his eyes lit with excitement. "The true line is safe! And that scheming woman has no right to rule. I am pleased you are free of her, my lady. I didn't hold with keeping people in line with magic, even before I knew of the Queen's treachery."

"My amulet," she continued, "now beats in time with the rightful queen's heart." She smiled. "The girl's name, you may be able to recall from your knowledge of the royal family, is..."

"Sasharia." he finished for her. "If she is only ten, she must be Sasharia, the youngest princess." His whole face seemed to glow. "This is wonderful news."

"And she was brought out of the chaos of that attack by her twelve-year-old brother who carried a babe in arms across the vastness of Kimora into the safety of Carrador."

"Twelve years old?" Morgan frowned with the effort of remembering. "So now he's be twenty-two? That would have had to be the youngest prince, Prince Jondarian." He shook his head in admiration. "And he managed that at twelve, did he, a soft-bred lad like that? Amazing."

Electra smiled warmly. "Yes, wasn't it?"

At the end of the row, Jon crossed his arms, shifting uncomfortably. He glanced to his left and right. "My lady, we cannot linger too long."

Morgan frowned at him, "It is not up to you, Jon..." He trailed off and turned a look of enquiry at Electra who nodded.

"Yes, Morgan. Jon is Sasharia's older brother."

As he returned his attention to Jon, Morgan's face spread into a grin, an expression rarely seen on the old man's face. "You young scamp! Well done. And fancy that! Me working with a prince all this time. You're such a friendly, helpful sort of character, no one would ever know." Still smiling, he went down on one knee and bowed his head. "Your Highness. It has been a privilege working with you."

With a final glance left and right, Jon came forward, grasped the old man's hands to raise him to his feet and grinned back. "The privilege is all mine, Morgan. You have been a great teacher and mentor for me... and will continue to be, I hope."

"I would be honoured, Sire."

"Just Jon, if you please. We are not out of the woods yet. Queen Toriana would have a vested interest in my demise, should she learn of my continued existence."

"And even more so, your little sister. Is she safe?"

"Yes, I think so," Jon gave a self-deprecating smile. "She is certainly safer now than she has been at some points in her past."

"So you see, Morgan," cut in Electra, "why I need a phaeton. It gives me a safe place to talk to Jon."

"I do, my lady." The old groom chuckled and gave Jon a friendly slap on the shoulder. "And I can also see that I'll have to keep bossing this young one around, just as I always have." He pulled a face. "Shame I can't share the joke with my wife, but I'll be able to one day."

"Wouldn't she support us?" asked Jon.

Morgan gave another chuckle. "Oh yes, she'd support you, but don't tell her until you want it spread all over town."

"Oh, I see." Jon grinned.

40

Two weeks after Sheldrake's party, Lady Electra drove out on a sunny afternoon to visit Batian House in her new phaeton, Jon seated behind her. As soon as the phaeton pulled up, Jayhan catapulted out of the front door almost cannoning into Jon, who was holding the door open for Electra to alight.

"Wow!" breathed Jayhan. "What a wonderful red. Can someone take me for a drive around in it? Look how high up it is."

Jon smiled down at him. "Hello rascal. Hop out of the way so her ladyship can alight."

Jayhan turned his face up to Electra who was laughing at his enthusiasm. "Lady Electra, can you take me for a drive before you get down...please?"

"Jayhan!" came a voice of displeasure from behind him.

"Uh oh" whispered Jayhan as he turned. "Yes, Dad?"

"You know what I'm going to say. Now move out of the way and let Electra get down. My word! You are cheeky sometimes."

"Maybe later, young man," said Electra kindly, as she was finally able to descend from her high perch.

Sheldrake nodded approvingly. "Very nice. I can see why Jayhan is so impressed."

Electra nodded, smiling, as she pulled off her gloves. "I'm glad you approve. Did Argyve buy your matched chestnuts?"

"He is still thinking about them. They would look very good between the shafts of your phaeton."

"Yes, wouldn't they?" Jon agreed. "Lady Electra is a skilled whipster so she could handle their spirit. In fact, I think she would enjoy them immensely."

"I'm sure Argyve enjoyed the spectacle of your arrival," said Maud mischievously. "I saw him watching through the parlour window."

"Oh."

"Now Electra," said Sheldrake, as he offered her an arm to lead her into the house, "I have someone I would like you to meet. She is, understandably, rather nervous about seeing you, but she has been of great assistance to Sasha."

"How intriguing."

Once Sheldrake, Maud, Jon and Electra had joined Argyve in the parlour and settled themselves, a knock came on the door.

"Come in," said Sheldrake.

Jayhan and Sasha poked their heads around the corner, then entered to stand either side of Yarrow as she entered. Although she was defiantly wearing her flamboyant clothes and jewellery, she looked, unusually for her, tense and awkward.

"This is Yarrow, my lady," said Jon. "She is worried about meeting you because she has been in hiding as an unregistered shaman for many years now. So she is taking a risk letting you know what she looks like."

Electra rose and walked over to clasp Yarrow's hands. "How do you do, Yarrow? If it is because of your knowledge that Sasha was able to overcome the enchantment that my amulet and I were under, then I thank you."

Yarrow breathed a quiet sigh of relief as she dropped a curtsey.

Sheldrake added, "She has also been teaching Sasha many other aspects of shamanism and about Kimora's history. We have all benefited from her efforts."

Once Yarrow had been guided to a seat and given a cup of tea, Electra asked, "Are there many unregistered shamans in Carrador and Kimora just waiting to rise up against the Queen?"

Yarrow eyes widened in alarm and she didn't answer.

"Don't worry, Yarrow," cut in Jon. "As soon as Lady Electra was freed from the amulet's fetters and realised what Toriana had done, she swore loyalty to Sasharia and me. I have worked for her for four years now and I trust her word." He took a sip of tea then set down his cup. "In answer to your question, the numbers are, of course, uncertain, but in Highkington alone there would be close to one hundred unregistered shamans and perhaps another three hundred spread throughout Carrador. Of course there are the shamans' families and other people who have escaped from persecution in Kimora. I would say that altogether, five thousand Kimoran refugees reside now in Carrador."

Sheldrake frowned. "That is a serious security matter for Carrador."

"Perhaps if we had eyes on taking over Carrador it might be, but all intention is aimed at protecting the people of Kimora." Jon looked puzzled. "But surely you must be aware of the influx of Kimorans into Carrador over the last few years?"

"I think" said Maud, "that we were not previously so clearly aware of the issue with shamans and current Queen. Hmm. In all conscience, I may have to chat to Gavin about it." Seeing the look of consternation on Jon's face, she added quickly, "But no names, I promise you."

Discussion turned to the events of the night of Sheldrake's party. Yarrow listened entranced as she heard how Sasha's amulet had affected Electra's.

"Well done, Sasha," she said at last, "Very well done." Yarrow turned to Electra, "How did you feel? It sounds gruelling. I am sorry you had to go through it."

Electra smiled. "Thank you for your concern. It was very disorienting, frightening; I had no idea what was happening." Her smile broadened. "But such a relief and a delight when I realised the cause."

"The process presents a few problems, though, doesn't it?" said Yarrow thoughtfully. "If your amulet affected a whole group of registered shamans, Sasha, you'd have all of them dropping like flies. Then you'd have to run around saying that phrase, 'Birth Life Death, Always,' to each of them to wake them up."

Sasha glanced at Sheldrake. "What do you think?"

"Why did you say it to Electra?" he asked in return.

Sasha shrugged. "It just came to me. I knew it would comfort her and bring her back more quickly."

"And would she have recovered without it?"

"Yes. But it would have been harder for her." Sasha frowned. "But we're not planning to try it on a big group of shamans, are we? Jon said I have to grow up first and that they, whoever they are, are not ready yet."

"True," said Yarrow. "I suppose I'm just getting ahead of

myself." She grimaced. "It's just sad for those people, like Electra, who have been constrained."

"Yes, it is," agreed Electra wholeheartedly. "You have no idea how much more clearly I am thinking now and how my spirits have lifted. It is a terrible thing to do to people. I didn't realise how bad, until I was free of it." Electra glanced at Yarrow then Jon. "Perhaps... What is your status with these refugee groups, Jon? Could you be instated as..." She turned to Yarrow. "Would he be accepted as regent until Sasha is older?"

"No one has any idea who Jon is," said Yarrow. "Sasha would have to be involved for them to accept who he is." She glanced at him but kept her eyes on Electra. "Saying that, he is a leader among them. He comes and goes between groups bringing them news of each other and nurturing a common purpose of looking after any who need help and working towards addressing the injustices within Kimora." She smiled at Jon. "You would make a fine regent."

"Absolutely not," exclaimed Jon. "I did not rescue Sasha all those years ago, just to usurp her." He ran his hand distractedly though his blond hair. "Besides, I will not have her placed in danger, just to verify my identity." He surged to his feet and began pacing. "And not only that, I don't want our people to end up in a bloody conflict with others of our people who are still in Kimora."

Argyve stood up and gripped the young man's shoulder as he strode by, bringing him to a standstill. "Now, Jon," he said quietly but with authority. "Listen to me. You have been carrying too much on your own for too long." He gestured around the room. "This room is full of powerful people. None of us is going to allow your sister to come to harm. Let's work out what you want, then how we can help you achieve it, and when."

Jon lifted his shoulders then dropped them, as he gave a huge sigh. Tears sprang to his eyes. "Thank you," he said thickly. He rubbed the heel of his right hand across his eyes. "Sorry." He felt a little hand in his left hand and looked down to see Sasha staring up at him solemnly.

"Jon, what is a regent? Do they want you to be king, instead of me being queen?"

He squatted down in front of her. "No, little one. Everyone here wants you to be queen... when you're old enough. A regent is someone who rules in the monarch's stead while they are still too young."

"And when I'm old enough, I would still become queen, even if there were a regent?"

Jon nodded. "The regent would step aside."

Sasha squeezed his hand. "Jon, if you could be a regent, we could help people sooner, couldn't we?"

"Yes, but you would have to become known to many people, which would place you in danger."

"She would only have to become known to a small representative group who could tell the others," suggested Maud. "This group would not even have to know where she resides."

"Having a regent would give our people more hope and more focus," pressed Electra. "You can't cajole them into opposing Toriana if there is no viable alternative. I agree with Sasha, if you accept the role of regent, we can begin sooner."

Jon squeezed Sasha's hand before standing up, a little dazed. "You were right, Argyve. There is a lot of power in this room." He looked down at his little sister. "Are you sure about this? It means handing over control until you are..." he frowned. "Hmm, Is it eighteen or sixteen? Electra, do you know?"

"Under Kimoran law, the regent shares the role when the monarch is between the ages of sixteen and eighteen. At eighteen, he or she relinquishes the role entirely, although he or she may stay on as advisor, of course."

Sasha beamed up at him. "Perfectly sure."

Jon shook his head. "Thank you for your confidence in me little one, although I fear you are too young to fully understand the ramifications of what you are agreeing to."

"She knows," said Jayhan, just as naïve as her. "Anyway, the room is full of people she trusts so she knows someone would tell her if they thought it was a bad idea." He grinned at Jon. "I think it's a great idea."

"And I think you must tell Sasha the story of her escape before she meets these representatives of yours," said Maud firmly. "They are bound to ask you and it would be better if she heard it in a place of safety first."

"Me too?" pleaded Jayhan.

Maud looked from one to the other of the children and gave a slight smile. "Yes. You too, but not now. We still have more to discuss."

"However, time for a break, I think," said Argyve decisively. "I need some fresh air," by which he meant the very unfresh air of his pipe.

41

A stiff breeze sent the smaller branches of the eucalyptus trees waving, their slender leaves seeming to flow and sparkle in the evening sunshine. The wattle trees among them were heavy with soft yellow pompom flowers. Honeyeaters darted among them, squawking at each other. High in the eucalypts, three sulphur-crested cockatoos swooped in to land, then called raucously, flipping up their crests and stomping along the branches as they settled.

Argyve sat on a bench in a sheltered spot in Sheldrake's front garden, drawing contentedly on his old briar wood pipe, while he contemplated the marvellous fact that here in Carrador, one wattle tree or another would be in flower at every time in the year. He turned his head as a young boy trundled a wheelbarrow around the corner of the stables, propped it under the trees and began to gather the fallen twigs and small branches that littered the lawn.

Argyve watched him for a few minutes then said, "Hello. You're doing a good job there. Are you gathering kindling for the fire?"

The boy nearly jumped out of his skin, making him drop the bundle of sticks he was just about to put in the wheelbarrow. Then he grinned from beneath an unruly thatch of light brown hair, as he saw Argyve sitting there. "Sorry. I didn't see you there. Am I disturbing you? Should I come back later?"

"Certainly not. You are doing a fine job. It is I who would not wish to disturb you."

"Oh." The boy, dressed in good quality brown working shirt and leggings, stared at him with piercing aqua eyes for a moment while he thought about the merit of this point of view. Then he shrugged and went back to work.

Once the boy had filled his wheelbarrow, Argyve asked him "What is your name?"

"I'm Edgar, sir. I'm just new. Started yesterday. My sister is Rose."

Argyve had no idea who Rose was. "Rose, eh?"

"Yes, she works here as a maid.' Edgar smiled proudly and pointed to his chest. "And now I work here too. And I have new clothes and I already had two meals yesterday and two today. The food is great. I've never eaten so much in my life. I wish mum could be here too. She would love the food as well."

"And how old are you?"

"I've just turned eight."

Argyve thought back to when he was eight, scampering around his parents' country mansion; lessons in the morning, sword craft or riding in the afternoons. He hadn't raked up a leaf in his life and, being a lord, he had started in the army as an officer so had only ordered others to gather kindling, never gathered it himself.

Suddenly Edgar's widened in fear and Argyve looked around to see that Jayhan had just entered the garden from the house. Jayhan hesitated in the face of Edgar's expression and dropped his eyes as he walked over to Argyve.

Argyve looked from Edgar to Jayhan and back again. "Now what's all this then? What has Master Jayhan done to you?" He frowned severely at Jayhan. "I hope you have not been abusing your position, Master Jayhan."

Jayhan waved a hand in a denial but kept his head down. "My father has asked you into afternoon tea and promises that they have stopped talking about shamans and amulets and things."

As Jayhan turned to walk away, Argyve said, "Just a moment." He turned to Edgar. "Now don't be afraid, Edgar. Tell me what is wrong."

"No. Please don't, Lord Argyve," pleaded Jayhan. "Just let it be. He will get used to me." When Argyve looked confused, he huffed impatiently and added, "It's my eyes, sir. I haven't done anything to him. He's just scared of my eyes."

"What nonsense!" declared Argyve. "Come here, young man," he ordered Edgar.

For a minute Edgar looked like he might cut and run, but Argyve frowned ferociously at him until finally he edged closer, not daring to look at Jayhan. Once he was standing before him, Argyve said, "Well done. Now, I want you to look into Jayhan's eyes. Jayhan, raise your head and look at Edgar."

Jayhan shrugged a sorry and raised his eyes, his face tight in anticipation of Edgar's reaction. Edgar did, in fact, flinch back but then stopped himself from retreating further.

"I can't help having these eyes, you know," said Jayhan crossly. "I don't think they mean anything. My great grandmother had eyes like mine and she wasn't very popular. That's all. As far as I know. Since everyone was so scared of them, I even tried making my eyes move or push things, but nothing happened." He put his hands on his hips. "Anyway, why didn't Rose tell you I'm not scary?"

"She said, 'Don't worry. As long as you do your work well, you'll be safe.'"

"She what???" Jayhan's face suffused with anger, making Edgar cower. Seeing that he had inadvertently frightened the boy, Jayhan backed away, waving his hands placatingly. "Sorry. I'm not mad at you. You can do as bad a job as you like, and no one here will hurt you..." He gave a wry smile. "But you mightn't keep your job, I s'pose."

"I think," interposed Argyve calmly, "that your sister probably meant your *job* would be safe if you did a good job."

Both boys looked at him then Jayhan returned his attention to Edgar. "Do you think?"

Edgar shrugged. "I don't know. Maybe." He thought for a while and shrugged. "Maybe she thought I was just nervous about the job and didn't realise I was scared of you." Suddenly his serious little face was transformed by a smile. "Sorry. I won't be scared any more, I promise. It's the kids in the village, see? They told me all this stuff about you being a walking corpse. They said you could strike them dead just by looking at them." He shuddered. "They got me really worked up."

"You were very brave to come here to work, in that case," said Argyve gravely.

"Yes, you were."

"Had to," Edgar looked down and scuffed his boot along the ground. "Mum's not well and we have to look after the little ones." He looked up and grinned cheekily at Jayhan,

"Anyway, except for you, I was looking forward to getting away from the house."

Suddenly a loud voice interrupted them. "Hoy Edgar, where the blazes have you gone? You should have finished long ago. I've been waiting to show you where to stack the kindling. Get your lazy arse over here." Leon strode around the corner into sight.

Jayhan smiled at him. "Hi Leon. Our fault. We're just meeting Edgar."

"Yes. Can't blame him. I ordered him over here. Little matter needed sorting out."

At these words, Leon frowned suspiciously at Edgar but Jayhan just shook his head and said briefly, "Eyes." Despite his best efforts to follow his father's admonishment to stand tall and meet people in the eye, his gaze dropped.

Leon ruffled Edgar's hair sympathetically. "Well, I'm glad we have that sorted then. Come along little fella. Bring that wheelbarrow you've filled and I'll show you where to put the twigs." He gave a nod of respect to Argyve before departing with Edgar trailing behind.

When they had gone, Argyve said, "Now look at me, young man. Let me study these eyes of yours." Taking a deep breath, Jayhan raised his face to find Argyve smiling encouragingly at him. "That's better. Hmm. When you look closely, your eyes are quite beautiful. The colour varies from white to lavender with small streaks of darker purple." He patted Jayhan on the shoulder. "You know, in my country, Eskuzor, there is a greater variety of eye colours. I haven't seen any like yours but the Prince Consort has bright purple eyes."

Jayhan grimaced. "I'm not sure that I want to be beautiful."

Argyve gave a crack of laughter. "Not all of you, young man. Just your eyes."

"And I definitely don't want to be scary."

"Well, Jayhan, No matter how big and scary an animal looks, it is only as frightening as its intention. Even a huge wolf is not frightening if it is sleeping in the sun, after a good meal. If people cannot look at you carefully enough to discern that your intention is to be kind and friendly, then that is their problem, not yours." His smile broadened. "Anyway, there are times in life when it is useful to appear frightening. If my soldiers were up to no good, my appearance in their midst would frighten them into better behaviour." He shrugged. "Though admittedly, it was my position rather than my appearance that frightened them. He grimaced self- deprecatingly. "I'm afraid I don't cut a very fearsome figure."

Jayhan chuckled then tilted his head as he looked the ex-colonel over. "I think you come across as strong and kind and solid as a rock," He coloured. "Whoops! I don't mean solid as in fat. I mean unmoving like a rock to cling to in the middle of a flood."

Argyve turned down the corners of his mouth. "That doesn't sound very dashing."

"That," said Jayhan with a flourish, pleased with himself for using the older man's own phrase. "is because of your intention. I bet you fight really well if you need to. It comes across in your... stillness."

Argyve stood up and rested his arm across Jayhan's shoulder as he started to walk. "Come on. We mustn't keep your father waiting. And in return, I can tell you that you come across as cheerful but with a streak of uncertainty, kind, brave and very perceptive about other people and how to react to them."

"Do I? What's perceptive?"

The older man laughed. "You notice things that other people might not. For instance, you noticed the times Edgar was scared and immediately changed what you were doing to make him feel safer."

Jayhan glanced up at him and grinned. "Well, I noticed that Lady Electra likes you quite a lot, even if you're not dashing."

The colour in Argyve's cheeks darkened. "Goodness, harrumph, um, you don't need to say everything you notice."

"Just thought you might like to know, just in case you didn't know already."

Argyve looked down at him as they rounded the corner of the stables and headed across the driveway into the house. "I didn't think boys your age were interested in romance."

"Oh, I'm not. Not at all. But older people are, aren't you?"

Argyve was saved from answering this by their advent into the parlour where Clive had just produced a tray of fresh tea accompanied by an assortment of tempting cakes and sandwiches. As they entered, Argyve particularly noticed that Electra's face lit up at the sight of him and to his horror, felt his cheeks warming. He hoped desperately that it didn't show.

PART VII

42

Jayhan knew when he was being left out of something. As he sat in the library preparing to answer a set of questions about the latest tedious reader, 'Daisy Gets Caught in the Rain', he gazed intermittently out of the window to see Sheldrake and Yarrow talking to Sasha. Then he watched Leon preparing the coach for a journey.

"You know I can read harder books now?" he complained, dragging his attention back inside.

Eloquin smiled at him. "The reader may be easy, but the questions are not."

Jayhan gave a little grunt of disbelief and returned his attention reluctantly to his work. He lifted his brows in surprise when he read the first question: *What ingredients would you use to help the girl get over the cold she caught in the rain?* He grinned as he looked up at his tutor. "Huh! I can answer that."

"I'm sure you can. You can put some of your magic training to use. Full grammatical sentences please." Her eyes twinkled. "Of course, I shall have to take your answer to your father or Yarrow for their opinions on your accuracy."

For the next half hour, he was distracted by actually completing some work so, by the time he looked back out the window, no one was in sight. But if he craned his neck, he could just see the carriage pulled up outside the front door. Someone was going somewhere, and no one had mentioned it to him at breakfast. Unusual.

He asked Eloquin, who had become more approachable over time, but either she didn't know or had been told not to say anything. Determined to find out more from Sasha in the afternoon, he turned back to the last question: *How could the girl have avoided being caught in the rain?* Hmm. Tricky.

Just as he emerged after his morning study session to cross to the stables, the coach, driven by Leon, rumbled slowly past him. He caught a glimpse of Maud, Sheldrake, Yarrow and Sasha inside it before they were past him and heading towards the gate. Outrage surged through him. How could they leave him behind like that? Without a word. Didn't they realise he was Sasha's protector?

Before good sense could intervene, he ran as fast as his small legs would carry him and jumped for the luggage rack at the rear. He just managed to grab it and, for a moment, hung dangling, holding his feet up, before hauling himself up.

Inside the coach, Sheldrake frowned as the coach gave a faint lurch, but only faint because the weight of four passengers softened its movements. "What was that?"

"I told you, dear," said Maud placidly. "The driveway needs attention. There are potholes forming everywhere."

Sheldrake raised his eyebrows. "Well, after that jolt, I shall heed your words."

Outside on the luggage rack, a large trunk took up most of the space but Jayhan was able to shove it over a little so that he could squeeze himself in beside it. He peered over the top of the carriage and spotted the back of Leon's head. Then he realised there was a rear window in the coach, only small and mostly blocked by the trunk, but he would have to stay low to avoid being spotted. Once they stopped, he had no idea what he would do but he had a strong feeling his father would not be happy to see him.

Inside the coach, Sasha peered out the window, her face tight, a small crease between her brows.

Yarrow patted her hand. "It's all right. They are friendly people. You have nothing to worry about. You'll see."

Sasha turned her head to look at the shaman. "I don't see why we couldn't bring Jayhan. We do everything together. He will feel like I've betrayed him."

Maud leaned forward. "Now Sasha, this is adults' business."

"I'm not an adult," protested Sasha, pouting.

"No. Clearly," retorted Maud acerbically. "And once we have handed over the regency to Jon, you will have nothing more directly to do with this rebellion until you are older and better prepared. I wouldn't be risking you outside the gates now, if we didn't have to support Jon. And I'm not risking Jayhan, if I don't have to."

"I still have my doubts about the wisdom of us accompanying Sasha," said Sheldrake, eyeing his wife. "If anyone among them is a spy for the Queen, our presence is like a beacon to Sasha's whereabouts."

"Nonsense, dear. We are merely Carradorian officials representing our king." Maud smiled at Sasha and patted her leg, "And we are the closest thing Sasha has to parents and I won't have her enduring this ordeal without us."

Regardless of whether he continued to think he was right, Sheldrake subsided, merely giving Sasha a rather whimsical smile.

As the minutes turned into slow hours of hunching down out of sight, Jayhan revised his impetuous decision to stow away and wished he could reverse it. The afternoon wore on in a tedious blur of open fields that gradually merged into patches of bush then thick looming forest on either side. Jayhan was glad he had Leon, Sheldrake and Maud with him, even if they didn't know he was there.

The vast forest they were now entering spread from fifteen miles east of Highkington, fifty miles to the border with Kimora, then another sixtty miles beyond. In the west, the trees were mainly eucalyptus, soft grey green leaves hanging in gentle swathes, scrubby wattles interspersed with yellow and red flowered grevilleas filling the space beneath them. As the forest became denser, tall mahogany and myrtle trees reached high, battling against each other to reach the sun light, great sinuous vines trailing from their branches, the screeches of strange birds echoing through the vast canopy. Tree ferns, dense tall grasses and bull rushes competed for the space along the creeks and rivers, where the sunlight could penetrate the canopy.

On the edges of the forest, loggers and farmers ventured in for timber, firewood, herbs, mushrooms and berries. Few people braved the depths of the forest, daunted by tales of travellers being lost, murdered, or robbed and left for dead. Few people dwelt there and those who did were considered strange and insular by those who lived outside.

The main Highkington to Manassa road, affectionately known as Park Lane, speared in a straight line through the forest but travellers then had to turn south, once they reached Kimora, and head across the Eastern Plains to reach the capital. A more direct route between the two capitals ran through the southern part of the forest but only determined or very experienced travellers could find their way along its obscure, narrow pathways. The rest of the forest was a maze of narrow winding tracks that would often end at an impassable tangle of undergrowth, the edge of a deep creek or sheer escarpment, or simply peter out in the middle of nowhere.

Twenty miles east of the forest's edge but still well within Carrador, the Creeping Vine Inn nestled beside Park Lane under a spreading river red gum, providing travellers with food, ale and changes of horses.

And it was outside this inn that Leon finally heaved on the reins, pulling up his team of horses so firmly that the decision about what to do next was taken from Jayhan as the sudden halt threw him from his perch. No one heard his yelp of pain above the jangling of the harnesses, as he landed on the stony ground behind the coach. He picked himself up and dusted himself off, inspecting his sleeve where it had torn at the elbow. He drew a sharp intake of breath when he tried to put weight on his left leg and realised his knee had been jarred by the fall. Suddenly, Jayhan heard Leon's feet on the gravel as the coachman walked along the lefthand side of the coach to open the door for his passengers. Wincing against the pain, Jayhan hobbled as fast as he could to the right, slanting backwards so that whoever was seated on the right couldn't see him. Once around the corner of the inn, he hid behind some beer barrels stacked against the wall. Heart hammering and panting for breath, he peeked back around the corner to watch.

Maud and Yarrow were walking arm in arm towards the inn, with Sasha and Sheldrake bringing up the rear. He could hear Maud saying, "We will have about an hour before Jon arrives. We will take a private parlour so that we don't run into anyone unexpectedly and I'll order some refreshments while we wait. I will change later, once we are out of sight of the inn."

Refreshments! Rats! Almost on cue, his tummy rumbled so loudly he was sure they would be able to hear it from across the yard. But no. No one looked his way. The four of them disappeared inside while Leon led the horses around to the stables on the other side of the inn.

Jayhan slid down against the wall and felt his knee for damage. Not much, he concluded with mixed feelings. He would be fine to walk and run, now that he was over the shock of falling.

He took stock of his surroundings. To his left, the inn stretched to the edge of the forest. Several windows on this side of the inn looked onto the road from Highkington and the yard he was in, so he would have to stay close to the wall and duck under them to gain the cover of the trees undiscovered. Even as he contemplated what to do, he saw another carriage appearing in the distance as it crested the rise in the road. Time to move.

He crept his way along the wall, past another stack of barrels and a woodpile before coming to an open door near the rear of the inn. He paused, listening for sounds of footsteps and when he heard none, peered around the corner. The door led into the kitchens and as he watched, someone moved across the light at the other end of a short corridor. He took a breath and scuttled past, quickly reaching the end of the side wall. A large gum tree stood only feet from the rear of the inn, its huge branches over-hanging its roof. Jayhan took a quick look around the corner then dodged the short distance to hide on the forest side of the tree.

The carriage he had seen in the distance was now pulling up at the inn and disgorging a motley group of men and women, many of them with the same dark colouring as Sasha. Jayhan surmised they were some of the Kimoran refugees. He saw them enter the inn but only twenty minutes later, they re-emerged and headed around the side of the inn straight towards where he was sitting. Jayhan scrambled backwards into the depths of what he now discovered was a rather prickly bush. After a quick re-think, he dodged to the far side of the huge gum tree and jumped for the lowest branch. He missed. He took a few steps back and with strength born of urgency, ran full tilt and threw himself upwards. As his hands grasped the branch, he swung his legs back and forth a couple of times until he had gained enough momentum to swing himself up onto the branch. He only just had time to settle himself when the motley group passed the other side of the tree. He forced himself to stop panting from the exertion and held his breath until they were several trees away. Jayhan frowned. *Why are they heading into those scary woods,* he wondered.

His attention was distracted by the appearance of a large cart on the brow of the far hill. As the cart drew nearer, he could see it was been driven by a woman holding the reins of a downtrodden old mare. Everything about them was grey; the woman's skirts, shawl, and hair. Even the old mare was grey. Two more women and two men were seated on the bare boards of the tray of the cart, leaning against the sides, their legs pulled up in front of them, with their arms wrapped around their knees. *Not very comfortable for a long distance,* thought Jayhan, *but better than a luggage rack shared by a travelling chest.*

Jayhan lost sight of them when they pulled up in front of the inn but could hear the sounds of them greeting other people who must have arrived from the other direction, either by vehicle or on foot. He could not hear any voices that sounded like members of his family's group, so he assumed Jon had not yet arrived. He certainly hadn't seen him.

This latest group of people did not linger but after a bit of chat, headed down beside the inn and took the same path into the forest that the previous group had followed.

For a while, nothing happened. Jayhan flicked away an ant that had begun the long climb up his hand. He noticed the bark felt rough under his legs below the leg line of his short leggings and ran his hand through some long thin leaves that were swaying in the breeze. Jayhan watched the progress of a black, yellow and white honey eater as it flitted in and out of the surrounding wattle trees. A shrieking trio of rainbow lorikeets shot overhead before zig-zagging at insane speeds between trunks and branches to swoop into a controlled landing in a distant tree.

Jayhan heaved a sigh. There was no doubt about it. He was bored. Being a spy was already turning out to be duller than he expected. Finally, a lone rider appeared on the road coming from the direction of Highkington. Jayhan squinted. The sun was starting to drop towards the horizon silhouetting the figure against the sky. Even so, he thought he recognised Jon. But maybe that was just wishful thinking. No. As the rider approached, Jayhan's guess was confirmed. He grinned to himself. Now, at last, his parents and Sasha and Yarrow would do whatever they were here to do. Jayhan guessed it was about making Jon a regent but he couldn't really believe they would leave him out of it when he had been present for so much of the planning.

Jon disappeared from Jayhan's view as he arrived at the front of the inn and by the time Sheldrake, Maud, Yarrow,

Sasha and Jon finally emerged, the western sky was streaked with gold and orange. They walked along the side of the inn, just as the other groups had, and headed off along the same path into the trees. But before they were out of sight, they halted while Maud separated from them into a nearby, denser grove of bushes. She re-emerged as a large, grey timber wolf; solidly built, Jayhan observed with an inward smile. He frowned. He had better stay upwind of them. A wolf had a keen sense of smell.

He was just about to climb out of his tree when eight people emerged quietly and walked down the side of the inn. Jayhan found them disquieting. They had an air of constraint about them and kept their voices low. As he listened, he realised with a trill of surprise that even though they were all dressed in men's clothing, two of them were women.

They passed directly beneath him, so that Jayhan could see that they were all dressed in black jackets and trousers, neat and in better repair than many outfits that he had seen pass by. They were more heavily armed than any others; each wore a sword on their left hip and a dagger on the right. Two of them carried what appeared to be long slender staffs, but when Jayhan spotted quivers of arrows on their backs, he realised he was looking at unstrung bows. A frisson of fear trickled down Jayhan's little body. He had heard how Sasha's father and brother had died.

He listened harder. He could just make out the words, "gathering," and "rumours." He thought he might have heard the word "amulet" but that may have been his imagination or expectation. He wasn't sure and now that they were moving into the trees, he couldn't hear them anymore.

Overhead the brilliance of the sunset was intensifying into streaks of deep orange. As dusk settled among the trees, the breeze died down. As soon as they were out of sight, Jayahn slithered down the tree on the side away from the forest, intent on overtaking them. He had to warn Sheldrake.

Suddenly a huge hand clamped down on his shoulder.

43

South of the inn, deep in the forest, a motley group of men and women sat in the dark around a campfire, clutching mugs of tea and talking quietly. They were clearly on edge, glancing frequently into the gloom around them, starting at faint noises. Some were well dressed while others wore worn tattered garments that suggested their owners had not been able to replace them for some time. For all that, the quality of clothing did not seem to correlate with differences in rank.

Suddenly, conversation froze as they all looked towards the north where definite sounds of people approaching emanated from the darkness. Some hands reached for weapons lying on the ground beside them.

A large solid man with a full but neatly trimmed beard shook his head and growled, "Nah. Don't bother. We're not surrounded. If this were a raid, they'd come from all sides."

Beside him, a taut young man, his sandy hair sticking out in tufts, brought his hand back onto his lap and flexed his thin fingers nervously. "What about the lookouts? Why haven't they alerted us? They should have alerted us, Argus."

Just then, an older woman dressed in dusty billowing brown skirts walked quickly into the clearing. She glanced at the taut young man. "I'm alerting you now, Shay. Stop fussing. Jon's arrived, that's all," She frowned slightly, "though he has brought a few more people with him than I expected." She shrugged. "Still, I suppose he knows what he's doing."

A minute later Jon entered the clearing, giving a wave of greeting and smiling disarmingly at them. "Thank you all for coming. As Rhoda said, I have brought some people to meet you; people who have your welfare, and that of Kimora, at heart." He cleared his throat and looked a little embarrassed. "They have a proposal to put to you."

Argus raised his eyebrows. "Do they now? And why haven't they come straight out and shown themselves?"

"I am here, Argus," said Yarrow, stepping into the firelight. "And the others will come out to meet you once I have had a chance to tell you about them first." She looked around the circle of faces. "Now, who among you are shamans? I know a few of you who are but possibly not all."

A show of hands indicated that eleven of the twenty-four people seated around the fire were shamans. Only three women weren't. Rhoda didn't raise her hand but said gruffly, "You know I am."

"Now, indulge me for a few minutes," said Yarrow. "Could each of you lift out your amulets and pace them on your hand so that everyone, shamans and non-shamans alike, can see them."

With a few mutterings under their breath and some narrowed eyes and frowns, they complied, making it clear they were not comfortable with the request.

Yarrow also produced her own before beaming at them, "Thank you." She swept her hand to indicate the revealed amulets. "Now, see that they are all gently pulsing in time with each other? Does their light seem a little stronger? Now I would like to present to you.... Sasharia, youngest daughter of Princess Corinna."

There was a collective gasp around the campfire as Sasha came forward from among the trees. Despite entreaties for her to wear a skirt, she had determinedly dressed in her usual leggings, her new leather jerkin worn over a white, neatly pressed shirt. Her only concession was the blue and orange ribbon, the colours of Kimora, which had been threaded through her dark wavy hair. She looked stiff, but otherwise hid her self-consciousness well.

"And," continued Yarrow, "may I also introduce Lord Sheldrake and Lady Maud Batian, who are here in an official capacity representing the Carradorian king's condemnation of the hunting of unregistered shamans within his borders?"

Sheldrake walked to her right with his arm around her shoulder, a great, grey timber wolf padded silently to her left. Murmurs around the fire passed the word from shamans that the wolf was a shapeshifter, although the introduction made that obvious. If anything, that knowledge made the wolf more intimidating since it meant she had the intelligence of a human combined with the strength and potential aggression of a wild predator.

Sasha stood uncertainly in the firelight, Yarrow and Jon, a little further to her left. She glanced at Yarrow for guidance who nodded. At the signal, Sasha drew forth her obsidian amulet. Immediately, her amulet sent forth a pulse of dark light. All around the campfire, the shamans' amulets flared with pale brilliance; some clear, some pale blue, some yellow, one a pale purple.

Excited babble broke out all around the clearing.

"I knew it."

"I knew she must still be alive."

"Oh thank heavens!"

"It's her! You found her."

Then, as the excitement died down, the murmurs began and slowly the volume rose again.

"Where has she been?"

"She's so young still."

"But at least she's here."

"Is it really her?"

"Maybe she stole the amulet?"

Jon raised both his hands in the air. "Please listen," he said quietly and after a few moments, they did. "I can understand both your joy and your scepticism. Let us address your uncertainty so that your pleasure in welcoming back your true monarch can be unrestrained. Would one of you shamans like to come forward to assist us?"

Rhoda glanced around the group and stomped forward. "I'll do it. What d'you want me to do?"

"Firstly, if you wouldn't mind holding out your wrist, Sasha?" He turned to Rhoda. "Feel her pulse and check whether it beats in time with your amulets."

Rhoda looked Sasha in the eyes and tilted her head as if to ask for permission. Sasha nodded. The pulsing of all the amulets quickened as Sasha' nervousness affected her heart rate. Rhoda gently took her wrist in her large seamed hand and concentrated for a full minute, during which Sasha's heart rate calmed and beat of the amulets slowed. Rhoda let go and smiled at her before turning to Jon.

"Anything else?"

"Now I would like you to put on Sasha's amulet. Sasha?"

Sasha removed her amulet and held it out to Rhoda, who looked at it doubtfully.

"Go on," urged Jon. "We'll get a non-shaman to do it too. Argus?"

Rhoda attempted to put the amulet over her head and cried out in pain as the amulet twisted away.

"Perhaps if you take your own amulet off first?" suggested Jon.

Rhoda frowned at him, knowing the outcome before she even tried. Nevertheless, she endured the reaction of Sasha's amulet a second time just to prove the point.

Argus took the amulet from her, then bowed to Sasha and said in his deep baritone, "If you will allow, my lady?"

Sasha's eyes widened at his respectful manner and she nodded quickly. As Argus placed the amulet over the top of his head as though to put it on, his hand burned and pains lanced through his head. With a yell he pulled it away from his head but managed to hold onto it and return it, rather abruptly, to Sasha.

"I think we have seen enough," growled Argus. "I believe, beyond the shadow of a doubt, that our rightful Queen stands before us. Does anyone disagree?"

People shook their heads and a few murmured, "No."

Argus lowered himself to one knee and placed his hand on his heart. "I pledge you loyalty and service, Sasharia, and will do all I can to restore you to your rightful throne."

Behind him, every single person around the campfire rose before going down on one knee, some quite stiffly, all offering pledges of loyalty. Their pledges were not in unison, so the result was ragged but heartfelt.

For a brief moment, Sasha looked panic-stricken but, after a glance at Jon, cleared her throat and said, "Please rise. Thank you. Um, could we sit down and talk to you please?"

A few people grinned but Argus said formally, "Of course. We would be honoured," and waved her to a seat on a log by the fire.

An old bloke, white whiskered and wizened, shifted over and patted the spot he had vacated. "Here y'are, girlie." He gave her a half toothless grin. "Me name's Berren but everyone calls me Beetlebrow. You can too, if you like. I s'pose I should call you Your Highness or some such, but you're a wee young thing and I haven't quite got my head around it yet."

Sasha gave him a nervous smile and sat down. "Thanks."

Maud paced back and forth a few times behind the row of people, deliberately making them nervous, before circling to the front of the log and settling down on the ground at Sasha's feet, while Sheldrake placed himself at the edge of the clearing near Jon, where he could keep his eye on everyone present.

Sasha noticed a woman in her twenties sitting across the fire from her and wondered how she had kept her long wavy brown hair so lustrous when the rest of her looked so ill kempt. The young woman looked her up and down with hard grey eyes before pronouncing, "Your existence will give us someone to fight for, to right the wrongs and overthrow the tyrant Queen." She flicked a twig into the fire. "But..." she added disparagingly, "you don't look like much of a warrior queen to lead us into battle."

Sasha felt like she'd been slapped in the face. Immediately, many voices around the fire rose to her defence.

"Draya, stop it."

"Don't be rude."

"Draya, mind your mouth."

As the recriminations died down, Sasha took a deep breath and said in a tight brittle voice, her hands held tightly on her lap, "I am ten years old and was brought up in an orphanage. I have been in hiding all my life. First I worked for a carter who beat me almost daily," this elicited a communal intake of breath and Jon, standing in the shadows, winced, "but now I have a job I love, working for a kind and clever family as a stable hand." She took another breath. "I only found out who I was, a couple of months ago. You can be as mean as you like, but it won't change who I am. But it might change whether I want to help you."

Voices came from everywhere; shocked and angry. Sasha glanced at the old bloke next to her who gave her a wink. She responded with the tiniest of smiles as she waited for the tumult to die down. Finally, when they were quiet, she continued as though no one had spoken. "My brother brought me out of Kimora when I was a baby. So, I remember nothing about Kimora. Nothing. Yarrow and my brother have been teaching me about her and explaining all the bad things that this new aunty of mine has been doing. I do not have, as my brother does, the inbred commitment to the Kimoran people, but for his sake and for the sake of what seems right, I will try to develop it." For the first time, she looked directly at Draya. "So don't make it too hard or I might just walk away."

A stunned silence was followed by another babble of voices. Finally, one question made itself heard above all the rest and was then taken up by everyone, "Who is your brother?"

Sasha gave a fond smile and gestured to Jon to come over to her. "Jondarian."

Spontaneous applause and shouts of approbation broke from the group.

"Ah Jon boy. We should have known," growled Argus. "You've done so much for all of us; organising shelter, food, introducing groups to each other. Yes, we should have known."

"Hardly our fault we didn't," snapped Draya. "We didn't even know he was still alive." She held up a hand to prevent another barrage of censure. "But I am glad he is. Really glad. And I'm glad our queen is, too."

"Thanks, Draya," Jon left his place on the clearing's edge and came forward to the fire, his smile diffident at first then broadening into a grin as people gathered around him slapping him on the back, smiling and laughing in delight. For a while, mayhem reigned, people handed out cups of tea while asking how he had escaped, how he'd rescued Sasha and how he'd lived in Carrador as a little boy. It did not seem to occur to any of them to demonstrate their allegiance to him as they had to Sasha, perhaps because they already knew him. Eventually someone remembered that a proposal was to be put to them.

"So come on, Jon, tell us, what is this proposal?" asked Rhoda.

Unaccountably for his onlookers, Jon looked a little embarrassed and turned to Yarrow. "I would rather this came from someone else."

Yarrow smiled understandingly at him, but before she could speak, Sasha said firmly, "I would like Jon to be regent until I come of age. That way, he can lead Kimora as soon as we get rid of my aunt." She shrugged. "Otherwise you will have to wait until I am old enough and know enough to rule myself... which will be ages," she added with a flash of childish language.

With no hesitation, Argus stood up. "I agree."

One after the other, they all stood and repeated his words. Angus glanced around himself and went down on one knee. The others followed his lead and the whole group pledged their faith in Jon, more closely in unison than their previous effort. Then Argus stood up and clapped Jon on the back. "You have earned our trust, young one." He smiled strongly at Sasha, "And you have all the makings of a great leader in the fullness of time."

Sasha blushed and looked down until the old bloke beside her nudged her and whispered, "Hold yer head high, girlie."

She grimaced at him but did as he directed. "Thanks Argus."

Just then, Maud stiffened and raised her snout to the wind, staring into the darkness beyond the clearing. A deep growl emanated from her throat. Around the fire, conversations died.

Sheldrake's eyes snapped to her. "What is it?'

In answer, her growl intensified. Suddenly she was gone, and a peregrine falcon shot out of the clearing, narrowly missing a tree branch, as she disappeared into the night.

"Careful Maud," murmured Sheldrake, as much to himself as to anyone else. He turned to the assembled people, unaware that his shadow loomed high and menacing against the trees behind him, and swept his arm overhead, creating a translucent lilac canopy over them.

"What on earth are you doing?" growled Argus.

Sheldrake looked mildly surprised. "I am merely

protecting us. Clearly someone or something is out there. While Maud investigates, I offer you all my protection."

"It's a shield, Argus," explained Rhoda impatiently "Haven't you seen one before?" She grimaced at Sheldrake. "Mages and wizards are not common in Kimora, only shamans."

Sheldrake nodded. "They are not so common in Carrador either, though I believe everyone in Eskuzor is a sorcerer to some degree. Perhaps I should explain. Maud has heard or sniffed people approaching. As a wolf, she can become aware of them much sooner than even your lookouts can. She senses they are a threat so has gone to investigate."

"Yes," growled Argus. "I gathered that much."

"So meanwhile," continued Sheldrake. "I have placed a translucent film of protection over you all, until we know what we are dealing with. Is that acceptable to you or do you feel too threatened by it? I assure you it merely blocks physical and magical attacks. It does nothing to the people within it."

Argus shrugged. "Good idea, I suppose."

"NO!" yelled Shay, his voice high with strain. "I hate being trapped. I can't stand it."

Before anyone realised what was happening, Shay had grabbed a long heavy branch from the woodpile and swung it into the back of Sheldrake's head. It connected with a dull thwack and Sheldrake dropped to the ground. The lilac shield winked out of existence.

"Shay, you idiot!" cried out Rhoda. "What have you done? This man is in the Carradorian government. If you've killed him, you'll hang."

"You bloody fool, Shay," bellowed Argus. "You'll get us all into trouble. He was protecting us."

Shay, wild-eyed, stood over Sheldrake's prone figure, still holding the branch, his breath coming in heaving gasps. Jon walked quietly over to him and held out his hand.

"Come on, Shay" he said gently. "Give me that stick. We don't want any more…"

Shay's eyes flew up to look at him and for a moment it looked as though he was thinking of swinging at Jon. Then he let out a breath and surrendered the branch.

"Good lad. Now sit down quietly by the fire and calm yourself down." Jon looked at Rhoda and Yarrow. "Can you attend to Sheldrake please?" He shook his head. "I hope he's all right." He looked across at Sasha, sitting stiff and frightened beside Beetlebrow, and gestured. "Come over here, little one."

44

Jayhan's heart nearly stopped with fright, thinking one of the fighters had returned. The hand propelled him around and he found himself staring into Leon's very grim face. Although this was not good, the alternative was so much worse that he breathed a sigh of relief.

"Oh hi, Leon. Thank goodness you're here. I need you."

"A good spanking is what you need," responded Leon severely.

"NO! Yes, well, maybe. But not now. Did you see those people? Eight of them. Two have bows and arrows and they're following Mum and Dad and everyone. Leon, they might kill them like they did to Sasha's family." His chest began to heave with panic as he worked himself up. "Leon, we have to do something."

"Not we. *I* have to..." Leon looked down into the panic-stricken little face and shook his head in exasperation. "Oh never mind! I haven't got time to make sure you stay here." He grabbed Jayhan's hand, none too gently, and dragged him towards the track through the trees. "Come on."

As Jayhan trotted along beside Leon, struggling to keep up with his captured hand, a little frown appeared between his eyes, "How come you didn't go with them to protect them?"

Leon glanced down at him and said impatiently, "Come on lad. Figure it out."

After a moment, Jayhan's brow cleared. "Oh! To check no one followed."

"Exactly." The family henchman explained between breaths as he jogged along. "I will send a flare up to warn Sheldrake but not while he ad Maud are still travelling within the tree canopy. They might not see it. I'll have to gauge when they have arrived in the clearing and find a gap through the trees to send it up then." He grimaced. "But I didn't expect eight attackers or any of them to be archers.

"We have to stop them, don't we, Leon?"

"Somehow," muttered Leon, tugging on the little boy's hand. "Come on," he said, picking up the pace.

Ten minutes later, the dusk had given way to full darkness, but their eyes had adjusted as the light faded. Nevertheless, it was becoming harder to see the path ahead. Jayhan was out of breath and dragging on Leon's arm.

"Sorry. I can't go as fast as you," he puffed. "I have to rest."

Leon stopped and stood over him, flustered, not knowing what to do. "Ah Jayhan! I have to go. I have to disarm those archers, at the very least. Stay here. Stay out of sight. Keep yourself safe. Please." Without another word, he let go of Jayhan's hand and sped off in pursuit of the attackers, at a much faster pace now that he was unencumbered.

Jayhan sat himself against a tree and waited until Leon had disappeared from view around a bend in the track. He had no intention of staying where he was, but how could he get there in time to be helpful? It didn't cross his mind for a minute that he might make things worse, by getting himself hurt or getting in the way.

He thought about the speed at which Leon could move compared to him and a stunning idea come to him.

He could shapeshift to be Leon… or better still Jon. Jon was even taller and younger, so probably faster. Then another idea occurred to him; maybe he could disguise himself as one of the attackers? No. He needed to know them pretty well to copy them. He'd only caught glimpses of the attackers as they'd passed beneath his tree. No. So, Jon it was.

Once he'd decided, he wasted no time.

He centred himself, focused inward, then visualized Jon as clearly as he could; how he stood, walked, waved his arms around, how he bent down. Slowly the image of Jon took over. For a few seconds, Jayhan nearly panicked and backed out. The differences in size and shape between Jon and him were far greater than the differences between Sasha and him had been. Well, except that she was a girl, but he didn't know that at the time… and now he thought about it, he didn't actually know in any detail, what those differences were. His wandering mind started to lose Jon's image and the sense of strangeness in his body faded.

Remembering the high stakes involved, Jayhan frowned at himself, refocused and prepared himself with grim determination, to accept the changes in his body. He visualized Jon again, ignoring the sensations in his body until, in his mind there was a small thunk as the change was completed.

He waved his hand and found it further away from him than he was used to. His feet looked huge and were on the end of long, proportionally slimmer, legs. It took him a couple of tries before he could grab a bit of his hair to see if it was blond; his hands kept not being where he expected them to be. Got it. Yes, he could see his hair was blond, even in the dark. He grinned.

Right. Time to stand up and get used to his limbs before setting off.

His first discovery was that it took more effort to raise a larger, taller body off the ground and when he straightened, he seemed a lot higher from the ground. His second discovery was that the branch he had been sitting under wasn't as far above him as he anticipated and he found himself entangled in it, his hair caught by small twigs and leaves.

When he brought his hand up to push away the twigs, the weight of his long arm swinging towards him sent him swaying backwards and only the fact that he was tangled in the branch saved him from hitting his head against the trunk or falling over. He grabbed hold of the foliage and after pushing it out of his hair, used it to give him something to hang onto while he took a few tentative steps.

At first, it felt like being on stilts. He stepped back and forth a few times, keeping hold of the tree for balance. Then leaning slightly forward, he took a breath for courage and walked away from the tree in the direction Leon had taken. Being young, fit and reasonably athletic, Jayhan soon got the hang of it and began to stride along with increasing confidence. In fact, it was fun. He realised the moon was rising behind the forest to the east and the path was now easier to see, although streaked with deep shadows of the trees. He began to experiment with jogging and was doing well until his toe hit a raised root on the path and he lurched forward. Unable to right himself quickly enough in his unfamiliar body, he crashed to the ground. This was when he discovered the ground was a lot further away to fall to and hurt more when he landed.

He sat disgruntled in the middle of the path, rubbing his bruised shoulder and inspecting his left hand which was grazed and oozing blood. The breeze had sprung up again and sent a fine cloud of dust into his face. His eyes blurred with tears and for a moment he thought it was maybe all too hard. But he was a determined little fellow and his family was in danger. So he gave a great big sniff and pulled himself together.

Gingerly, he pushed himself up onto his feet again and set off, quickly increasing his pace again to a jog, but this time more alert to the path's undulations and more wary of bumps concealed within the trees' shadows. He was just beginning to lengthen his stride when he rounded a corner to be confronted by a mound in the middle of the path. His momentum almost carried straight him onto it, but he was able to grab hold of a low-slung branch to stop himself in time. As he drew nearer, he could see the lump was a large man sprawled face-down in the middle of the path.

It was Leon.

Filled with dread, Jayhan carefully crouched down beside him. At first, Jayhan just looked at him, taking in his closed eyes and the dark wet patch on the side of his head. After a moment, he slowly reached out a shaky hand to touch Leon's chest. He felt almost giddy with relief when he felt Leon's chest rise and fall beneath his fingers. The movement was faint, but it was there.

Jayhan sat back on his heels and pondered what to do. After a bit of thought, he decided that no one was likely to hurt Leon, any more than he already had been and, in fact, if someone else came along the path and found him, they might be able to help him. On the other hand, if Jayhan tried to move him, he might hurt him more. Jayhan vaguely remembered it could be dangerous to move people with head injuries... or was that back injuries? He gave a faint shrug and decided to leave Leon where he was and tell Sheldrake as soon as he could.

As he leaned his weight forward, ready to stand up, he noticed a slim, smooth, slightly tapered stick poking out from beneath Leon. He pulled it free and found the other end was jagged. After a moment, he rubbed his hand along the tapered end and found a notch. Hmm. So at least Leon had disarmed one archer before being knocked out. One archer left.

Giving Leon a farewell pat on the back, Jayhan unfolded himself to his greater height, taking noticeably longer to straighten. He realised he still had the broken half-bow in his hand. He decided he might as well keep it. It wasn't much, but it was the only weapon he had. With a last glance at Leon, he set off down the track.

After his encounter with Leon's body, Jayhan decided to lope as fast as he could in the low light, on the straight parts of the path, but to creep around the corners in case any of the attackers were lying in wait for him. This had the added advantage of giving him periods of rest. He was nearing the end of a straight section when he thought he heard a voice. He stopped dead and listened. Nothing. Realizing that he had probably been making too much noise, he crept to the side of the path and hid behind a large tree. He stood silently, trying to hear above the hammering of his heart.

There it was. The soft sound of a shoe shuffling on the dirt of the track. Jayhan desperately wanted to peek around the side of the tree and see what was happening but he couldn't risk his pale face and blond hair being visible in the gloom. Anyway, he knew what he would see; one or two of those people creeping back along the track, looking and listening for anyone following them.

After what seemed an eternity, he heard a low murmur of voices and the sound of unguarded footsteps as the rear guard walked back to re-join their companions. Jayhan let out a slow breath of relief. Well, he had caught up with them but now what to do? After a bit of thought he decided to change back to his own familiar body. Less chance of making a noise inadvertently. Less concentration on himself, too, which meant he could focus more on these armed interlopers. He slid down the trunk of the tree until he was seated on the ground, noting but ignoring a couple of sharp rocks under his bottom. Then he closed his eyes and remembered how he felt usually.

The sense of strangeness came and went more quickly this time and his back slid further down the tree as he decreased in size. With a mental thunk, Jayhan was back as his own body. He smiled, enjoying its familiarity, although he realized he was feeling tired after the changes, the concentration and running to catch up. Never mind. Not so tired that he couldn't keep going.

He rose quietly and crept along the side of the path, keeping within the shadows of the trees. Because of the density of the forest, there were only a few patches where the moonlight shone brightly, and he was mostly able to avoid them by keeping to the easterly side of the path. Every now and then, he stopped to listen. Sometimes he caught the sound of lowered voices up ahead.

A short time later, he heard the unmistakable sound of a large group chatting and laughing together, making little effort to lower their volume. Clearly Jayhan and his interloper companions were close to their destination. Jayhan drew up as close to the intruders as he could risk, keeping himself hidden in the undergrowth, but looking for the archer among them. He could only see six of them. Maybe the other two had gone ahead. He hoped the archer was among the remaining six. The interlopers began to spread out, three to the right, three to the left. Then Jayhan spotted the archer. One man had stopped before reaching the deep shadows to string his bow, grunting with the effort of curving the wood enough to slot the string into the notches at either end. The archer straightened and crept forward, until he reached the base of a huge spotted gum tree. Then he began to climb.

Suddenly a peregrine falcon flew in low, angling swiftly to avoid low branches. In a trice it was gone, winging up the track the way they had come. A minute later it was back, swooping low under the tree canopy before gaining height and flying off in the direction of the voices. Jayhan was pretty sure it hadn't seen him, or the archer, but it had seen the other five, at least. He thought the falcon was behaving strangely and he wondered whether, *hoped,* it was his mother.

But even if it were, she had not seen the archer. Jayhan waited until the other five had disappeared into the trees on either side of the path and crept forward, with no clear plan except to follow the archer and stop him if he could. As he drew nearer, he caught glimpses of firelight flickering through the trees. He reached the foot of the spotted gum that the archer had climbed and looked up. He could see no sign of him. Maybe, probably, he had climbed around the other side of the tree nearer to the campsite ahead of them.

The lower branches were within easy reach. Pushing his broken bow into the belt of his leggings, Jayhan swung himself easily up onto a long low branch then stopped to listen. He could hear nothing but the swishing of leaves swaying in the breeze. He eased himself onto his feet and climbed quietly to the next level. Every move he made sounded loud in his ears, but the breeze had quickened, and leaves were rattling all around him, masking the sound of his movement. After he had pulled himself up onto the third level of branches, now about twenty feet off the ground, he peered cautiously around the trunk. There, straight ahead of him, lay the archer, stretched out over a fork in the branches directly over the near side of the clearing, his nocked arrow aimed at Sasha, who was sitting on the other side of the fire. Even as he watched, Sasha moved around the fire to stand beside her brother, bringing herself even more conveniently into range. The bowman adjusted his aim and pulled back the string of his bow, ready to release.

Jayhan had no time to think. He simply threw himself at the bowman, desperate to disrupt his shot. The bowman grunted, there was a loud crack and the two of them fell through the branches to land at Sasha's feet; the archer landing on the broken branches, Jayhan happily cushioned by the archer.

They were immediately surrounded by a circle of drawn knives.

Jayhan didn't care. His only concern was whether the arrow had missed its mark. He blew a sigh of relief when he saw the arrow stuck in the ground three feet from Sasha's side.

But from his new vantage point on the ground, Jayhan could also see his father sprawled on the ground close to him. He did care about that. The crash of their landing seemed to have roused Sheldrake, who lifted his head groggily, struggling to make sense of the vision of his son lying beside him on the back of an unknown black-clad man.

Even though he was feeling jarred by the fall, Jayhan managed to give him a sheepish smile. "Hi Dad."

Sheldrake rolled his eyes and passed out again.

45

"Jayhan!" chorused Jon and Sasha, staring at him in astonishment. This was followed by a garble of questions that Jayhan couldn't make out; his mind was so taken up by the sight of his stricken father that he barely registered them.

"What's wrong with Dad?" asked Jayhan in alarm.

"Hit in the head," replied Jon briefly. "A shaman looked at him. I think he'll be all right." He waved his hand. "Worry about him later. Maud's just told us there are five people about to attack us."

Still lying on the prone archer, Jayhan lifted his torso up on his arms, his elbows digging into the back of the man below him, who still hadn't moved. "Seven actually. Eight to start with, all with swords and knives, two of them archers. One's bow is broken, the other one..." he pointed downwards. "Don't know what happened to the other two that Mum didn't see. They disappeared a while ago."

"Where are the sentries?" asked Jon suddenly. "Maud sensed intruders, but we've still had no word from the sentries... or Leon."

"Leon is back on the track. Uncons..." Jayhan couldn't remember the word and settled for, "Like he's sleeping but won't wake up. He broke one of the bows, though."

Jon's eyes widened. "Right. Argus and you three, go and check the sentries. Bring them back if you find them. Come straight back yourselves. We all need to be here together." He looked at the people standing around Jayhan and waved his hand impatiently at them. "Get your knives away from Jayhan. He just saved Sasha's life." He used his foot to gently prod the archer's head, which rolled with sickening ease. "And he's dead. So you don't have to worry about him."

"He's dead?' yelped Jayhan, throwing himself off the dead man as though he'd been scalded.

Despite the gravity of the situation, Jon grinned. His grin faded when he saw the four he had sent off return at a run, panting.

"One's knocked out. The other, Morin, his throat's been slit." The speaker, a young lad with hair and skin dark like Sasha's, looked like he was about to be sick. Sure enough, a moment later, he doubled over and retched.

Jon put his hand briefly on his back but was distracted by the sight of Maud, back in human form, storming across the clearing.

"Uh oh. You're in trouble now, Jayhan," Jon left him to it, turning away to deploy people defensively; some close to Sasha, others around the perimeter.

Jayhan jumped up, staggering from the stiffness in his muscles. "Hi Mum," he tried cheerily, knowing it would be futile.

"And exactly what are you doing here, Jayhan?" his mother growled at him, standing over him with her hands on her hips.

He was tempted to say, "Saving Sasha's life," but instead settled for, "No one said I couldn't come."

This turned out to be a poor response. Maud's face turned an interesting shade of dark pink. "I've brought up an idiot, have I, who can't read the signs that he's not wanted on a trip?"

Jayhan hung his head. "No, Mum."

His mother snorted with exasperation, then suddenly reached forward and grabbed him into a huge hug. "Oh, my wilful little son! What would we have done without you? Sasha would be dead by now, if not for you."

Jayhan's eyes widened in surprise as he was enveloped by his mother. He hugged her back fiercely and mumbled, "Sorry Mum," but they both knew he would do it again.

Sounds of fighting drew them apart. They swung around to see two black-clad fighters, a lithe whip-strong woman and a heavier man, run from the cover of the trees to cut at Jon, who dodged out of the way, drawing his own sword as he backed up. Above him, balanced on the fork of two branches, stood another man waiting for his opportunity to drop on Jon or throw his knife. Jon's actions in ordering men out to search for the lookouts had designated him as leader and it was clear they were targeting him.

Intent on reaching Jon, another intruder was attacking Argus, who barely drew his sword in time to parry the first blow. He was staggering back under the onslaught of an experienced fighter, when suddenly a bulky shadow emerged from the path to grab the intruder from behind and hoist him, sword flailing, away from Argus. It was Leon, battered and bloody, but back in good fighting fettle. Leon wrested the man's sword from him and swung the sword's hilt to connect solidly with the man's temple, dropping him like a stone.

Maud thrust Jayhan aside and started towards the attackers, changing between one step and the next into a snarling mountain lion. She dodged between the fighters and out of the clearing. In three fluid jumps, she reached the height of the assailant in the tree above Jon. With a roar, she lunged at the man balanced in the fork of the tree. The intruder had no chance to turn or to use the sword in his left hand. The knife he held ready in his right hand, clattered to the ground below. The sheer momentum of Maud's leap thrust the intruder from his perch and sent him crashing through the branches to land, broken and unconscious, at Jon's feet. Maud, however, did not fall with him as Jayhan had, but braced herself on the branches and considered her next move. Below her, Jon was so hard-pressed, he could barely afford the time to glance at the man's body as it thudded to earth beside him.

Now, three black-clad figures lay sprawled on the ground, but two were still advancing on Jon while several refugees, sporting deep gashes or clutching bruised or broken limbs, struggled to intervene. Even though the marauders were outnumbered three to one, they were trained and merciless while the refugees were used to eluding capture rather than standing and fighting. Many bore weapons but few really knew how to use them.

Two attackers were still pressing Jon when another man and woman leapt into the clearing, slashing their way towards Jon, aiming to force him, in a pincer movement, towards the edge of the clearing. Draya threw herself into the fray, roaring her own fearsome battle cry as her sword clashed with that of a solidly built man. Her attack was so ferocious that her opponent staggered before regaining his footing and pressing forward again.

Beetlebrow reached down and grabbed a large stone.

Squinting his eyes for a moment, he threw it with such uncanny accuracy that he hit the heavy man who had been pressing Jon from the start, in the middle of his forehead. The man's legs folded beneath him.

A second female attacker was holding other defenders at bay, swinging her sword in an arc before her as the man fighting Draya edged his way towards Jon. Suddenly the swordswoman's eyes widened as a pale yellow glow shone up through the neckline of her black clothing. The yellow light began to pulse steadily at first, then randomly, before a new firm rhythm took over. Sweat glistened on the woman's forehead and she staggered.

"She's a shaman," shouted Yarrow. "Sasha, focus on her."

From within her ring of protectors, Sasha concentrated instead on her own heartbeat unitl a swathe of black power speared towards the enemy swordsman, encasing her in a black cloud. Unnerved by what was happening to the shaman, other defenders edged away from her, rather than taking advantage of her distraction. The blackness grew in intensity until, within a blinding flash of light, the woman gasped and crumpled to the ground.

"Wow. Sasharia just broke through the Queen's binding spell. Amazing," yelled Rhoda triumphantly. "That's five down now. Two here. If that boy is right, there's another one somewhere. We're winning. Keep going."

Maud was just bunching her muscles to leap down onto Jon's attacker when a tall wiry man broke cover behind Jon and grabbed him around the neck. Suddenly, Jon felt the coldness of metal against his throat. From either side of Jon, the other two attackers calmly disengaged from their opponents and converged on him. As he stilled, the first assailant stepped forward with cool efficiency and relieved Jon of his sword, then stood close by, ready to help his accomplices, if needed.

"Stop!" the wiry man commanded, "Or he dies."

Everyone froze.

To the refugees' shock, Shay stood up and strode over to join them before turning to face those in the centre of the clearing crowded around Sasha. In a hard, forceful voice, completely different from his usual stressed whine, he ordered, "If you don't want to lose your so-called regent, hand over the girl... and her amulet. We won't hurt her. You have my word. You shamans, line up over there," he added, indicating the base of the gum tree that Jayhan had catapulted out of previously.

Before anyone could move, Jon shouted, "NO! They'll take her back to Toriana, Keep her s..." His voice was strangled off as his attacker applied pressure to his throat, pressing the blade harder until a row of tiny droplets of blood appeared on Jon's neck.

Jayhan's eyes widened in horror and he screamed, "Nooo!"

All heads turned to him, expecting a hysterical little boy. Instead, they saw a fearsome sight. A small figure with ghoulishly white eyes, far whiter than they had been before, shining so brightly that they bathed Jon and the assailants in a sickly pale light. Shay and his henchmen stared at him in stark terror, their bodies frozen rigid with fear.

Yarrow calmly walked over and took the knife from the wiry man's now unresisting hand. "Beetlebrow, Argus and you people, secure these bastards. Draya and Rhoda, secure Shay. Jon, go to your sister where you have more protection. Quickly."

People leapt to do her bidding, completely unaffected by the white light. Within seconds, they had bound Shay's and the assailants' hands and shoved them roughly against a tree where they were secured firmly with lengths of rope.

Maud leapt down from the tree and padded into the clearing. As she passed the prisoners, she growled threateningly at them, her fearsome teeth shining white in the gloom. Then she and everyone else returned their attention to Jayhan.

Yarrow approached him, walking unscathed through the bright light of his eyes, and squatted down in front of him. "It's all right now, little one," she crooned, "We are safe."

Slowly the light faded, leaving behind a rather dazed little boy. He blinked a few times and looked uncertainly at Yarrow. "What happened? Did I hurt them?" His gaze shifted to his mother who was padding slowly towards him. His face crumpled and he sobbed at her, "Oh no! Now you'll hate me, 'cause I'm like my great grandmother."

Maud had no time to respond before Sasha dodged between her minders and threw her arms around Jayhan. "Jayhan, it finally worked. But you didn't throw them backwards. You just frightened them, almost to death. Fantastic!"

"No, it's not," he wailed. "Mum hates me now."

"Mum does not hate you now and never will," said Maud firmly, back in her human form, although a little shaky from so many recent shape changes. She enclosed both of them in her arms. "I am very proud of you and love you very much."

He hiccoughed on a sob and looked up. "Do you? Really? Even though I..." he half-waved a trapped arm, "you know...everything?"

Maud smiled down at him. "Yes, even though, and maybe especially because of, everything."

"Oh." And because he was so young and had been through so much on his own and was so relieved his mother still loved him, he let go and had a good long cry, oblivious to the cheering around him.

46

Sheldrake sat on the ground with his back against a log. His head was wrapped in a bandage that secured a poultice to the bruised bump on the back of his head. Earlier, Rhoda had held his head between her hands, easing the pain and apparently healing a hairline skull fracture before applying the bandage. He was still pale and lethargic but was doing his best to get a grip on the situation. Maud was sitting beside him and, in an uncharacteristic display of public affection, held his hand in hers, a gesture that told Jayhan how serious his father's injury had been.

On her left side, Jayhan leaned in against her within the circle of her arm, exhausted but too tense to sleep. Every time his eyes drooped, the memory of the dead man beneath him or Jon with the knife to his throat would jerk him awake again. Each time this happened, his mother would hug him closer or pat his side, soothing him until his tense little body relaxed again.

Only a few yards away, Sasha was curled up on Jon's knee, her head against his shoulder, sound asleep. But from time to time, her limbs would twitch or her eyelids would flutter, as her sleep was disturbed by dark memories. After a particularly noticeable jerk of her leg, Jon looked at the others around the fire and said, "This why I don't want Sasha involved until she is older."

A few of the refugees glanced at each other.

"What?" demanded Jon, his gaze coming to rest on Argus whose left cheek was swollen and bruised.

Argus wrung his hands, looking uncomfortable before he straightened up and said, "Many of us have children who have been through a lot worse than this." He held up a hand to forestall Jon's protest. "Don't worry. I agree with you that we should protect Sasharia from such unpleasantness as much as we can, just as we do with our own children. But..."

"But what, Argus?" Jon pressed, but not unkindly.

"But she has great power, Jon. Power that none of us has. She alone can unleash those poor fettered shamans." He nodded in the direction of the tree where the attackers were being held captive with a dazed shaman sitting amongst them. He waved his hand and subsided. "Just saying, is all."

Jon gazed down at his sister in his arms and stroked her hair. After a minute, he said softly, "Yes she does. And you're right, we will need that power, but not yet. At the very least, we need to build our strength, organise ourselves and plan very, very carefully before we take her anywhere near Toriana." He looked up. "Tonight was the first step towards that. Knowing that Sasharia lives and can break though the binding between Toriana and her shamans will give our cause hope and focus." He gave his self-deprecating grin, "And to a lesser extent, so will I."

"Ah, Jon boy. You've already given us more than hope. You and your sister have given us back our faith in our cause, in our people and in our country," Beetlebrow flicked a stick into the fire. "And what you say makes sense. We can't afford to risk the little princess, not just for her sake, but for the sake of all of us."

"On which topic, how did they know Sasharia was here?" asked Sheldrake quietly as though trying not jolt his head. Even so, he winced slightly as he spoke. "Where is the leak in your organisation?"

Jon glanced around at his companions and grimaced. "Well, Shay obviously. But I don't know how he knew Sasha was going to be here."

"He didn't," said Rhoda flatly. "He and his cutthroats were after shamans. All he knew was that we'd be gathered here and that he could capture several of us at once. He just grabbed the opportunity... or tried to."

"I bet he couldn't believe his luck when Sasharia was introduced to us," added Argus.

Jon nodded. "Toriana wants control of all shamans but more than that, she wants the black amulet in her hand and to make sure Sasha is dead. Only then will her rule be secure. Shay would have been richly rewarded."

"Well, now they will moulder in a Carradorian prison instead," said Maud with relish. "Jon, set some of your people to guard them. We will send soldiers as soon as we can, to take them into custody."

She looked around the clearing, seeing the gouges in the dirt and broken branches strewn on the ground. Two men were digging a grave for the dead archer after Jon's insistence that the man was still Kimoran, serving his country even if misguidedly. Not everyone had agreed with this view, but they had still acquiesced to Jon's request. Another grave was being dug under the overhang of a soft flowing vine for the murdered lookout.

The other unconscious attackers had been dragged

close to their comrades, securely tied in preparation for them regaining consciousness. Shamans had checked them over and made sure their injuries were not slowly killing them. Other than that, they were left to heal on their own.

Yarrow followed her gaze and said, "I'm afraid we will have to find a new meeting place if we wish to escape notice. Too many will know of this place now,"

"No great loss," grumbled Beetlebrow. "Wouldn't feel safe here after this, anyway."

Sheldrake glanced at Maud and in response to some unspoken understanding, Maud said, "You realise that the actions of those Kimoran soldiers on Carradorian soil is an act of aggression against our state?"

"But we are not Carradorians," protested Rhoda.

"Sheldrake is indisputably Carradorian, and while you are within our borders, unless you are criminals, which you are not, you are under our protection. I stated explicitly to the Kimoran ambassador that we would not sanction the hunting of shamans within our borders."

"And we now have a foreign regent living within our borders," added Sheldrake.

Maud gave a rueful grimace, knowing they would not like what she was about to say, "I'm afraid I will have to inform King Gavin of tonight's events."

47

Sasha wiped her hands nervously down the side of her beautifully tailored tan leggings. In her continued masquerade as a stableboy, she was wearing leggings, a white shirt and her new jerkin. Her palms were sweaty, and her chest heaved with anxious breaths.

Her brother, Jon, stood beside her, tense but in control. His blonde hair was tied back neatly at the nape of his neck and his court dress of grey and yellow accentuated his tall willowy frame. He glanced down as she drew in yet another deep breath, and leant down to say, "Sasha, he won't eat us. You're working yourself up. Breath out and don't breath in for a few moments." He took her hand and squeezed it "Hold it... Okay. Breath in slowly." He smiled encouragingly at her. "Good girl. You'll be fine. Try to breathe normally or you'll start to feel a bit strange."

They were distracted by the huge cream and gold doors gliding open before them. Even though she was only ten years old, Sasha pulled her hand away and straightened herself up.

The footmen who had been standing before them in

their red and gold livery, moved aside to reveal an intimidating, rotund, old woman. She was dressed in severe black relieved by two thin lines of colour, one gold, one red, running down either side of her bodice, denoting her as a staff member without being too obvious about it. She glared them up and down, then ushered them through into the King of Carrador's presence, before leaving and closing the doors behind herself.

The room they entered was not the audience chamber but a comfortable sitting room, several arm chairs placed in a loose semi-circle around a small, highly polished wooden desk that had been placed facing into the room so that its occupant could look out the window into the gardens leading down to the lake. Bookcases filled with leather bound books lined three of the walls.

King Gavin was only a year or two older than Jon. His long russet coat and cream shirt were of the finest materials but, given that they were court clothes, not overly ostentatious. He wore his wavy auburn hair a little shorter than many, just resting on his shoulders and he wore no crown or sign of his rank, except for the signet ring on his right ring finger. Gavin was noticeably shorter and slighter than Jon but held himself with an unconscious authority. As they entered, he rose from the desk and walked into the centre of the room to greet them.

Jon's quick eyes noted that no one else was apparently in the room.

Jon and Sasha both bowed neatly from the waist but did not genuflect as one of the king's subjects would have done. A lot of thought had gone into the gesture. They owed the king a gesture of respect for sheltering them within his borders even if, until very recently, he had been unaware of it. On the other hand, they knew Maud had revealed their identities to him, and even if they were not currently officially recognised as the rulers of Kimora, they too were royal. It had been a long, and Sasha thought, tedious discussion.

As they straightened, Gavin inclined his head briefly in recognition of their gesture and status. Maud had reported that the king's blue eyes twinkled benignly at people, but they were not twinkling now. His face looked closed and wary.

"So, we meet at last, even though I am given to understand that you have been within the borders of my kingdom for nearly ten years." The king gestured to the armchairs, as he himself sat in one to the right of his desk that gave him the view of his garden. "Please. Take a seat."

"Thank you, Sire," said Jon, sitting down and crossing his legs, still formal although not obviously nervous.

Sasha chose a chair two away from Jon so that she did not appear too clingy. She did, however, looked ill at ease despite her best efforts, sitting bolt upright on the edge of the chair.

There was a short uncomfortable silence before Jon uncrossed his legs, leaned forward and smiled, not his usual sunny smile but a smile, nevertheless. "I suppose I must apologize to you, Your Majesty, for not coming to you... or your father, sooner. As Maud may have told you, the situation has been vexed. I fled from the slaughter of my family when I was twelve, carrying Sasha, the rightful successor to the throne, as a babe in arms. I was running from betrayal at the highest level. I wasn't running *to* anywhere. It never occurred to me to seek sanctuary from the Carradorian crown. I just hid from everyone." He gestured at Sasha. "I did not even tell my own sister until four months ago. The only person I told in all that time was Old Tom. He's..."

"I know who Old Tom is," interrupted the king, firmly but not unkindly. "Maud has briefed me comprehensively." He glanced outside at the sunlit garden then at Sasha. "Perhaps you two would like to accompany me for a stroll in my garden?"

Sasha's face brightened immediately.

"Of course, Sire," responded Jon stiffly, feeling he had been snubbed.

He rose to his feet and Sasha bounced over to his side as the king opened the French windows leading into the garden and gestured, "This way." As a fresh breeze blew in, he asked, "Not too cold?" When Sasha shook her head, Gavin stepped out onto the broad pale yellow gravel path that led down to the lake and said to her, "Do you think you could race down to that tree by the lake and pick one of those lovely pink flowers for me?"

Sasha stared at him for a moment, but the urge to explore overcame any qualms she might have had that this wasn't what a future queen should be doing.

As Jon joined him, Gavin turned to him. "I believe I was too abrupt. Sasha's worried eyes were distracting me, and I was racking my brains trying to think how to put her at ease." He gave the slightest of bows. "You have my apologies."

Jon took in a long breath and let it out slowly, letting the resentment dissipate. He stared at Gavin for a long moment before breaking into a genuine smile. "I don't know about you, Sire, but I have no idea how to act in this situation. None of my court training, which was cut short at twelve, prepared me to meet a monarch, while I am both regent of a neighbouring power and, at the same time, an untitled refugee and footman."

Suddenly, Gavin stopped being formal and smiled at

him. "No. Neither do I. It is, as you say, a most peculiar set of circumstances. It is really most reprehensible, both on your part and mine, that you have been living, unacknowledged, in fear within my realm all these years." Gavin raised his hand to forestall Jon's protest. "I understand why you didn't approach the throne before. In fact, I doubt that you could have broached the citadel of palace officials to gain an audience without Maud's intercession. But I have been extremely disturbed to discover that such a significant number of foreign agents have been hunting down Kimoran shamans and searching for Sasharia without my knowledge. That degree of interference within my realm is close to a justification for a declaration of war on Kimora. They have no right to hunt down residents of Carrador without my permission."

Whatever Jon had been going to reply was forestalled by Sasha who arrived at a run, flushed and slightly out of breath, bearing a large pink bottlebrush flower. She held it out to the king. "Here you are, Sire. The bush is full of them and there's a wren's nest right in the middle. Did you know that?"

"Thank you." Gavin smiled and accepted the flower. "No, I didn't know. Are there any eggs in it?"

Sasha grimaced. "I don't know. It was too high for me to see."

Gavin pointed to a mass of reeds further along the shore of the lake, "See over there? Inside that clump of reeds is swan's nest. Shall we go and inspect it?"

"Jayhan was right. You are just like other people."

Gavin raised his eyebrows. "Were you expecting horns?"

Sasha giggled. "No. That's just what I asked Jayhan when he thought I should be different if I were a queen."

"Did you indeed? That's a coincidence. Maybe we think the same way because we're related." Gavin veered off the path and walked across the lawn towards the reeds. The grass underfoot was neatly trimmed but damp, glistening in the morning sunshine.

"Are we?" asked Sasha, surprised.

"Yes. We share grandparents on our fathers' side. My father's younger brother married your mother. We are, in fact, cousins."

Jon glanced at Gavin speculatively. "So you believe Sasha's claim to the Kimoran throne?"

"Yes. I trust Maud implicitly. She and Sheldrake would have made very sure of their facts before presenting such a claim." He reached the side of the lake and began to pace along its shore, peering into the reeds, now and again pushing some aside. Then he stopped. "Ah, here we are." He gestured to Sasha then pointed through the reeds.

On a raised piece of land inside the reeds, a black swan sat on a large untidy collection of straw, old reeds and sticks. As they watched, her mate glided through the reeds from the other side and clambered up onto the nest, waggling his tail and shaking out his wings, showing off the panels of white on the underside of his wings.

Sasha smiled up at Gavin. "They're wonderful. I've never seen swans up close before." She chortled, her self-consciousness completely forgotten. "Wait 'til I tell Jayhan. He'll be so jealous."

Now the king's blue eyes did twinkle as he laughed in response. "I gather you two are very good friends."

Jon smiled wryly. "They are almost inseparable. We tried to leave Jayhan behind when we drove into the forest to introduce Sasharia to the Kimoran refugees, but he just stowed away on the back of the coach."

"I told you we shouldn't have left him out. It wasn't fair after he'd been with us for all the planning." Sasha turned earnest dark eyes up to Gavin. "Jayhan said you used to be nervous of his pale eyes, just like everyone else, but you don't need to be. He is brave and strong and kind, and a bit silly at times, well often, but," she shrugged, from her mature standpoint as a ten-year-old, "he *is* only eight. He's not evil."

A faint blush coloured the king's cheeks. "Oh dear. I tried not to show it, you know."

Sasha grinned. "I know. Jayhan told me."

Gavin rolled his eyes.

Jon laughed. "Whether his eyes are unnerving or not to his friends, they hold great power against his enemies. Did Maud tell you how he saved Sasha's life by pure desperate courage and mine with his eyes?"

"No. Maud didn't go into details. She merely told me that eight Kimoran agents had attacked a group of peaceful refugees within the forests to the east, while you, Sasha, Sheldrake and Maud were present. I believe people had gathered so that Sasharia could be introduced to them as their true queen and you could be instated as regent. Am I correct?" When Jon nodded, Gavin added with a hint of censure, "All without my knowledge."

"Again, I apologize," began Jon.

Gavin turned to head back towards the palace. "It is not just you. I am disappointed in Maud. Her loyalty to me should be paramount."

"It is, Sire. As soon as she knew, she told you about the shaman hunters and the number of shamans and refugees living within your borders."

Gavin was implacable. His anger was betrayed by the length of his stride, which made Sasha have to run a bit to keep up. "She did not tell me about you and Sasharia, not until last week."

"Had she considered us a threat, she would have. But when she first employed Sasha, Maud had no knowledge of her true identity and in fact, thought she was a boy."

"But she has known for some time now, I think." Gavin stopped and turned to Jon. "Don't play games with me. We both know that Maud should have informed me of a claimant to the Kimoran throne living within my realm, as soon as she knew. Think as a regent, before you reply."

Jon sighed. "You are right, of course." He frowned as he thought back to a conversation he had had with Maud and Sheldrake. "Sheldrake said it would be... awkward for you or them to be seen as complicit in undermining Toriana. They thought that it would be less problematic if Sasha's identity remained hidden. However, they did think through whether supporting Sasha compromised their loyalty to Carrador and decided that a more stable monarchy in Kimora would, in fact, be in Carrador's best interests, since the unrest in Kimora is affecting your trade relations with her."

Gavin's mouth was set in a thin line. Clearly, he was not impressed by their reasoning. Suddenly he was distracted by a little hand taking hold of his. He looked down to see Sasha gazing up at him with big worried eyes. "Please don't be mad at Maud. I was with a carter who beat me every day before they rescued me and took me on as their stable boy. It was my first good home outside the orphanage. Jon would have left his job and taken me on the road, but Sheldrake and Maud just wanted to keep me safe until they worked out what to do."

"Oh, for goodness sakes," exclaimed Gavin, rolling his eyes in exasperation. "No wonder they wanted to look after you. You both wear your hearts on your sleeves. Whether you intend it or not, you two are a force to be reckoned with." The king shook his head and turned once more for the palace, still holding Sasha's hand. "Come on. Let's go inside and have morning tea."

48

When they re-entered the study, they found a low table set out in the middle of the room with freshly brewed tea and coffee, a jug of lemonade and a wonderful variety of little cakes, savoury morsels and sandwiches. Small side tables had been placed near the chairs so that the guests could help themselves and take their booty back to where they chose to sit.

"Wow!" breathed Sasha. She dragged her eyes away to look at the king. "Do you eat this *and* breakfast *and* lunch?"

Gavin laughed. "Not usually to this extent, no. Only when I have very honoured guests."

"Oh." Sasha blushed.

Gavin nodded at the food. "Go on. Help yourself to whatever you want. We'll let you go first."

With great restraint, Sasha did not overload her plate, although she looked longingly at a couple of little jelly cakes she couldn't fit on it, as she headed to her seat.

"Don't worry, "said Gavin, as he chose a bacon and egg tart and a cheese twist for his own plate. "You may come back for more."

Sasha beamed at him as she sat down.

"No wonder so many pictures of kings show them as overweight." Jon smiled at Gavin. "No reflection on you. You look pretty trim."

Gavin smiled and shook his head. "What is it about families? Even though we have never met, we still feel familiar to each other."

Jon looked surprised. "Yes, we do, don't we?"

Once they were seated and Sasha had had a few minutes to take the edge of her hunger, Gavin asked, "So tell me about your heroic little friend Jayhan. I think Maud must have been too modest to blow her own son's trumpet by telling me."

Sasha nearly choked herself trying to quickly finish the mouthful of cream cake she was eating.

Gavin held up his hand. "No rush. Please don't die on my account."

Sasha just managed to swallow rather than spit the cake she was eating as she laughed. She took a big breath and said, "Okay. I'm ready now." She gave her mouth a neat swipe with a serviette then began. "Jayhan followed the bad people from the inn into the forest. He knew two of them had bows and was worried they would shoot us as they had our family." She shot a sympathetic glance at Jon as she said this. She didn't remember her family being killed but she knew he did. "Leon, that's our coachman and Sheldrake's righthand man, discovered Jayhan but told him to stay put while he went ahead to warn Sheldrake. Jayhan didn't, of course. He followed and found Leon unconscious on the path with a broken bow under him.... Which still left one more bowman."

"...and seven other attackers," put it Jon.

"So Jayhan followed them and saw the archer climb a

tree. He snuck up after him... Jayhan and I climb trees a lot... and saw him about to shoot an arrow at me." She grinned. "So then he did the only thing he could. He threw himself on the archer and they both fell out of the tree, landing right next to me. Luckily," she added, wiping a bit of cream off her fingers with her napkin, "Jayhan landed on the bad man, who died."

"My word!" exclaimed Gavin who had been listening with rapt attention. "What a brave little lad."

Sasha beamed. "Yes, wasn't he? Mind you, I'd have done the same for him." This was not said to raise herself in Gavin's esteem, but simply as a statement of her friendship with Jayhan.

Gavin understood its intention and turned to Jon. "And how did our fearless young man save your life?"

Jon laughed. "By being terrified. When it looked like an attacker was about to slit my throat, Jayhan screamed out in pure terror and suddenly his eyes blazed forth with an amazing white light that froze our attackers with fear, horror... I'm not sure what... but did not affect any of his friends."

"Extraordinary. So his eyes are something to fear, after all," said the king thoughtfully. "No wonder they seem so uncanny. Can he do this at will or only *in extremis*?"

"I *like* Jayhan's eyes," said Sasha, quick to defend her friend.

"At this stage, he has only done it once, as far as I know," replied Jon, ignoring Sasha's outburst. "I doubt that he can do it at will."

Sasha looked from one to the other and frowned. "Jayhan doesn't like people being frightened of him. So he wouldn't want to, anyway."

Gavin sipped his coffee before setting his cup down,

giving her time to calm down. "I think he might want to, if it protected people he cares about. Don't you?" He gestured at the central table. "More cakes?" When Sasha had helped herself to a jelly cake and a small chocolate cupcake, Gavin continued. "So, I have heard a little of your past, although I would be interested to hear a more detailed account of your flight from Kimora, Jon, and something of your life there at another time. Now, I would like you to explain your current living and working arrangements. Sasha?"

"I live at Maud and Sheldrake's and work as a stableboy."

"Light duties, I presume. Only a ruse, a front for visitors?"

Sasha shook her head. "Oh no. I muck out all the stables, clear the horse dung from the paddocks, feed, groom and help exercise the horses. And I'm learning how to mend the tack. Then in the afternoon, I have magic lessons with Lord Sheldrake and Jayhan... *then* Jayhan and I can play."

Gavin looked pole axed. "But Maud and Sheldrake know who you are. How dare they continue to treat you as though you were a servant?"

"Jayhan worried about that too, but they care more about keeping me safe and I agree with them. I love what I do. Besides, they are always kind and polite to me."

"Well, I presume your accommodation at least befits your station?" asked Gavin, slightly mollified.

Sasha grinned. "As a stableboy, yes. I sleep in amongst the hay above the stables. I have a little bed and a wooden crate as a side table and a small cupboard for my clothes and belongings."

The king's face darkened. "That is outrageous. Even if your throne has been stolen from you, you are still royalty and my kin. This cannot be allowed to continue." As Sasha began to protest, he held up his hand and turned his gaze to Jon "And you?"

"As Maud may have mentioned, I work as a footman in the Kimoran Embassy. I serve at table, ride behind the carriage, clean the silverware, horse's tack and carriages, and generally run errands and fetch things as required by Lady Electra. I have a small bedroom in the servant's quarters." He hurried on before Gavin could react. "My position has provided me with a wealth of information about the state of affairs in Kimora."

"Pah! I imagine it has, but at what cost? The humiliation of being in service to someone whom you outrank. Unconscionable!" Gavin leapt out of his chair and strode back and forth across the room, driven by his outrage. He no longer looked amiable and easy-going. He waved his hand and turned to look at them, a severe line cutting between his eyebrows. "You realise this cannot be allowed to continue? I will not have my kin working as mere servants. You will come to the palace and reside here. You will have your own apartment, servants and an allowance."

Far from being delighted, Jon face was tight-lipped and Sasha was clearly dismayed. Jon stood up and waited, stifflimbed, until he could trust himself to speak. Finally he said, forcing himself to be courteous. "I thank you for your offer. But I did not come here to throw myself, ourselves, on your charity." When Gavin waved away his objection, he continued forcefully, "And I do not feel obliged to follow your dictates nor to act merely to suit your feelings of nicety."

The king put his hands on his hips. "You are in my kingdom. You will do as I say."

Jon realised that Gavin could, in fact, place them under house arrest within the palace, or worse, in the dungeons, if he chose to. He forced himself to calm down. After a long moment, where Gavin's last words hung in the air between them, he said quietly, "Are we to be your servants instead, but with no say in our fates, if we must do as you command?"

"No." Gavin seemed perplexed. He let his hands drop form his hips and walked over to pour himself another cup of coffee, giving himself time to think. "These cups are annoyingly small," he said tetchily to himself. He spoke once more to Jon. "I had thought you would be pleased. I may have phrased it rather more vehemently than I intended, because I was shocked by what you have had to deal with. I do not wish us to be at odds." He sipped his coffee and looked at them over the rim of the cup, noticing the strain in Sasha's eyes, before replacing the cup in its saucer. "I like what I have seen of you two or I would not have extended that invitation." He smiled self-deprecatingly. "I know. It sounded more like a command than an invitation. In fact, it was, which, as you have so carefully pointed out, rather defeats the purpose of delivering you from your servitude." He sat down, indicating that Jon should do likewise, and spoke in a calm but authoritative voice. "Very well. Let us start again and discuss this as equals. You know my thoughts on your immediate future. Let me hear yours. Sasha?"

Sasha knew he was addressing her as a future queen and was imposing on her a greater expectation of mature thought than the less complicated wishes of a ten-year-old. She took a deep breath. "I have only been with Lady Maud and Lord Sheldrake for about six months. Even though I act as their stableboy, I know they care about me and it is the first true home I have ever known. I really need to learn magic, which Sheldrake has organised for me, both from himself and from Yarrow, a shaman from Kimora. Yarrow also teaches me about Kimora, its history, customs and expectations. She is an unregistered shaman and in constant danger from the shaman hunters, so has been living in hiding for years. Beth, the head groom, has taught me reading in the evenings. I suppose I have had little training in numbers other than what I learnt in Stonehaven, the orphanage. In the afternoons, between magic lessons and dinner, Jayhan and I are allowed out to play." She smiled. "With all that, I have learnt to work hard and to make the most of every second. Also, I have recently discovered I have a brother. I have never been happier in my life."

Sasha looked around the room at the ornate cornices, the exquisite furniture and the oil painting on the walls and said, "I can see, though, that there is a whole way of life in a palace that I can't really learn at home. They have all been trying to teach me but when I look around here, I realise that it is not the same as being here. It feels completely different." She glanced at Jon then back to Gavin, her brow puckered in a frown. "But..."

"But she needs the warmth and stability she has found there," finished Jon for her, "At least for the time being, or for some of the time."

"I see." Gavin sipped his coffee. "And you?"

"Ah. Well, things have changed recently for me." When Gavin looked enquiringly at him, Jon continued, "After a little experiment we conducted at Sheldrake's birthday party, Lady Electra's amulet was released from the spell binding her will to Queen Toriana. She is, unbeknownst to Toriana, a free agent... and she knows who Sasha and I are and has sworn her loyalty to us." He gave a little chuckle. "And she now finds it embarrassing having me working for her. But she is bravely, and with some effort, continuing as before, to protect my identity." He grinned. "She has even gone so far as to purchase a phaeton so that she can talk to me without others around, while I act as her footman sitting behind her."

Gavin nodded. "I think I saw it the other day, barrelling up the High St. It has red enamelled panelling, doesn't it? Was that you up behind?"

"Yes. Dashing outfit, isn't it?" He grimaced. "Anyway, I would have to admit it is a bit awkward, now that she knows who I am. And now that she and her coachman support me, I could get most of the updates about Kimora without actually having to be in the Embassy myself."

"So, are you saying you will accept my *offer* after all?"

Jon smiled wryly. "Yes, I believe I will, but," he almost winced, "with two considerations." Gavin merely raised his eyebrows, becoming used to the fact that these two were indeed on a par with him. "I'm afraid my pride dictates that I need to be useful to you in some role so that I am paying my way, at least to some extent..."

"He's good with horses," put in Sasha helpfully.

"He cannot be a stableboy or a groom," said Gavin firmly. "And secondly?"

"Secondly, we need to consider whether I should be residing with you under my own name or incognito; for your safety, for mine and for the future of Kimora."

Gavin stood up and walked over to the window and stood, staring out across the lawns at the lake. After a moment, he looked at Jon over his shoulder and said, "My first instinct was to present you to the world with my support behind you. After all, in normal circumstances, an ousted monarch could live reasonably safely in a foreign court..." He turned to face them "But we have a complication: According to Kimora's constitution, the existence of

Sasharia and her amulet actually invalidates Toriana's right to rule. When Kimorans discover they have been duped by a false amulet, they will rise against their false queen. And Toriana's response will be ruthless. Thousands will be killed... and all those spellbound shamans will be compelled to fight on her side." Gavin shook his head. "I don't think either," he glanced at Sasha and amended, "*any* of us wants that."

Jon gave a sigh of relief. "No. No, I'm so glad you see that. We have to keep Sasharia secret until the resistance is better organised and she is older, surer of her power, better trained in court craft and," he threw his hand up, "so many other things." He gave a wan smile. "I have tried to rally our refugees over recent years but until now I have had no recognised status. And well, for the first few years..." His eyes slid away from Gavin's.

Gavin walked over and laid a hand on his shoulder. "Jon, do not blame yourself. I only regret that I could not have helped you sooner. A boy of twelve, alone and penniless on the streets of Highkington..." He shook his head. "It does not bear thinking about." He patted Jon's shoulder bracingly. "I am lost in admiration at what you have achieved; saving Kimora's true monarch, setting up networks," At Jon's look of surprise, Gavin nodded. "Oh yes, I know about them - and your camps of refugees placed strategically though the forest. I'm glad you're not planning to overthrow my throne; you would make a formidable foe."

"Thanks." Jon grinned, his air of gloom dissipating. Then he frowned. "Hmm. It does sound rather intrusive, doesn't it, having all those networks and refugee camps within your borders. I can see why you might have been upset."

The king merely raised his eyebrows.

"If you wish it," said Jon magnanimously, "I will undertake to keep you informed of all developments related to Kimora within your borders."

He looked so much like an eager puppy hoping for praise that Gavin laughed. "Very good of you, I'm sure." He glanced at Sasha who was now roving the bookcases, peering at the spines of the leather-bound books. "Hmm. I think we may be boring our future queen."

She turned quickly, her face reddening with chagrin. "Sorry."

Gavin waved a dismissive hand. "Quite all right. Let me know if you find something you would like to borrow." He poured himself yet another cup of coffee, which was cooler now than most people would drink it. He took a sip as he sat down and didn't seem to mind. "And now to your immediate futures. Having taken your views into account, I intend to introduce Jon to the court as Lord Johnson, my new Minister for Transport. The role will encompass oversight of roads, horses and coaches, about which, Jon, you will already know a great deal, but it will also cover the rivers, coastline and seafaring vessels, about which I suspect you may have to learn." He gave a slight smile. "The role will also give you reason to travel around the kingdom." He took another sip as he waited for a reaction.

Jon's head nodded slowly up and down as he thought about it. Gradually a smile appeared on his face that grew until he was grinning from ear to ear. "That sounds marvellous, sire. But who do I replace, and will my persona bear up under scrutiny?"

"You will replace Sheldrake, as it turns out." At Jon's look of shock, Gavin raised his hand. "No. I am not doing away with Sheldrake's services. It is just that he has been holding that portfolio on top of his own since late last year when the previous Minister died unexpectedly. He will be delighted to be released from it. Sheldrake is also organising your persona." He smiled. "Unbeknownst to you, you own a moderately-sized holding up in the north of the country but have been travelling abroad for several years and have just recently returned."

Jon sat back in his chair, his expression wandering from amazement to suspicion to anger. "You had this all planned with Sheldrake from the start."

Gavin shrugged unapologetically. "Well, yes. I was planning on inviting you to reside in the palace, if you remember, and I had come to the same conclusion as you, that you should hide your identity for the time being. So, there we are."

"Huh." Jon's brow cleared. "Huh, there we are indeed. Thank you."

Gavin smiled. "A pleasure. Sheldrake and I had an enjoyable time inventing your persona. Now all he has to do is create it."

"And me?" asked a small voice from the side, "What about me?"

"You, my young cousin, will stay at Maud and Sheldrake's for another two years, at which time we will review it." As Sasha's face lit up, he raised his hand, "But, you must have a proper bed and bedside table, even if it must be up in the loft. You will need a wardrobe and clothes befitting a young princess, perhaps kept somewhere in the house to protect the expensive court dresses." As she went to protest, he overrode her, "You must learn the ways of court. No one can teach you that while you are dressed as a boy. I am not stipulating that you wear dresses while you are at home, but you will wear them when you come to court." With a flash of acumen, he added, "And tell your little friend that I forbid him from teasing you."

When she had nodded her agreement, he continued, "Over the next two years, you will visit me for several days at least once a month. While you are here, you will learn the ways of court and the nobility. My mother's Lady-in-Waiting has a daughter your age, who may bear you company while you are here. Her name is Lady Teresa." He gave another smile, his eyes crinkling in the corners. "And your name is Lady Natasha."

Sasha smiled back. "Clever. Then I can still be called Sasha?"

Gavin nodded. "And one last thing, which I think you two and your little friend may like above all else." He paused to give his announcement a sense of occasion. "I will employ a master at arms to teach Jayhan and you armed and unarmed combat. He will also provide extra security at Maud and Sheldrake's house while you are there. You, Jon, may join me in my training sessions here and have extra training as you choose and have time for. After all, I have been training for years whereas you, presumably, have not."

"Not formally, no. At least, not since I was twelve." He grinned. "I picked up a few tricks on the streets, but all help will be gratefully received. Thank you."

From there, their conversation turned to less weighty topics until next half an hour later, the indomitable woman in the black gown returned to usher them out.

49

The trumpets blared and the huge doors swung slowly open, revealing a small, neatly turned-out boy accompanied by his parents. His father wore a black long coat reaching halfway down his thighs over a deep blue shirt and black breeches while his mother sailed beside him in a sapphire-studded deep emerald gown.

Jayhan, wedged between his parents, trod resolutely down the length of the audience chamber, his eyes lowered to avoid meeting anyone's gaze. When they reached the dais, Maud gave a low graceful curtsey while the two males bowed deeply as they stood before King Gavin whose eyes, once more, were twinkling benignly. Next to him, the herald thumped his gold staff twice on the floor and announced sonorously, "Jayhan Batian, accompanied by his parents, the Lady Maud Batian and Lord Sheldrake Batian."

Maud and Sheldrake stepped back and melted into the crowd of finely dressed lords and ladies on either side, who were looking on with mild curiosity, waiting to see why the small boy had been summoned.

"Look up, Jayhan," said the king softly. He rose and smiled down at Jayhan, resolutely meeting his pale eyes, before sweeping the audience with his gaze. Once he was sure he had everyone's attention, he spoke. "Today we honour a brave hero, who fought, with no thought for his own safety... "

"A bit of thought," muttered Jayhan. "I was scared to death."

"Shh," Sheldrake hissed from the sidelines.

Gavin gave a slight frown and amended, "who, although in fear of his life, persevered against almost impossible odds to stop an archer who had an arrow aimed at his friend. Jayhan Batian launched himself at the archer who was lying, bow string drawn, in the overhanging branches of a tree, sending himself and the archer plummeting twenty feet to the ground, thus saving the life of his friend." Gavin crooked his finger. "Come forward, Jayhan."

Jayhan stepped closer to the king, who took a medal suspended on a gold and red lanyard from a tray held by the herald and placed it over Jayhan's head so that the medal dangled on his small chest.

"Thank you," said Jayhan, beaming up at Gavin, who met his gaze stalwartly, his smile never faltering.

Then, amid the cheers and clapping of the audience, the king placed his hand on Jayhan's shoulder and turned him for all to see. "I give you, Jayhan who, at eight years old, is the youngest recipient of our nation's Star of Courage."

As Jayhan turned, the crowd's applause faltered, and a ripple of unease swept through the lords and ladies as they saw his pale eyes. Gavin felt the boy's chest heave beneath his hand as Jayhan lifted his chin and stared back defiantly. Gavin gave Jayhan's shoulder a reassuring squeeze and said loudly, "I can see you are all stunned by the beauty of

Jayhan's pale lavender eyes. They are unique, as far as I know, and are the sign of a kind, brave, loyal friend. If you ever gain his friendship, feel privileged, as I do."

The crowd erupted into renewed applause and Gavin felt the tension drain from Jayhan's shoulders. Jayhan looked up at Gavin, his eyes shiny with tears, and whispered, "Thank you," knowing that for him, this was a far greater reward than the medal.

END OF BOOK 1

Dear reader,

We hope you enjoyed reading *The Pale-Eyed Mage*. Please take a moment to leave a review, even if it's a short one. Your opinion is important to us.

Discover more books by Jennifer Ealey at https://www.nextchapter.pub/authors/jennifer-ealey

Want to know when one of our books is free or discounted? Join the newsletter at http://eepurl.com/bqqB3H

Best regards,

Jennifer Ealey and the Next Chapter team

You might also like:
Bronze Magic by Jennifer Ealey

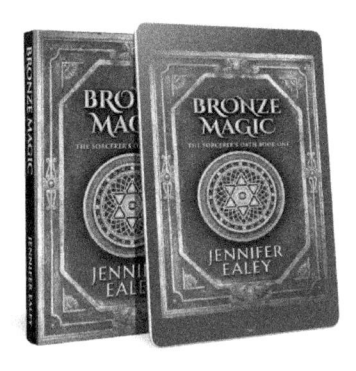

To read the first chapter for free, please head to:
https://www.nextchapter.pub/books/bronze-magic

CPSIA information can be obtained
at www.ICGtesting.com
Printed in the USA
BVHW041019061120
592698BV00011B/644